The Collected Stories of Ellen Glasgow

The Collected Stories of Ellen Glasgow

EDITED BY *Richard K. Meeker*

Louisiana State University *Press*

Editor's Preface

‎UNFORTUNATELY, IT has not been possible to determine exactly the order in which Ellen Glasgow wrote her stories, much less their dates of composition. The only reasonable course has been to arrange them in the order of their original publication. The manuscript story, "The Professional Instinct," appears last because in theme and style it is a late story, of the same vintage as "The Difference" and "Romance and Sally Byrd." This order is sufficient to reveal the growth of her technique and ideas.

The four unreprinted stories are presented just as they appeared in their respective magazines. The choice of a definitive text for the collected stories, however, has been a problem because Miss Glasgow revised the magazine versions once for *The Shadowy Third* of 1923 and again, slightly, for *Dare's Gift,* the English edition of 1924. In a letter to Joseph Hergesheimer, Miss Glasgow regretted not sending him the English edition because she had been able to correct the proof for it more thoroughly than she had for the American edition.

The text presented here is that of *The Shadowy Third* of 1923. I have corrected one misprint that occurred in both the American and English editions: "Have you see[n] Dr. Brandon?" *Dare's Gift* contains thirty variations from the American text, all in spelling and punctuation. In neither revision did Miss Glasgow make significant changes on the scale that Henry James did for *The Portrait of a Lady.* She might substitute "leafless" for "bare," but she did little rewriting. The only important changes are removals of phrases or sentences which she considered too explicit. Miss Glasgow often caught herself overstating where an allusion would be sufficient. Textual notes for the individual stories will indicate her excisions.

A careful study of Miss Glasgow's revisions shows that half of those for *The Shadowy Third* and all but a few of those for *Dare's Gift* are orthographic. Although there is some rephrasing of the magazine versions for the American collection, not a word has been changed in the English edition, except for spelling. Miss Glasgow kept altering the American to the English spelling of "centre," "sombre," "afterwards," "towards," "labour," "neighbours," "honour," "ardour," "odour," "colour," "dishevelled," "travelling," "cheque," "moustache," "gayety," "spelt," "axe," and "storey." *Dare's Gift* is more consistent in this respect than *The Shadowy Third*.

Furthermore, Miss Glasgow's punctuation grew more conservative with revision in accordance with what she presumed was the English taste. She cut down on dashes and colons, replacing them with simple commas and periods. She seems to have worried a good deal about hyphens, putting them back into words that might not be acceptable compounds and splitting up words that were originally hyphenated.

According to her English publisher, John Murray, the 1924 edition had to be named *Dare's Gift* because there was already in print an English book, *The Shadowy Third,* by H. A. Vachell. In the English text "Dare's Gift" replaces "The Shadowy Third" as the first story, but the sequence is otherwise unchanged. There was a second printing of the English edition in 1926, and a total of two thousand copies were sold before *Dare's Gift* went out of print in 1942.

Acknowledgments

I AM first of all grateful to Mrs. Irita Van Doren and Mr. Frank Morley, Ellen Glasgow's literary executors, and to the First and Merchants National Bank of Richmond, Miss Glasgow's trustee, for their interest in this project. Their kind co-operation in obtaining or giving permission to publish these stories made the collection possible. Neither would it have been possible without the co-operation of Harcourt, Brace & World, Inc., which by special arrangement now holds rights to the seven stories originally published by Doubleday, Page & Company in the 1923 collection, *The Shadowy Third and Other Stories.*

A note of gratitude is due the magazines in which Miss Glasgow's stories first appeared. Some—for example, *Harper's Magazine, Good Housekeeping,* and the *Saturday Evening Post*—are still very much around; others—*McClure's Magazine, Scribner's Magazine,* and *Woman's Home Companion*—unfortunately are not. The credits for specific stories are given in the Editor's Notes.

For their helpfulness in obtaining permissions or clearing up the matter of copyrights, I am grateful also to Mr. C. Coleman McGehee and Mr. George V. Moncure of the First and Merchants National Bank of Richmond, the latter the Glasgow trust officer, and the Copyright Office of the Library of Congress. Their assistance was invaluable.

I am also indebted to the Institute of Southern Culture at Longwood College for use of my essay from their 1961 volume and to the University Center in Virginia for a research grant which helped make this project possible.

To Mr. John Cook Wyllie and Mr. Robert E. Stocking of the Alderman Library at the University of Virginia, I offer my thanks for the free access they gave me to the invaluable Ellen Glasgow papers housed there.

Mr. John Murray kindly sent me detailed information about the English edition of the stories, entitled *Dare's Gift*. Professors William W. Kelly of Michigan State University, Louis D. Rubin, Jr., of Hollins College, and Willard Thorp of Princeton University all generously took time from their own projects to give me criticism and encouragement. I have acknowledged specific debts to these men elsewhere.

Finally, I am grateful to Miss Judith Van Detrich for patiently collating the various versions of these stories.

R.K.M.

Contents

THE COLLECTED STORIES OF ELLEN GLASGOW

1

Introduction

ON NOVEMBER 22, 1897, after publishing her first novel, *The Descendant,* Ellen Glasgow wrote to Walter Hines Page, then an editor on the *Atlantic Monthly,* "As regards my work I shall follow your advice in full. I shall write no more short stories and I shall not divide my power or risk my future reputation. I will become a great novelist or none at all." [1] Literary history has already recorded and applauded the eighteen novels which she wrote thereafter; however, history has failed to notice how often Miss Glasgow broke that promise to Page. As a matter of fact, she published eleven short stories by 1925 and left another one in manuscript. [2] Nevertheless, only a few paragraphs have been written about them, and editors of anthologies usually have passed them by for a piece from *The Sheltered Life,* if they have represented her at all. [3] A partial collection, *The Shadowy Third and Other Stories* (1923), has been out of print for over twenty years. It is time to consider whether such neglect of Ellen Glasgow's short stories is justified.

Miss Glasgow's letter to Page calls for further explanation. To begin with, Page, on the inside of the New York publishing world, was perfectly right in asserting that the novel was the thing, and Miss Glasgow was only being prudent in agreeing to his advice. The reading public

[1] *Letters of Ellen Glasgow,* ed. Blair Rouse (New York, 1958), 25.

[2] Miss Glasgow began writing poetry before she tried either long or short fiction. The *Atlantic Monthly* published her first poem, "The Freeman," in December, 1897. The following year she had enough poems to make a small volume, which finally appeared in 1902. Although her publisher said that only nine copies were sold, she continued to write occasional verse until about 1920.

[3] One commendable exception is Sculley Bradley, Richard C. Beatty, and E. Hudson Long (eds.), *The American Tradition in Literature* (2 vols.; New York, 1956, 1961), which reprints "Jordan's End." The fullest discussion of the stories is in Frederick McDowell's *Ellen Glasgow and the Ironic Art of Fiction* (Madison, Wis., 1960), 144–45.

was still conditioned by the assumption that seriousness required bulk. The literary giants of the late nineteenth century were largely novelists, such as Howells, James, Hardy, Galsworthy, Balzac, and Tolstoy. The short story was still in the hands of the sentimentalists and the local colorists. The best of them—Mary Wilkins Freeman, Sarah Orne Jewett, Margaret Deland, and George Washington Cable—had not yet made the world safe for the realistic short story. Stephen Crane achieved his reputation with a novel, *The Red Badge of Courage,* although he preferred his poetry in *The Black Riders* to any of his fiction. E. A. Robinson, born too soon, had just destroyed the manuscript of his short stories and resolved to be a great poet or nothing.

In short, Page was accurately reflecting the official attitude toward short fiction. But a few weeks later, when he replied to Miss Glasgow's letter, he showed that he was really warning her against spreading herself too thin:

. . . it is an everyday occurrence that authors of promise scatter the influences that ought to go towards the firm and steady building of a great reputation, by appearing in print here, there, and everywhere. Even if all the minor literature that they put forth be excellent of its kind, the public comes after a very little while to regard the author as a sort of "professional" writer who turns up with poems or short stories, or essays and other things so often as to cause one to regard the writer rather as a "literary operative" than as a person who is bent upon doing only great pieces of work. . . . Of course after a little when you have more firmly established your reputation, you can better afford to amuse yourself with smaller things.[4]

Actually, Ellen Glasgow did follow Page's advice, as much as she followed the advice of any man. She had already written at least two short stories and sent them to her New York literary agent, Paul R. Reynolds, before she promised not to write any more of them. On November 1, 1897, she had suggested that Reynolds offer one of her stories to *McClure's Magazine.* Reynolds apparently sent "Between Two Shores," which was published there in February, 1899. Then, on January 27, 1898, reassured by Page's advice and the successful completion of her second novel, Miss Glasgow announced firmly, "I have decided to write no more short articles—and I wish I could recall them all." Perhaps her decision was reinforced by the fact that another of her stories remained unpublished. She asked Reynolds to return it, but he succeeded in placing "A Point in Morals" with *Harper's Magazine* for May, 1899, and made several efforts to sell her poems.

---

[4] Burton J. Hendrick, *The Training of an American: the Earlier Life and Letters of Walter H. Page, 1885–1913* (Boston, 1928), 336–37. The letter is dated December 8, 1897.

For the next fifteen years Ellen Glasgow concentrated on novels. Her determination was still firm on May 9, 1913, when she wrote to Reynolds, "As for short stories—well, I've tried hard to interest myself in them, but simply can't. The work is so tiresome that I'd rather not have the money they bring than try to write them." [5] Then something happened. On July 1, 1916, she wrote Reynolds that she was working on a story about a haunted house and wondered if there happened to be any particular demand for short fiction just then.

Reynold's reply was encouraging. He said that there was presently a great demand for short stories and that with her reputation she could command a good price for one. He asked to see it as soon as it was ready. This story was undoubtedly "The Shadowy Third," which *Scribner's Magazine* published in December, 1916. During the next eight years Miss Glasgow produced nine more stories and sold all but one.

II

Why did Ellen Glasgow, in the middle of her career as a novelist, just when *Life and Gabriella* had reached fifth place on the *Publishers' Weekly* best-seller list, turn back to writing short stories? An obvious answer, which her correspondence with Reynolds bears out, is that she needed the money. While hardly poor by ordinary standards, Miss Glasgow had large medical bills, traveled extensively, and had to maintain One West Main Street in Richmond after her father's death in 1916. For this reason, she would even sell stories to women's magazines if they paid well, although she did balk at appearing in the *Ladies Home Journal*. Another answer is that she could afford to follow Page's advice and amuse herself now that she was an established novelist.

The full explanation is more complicated, however. The first hint comes from an interview Miss Glasgow gave in New York in 1916 shortly after the publication of *Life and Gabriella*: "When I began *Virginia* I had in mind three books dealing with the adjustment of human lives to changing conditions. . . . Virginia was the passive and helpless victim of the ideal of feminine self-sacrifice. . . . Gabriella was the product of the same school, but instead of being used by circumstances, she used them to create her own destiny." Then she added, "The third book may never be written. If it should be, it will deal with a woman who faces her world with weapons of indirect influence or subtlety." [6] It is hard to

[5] The correspondence from Ellen Glasgow to Paul Revere Reynolds has been published, with notes, by James B. Colvert in *Studies in Bibliography*, XIV (1961), 177–96. The two quotations from her letters are taken from that article.

[6] Grant M. Overton, *The Women Who Make Our Novels* (New York, 1918), 32–33.

find the prescribed character in *The Builders* of 1919 or *One Man in His Time* of 1922.

There is both biographical and critical evidence that Miss Glasgow faltered between *Life and Gabriella* and *Barren Ground,* that is, between 1916 and 1925. In a letter to Hugh Walpole, dated August 23, 1923, she summarizes her ordeal:

Ah, I've been through the Slough of Despond about my work. After I wrote *Life and Gabriella* about 8 or 10 years ago, I let go and gave up. I was passing through an experience that seemed to drain everything out of me—vitality, imagination, interest, everything. In that time I lost a great deal, and I slipped somehow, naturally, I suppose, away from what I had won. Now, I have boiled up, I hope, out of those depths, and I am trying to win back what I have lost.[7]

She goes on to describe her plans for *Barren Ground.*

Plainly, Miss Glasgow was struggling to re-orient herself following several disillusionments, public and private, after World War I. But why write short stories during this Slough of Despond? Ironically, the answer may lie in her own deprecation of the short story form during her 1916 interview:

I cannot write short stories. They bore me excruciatingly. The whole technique of the short story and the novel is different. All the best of the short stories must be painfully condensed with slight regard for the evolutionary causes bringing about this or that effect. Everything I see, I see in the form of a novel—as a large canvas. I want to trace the process of cause and effect.[8]

In other words, the novel calls for a comprehensive view of life, a coherent philosophy to motivate the characters. It is evident that following World War I Miss Glasgow temporarily lost her ability to compose large canvases, that is, lost her sense of evolution. Her writings at this point contain increasing references to a world gone mad, uncivilized barbarians, and ugly deviations from human decency. The modern world began to mystify, even horrify Miss Glasgow. It became increasingly hard for her to write on a large scale, to trace the causes and effects that had so fascinated her.

Professor Willard Thorp has pointed out to me that Miss Glasgow was preceded by her distinguished rival Henry James in the literary Slough of Despond. James, too, wallowed in frustration during the nineties after a string of successful novels. When he had consolidated his art through

---

[7] Rouse (ed.), *Letters of Ellen Glasgow,* 69. This letter and the previous interview recorded by Overton contain no reference to her famous "social history of Virginia." The master plan does not seem to have occurred to her yet, verifying James Branch Cabell's contention that he suggested the idea to her in 1925.

[8] Overton, *The Women Who Make Our Novels,* 26.

writing short stories and plays, he emerged into the "major phase" with *The Ambassadors.* To complete the parallel, we can easily say that Miss Glasgow's major phase began with *Barren Ground,* after she had stabilized herself through short fiction. Like Henry James, Edith Wharton, Willa Cather, and James Branch Cabell, she found the short story a medium perfectly adapted for catching isolated moments in time, when causes are impossible to trace and results are hard to measure. With her talent for epigram, Miss Glasgow found condensation no great strain either.

Furthermore, the short story was rapidly becoming a respectable and profitable literary form in the periodicals. Quality magazines like *Scribner's* and *Harper's* were carrying serious fiction by writers of stature like Mark Twain, Theodore Dreiser, Henry James, and Hamlin Garland. Even the family magazines were competing for stories by established novelists—magazines like *Woman's Home Companion, Good Housekeeping,* and the *Saturday Evening Post.* Ellen Glasgow may have blushed to admit it, but she sold stories to all these magazines. Moreover, she took her stories seriously enough to collect seven of them in 1923 into a volume entitled, after the first story, *The Shadowy Third.* Probably, as Arthur H. Quinn has commented, these seven represent those of which she was proudest. It is significant that all but one of the reprinted stories came from the "quality" magazines, *Harper's* and *Scribner's.*

If Miss Glasgow had had her way, as she usually did with her publishers, *The Shadowy Third* would have been included in the monumental Virginia edition of her works in 1938, but according to Edward Wagenknecht, Scribner's insisted on novels only.[9] Otherwise, we might have had a preface for her short stories, like those collected later in *A Certain Measure.* There Miss Glasgow might have told us where she got the ideas for her stories and what technical problems she encountered. She also might have, characteristically, pointed out the beauties of style and structure, lest we miss them. While we are lacking some useful information, we have also been spared some embarrassment, for Miss Glasgow is inclined to tell us not only how she wrote her stories but what she wants us to think of them. Her prefaces are sometimes like a guided tour in which certain rooms are lingered in too long and other doors kept suspiciously closed. Today, critics like Northrop Frye warn us, "The poet speaking as critic produces not criticism, but documents to be examined by critics."[10]

[9] Wagenknecht, *Cavalcade of the American Novel* (New York, 1952), 270.
[10] Northrop Frye, *Anatomy of Criticism* (Princeton, 1957), 6.

In addition to those previously quoted, we have only a few brief statements by Miss Glasgow about her short stories. One is contained in a letter she wrote to Mrs. Robert C. Taylor on February 8, 1924: "It makes me happy that you love my Shadowy Third stories. They are very near to my heart, those stories, and I lived in that atmosphere when I was writing them." [11] To Joseph Hergesheimer she wrote on January 7, 1924, "I am sending you the short stories, and I only wish the book could be of the English edition because I was able to correct the proof more thoroughly. Several of these you may like. 'Dare's Gift' is, I think, a perfectly true picture of the closing days of the Confederacy." [12]

III

Every review of *The Shadowy Third* was favorable, and every reviewer pointed out the preponderance of the supernatural in the stories.[13] Ellen Glasgow obviously arranged them to emphasize this effect. The Shadowy Third is the spirit of a dead child who is visible only to sensitive persons; scientifically minded people never see the spirit. Two other stories have spirit characters. In "The Past" Vanderbridge's first wife returns to haunt him and his second wife. In "Whispering Leaves" Mammy Rhody [14] returns to protect little Pell from harm. These three spirits are all seen by objective narrators with a reputation for reliability. A fourth story, "Dare's Gift," contains a house haunted by the spirit of treachery, which corrupts every inhabitant. These, the first four stories in the book, are plainly intended to dominate it.

No one who has pictured Ellen Glasgow as a sharp-eyed realist can read these four stories without surprise. Ghosts are not fashionable in the twentieth century, least of all visible ones, and yet we are urged to believe in them here, because the narrators all believe in them; all the good people in the story believe in them. Furthermore, the ghosts actually perform; the little girl seems to trip up her father with a jump rope; the second wife sits at the dinner table with the Vanderbridges; Mammy Rhody actually saves little Pell from falling. Why is a Darwinian determinist urging belief in phantoms?

[11] From a letter pasted in the Taylor copy of *The Shadowy Third* at Alderman Library, University of Virginia.

[12] Rouse (ed.), *Letters of Ellen Glasgow,* 70.

[13] Ellen Glasgow's talent for eliciting favorable reviews has been commented on frequently, especially by James Branch Cabell. Several of these reviews, in *The Bookman* and the Greensboro (N.C.) *Daily News,* for example, have an "inspired" look. They may be said to constitute an official interpretation.

[14] The Negro mammy who brought up Ellen Glasgow's mother was named Mammy Rhoda. There is also a Mammy Rhoda in *The Sheltered Life.*

Ellen Glasgow had both personal and ideological reasons for believing in ghosts. She has testified in several places to her frail, sensitive girl-hood, where she was protected from harsh realities by the world of her imagination. In an essay she wrote for *I Believe,* she said, "As a very small child I was a believing animal. I believed in fairies; I believed in Souls—not only the souls of men and women and children, but the souls, too, of trees and plants, and winds and clouds."[15] She tells in *The Woman Within* of her happy summers at Jerdone Castle, a farm where the Glasgows lived before moving to Main Street in Richmond. On the farm, accompanied by her Mammy Lizzie, she invented "Little Willie" stories at bedtime, and all of nature came alive for her:

Every vista in the woods beckoned me; every field held its own secret; every tree near our house had a name of its own and a special identity. This was the beginning of my love for natural things, for earth and sky, for roads and fields and woods, for trees and grass and flowers; a love which has been second only to my sense of an enduring kinship with birds and animals, and all inarticulate creatures. Mammy and I gave every tree on the big blue-grass lawn a baptism. We knew each one by name, from Godwin, the giant elm, to Charles, the oak, and Alfred, the shivering aspen.[16]

One of her most painful experiences there was the sale of her dog Pat, whom her farther refused to take with them to Main Street.

Out of this period in Miss Glasgow's childhood comes her first written story, "Only a Daisy," which she carefully put on paper when she was either seven or eight years old:[17]

In a garden full of beautiful flowers there sprung up a little daisy. Every-thing was bright and cheerful around it, but the daisy was not content. "If I were only one of those roses[,]" it said[,] "then I would be happy, but I am only a little daisy[,]" and the daisy sighed and hung its head.

Days passed and the roses were carried away. There was to be a grand ball in the castle[,] for the you[ng] earl was going away. "If I could only be there but no one would think of taking me[,]" said the daisy when the other flowers were carried away to grace the stands and vases on the night of the ball. "But I am only a little daisy[,]" and it sighed again.

It was the evening before he should go away and the Earl was walking in the garden with a young girl. "Let me give you a flower before you go[,]"

<hr>

[15] Clifton Fadiman (ed.), *I Believe* (New York, 1939), 93.

[16] *The Woman Within* (New York, 1954), 27.

[17] The degree of her precocity will probably never be established. A notation in the upper left hand corner of the MS in Miss Glasgow's handwriting says she was seven. In *The Woman Within,* she says she was seven. However, she told her friend, Sara Haardt (later Mrs. H. L. Mencken), that she was eight. One of Miss Glasgow's notebooks says that she was eight. "Only a Daisy" has never before been published. I have supplied essential punctuation and corrected a few obvious mistakes.

she said[,] "for it is the last time I will see you before you go[,]" and she stooped to pluck a tall white lily that grew near, but the young man stopped her[.] "No," he said[,] "I will have this little daisy[.] I will keep it and it will remind me of you[.]" She plucked the daisy and handed it to him. They stood together and talked for a little while and then the girl turned and went into the house. The young [man] stood still a moment[,] pressed the daisy to his lips[,] then hurried away and was soon lost to sight in the darkness. And the little daisy was content at last to be "only a daisy[."]

In this charming little Cinderella myth, there is no mistaking Ellen Glasgow's early sense of being an outcast.

Another story most reminiscent of her childhood is "Whispering Leaves." On a visit to an old house of that name, the narrator finds little Pell, a frail, imaginative boy who is ignored by his stepfather, Mr. Blanton, and his stepbrothers and sisters, exactly as Miss Glasgow apparently was by her brothers and sisters. Pell's only companion is the ghost of Mammy Rhody, who, like Ellen's Mammy Lizzie, comforts the child with stories at night. Because of Mammy Rhody's skill at training birds, "Whispering Leaves" has gained its name as a bird paradise. Little Pell also has that "enduring kinship with birds and animals" of which Miss Glasgow has spoken. He is actually birdlike in appearance and appetite, and he spends his waking hours outdoors, mostly in the trees. Like Ellen, too, Pell loses his beloved dog through the cruelty of his stepparent. It is not too much to say, then, that in "Whispering Leaves" Ellen Glasgow is reliving her childhood at Jerdone Castle.

The other ghost stories would not be so rewarding if interpreted biographically, but no reader can miss the preoccupation with illness, especially nervous illness, in them. In *The Woman Within,* Miss Glasgow tells us about her mother, who, worn out from child-bearing, lived in a state of anxiety that baffled her doctors for years. The autobiography also chronicles the long list of brothers, sisters, and other relatives whom she saw die around her. More specifically, the nurse who narrates "The Shadowy Third" and the secretary who narrates "The Past" probably derive from Anne Virginia Bennett, a trained nurse, who was Miss Glasgow's companion and secretary for many years.

Thus Miss Glasgow's personality and childhood experiences would have disposed her to take ghosts and native spirits seriously. But her reading in science and philosophy suggests another rationale. It is significant that the spirits are always manifested through an act of will by one of the characters. Miss Glasgow is plainly suggesting that ideas can be more real than objects, a concept as old as Plato. The reviewer in the Greensboro (North Carolina) *Daily News* explained her system in a way that would have appealed to both Ellen Glasgow and Edgar Allan Poe:

". . . ideas once definitely and strikingly resolved into action do not die, but manifest themselves as still living long after the individual who put his own compelling idea into vivid action has ceased to live. . . ."[18] Primitivism is involved, too, because innocent, young, or uneducated people are the most likely to "see" these ideas. As Miss Glasgow's old friend, Louise Collier Willcox, explained in *The Bookman,* "There may be a stage in training before the mind takes entire control of the nerves, when the *whole* body 'thinks,' and we are aware of more than a densely physical atmosphere."[19]

This is a romantic philosophy, but it is a post-Darwinian romanticism, and it is meant to be taken seriously. The opponents of the believers in spirits are, naturally, scientists—usually doctors. However, it is the specialist—the psychiatrist, the surgeon—not the general practitioner, that Ellen Glasgow attacks in these stories. The famous alienist, Dr. Roland Maradick, in "The Shadowy Third" is unable to minister to his own wife, but his young, sympathetic nurse knows intuitively that Mrs. Maradick is not insane, that she is only preserving the memory of her dead daughter. Dr. Drayton, a Washington nerve specialist, can only prescribe a rest in the country for Mrs. Beckwith, but old Dr. Lakeby, a general practitioner from Chericoke Landing, knows immediately that she is under the spell of "Dare's Gift" and predicts a speedy recovery once she leaves that contaminated house. Mrs. Vanderbridge in "The Past" has had a succession of doctors for her nervous ailment, but Miss Wrenn, her new secretary, soon learns that the spirit of the first Mrs. Vanderbridge is the cause of it. Dr. Estbridge, a psychiatrist in "The Professional Instinct," is unable to meet his wife's needs and ignorant of his own selfish motives until they are revealed to him by a friendly journalist.

Actually, Miss Glasgow was working in a familiar literary tradition. Although she might have been reluctant to admit it, she was exploring the same psychological vein that Rudyard Kipling and Henry James had explored a decade before. Kipling in "They" and James in such stories as "The Turn of the Screw," "The Jolly Corner," and "The Beast in the Jungle" were fascinated by the power that ideas, especially fears, have over men's minds. As their stories show, a fear or a wish can be so strong that the object takes on a concrete existence. However, their symbolic ghosts are visible only to the afflicted characters; Miss Glasgow's ghosts are more "real" than that, as I have shown. They take us nearer to

[18] Greensboro (N.C.) *Daily News,* December 16, 1923, p. 10. The author was probably Gerald W. Johnson, the associate editor, who knew Miss Glasgow through their mutual interest in *The Reviewer,* a Richmond little magazine, 1921–24.
[19] *The Bookman,* LVIII, No. 5 (January, 1924), 573.

modern ghost stories, like Kafka's, where the ghost becomes human and
the dream completely displaces reality. For Kipling, James, and Glasgow,
ghosts could have either good or bad influences; modern ghosts, supported by Freud and Jung, are consistently frightening because they represent the unconscious levels of the mind.

<h1 style="text-align:center">IV</h1>

The first four stories in *The Shadowy Third* have another feature in
common: the influence of Edgar Allan Poe. In a letter to Van Wyck
Brooks in 1944, Miss Glasgow recognized the unlikely relationship herself: "I have always felt a curious (because improbable) kinship with
Poe." [20] This kinship is worth exploring. We might begin by noticing
the parallel in plot between Poe's "Ligeia" and Glasgow's "The Past."
In both stories the first wife tries to destroy the second by supernatural
means. The Glasgow approach differs in that the first Mrs. Vanderbridge,
who appears in her own body, retires in defeat when the second Mrs.
Vanderbridge proves her own moral superiority. However, Poe might
well have preferred the first wife.

Whereas "Ligeia" is similar only in plot, "The Fall of the House of
Usher" must be admitted as a deep and pervasive influence on all four
ghost stories in the Glasgow collection. First, observe that three of the
four stories—"Dare's Gift," "Whispering Leaves," and "Jordan's End"—
are set in symbolic country houses that supply the titles for their stories.
All four houses exert a definite moral influence over their inhabitants.
The treachery of Sir Roderick Dare in Bacon's Rebellion causes the betrayal of a Union soldier by his Confederate sweetheart and the deception of a corporation lawyer by his wife. Successive acts of treachery have
corrupted the very walls of the house. Dr. Lakeby makes this point clear:
"Did you ever stop to wonder about the thoughts that must have gathered within walls like these?—to wonder about the impressions that must
have lodged in the bricks, in the crevices, in the timber and the masonry?
Have you ever stopped to think that these multiplied impressions might
create a current of thought—a mental atmosphere—an inscrutable power
of suggestion?" This is identical with Roderick Usher's theory of the
"sentience of vegetable things." Even the architecture of "Dare's Gift"
prepares us for the thematic moral decay. The present owners discover,
too late ". . . architectural absurdities—wanton excrescences in the modern additions, which had been designed apparently with the purpose of
providing space at the least possible cost of materials and labour."

[20] Rouse (ed.), *Letters of Ellen Glasgow,* 352.

"Whispering Leaves" makes the same point in the same way. The spirit of the first Mrs. Blanton prevails, despite the neglect of the present owners, in the splendid house and flourishing garden, just as the birds remain in their sanctuary after the death of Mammy Rhody. But decadence is inevitable. It is already perceptible in the character of Pelham Blanton, "a tall, relaxed, indolent-looking man of middle age, with grey hair, brilliant dark eyes and an air of pensive resignation. . . ." The narrator concludes, "I had heard, or had formed some vague idea, that the family had 'run to seed', as they say in the South, and my first view of Cousin Pelham helped to fix this impression more firmly in my mind. He looked, I thought, a man who had ceased to desire anything intensely except physical comfort." Cousin Pelham is plainly a cousin to Roderick Usher, too.

By now the analogy with Poe's "Fall of the House of Usher" should be clear. There, too, the decaying house contributed to the decay of Roderick and his sister, just as the Usher family had contributed to the decay of the house itself. The tonal unity achieved by the identification of house and occupants has been one of the most admired features of the Poe story.

The prize demonstration of the House-of-Usher influence is reserved for the last story in *The Shadowy Third* collection, "Jordan's End." Even the title bears the same dual symbolism as the Poe story. Jordan's End is simultaneously the name of the crumbling old Virginia plantation and the epitome of the decaying family that inhabits it. The narrator, a young doctor, has been called to treat Alan Jordan, who seems to have fallen prey to the ancestral insanity. Our narrator, like Poe's, arrives at the house as the sun is setting. It is dusk in November, and the doctor pauses at a fork in the road, where there is a dead tree with buzzards roosting in it. Only a sunken, untraveled trail leads to Jordan's End. An old Negro tells him that all the male Jordans have died insane, and now young Alan must be confined and guarded. Carstairs, the famous alienist from Baltimore, is to decide tomorrow whether Alan is, like his ancestors, incurable.

With this information in his mind, the doctor emerges from the gloomy woods.

The glow in the sky had faded now to a thin yellow-green, and a melancholy twilight pervaded the landscape. In this twilight I looked over the few sheep huddled together on the ragged lawn, and saw the old brick house crumbling beneath its rank growth of ivy. As I drew nearer I had the feeling that the surrounding desolation brooded there like some sinister influence.

But the narrator also recognizes that both the house and its inhabitants once had charm, even distinction. Although the eaves are now falling away, the shutters sagging, the windows broken, and the boards rotting, the house was once of an impressive Georgian design with beautiful details. "A fine old place once, but repulsive now in its abject decay, like some young blood of former days who has grown senile," the doctor muses. Similarly, the Jordan family was once the proudest in the county until the Civil War. "Jest run to seed," Father Peterkin, the old Negro says. Intermarriage is a partial explanation.

But Miss Glasgow uses the House-of-Usher theme to make a point that Poe was unable to make about the South because he was too close to it. The degeneration which the house always symbolizes is brought about by the refusal of the inhabitants to trust more than their senses. The families that go to seed are those that refuse to believe in the intangible. They love material comfort more than beauty; they love tradition more than progress. "Dare's Gift" and "Whispering Leaves," Ellen Glasgow's most ambitious stories, show both the necessity and the difficulty of believing in the intangible. The ghosts are only objective correlatives for this idea. We need not believe in them so long as we believe in what they stand for.

The house that destroys its occupants had, we might guess, a real-life parallel in One West Main Street, a house that both attracted and repelled Miss Glasgow because of its burden of memories. Although she left it from 1911 to 1916 and frequently went away during the hot summers after that, it was always her home address, and *The Woman Within* testifies to its powerful impression on her. "The fibers of my personality are interwoven, I feel, with some indestructible element of the place." [21] In 1942 she could say that out of ten children only she and two others remained alive, but still the house stood. Ever since Poe a trademark of Southern literature has been the house that is an image of the family and in turn becomes an image of the society. Ellen Glasgow's character with the vein of iron belongs in a solid gray house like One West Main Street.

V

All four of the ghost stories in *The Shadowy Third* collection have another feature in common: the use of a first-person narrator. Again, the influence of Poe is possible. However, in her preface to *The Romance of a Plain Man* (1909), her only novel told from a first-person point of view, Miss Glasgow testifies to her discomfort: "The question of the proper use of the first person has been frequently discussed in criticism, and either approved or condemned according to the preferences of the critic. For my part, I have always thought that the method contained

[21] *The Woman Within,* 26.

almost insurmountable disadvantages, even when it was employed by the great masters of prose fiction." Then she adds apologetically, ". . . I think my one and only adventure with the first person singular is likely to have been the sad result of my youthful fondness for the heroes of romance." [22]

Miss Glasgow does not list the disadvantages of the method or the names of the famous practitioners, nor does she mention her short stories. However, one insurmountable disadvantage to her must have been the sacrifice of the godlike, ironic perspective from which she liked to write. It is possible that she would have been an even better artist if she had been able to restrain herself within the limits of the first-person narrator; her love of epigram frequently becomes intrusive editorial comment in fiction.

But why, then, did she deliberately choose an uncomfortable point of view for most of her short stories? She had two distinguished guides in Poe and James, both of whom realized that a first-person viewpoint can plausibly convey the most bizarre details. Because the narrative is told by someone to whom it is actually happening, we are more likely to suspend our disbelief. Where spirits are supposed to be visible, it also helps to have an intelligent, objective eyewitness, such as a secretary, a nurse, a lawyer, or a family doctor.

Poe invariably chose a first-person narrator for his horror stories; James had even better equipment. In his preface to *The Altar of the Dead* (1909) where he collected all his ghost stories except "The Turn of the Screw," James complained that the sensational white vision at the end of *Arthur Gordon Pym* failed because Poe had made Pym merely the reporter rather than the perceiver of the vision. For James the success of the supernatural depended on its being filtered through the consciousness of a central character. "We want it clear, goodness knows, but we also want it thick, and we get thickness in the human consciousness that entertains and records, that amplifies and interprets it." [23] James used a first-person percipient in "The Turn of the Screw," but elsewhere he achieved supernatural effects by means of his famous central intelligence viewpoint.

Only one story in *The Shadowy Third*, "The Difference," is narrated from Ellen Glasgow's favorite point of view, the central intelligence. However, James would have found little to praise in her use of it. For example, the viewpoint in "The Difference" shifts abruptly from Margaret Fleming to her opponent Rose Morrison so that we can see how

---

[22] *A Certain Measure*, 70.
[23] R. P. Blackmur (ed.), *The Art of the Novel* (New York, 1953), 256.

Margaret looked to Rose. Four out of the five uncollected stories are also handled from the central intelligence viewpoint, but there is no hint yet of Miss Glasgow's concentrated use of it in *Barren Ground,* or of the multiple viewpoint which she was to use so brilliantly in *They Stooped to Folly, Vein of Iron,* and *The Sheltered Life.*

VI

All five of the uncollected stories and "The Difference" from *The Shadowy Third* have as their theme that limitless subject—the relationship between men and women. Although Ellen Glasgow's "social history" of the South appears to have been her main concern, the real focus in all her fiction seems to be the struggle of women for respect in a world dominated by men. Her short stories dramatize a complete cycle of relationships, from the first apprehensive encounter to the last bitter rejection. To a Darwinian, love is apparently a struggle for dominance. Miss Glasgow's women hope that love is something better than that, but they are usually disappointed. Her typical plot sequence runs: girl meets boy; girl is taken advantage of by boy; then girl learns to get along without boys, or, girl gets back at boy.

The cycle begins in Ellen Glasgow's first published story, "Between Two Shores." Here fate has placed, on a ship bound for England, a shy, sensitive young widow, Lucy Smith, in a stateroom next to a confident, attentive young man who calls himself Lawrence Smith. Because of the coincidence of names, everyone on the ship considers them married, and "Lawrence Smith" encourages the deception, since he is fleeing from the American police under an alias. Unaware of his past Lucy is alternately frightened and attracted by this strong, impulsive man, who seems devoted to her during her many spells of sickness. In Lawrence she sees ". . . the face of a man of strong will and even stronger passions, who had lived hard and fast. . . . If one were in his power, how quietly he might bend and break mere flesh and bone."

Here the allegory sets in. Lucy has never loved her husband and has never really immersed herself in life. She is obviously ". . . a woman in whom temperamental fires had been smothered rather than extinguished, by the ashes of unfulfillment. To existence, which is a series of rhythmic waves of the commonplace, she offered facial serenity; to life, which is a clash of opposing passions, she turned the wistful eyes of ignorance."

The combination of Lawrence's gentle hands and his passionate nature soon undermines Lucy's restraint, until she confesses, "I should choose to be broken by you to being caressed by any other man—." In fact, when they reach Liverpool Lucy is inspired to protect her "husband" from possible arrest by playing the role of his wife. This symbolic act links her with him and with real life.

"Between Two Shores" means literally a happening between New York and Liverpool, but the title also describes Lucy's state of suspense between repression and indulgence, between ignorance and experience. We might say she began to live at Liverpool. The Freudian critic will see here an ego torn between the id and the superego. Other readers will be reminded of such symbolic works as Conrad's "The Secret Sharer," James's "The Beast in the Jungle," or O'Neill's *The Hairy Ape*.

However, after reading *The Woman Within*, we can see that Miss Glasgow was actually dramatizing her spiritual withdrawal following the death of her mother in 1893. She loved her mother so deeply that she might actually feel widowed after such a loss. She had barely abandoned mourning in June, 1896, when, thanks to the generosity of her brother Arthur, who had become a successful engineer in London, she embarked for a summer in England. She confesses:

Never before in my life had I felt so suffocated by melancholy as I felt when I sailed, alone, among strangers, to England. I know that I was in a cloud of nervous depression; but it was impossible for me to break through the restraint, or to be natural. . . . I had never looked worse in my life, and I knew that whatever charm I possessed was dimmed by the terror of not hearing strange voices, and of not understanding strange words that were said to me.[24]

Her story dramatizes clearly her need for and fear of emotional commitment. While here she stresses the rewards of such commitment, later she was to concentrate on the dangers.

Four stories constitute a "marriage group," and three of them preach a similar moral: in marriage the woman gives up everything, while the man gains himself a servant. Three husbands are depicted as selfish brutes, ranging from Stanley Kenton in "Romance and Sally Byrd," a philanderer who deceives an innocent kindergarten teacher, to George Fleming, who includes both golf and adultery among his favorite recreations in "The Difference," to Dr. John Estbridge in "The Professional Instinct," who self-righteously decides to abandon his domineering wife. Since these particular stories were written just after Miss Glasgow's unsatisfactory engagement to Colonel Henry W. Anderson, a biographical excursion is tempting here. The self-sacrificing wives in these stories explain well enough why Ellen Glasgow never married. Elsewhere she has celebrated her independence in this way: "I have had much love and more romance than most women, and I have not had to stroke some

[24] *The Woman Within*, 118.

man the right way to win my bread or the wrong way to win my freedom." [25]

"The Difference" and "Romance and Sally Byrd" present the double standard in marriage that irked Miss Glasgow so much. The patient wives endure their husbands' unfaithfulness as if there were no hope for a fairer relationship. Stanley Kenton's wife consoles his latest victim, Sally Byrd: "When your heart is really broken, it lies still and dead like mine. You can't imagine what a relief it is . . . to have your heart break at last." She sits darning a symbolic pair of Stanley's seven-dollar socks as she remarks, "Men are so careless about their things." Margaret Fleming in "The Difference" suffers an even worse fate. She loses both her pride in her husband and in herself when she learns, after a visit to his mistress, that he has never loved anybody but himself.

In "The Professional Instinct" Miss Glasgow ironically presents the same theme, this time from the point of view of the selfish husband. Dr. Estbridge, a psychoanalyst, is prepared to elope with Judith Campbell, a philosophy professor and author of *Marriage and Individuality*, but when he hears at the last minute of a chance at the chair in physiology at the state university, he leaves Judith waiting at the station. Judith, incidentally, has given up a chance at a college presidency in order to elope with Estbridge. The story fairly bristles with such obvious irony. Like George Fleming, Estbridge loves only his own reflection in women.

"Thinking Makes It So" catches Miss Glasgow in a rare sentimental mood about marriage. Here she describes a romance by correspondence between two middle-aged lovers who have been bruised and worn by life. They still have their dreams, however, and thinking makes them so. The distant echo of "Only a Daisy" can be heard here. It is unquestionably the weakest of the Glasgow stories, made up of leftovers from *Life and Gabriella*. Its only interest is biographical.

A more successful attempt to take a comic view of romance is "The Artless Age," which describes a teenage courtship, or rather, two of them. This story is a symbol-hunter's paradise, because the Old-Fashioned Girl, Mary Louise Littleton, and the Modern Girl, Geraldine Plummer, are competing for the affection of the American Boy, Richard Askew. At a costume ball, Mary Louise goes as an angel, Geraldine as a devil. At the end of the story we learn that there is no such thing as an artless age; every age has its own arts. Mary Louise, although protected in a French convent and in the Blue Ridge Mountains, is just as artful as Geraldine, but her wiles are outmoded. The hopeless conflict is well

[25] From "Miscellaneous Pungencies," Miss Glasgow's private collection of epigrams in the Alderman Library, University of Virginia.

demonstrated by the following dialogue. Mary Louise: "I am so fond of Ruskin." Geraldine: "What's a Ruskin? Do you make it with gin?"

Inevitably, Richard is trapped by the more aggressive Geraldine and led unprotesting to the altar. Poor Mary Louise is sacrificed to the allegory; she marries Geraldine's father, who is an archeologist!

The observant mothers, who play the part of a Greek chorus, deplore Geraldine's tactics, but admit that they are well suited to the modern world. Here and in two novels, *The Romantic Comedians* (1926) and *They Stooped to Folly* (1929), Miss Glasgow managed to take a comic view of the world in the 1920's, but her heart was not really in it. At any rate, in "The Artless Age," her analysis of love has come full circle. In twenty-five years, Lucy Smith has been replaced by Geraldine Plummer.

VII

Two more stories focus on an abstract moral problem—what we now call mercy killing, or euthanasia. Two persons with no reason for living are put out of their misery with the assistance of their fellow men. Is this a crime? There are subtleties in each case which complicate the moral decision. In "A Point in Morals" an alienist is asked for a package of opium by a passenger on a train, who has botched his life and wants to commit suicide. The alienist, finally convinced by the young man's story that he has no reason for living and many reasons for dying, leaves the fatal package on the seat when he gets off the train.

Because she has effaced herself completely from the story by means of a dramatic framework, Miss Glasgow makes evaluation of the doctor's act very difficult. The story begins as a dialogue among the five characters around a dinner table on a ship: a journalist, a lawyer, an Englishman, a girl in black, and the doctor. The discussion turns to whether the saving of a human life might become positively immoral. At this point the alienist begins his story, into which he inserts the unhappy man's biography, making a story-within-a-story-within-a-story. The reaction of the audience gives us no clue as to an official interpretation. Each of the characters is ridiculed at some point. Perhaps Miss Glasgow had no stand here but merely wanted to embarrass all these sophisticated observers with a moral problem beyond the reach of science. If we assume that she disliked this alienist as much as those in the other stories, then the doctor must be labeled a monster. We should recall, however, that this is an early story, written before Miss Glasgow had rejected science in favor of philosophy.

An answer may be easier after we consider a parallel situation in the previously discussed "Jordan's End." Alan Jordan, incurably insane, dies mysteriously after an overdose of the opiate that the doctor-narrator has prescribed. The doctor knows that Jordan's wife must be to blame, but he cannot bring himself to question her. Jordan's death solves many problems and will cause none, so long as everyone remains silent. The doctor and Mrs. Jordan are described so sympathetically that one is tempted to condone this mercy killing.[26] Taken together, the two stories reflect Ellen Glasgow's early realization that the most serious human problems lie beyond the reach of science. This theme, too, links her with Poe and with the agrarian branch of the Southern literary tradition.

VIII

Two questions remain: what is the relationship of Ellen Glasgow's stories to her novels? And what is the artistic merit of the stories in themselves? The stories are both the causes and the effects of her other fiction. The four stories previously discussed in the "marriage group" may be recognized as pencil sketches for the three full-scale studies of love and marriage: *The Romantic Comedians, They Stooped to Folly,* and *The Sheltered Life.* In George Fleming, Stanley Kenton, and Dr. Estbridge, all fatuous, frustrated, middle-aged husbands, we see trial sketches for Judge Honeywell, Virginius Littlepage, George Birdsong, and even General Archbald, although it would be fairer to call Dr. Lakeby in "Dare's Gift" *his* prototype. On the female side, the romantic competition between Mary Louise Littleton and Geraldine Plummer in "The Artless Age," between Margaret Fleming and Rose Morrison in "The Difference," between Sally Byrd and Mrs. Kenton in "Romance and Sally Byrd," and between Mrs. Estbridge and Judith Campbell in "The Professional Instinct" reveal simultaneously the male refusal to grow old gracefully and the female refusal to get along without men.

The conflict within as well as between the sexes is enacted on a larger scale in the novels, but with similar results. The conflicts between Anna-bel Upchurch and Amanda Lightfoot over Judge Honeywell in *The Romantic Comedians,* between Victoria Littlepage and Amy Dalrymple over Virginius Littlepage in *They Stooped to Folly,* and between Jenny Blair Archbald and Eva Birdsong over George Birdsong in *The Sheltered Life,* are all prepared for by romantic triangles of the same kind in the short stories. Mrs. Kenton is the first of many Glasgow women to cele-brate the end of her need for sexual love, and, hence, for men. Later, in *Barren Ground,* Dorinda Oakley exults after repulsing Jason Greylock,

[26] Professor William W. Kelly suggests that her interest in euthanasia may derive from the long illnesses which her mother and favorite sister Cary suffered before their deaths.

"Oh, if the women who wanted love could only know the infinite relief of having love over!" [27] Then in *The Romantic Comedians* Edmonia Bredalbane horrifies her twin brother, Judge Honeywell, by asking, "After all the fuss that has been made about marriage, isn't there something more in it than this?" [28] Four husbands have not changed her opinion.

The most complex discussion of the marriage problem is in *The Sheltered Life*. There are no villains here; as in the short stories, there are only weak, selfish people. Jenny Blair and George Birdsong would rather die than bring pain to George's wife, Eva, but their innocent flirtation brings disaster to both of them. Several awkward encounters between Jenny Blair and Eva are anticipated by the climax of "The Difference," where the wife and the "other woman" try to reach an understanding about a man not worth understanding. The exemplary women are held in their places only by a sense of duty; the exemplary men have preserved their status only accidentally. For example, only an accident prevented General Archbald from running off with a married woman in England, but the world knows him as a model husband.

The most substantial transfer of theme and setting from story to novel is from "Jordan's End" to *Barren Ground*.[29] The disintegration of Jordan's End prepares us for the deterioration of Five Oaks; there is a difference only in degree. The derangement of all the Jordans is matched by the decadence of all the male Greylocks and the madness of Geneva Greylock. Even the descriptions of the two houses are similar, although there is still hope for Five Oaks: "It was a fairly good house of its period, the brick building, with ivy-encrusted wings, which was preferred by the more prosperous class of Virginia farmers. The foundation of stone had been well laid; the brick walls were stout and solid, and though neglect and decay had overtaken it, the house still preserved, beneath its general air of deterioration, an underlying character of honesty and thrift."

The beginnings of "Jordan's End" and *Barren Ground* are almost interchangeable. A doctor in a buggy pulled by a mare approaches a ruined house at sunset in late autumn, after traveling over a mile of rutted track from the Old Stage Road, where a large, dead tree stands. His passenger in one story is Dorinda Oakley, in the other, Father Peterkin.

Judith Yardley Jordan embodies the qualities of both Dorinda Oakley and Geneva Ellegood Greylock. Like Geneva, she was a famous beauty

[27] *Barren Ground* (Sagamore Press edition, 1957), 238.
[28] *The Romantic Comedians* (New York, 1926), 36.
[29] The relationship between "Jordan's End" and *Barren Ground* has been pointed out to me by Professors William W. Kelly and Louis D. Rubin, Jr.

from an adjoining farm before she married into a decadent family. Like
Geneva, she drooped under the gloom of the place, but like Dorinda, she
found the necessary iron vein when a bold stroke was necessary. Judith's
husband, Alan Jordan, is the original of Jason Greylock. Both are the
last limbs on a decaying family tree and both succumb to their in-
heritance.

It would not be too much to say that *Barren Ground* is a continuation
of "Jordan's End" because Dorinda and Nathan Pedlar reclaim Five
Oaks from a state similar to that of Jordan's End as visible proof that
the vein of iron can prevail over the temptations of the flesh. In *Barren
Ground* Miss Glasgow is celebrating the suppression of sex and of male
tyranny. She was thus enabled to take a comic view of human relations
in her next two novels; but it is hard to find much comedy in the
"evasive idealism" of the "happiness hunters" because the attitudes she
mocks are her own discarded ideas.

What makes "Jordan's End" and *Barren Ground* such impressive
stories is that in both of them Miss Glasgow has tried to dissect the
grandeur that was the South. Family pride, refusal to abandon agrarian
ways, rutted absorption in the past, inbreeding, sensuality—all are drama-
tized through plot, character, and setting. "Jordan's End" is a tragedy, or
the outline of one. *Barren Ground* converts tragic material into tragi-
comedy. Ironically, another salvation besides the famous iron vein is
implicit in a striking scene from "Jordan's End," but Miss Glasgow
missed its significance. Two Negroes are sitting beside the fireplace in
Alan Jordan's room as the doctor enters. "They had simple, kindly faces,
these men; there was a primitive humanity in their features, which
might have been modelled out of the dark earth of the fields . . . but
the man in the winged chair neither lifted his head nor turned his eyes
in our direction. He sat there, lost within the impenetrable wilderness
of the insane. . . ."

The short stories not only influenced the novels but they occasionally
show the effects of them. *Life and Gabriella* supplied not only the middle-
aged romance in "Thinking Makes It So," but the Richmond-to-New
York setting of "Romance and Sally Byrd." Fiery old Colonel Dare in
"Dare's Gift" has his original in General Battle from *The Voice of the
People* (1900) and in Major Lightfoot from *The Battleground* (1902).
The newspaper board meetings in *The Descendant* (1897) and the
boarding-house arguments in *Phases of an Inferior Planet* (1898) are
models for the dialogue with allegorical characters in "A Point in
Morals." Even Miss Glasgow's experiment with first-person narration be-

gan with *The Romance of a Plain Man* (1909) rather than in the short stories.

But Ellen Glasgow's best stories are those which owe nothing to her novels. They are independent moral and philosophical analyses of the nature of reality and of man's relationship with his fellow man. "A Point in Morals," "The Difference," and "Jordan's End" are not so daring today as they once were, but they are the products of a bold mind, and "Jordan's End," at least, escapes being a period piece. The device of making ideas visible in the four "ghost" stories is psychologically sound, if not artistically successful.

It is unfortunate for the artistic stature of her short stories that Miss Glasgow did not continue writing them after 1924. Although she dated *Virginia* (1913) as her first mature work, it is generally agreed that her "major phase" began with *Barren Ground* (1925). This novel, together with *The Sheltered Life* (1932) and *Vein of Iron* (1935), remains unchallenged by anything she wrote in a shorter form. "Jordan's End" gives us a hint of what she might have done if she had taken the short story as seriously as she took the novel, if she had not been so obsessed with her "social history of Virginia."

From our perspective today, we can see that Ellen Glasgow kept maturing stylistically, but that her moral and social concepts solidified in the middle of the 1920's. The rebel of the nineties found herself the conservative of the twenties. Nevertheless, the advice of Walter Hines Page and her own iron vein kept her writing fiction even after she had lost faith in her readers, even when she knew she was celebrating lost values. For this she had earned her status as one of America's leading woman novelists.

But her twelve short stories prove that, contrary to what Miss Glasgow believed about herself, her literary talents were not confined to large-scale evolutionary studies. This prejudice she acquired from her early models. She was fundamentally a moralist rather than a historian. Her epigrams reveal a dazzling talent for condensation. Her inclination toward irony and paradox shows up particularly well in a small space. In short, she had all the equipment of a great short story writer, except a respect for the form.

Between Two Shores

SHE WAS leaning against the railing of the deck, gazing wistfully down upon the sea of faces on the landing below. She wore a skirt and coat of brown cloth, and her veil was raised in a white film above her small hat.

In the crowd clustering about her eager for the last glimpse of friends she looked shy and nervous, and her brown eyes were dilated in alarm. Despite her thirty years, there was something girlish in her shrinking figure—a suggestion of the incipient emotions of youth. The fine lines that time had set upon brow and lips were results of the flight of undifferentiated days, and lacked the intensity of experimental records. One might have classified her in superficial survey as a woman in whom temperamental fires had been smothered, rather than extinguished, by the ashes of unfulfilment. To existence, which is a series of rhythmic waves of the commonplace, she offered facial serenity; to life, which is a clash of opposing passions, she turned the wistful eyes of ignorance.

A tall girl, carrying an armful of crimson roses, pressed against her, and waved a heavily scented handkerchief to some one upon the landing. On the other side, a man was shouting directions in regard to a missing piece of baggage. "I marked it myself," he declared frantically. "It was to have been shipped from New Orleans to the Cunard dock. I marked it 'Not Wanted' with my own hands, and, by Jove, those dirty creoles have taken me at my word."

She rested her hand upon the railing, and leaned far over. Down below, a pretty girl in a pink shirt waist was kissing her gloved finger tips to a stout gentleman on deck. An excited group were waving congratulations to a bride and groom, who looked fatigued and slightly bored. She yawned and bowed her head to avoid the spoke of a black parasol sheltering the lady on her right. For the first time she recognized in this

furtive shrinking a faint homesickness, and her thoughts recoiled to the
dull Southern home, to the sisters-in-law who made her life burdensome,
and to the little graveyard where the husband she had never loved lay
buried. The girl with the crimson roses jostled her rudely, and from behind, some one was treading upon her gown. The insipid heat of the
July sun flashed across her face, and in a vision she recalled the sweeping
pastures of the old plantation, with the creek where the willows grew
and the thrushes sang. Then the odor of the heavily scented handkerchief half sickened her. From the crowd some one was calling to the
girl in tones of reassurance: "See you in London? Of course. Booked for
'Campania,' sailing twenty-sixth."

Suddenly the steamer gave a tremor of warning, and a volley of
farewells ascended from below.

"Pleasant voyage!" called the man to the girl beside her. "Pleasant
voyage!" called some one to the lady on her right. Then she realized that
she was alone, and for the first time regretted that her father-in-law had
not come. When the news of his delay had first reached her and she had
volunteered to start alone, she had experienced a vivid elation. There was
delight in the idea of freedom—of being accountable to no one, of being
absolutely independent of advice. Now she wished that she had an acquaintance who would wish her godspeed, or shout an indistinct pleas-
antry from the crowded landing.

The steamer moved slowly out into the harbor, and the shore was
white with fluttering good-byes. The girl still waved the scented cambric.
Then the distance lapsed into gradual waves of blue.

She left the railing, and stumbled over a group of steamer chairs
placed midway of the deck. She descended to her state-room, which was
in the center of the ship. At the door she found the stewardess, who inquired if she was "Mrs. L. Smith."

"That is my name, and I am going to be ill. I know it."

"Lie down at once. And about this bag? I thought it would give you
more space if I put it in the gentleman's room. He hasn't much lug-
gage."

Lucy Smith looked up in mystification. "But it is mine," she explained,
"and I want it."

Then the boat gave a lurch, and she undressed and climbed into her
berth.

The next day, after a sleepless night, she struggled up and left her
state-room, the stewardess following with her wraps. At the foot of the
stairs she swayed, and fell upon the lowest step. "It's no use," she said
plaintively, "I can't go up. I can't indeed."

The stewardess spoke with professional encouragement. "Oh, you're all right," she remonstrated. "Here's the gentleman now. He'll help you."

"Isn't there but one gentleman on board?" Mrs. Smith began, but her words failed.

Some one lifted her, and in a moment she was on deck and in her chair, while the stewardess wrapped rugs about her and a strange man arranged the pillows under her head. Then they both left her, and she lay with closed eyes.

"Perhaps you would like yesterday's 'Herald'?" said a voice.

She started from an uncertain doze, and looked around her. Hours had passed, and since closing her eyes the sea had grown bluer and the sun warmer. A pearl-colored foam was glistening on the waves. "I beg your pardon," she replied, turning in the direction whence the words came, "did you speak?"

The man in the next chair leaned towards her, holding a paper in his hand. He was tall and angular with commonplace features, lighted by the sympathetic gleam in his eyes.

"I asked if you would like a 'Herald'?" he repeated.

She looked at him reproachfully. "I am ill," she answered.

He smiled. "Oh, I beg your pardon," he said. "You didn't look it, and it is so hard to tell. I offered a lemon to that gray-green girl over there, and she flew into a rage. *But are* you ill in earnest?"

"I shouldn't exactly choose it for jest," she returned; "though, somehow, it does make time pass. One forgets that there are such divisions as days and weeks. It all seems a blank."

"But it is very calm."

"So the stewardess says," she answered aggrievedly, "but the boat rocks dreadfully."

He did not reply, and in a moment his glance wandered to the card upon her chair. "Odd, isn't it?" he questioned.

She followed his gaze, and colored faintly. The card read: "Mrs. L. Smith." Then he pointed to a similar label upon his own chair, bearing in a rough scrawl the name, "L. Smith."

"It is a very common name," she remarked absently.

He laughed. "Very," he admitted.

"Perhaps your husband is Lawrence Smith also."

The smile passed from her lips.

"My husband is dead," she answered; "but his name was Lucien."

He folded the newspaper awkwardly. Then he spoke. "Nicer name than Lawrence," he observed.

She nodded. "A name is of very little consequence," she rejoined. "I have always felt that about every name in the world except Lucy. Lucy is mine."

He looked into her eyes. Despite her illness, they shone with a warm, fawn-like brown. "I think it a pretty name," he said. "It is so soft."

"It has no character," she returned. "I have always known that life would have been different for me if I hadn't been called Lucy. People would not treat me like a child if I were Augusta or even Agnes—but *Lucy!*"

"People change their names sometimes," he suggested.

She laughed softly. "I tried to. I tried to become Lucinda, but I couldn't. Lucy stuck to me."

"It wouldn't be so bad without Smith," he remarked, smiling.

"That was a horrible cross," she returned. "I wonder if you mind Smith as much as I do."

At first he did not answer. To her surprise his face grew grave, and she saw the haggard lines about his mouth which his smile had obscured. "It was a deuced good chance that I struck it," he said shortly, and opened his paper.

For a time they sat silent. Then, as the luncheon gong sounded and the passengers flocked past, he rose and bent over her chair. "You will have chicken broth?" he said distinctly. "I will send the steward." And before she recovered from her surprise he left her.

A little later the broth was brought, and soon after the steward reappeared bearing iced prunes. "The gentleman sent you word that you were to eat these," he said. And she sat up in bewilderment, and ate the prunes silently.

"You are very kind," she remarked timidly, when he came up from the dining-saloon and threw himself into the chair beside her.

For an instant he looked at her blankly, his brow wrinkling. She saw that he was not thinking of her, and reddened.

"You were kind—about the prunes," she explained.

"The prunes?" he repeated vaguely. Then he brought himself together with a jerk. "Oh, you are the little woman who was sick—yes—I remember."

"They were very nice," she said more firmly.

"I am glad you liked them," he rejoined, and was silent. Then he broke into an irrelevant laugh, and the lines upon his forehead deepened. She saw that he carried an habitual sneer upon his lips. With a half-frightened gesture she drew from him.

"I am glad that you find life amusing," she observed stiffly. "I don't."

He surveyed her with a dogged humor. "It is not life, my dear lady, it is—you."

She spoke more stiffly still. "I don't catch your meaning," she said. "Is my hat on one side?"

He laughed again. "It is perfectly balanced, I assure you."

"Is my hair uncurled?"

"Yes, but I shouldn't have noticed it. It is very pretty."

She sat up in offended dignity. "I do not desire compliments," she returned. "I wish merely information."

Half closing his eyes, he leaned back in his chair, looking at her from under the brim of his cap. "Well, without comment, I will state that your hair has fallen upon your forehead and that a loosened lock is lying upon your cheek—no, don't put it back. I beg your pardon——"

A pink spot appeared in the cheek next to him. Her eyes flashed. "How intolerable you are!" she said.

The smile in his eyes deepened. "How delicious you are!" he retorted.

She rose from her chair, drawing herself to her full stature. "I shall change my seat," she began.

Then the steamer lurched, and she swayed and grasped the arm he held out. "I—I am so dizzy," she finished appealingly.

He put her back into her chair, and wrapped the rugs about her. As she still shivered, he added his own to the pile. When he placed the pillow beneath her head, she noticed that his touch was as tender as a woman's. The sneer was gone from his lips.

"But you will be cold," she remonstrated from beneath his rug.

"Not I," he responded. "I am a tough knot. If the fiery furnace has left me unscathed, a little cold wind won't do more than chap me."

His voice had grown serious, and she looked up inquiringly. "The fiery furnace?" she repeated.

"Oh, predestined damnation, if you prefer. Are you religious?"

"Don't," she pleaded, a tender light coming into her eyes, and she added: "The damned are not kind—and you are very kind."

Her words faltered, but they chased the recklessness from his eyes.

"Kind?" he returned. "I wonder how many men we left in America would uphold that—that verdict—or how many women, for that matter?"

Her honest eyes did not waver. "I will stand by it," she replied simply.

A sudden illumination leaped to his face. "Against twelve good and true men?" he demanded daringly.

"Against a thousand—and the President thrown in."

He laughed a little bitterly. "Because of the prunes?" He was looking down into her face.

She reddened. "Because of the prunes and—and other things," she answered.

A ghost of the sneer awoke about his mouth. "I never did a meaner thing than about the prunes," he said hotly. Then he turned from her, and strode with swinging strides along the deck.

That evening he did not speak to her. They lay side by side in their steamer chairs, watching the gray mist that crept over the amber line of the horizon. She looked at his set and sallow face, where the grim line of the jaw was overcast by the constant sneer upon his reckless lips. It was not a good face, this she knew. It was the face of a man of strong will and stronger passions, who had lived hard and fast. She wondered vaguely at the furrowed track he must have made of his past years. The wonder awed her, and she felt half afraid of his grimness, growing grimmer in the gathering dusk. If one were in his power, how quietly he might bend and break mere flesh and bone. But across the moodiness of his face she caught the sudden warmth of his glance, and she remembered the touch of his hands—tender as it was strong. She moved nearer, laying her fragile fingers on the arm of his chair. "I am afraid you are unhappy," she said.

He started nervously, and faced her almost roughly. "Who is happy?" he demanded sneeringly. "Are you?"

She shrank slightly. "Somehow I think that a woman is never happy," she responded gently; "but you——"

He leaned towards her, a swift change crossing his face, his keen glance softening to compassion. "Then it is dastardly unfair," he said. "What is goodness for, if it does not make one happy? I am a rough brute, and I get my deserts, but the world should be gentle to a thing like you."

"No, no," she protested, "I am not good."

His eyes lightened. "Any misdemeanors punishable by law?"

"I am discontented," she went on. "I rage when things go wrong. I am not a saint."

"I might have known it," he remarked, "or you wouldn't have spoken to me. I have known lots of saints—mostly women—and they always look the other way when a sinner comes along. The reputation of a saint is the most sensitive thing on earth. It should be kept in a glass case."

"Are you so very wicked?" she asked frankly.

He was gazing out to sea, where the water broke into waves of deepening gray. In the sky a single star shone like an emerald set in a fawn-colored dome. The lapping sound of the waves at the vessel's sides came softly through the stillness. Suddenly he spoke, his voice ringing like a jarring discord in a harmonious whole.

"Five days ago a man called me a devil," he said, "and I guess he wasn't far wrong. Only, if I was a single devil, he was a legion steeped in one. What a scoundrel he was!"

The passion in his tones caused her to start quickly. The words were shot out with the force of balls from a cannon, sustained by the impulse of evil. "Don't," she said pleadingly, "please, please don't."

"Don't what?" he demanded roughly. "Don't curse the blackest scoundrel that ever lived—and died?" Over the last word his voice weakened as if in appeal.

"Don't curse anybody," she answered. "It is not like you."

He turned upon her suspiciously. "Pshaw! how do you know?"

"I don't know. I only believe."

"I never had much use for belief," he returned; "it is a poor sort of thing."

She met his bitter gaze with one of level calm. "And yet men have suffered death for it."

Above her head an electric jet was shining, and it cast a white light upon her small figure buried under the mass of rugs. Her eyes were glowing. There was a soft suffusion upon her lashes, whether from the salt spray or from unshed tears, he could not tell.

"Well, believe in me if you choose," he said; "it won't do any harm, even if it doesn't do any good."

During the next few days he nursed her with constant care. When she came out in the morning, she found him waiting at the foot of the stairs, ready to assist her on deck. When she went down at night, it was his arm upon which she leaned and his voice that wished her "Good-night" before her state-room door. Her meals were served outside, and she soon found that his watchfulness extended to a host of trivialities.

It was not a confidential companionship. Sometimes they sat for hours without speaking, and again he attacked her with aggressive irony. At such times she smarted beneath the sting of his sneers, but it was more in pity for him than for herself. He seemed to carry in his heart a seething rage of cynicism, impassioned if impotent. When it broke control, as it often did, it lashed alike the just and the unjust, the sinner and the sinned against. It did not spare the woman for whose comfort he sacrificed himself daily in a dozen minor ways. It was as if he hated himself for the interest she inspired and hated her for inspiring it. He appeared to resent the fact that the mental pressure under which he labored had not annihilated all possibility of purer passion. And he often closed upon a gentler mood with burning bitterness.

"How about your faith?" he inquired one day, after a passing tenderness. "Is it still the evidence of virtues not visible in me?"

She flinched, as she always did at his flippancy. "There is circumstantial evidence of those," she replied, "sufficient to confound a jury."

There was a cloud upon his face. "Of the 'ministering angel' kind, I suppose," he suggested.

"Yes."

"Your judgment is warped," he went on. "Do you expect to convince by such syllogisms as: It is virtuous to make presents of prunes. He makes me presents of prunes. Therefore he is virtuous."

She looked at him with wounded eyes. "That is not kind of you," she said.

"But, my dear lady, I am not kind. That is what I am arguing for."

Her lips closed firmly. She did not answer.

"Is the assertion admitted?" he inquired.

Her mouth quivered. He saw it, and his mood melted.

"Do you mean to say," he asked, adjusting the rug about her shoulders and regarding her with an intent gaze, "that it makes any difference to you?"

The fragment of a sob broke from her. "Of course it makes a difference," she answered, "to—to be treated so."

His hand closed firmly over the rug, and rested against her shoulder. "Why does it make a difference?" he demanded.

She stammered confusedly. "Because—because it does," she replied.

His face was very grave; the hand upon her shoulder trembled. "I hope to God it does not make a difference," he said. "Look! There is a sail."

They rose and went to the railing, following with unseeing eyes a white sail that skirted the horizon. At the vessel's side porpoises were leaping on the waves. She leaned over, her eyes brightening, her loosened hair blowing about her face in soft, brown strands. There was a pink flush in her cheeks. "I should like to be a porpoise," she said, "and to skim that blue water in the sunshine. How happy they are!"

"And you are not?"

The flush died from her cheeks. "I? Oh, no," she answered.

He leaned nearer; his hand brushed hers as it lay upon the railing.

"Did love make you happy?" he asked suddenly.

She raised her lashes, and their eyes met. "Love?" she repeated vaguely.

"That husband of yours," he explained almost harshly, "did you love him?"

Her gaze went back to the water. A wistful tremor shook her lips. "He was very good to me," she replied.

"And I suppose you loved him because he was good. Well, the reason suffices."

She looked at him steadily. "Because he was good to me," she corrected. Then she hesitated. "But I did not love him in the way you mean," she added slowly. "I know now that I did not."

"Eh!" he ejaculated half absently; and then: "How do you know it?"

She turned from him, looking after the vanishing sail, just visible in the remote violet of the distance. "There are many ways——"

His eyes rested upon the soft outline of her ear, half hidden in her blown hair. "What are they?"

She turned her face still further from him. "It made no difference to me," she said, "whether he came or went. It wearied me to be with him —and I was very selfish. When he kissed me it left me cold."

His gaze stung her sharply. "And if you loved some one," he said, "it would make great difference to you whether he came or went? It would gladden you to be with him, and when he kissed you it would not leave you cold?"

"I—I think so," she answered.

He bent towards her swiftly; then checked himself with a sneering laugh. "I'll give you a piece of valuable advice," he said; "don't allow yourself to grow sentimental. It is awful rot."

And he threw himself into his chair. He drew a note-book from his pocket, and when she seated herself he did not look up. There was a gray cast about his face, and his lips were compressed. She noticed that he was older than she at first supposed and that the hand with which he held the pencil twitched nervously. Then she lay watching him idly from beneath lowered lids.

An hour later he looked up, and their glances met. With sudden determination he closed the book and replaced it in his pocket. "You look pale," he remarked abruptly.

"Do I?" she questioned inanimatedly. "I do not see any reason why I should not."

"Perhaps—so long as it is not unbecoming to you."

"Why will you say such things?" she demanded angrily. "I detest them."

"Indeed? Yes, pallor is not unbecoming to you. It gives you an interesting look."

She rubbed the cheek next him with the edge of her rug until it glowed scarlet. "There!" she exclaimed in resentment.

"That gives you a radiant look," he remarked composedly.

Her eyes flashed. "You will make me hate you," she retorted.

He smiled slightly, his eyes half sad. "I am trying to," he responded.

She stamped her foot with impatience. "Then you won't succeed. I will not hate you. Do you hear? I will not!"

"Is it a question of will?"

"In this case, yes."

"Do you hate as you choose—and love?" he asked.

"I don't know," she replied. "I hardly think I could hate you if I would. Despite your—your hatefulness."

"Not though it were a part of wisdom?"

"Wisdom has nothing to do with——"

"With what?" he questioned.

"With hate."

"Nor with love?"

"Nor with love."

He shook himself free from an imaginary weight, passing his hand across his contracted brow. "Then so much the worse for hate," he responded, "and for love."

As she did not answer he spoke fiercely. "When you love, love a virtuous, straightaway plodder," he said. "Love a man because he is decent—because he is decent and plain and all the things that the romancers laugh at. Love a fool, if you will, but let him be a fool who goes to his office at nine and leaves it at six; who craves no more exciting atmosphere than the domestic one of house-girl worries and teething babies. If you ever find yourself loving a man like me, you had better make for the nearest lamp-post and—hang——"

"Hush!" she cried, her cheeks flaming. "How—how dare you?" Her voice broke sharply, and she fell to sobbing behind her raised hands.

"My God!" he said softly. She felt his breath upon her forehead, and a tremor passed over her. Then his hands fastened upon hers and drew them from her eyes. He was panting like a man who has run a race.

She was looking straight before her. A small homing bird alighted for a swift instant on the railing near them, scanning suspiciously the deserted corner—and she knew that that bird would be blazoned on her memory forever after. Then she felt the man's lips close upon her own.

"You shall love me," he said, "and right be damned!"

II

She stepped out upon the deck, her eyes shining. He met her moodily. "Shall we walk up into the bow?" he asked.

She nodded. "This is our last evening," she said. "We will make it long."

"However long we make it, there is always to-morrow."

Her face clouded. "Yes, there is to-morrow," she admitted.

She fell into step with him, and they walked the length of the deck. Once she lost her balance, and he laid his hand upon her arm. When she recovered herself, he did not remove it.

"We will go far up," she said. "We will look straight out to sea and forget what is behind us."

"Can we forget it?" he asked gloomily.

She smiled into his face. "I will make you," she answered. "Put your hands upon the railing—so—and watch the boat as it cuts the waves. Is it not like a bird? And see, the stars are coming out."

The salt spray dashed into their faces as they leaned far over. A wet wind blew past them, and she put up her hand to hold her hat. Her skirts were wrapped closely about her, and her figure seemed to grow taller in the gray fog that rose from the sea. The ethereal quality in her appearance was emphasized.

He drew away from her. "You are too delicate for my rough hands," he said.

"Am I?" she laughed softly; then a rising passion swelled in her voice: "I should choose to be broken by you to being caressed by any other man——"

His face whitened. "Don't say that," he protested hoarsely.

"Why not, since it is true?"

"It is not true."

A half-moon was mounting into the heavens, and it lit the sea with a path of silver. The pearl-colored mist floated ahead of the steamer, fluttering like the filmy garments of a water sprite. A dozen stars hung overhead.

"But it is true," she answered. Her words rang clearly, with a triumphant note. For a time he did not speak. In the light of the half-moon she saw the deepening furrows upon his face. His hands were clenched.

"There is time yet," he said at last, "to withdraw a false play. Take your love back."

She trembled, and her lips parted. "I cannot," she replied, "and I would not."

He stretched out his arms, as if to draw her towards him, and she faltered before the passion in his glance. Then he fell back. "What a mess you are making of your life!" he said.

But his warming eyes had reassured her. "The mess is already made," she responded.

"But it is not," he returned. Then he summoned his flagging force. "And it shall not be."

"How will you prevent it?"

"By an appeal to reason——"

She laughed. "What love was ever ruled by reason?"

"By proofs."

She laughed again: "What proof ever shattered faith?"

"Great God!" he retorted passionately. "Stop! Think a moment! Look things in the face. What do you know of me?"

"I know that I love you."

"I tell you I am a devil——"

"And I do not believe you."

"Go back to America, and ask the first man you meet."

"Why should I respect his opinion?"

"Because it is the opinion of the respectable public——"

"Then I don't respect the respectable public."

"You ought to."

"I don't agree with you."

Again he was silent, and again he faced her. "What is it that you love in me?" he demanded. "It is not my face."

"Certainly not."

"Nor my manners?"

"Hardly."

"Is there anything about me that is especially attractive?"

"I have not observed it."

"Then I'll be hanged if I know what it is!"

"So will I."

He sighed impatiently. "No woman ever discovered it before," he said, "though I've known all sorts and conditions. But then I never knew a woman like you."

"I am glad of that," she responded.

"I would give two-thirds of my future—such as it is—if I had not known you."

"And yet you love me."

He made a step towards her, his face quivering. But his words were harsh. "My love is a rotten reed," he said. Then he turned from her, gazing gloomily out to sea. Across the water the path of moonlight lay unrolled. Small brisk waves were playing around the flying steamer. Suddenly he faced her. "Listen!" he said.

She bent her head.

"From the beginning I have lied to you—lied, do you hear? I singled you out for my own selfish ends. All my kindness, as you call it, was because of its usefulness to me. While you looked on in innocence I made you a tool in my hands for the furtherance of my own purposes. Even those confounded prunes were sent to you from any other motive than sympathy for you——"

She shivered, supporting herself against the railing. "I—I don't understand," she stammered.

"Then listen again: I needed you, and I used you. There is not a soul in this boat but believes me to be your husband. I have created the impression because I was a desperate man, and it aided me. My name is not even Lawrence Smith——"

"Stop!" she said faintly. For an instant she staggered towards him; then her grasp upon the railing tightened. "Go on," she added.

His face was as gray as the fog which shrouded it. "I left America a hunted man. When I reach the other side, I shall find them still upon my tracks. It is for an act which they call by an ugly name; and yet I would do it over again. It was justice."

She was shivering as from a strong wind. "I—I don't think I understand yet," she said.

"I have led a ruined life," he went on hurriedly. "My past record is not a pretty one—and yet there is no act of my life which I regret so little as the one for which they are running me down. It was a deed of honor, though it left blood upon my hands——"

Her quivering face was turned from him.

"I reached New York with the assistance of a friend—the only man on earth who knows and believes in me. He secured a state-room from an L. Smith, who was delayed. I took his name as a safeguard, and when I saw yours beside me at table, I concluded he was your husband, and I played his part in the eyes of the passengers. It succeeded well." He laughed bitterly. "Lawrence was a guess," he added.

Then before her stricken eyes his recklessness fell from him. "Oh, if I could undo this," he said, "I would go back gladly to stand my chances of the gallows——"

A sob broke from her. "Hush," she said wildly. "Have you no mercy—none?"

"You must believe this," he went on passionately, "that at the last I loved you. You must believe it."

She shook her head almost deliriously.

"You must believe it," he repeated savagely. "If I could make you believe it, I would lie down to let you walk over me. You must believe that I have loved you as I have loved no other woman in my life—as I could love no other woman but you. You must believe that, evil as I am, I am not evil enough to lie to you now. You must believe it." He put out his hands as if to touch her, but she shrank away.

"No—no!" she cried. And she fled from him into the obscurity of the deck.

All that night she sat up on the edge of her berth. Her eyes were strained, and she stared blankly at the foam breaking against the porthole. Thought hung suspended, and she felt herself rocking mentally like a ship in open sea. She saw her future brought to bay before the threatening present, and she glanced furtively around in search of some byway of escape. The walls of the little state-room seemed closing upon her, and she felt the upper berth bearing down. She sobbed convulsively. "It was so short," she said.

When she came upon deck next day, it was high tide and the steamer was drawing into Liverpool. She wore a closely fitting jacket, and carried a small bag in her hand. Through her lowered veil her eyes showed with scarlet lids as if she had been weeping. The crowd of passengers, leaning eagerly over the railing, parted slightly, and she caught a glimpse of the English landing, peopled by strange English faces. A sob stuck in her throat, and she fell hastily into a corner. She dreaded setting foot upon a strange shore. She heard the excited voices vaguely, as she had heard them seven days ago upon sailing. They grated upon her ears with the harsh insistence of unshared gaiety, and made her own unhappiness the more poignant.

"Why, there is Jack!" rang out the voice of a woman in front of her. "Lend me the glasses. Yes, it is Jack! And he came up from London to meet me."

Then the steamer drifted slowly to the landing, and the voyage was over. She saw the gangways swung across, and she saw a dozen men stroll leisurely aboard. Yes; the end had come. "There is no harm in good-bye," said a voice at her side.

She turned hastily. He was looking down upon her, his eyes filled with the old haunting gloom. "Good-bye," she answered.

He held out his hand. "And you will go home like a sensible woman and forget?"

"I will go home."

His face whitened. "And forget?"

"Perhaps."

"It is wise."

She looked up at him, her eyes wet with tears. "Oh, how could you?" she cried brokenly. "How could you?"

He shook his head. "Don't think of me," he responded; "it is not worth the trouble."

The hand that held her bag shook nervously. "I wish I had never seen you," she said.

Then a voice startled them.

"So you have got your wife safely across, Mr. Smith," it said, "and no worse for the voyage. May I have the pleasure?"

It was the ship's surgeon, a large man with a jovial face. "I am afraid it was not the brightest of honeymoons," he added with attempted facetiousness. She looked up, her face paling, a sudden terror in her eyes.

A man with a telegram in his hand passed them, glancing from right to left. He stopped suddenly, wheeled round, and came towards them.

All at once her voice rang clear. She laid her hand upon the arm of the man beside her. "It is a honeymoon," she said, and she smiled into the surgeon's face, "so bright that even seasickness couldn't dim it. You know it has lasted eight years——"

The surgeon smiled, and the strange man passed on.

Some one took her hand, and they descended the gangway together. As she stepped upon the landing, he looked down at her, his eyes aflame.

"For God's sake," he said, "tell me what it means?"

Her glance did not waver. "It means," she answered, "that I am on your side forever."

His hand closed over the one he held. "I ought to send you back," he said, "but I cannot."

"You cannot," she repeated resolutely.

Then her voice softened. "God bless that detective," she added fervently.

Across the passion in his eyes shot a gleam of his old reckless humor. "It was Cook's man after a tourist," he said, "but God bless him."

Editor's Note

This is undoubtedly one of several stories which Ellen Glasgow had completed by November, 1897, and to which she referred in her letter to Paul R. Reynolds. Through Mr. Reynolds' efforts, the story was published in the now defunct *McClure's Magazine,* for February, 1899.

Miss Glasgow's first published story draws from her first summer abroad in the summer of 1896. The loneliness and shyness of Lucy Smith are identical with the feelings Miss Glasgow described in *The Woman Within*. Lucy's ambivalent feelings toward "Lawrence" are the most interesting aspect of the story; she is alternately attracted and frightened by him. Using Freudian insights and *The Woman Within,* we can trace this ambivalence back to Miss Glasgow's feelings toward her father, whom she both loved and feared. She learned from her mother that submission was expected from women, but this submission was, from Miss Glasgow's viewpoint, the death of her mother. How could one be loved as a woman without submitting as her mother did? This problem continued to puzzle Miss Glasgow. She did not reprint "Between Two Shores" in *The Shadowy Third* collection, probably because she found Lucy Smith's answer unsatisfactory.

III

A Point in Morals

〜 "THE QUESTION seems to be——" began the Englishman. He looked up and bowed to a girl in black who had just come in from deck and was taking the seat beside him. "The question seems to be——" The girl was having some difficulty in removing her coat, and he turned to assist her.

"In my opinion," remarked the distinguished alienist, who was returning from a vacation in Vienna, "the question is whether or not civilization is defeating its own aims in placing an exorbitant value on human life." As he spoke he leaned forward authoritatively and accented his words with foreign precision.

"You mean that the survival of the fittest is checkmated," remarked a young journalist travelling in the interest of a New York daily, "that civilization should practise artificial selection, as it were?"

The alienist shrugged his shoulders deprecatingly. "My dear sir," he protested, "I mean nothing. It is the question that means something."

"Well, as I was saying," began the Englishman again, reaching for the salt and upsetting a spoonful, "the question seems to be whether or not, in any circumstances, the saving of a human life may become positively immoral."

"Upon that point——" began the alienist; but a young woman, in a white dress, who was seated on the Captain's right interrupted him.

"How could it?" she asked. "At least I don't see how it could. Do you, Captain?"

"There is no doubt," remarked the journalist, looking up from a conversation he had drifted into with a lawyer from one of the Western States, "that the more humane spirit pervading modern civilization has not worked wholly for good in the development of the species. Probably, for instance, if we had followed the Spartan practice of exposing unhealthy infants, we should have retained something of the Spartan hardihood. Certainly if we had been content to remain barbarians both our digestions and our nerves would have been the better for it, and melancholia would perhaps have been unknown. But, at the same time, the loss of a number of the more heroic virtues is overbalanced by an increase of the softer ones. Notably, human life has never before been regarded so sacredly."

"On the other side," observed the lawyer, lifting his hand to adjust his eyeglasses, and pausing to brush a crumb from his coat, "though it is all very well to be philanthropic to the point of pauperizing half a community and of growing squeamish about capital punishment, the whole thing sometimes takes a disgustingly morbid turn. Why, it seems as if criminals were the real American heroes! Only last week I visited a man sentenced to death for the murder of his two wives, and, by Jove, the place was literally besieged by woman sympathizers. I counted six bunches of roses in his cell, and at least fifty notes."

"Oh, but that is a form of nervous hysteria!" said the girl in black, "and must be considered separately. Every sentiment has its fanatics, philanthropy as well as religion. But we can't judge a movement by a few over-wrought disciples."

"Why not?" asked the Englishman, quietly. He was a middle-aged man, with an optimistic expression and a build of comfortable solidity. "But to return to the original proposition. I suppose we all accept as a self-evident truth the axiom that the highest civilization is the one in which the highest value is placed upon individual life."

"And happiness," added the girl in black.

"And happiness," assented the Englishman.

"And yet," commented the lawyer, "I think that most of us will admit that such a society, where life is regarded as sacred because it is valuable to the individual, not because it is valuable to the state, tends to the non-production of heroes."

"That the average will be higher and the exception lower," observed the journalist. "In other words, that there will be a general elevation of the mass, accompanied by a corresponding lowering of the few."

"On the whole, I think our system does very well," said the Englishman, carefully measuring the horseradish. "A mean between two extremes is apt to be satisfactory in results. If we don't produce a Marcus Aurelius or a Seneca, neither do we produce a Nero or a Phocas. We may have lost patriotism, but we have gained humanity, which is better. If we have lost chivalry, we have acquired decency; and if we have ceased to be picturesque, we have become cleanly, which is considerably more to be desired."

"I have never felt the romanticism of the Middle Ages," remarked the girl in black. "When I read of the glories of the Crusaders, I can't help remembering that a knight wore a single garment for a lifetime, and hacked his horse to pieces for a whim. Just as I never think of that chivalrous brute, Richard the Lion-Hearted, that I don't see him chopping off the heads of his prisoners."

"Oh, I don't think that any of us are sighing for a revival of the Middle Ages," returned the journalist. "The worship of the past has for its devotees people who have known only the present."

"Which is as it should be," commented the lawyer. "If man were confined to the worship of the knowable, all the world would lapse into atheism."

"Just as the great lovers of humanity were generally hermits," added the girl in black. "I had an uncle who used to say that he never really loved mankind until he went to live in the wilderness."

"I think we are drifting from the point," said the alienist. "Was it not: Can the saving of a human life ever prove to be an immoral act? I once held that it could."

"Did you act upon the theory?" asked the lawyer, with rising interest. "I maintain that no proposition can be said to exist until it is translated into action. Otherwise it is in an embryonic state merely."

The alienist laid down his fork and leaned forward. He was a notable-looking man of some thirty-odd years, who had made a sudden leap into popularity through several successful cases. He had a nervous, muscular face, with singularly penetrating eyes and hair of a light sandy colour. His hands were white and well shaped.

"It was some years ago," he said, bending a scintillant glance round the table. "If you will listen——"

There followed a stir of assent, accompanied by a nod from the young woman on the Captain's right. "I feel as if it would be a ghost story," she declared.

"It is not a story at all," returned the alienist, lifting his wineglass and holding it against the light. "It is merely a fact."

Then he glanced swiftly round the table as if challenging attention.

"As I said," he began, slowly, "it was some few years ago. Just what year it was does not matter; but at that time I had completed a course at Heidelberg, and expected shortly to set out with an exploring party for South Africa. It turned out afterward that I did not go, but for the purpose of the present story it is sufficient that I intended to do so, and had made my preparations accordingly. At Heidelberg I had lived among a set of German students who were permeated with the metaphysics of

Schopenhauer, Von Hartmann, and the rest, and I was pretty well saturated myself. At that age I was an ardent disciple of pessimism. I am still a disciple, but my ardour has abated, which is not the fault of pessimism, but the virtue of middle age——"

"A man is called conservative when he grows less radical," interrupted the journalist.

"Or when he grows less in every direction," added the Englishman, "except in physical bulk."

The alienist accepted the suggestions with an inclination, and continued. "One of my most cherished convictions," he said, "was to the effect that every man is the sole arbiter of his fate. As Schopenhauer has put it, *'that there is nothing to which a man has a more unassailable title than to his own life and person.'* Indeed, that particular sentence had become a kind of motto with our set, and some of my companions even went so far as to preach the proper ending of life with the ending of the power of individual usefulness."

He paused to help himself to salad.

"I was in Scotland at the time, where I had spent a fortnight with my parents, in a small village on the Kyles of Bute. While there I had been treating an invalid cousin who had acquired the morphine habit, and who, under my care, had determined to uproot it. Before leaving I had secured from her the amount of the drug which she had in her possession —some thirty grains—done up in a sealed package, and labelled by a London chemist. As I was in haste, I put it in my bag, thinking that I would add it to my case of medicines when I reached Leicester, where I was to spend the night with an old schoolmate. I took the boat at Tighnabruaich, the small village, found a local train at Gourock, to reach Glasgow, with one minute in which to catch the first express to London. I made the change, and secured a first-class smoking-compartment, which I at first thought to be vacant; but when the train had started a man came from the dressing-room and took the seat across from me. At first I paid no heed to him, but upon looking up once or twice and finding his eyes upon me, I became unpleasantly conscious of his presence. He was thin almost to emaciation, and yet there was a suggestion of physical force about him which it was difficult to account for, since he was both short and slight. His clothes were shabby, though well made, and his tie had the appearance of having been tied in haste, or by nervous fingers. There was a trace of sensuality about his mouth, over which he wore a drooping yellow moustache tinged with gray, and he was somewhat bald on the crown of his head, which lent a deceptive hint of intellectuality to his uncovered forehead. As he crossed his legs, I saw that his boots were carefully blacked, and that they were long and slender, tapering to a decided point."

"I have always held," interpolated the lawyer, "that to judge a man's character you must look at his feet."

The alienist sipped his claret and took up his words:

"After passing the first stop, I remembered a book at the bottom of my bag, and unfastening the strap in my search for the book, I laid a number of small articles on the seat beside me, among them the sealed package bearing the morphine label and the name of the London chemist. Having found the book, I turned to replace the articles, when I noticed that the man across from me was gazing attentively at the labelled package. For a moment his expression startled me, and I stared back at him from across my open bag, into which I had dropped the articles. There was in his eyes a curious mixture of passion and repulsion, and, beyond it all, the look of a hungry hound when he sees food. Thinking that I had chanced upon a victim of the opium craving, I closed the bag, placed it in the net above my head, and opened my book.

"For a while we rode in silence. Nothing was heard except the noise of the train and the clicking of our bags as they jostled each other in the receptacle above. I remember these details very vividly, because since then I have recalled the slightest fact in connection with the incident. I knew that the man across from me drew a cigar from his case, felt in his pocket for an instant, and then turned to me for a match. At the same time I experienced the feeling that the request veiled a larger purpose, and that there were matches in the pocket into which he had thrust his fingers.

"But, as I complied with his request, he glanced indifferently out of the window, and following his gaze, I saw that we were passing a group of low lying hills sprinkled with stray patches of heather, and that across the hills a flock of sheep were filing, followed by a peasant girl in a short skirt. It was the last faint reminder of the Highlands.

"The man across from me leaned out, looking back upon the neutral sky, the sparse patches of heather, and the flock of sheep.

" 'What a tone the heather gives to a landscape!' he remarked, and his voice sounded forced and affected.

"I bowed without replying, and as he turned from the window, and a draught of cinders blew in, I bent forward to lower the sash. In a moment he spoke again:

" 'Do you go to London?'

" ' To Leicester,' I answered, laying the book aside, impelled by a sudden interest. 'Why do you ask?'

"He flushed nervously.

" 'I—oh, nothing,' he answered, and drew away from me.

"Then, as if with swift determination, he reached forward and lifted the book I had laid on the seat. It was a treatise of Von Hartmann's in German.

" 'I had judged that you were a physician,' he said, 'a student, perhaps, from a German university?'

" 'I am.'

"He paused for an instant, and then spoke in absent-minded reiteration, 'So you don't go on to London?'

" 'No,' I returned, impatiently. 'Can I do anything for you?'

"He handed me the book, regarding me resolutely as he did so.

" 'Are you a sensible man?'

"I bowed.

" 'And a philosopher?'

" 'In amateur fashion.'

"With feverish energy he went on more quickly, 'You have in your possession,' he said, 'something for which I would give my whole fortune.' He laid two half-sovereigns and some odd silver in the palm of his hand. 'This is all I possess,' he continued, 'but I would give it gladly.'

"I looked at him curiously.

" 'You mean the morphine?' I demanded.

"He nodded. 'I don't ask you to give it to me. I only ask——'

"I interrupted him. 'Are you in pain?'

"He laughed softly, and I really believe he felt a tinge of amusement. 'It is a question of expediency,' he explained. 'If you happen to be a moralist——' He broke off.

" 'What of it?' I inquired.

"He settled himself in his corner, resting his head against the cushions.

" 'You get out at Leicester,' he said, recklessly. 'I go on to London, where Providence, represented by Scotland Yard, is awaiting me.'

"I started. 'For what?'

" 'They call it murder, I believe,' he returned; 'but what they call it matters very little. I call it divine justice—that also matters very little. The point is—I shall arrive, they will be there before me. That is settled. Every station along the road is watched.'

"I glanced out of the window.

" 'But you came from Glasgow,' I suggested.

" 'Worse luck! I waited in the dressing-room until the train started. I hoped to have the compartment alone, but—' He leaned forward and lowered the window-shade. 'If you don't object,' he said, apologetically; 'I find the glare trying. It is a question for a moralist,' he repeated. 'In-

deed, I may call myself a question for a moralist,' and he smiled again
with that ugly humour. 'To begin with the beginning, the question is
bred in the bone and it's out in the blood.' He nodded at my look of
surprise. 'You are an American,' he continued, 'so am I. I was born in
Washington some thirty years ago. My father was a politician, whose
honour was held to be unimpeachable—which was a mistake. His name
doesn't matter, but he became very wealthy through judicious specula-
tions in votes and other things. My mother has always suffered from
an incipient hysteria, which developed shortly before my birth.' He
wiped his forehead with his handkerchief, and knocked the ashes from
his cigar with a flick of his finger. 'The motive for this is not far to
seek,' he said, with a glance at my travelling-bag. He had the coolest
bravado I have ever met. 'As a child,' he went on, 'I gave great promise.
Indeed, we moved to England that I might be educated at Oxford. My
father considered the ecclesiastical atmosphere to be beneficial. But while
at college I got into trouble with a woman, and I left. My father died, his
fortune burst like a bubble, and my mother moved to the country. I was
put into a banking office, but I got into more trouble with women, this
time two of them. One was a variety actress, and I married her. I didn't
want to do it. I tried not to, but I couldn't help it, and I did it. A month
later I left her. I changed my name and went to Belfast where I resolved
to become an honest man. It was a tough job, but I laboured and I succeeded for a time. The variety actress began looking for me, but I escaped
her, and have escaped her so far. That was eight years ago. And several
years after reaching Belfast I met another woman. She was different. I
fell ill of fever in Ireland, and she nursed me. She was a good woman,
with a broad Irish face, strong hands, and motherly shoulders. I was
weak and she was strong, and I fell in love with her. I tried to tell her
about the variety actress, but somehow I couldn't, and I married her.' He
shot the stump of his cigar through the opposite window and lighted
another, this time drawing the match from his pocket. 'She is an honest
woman,' he said, 'as honest as the day. She believes in me. It would kill
her to know about the variety actress and all the others. There is one
child, a girl, a freckle-faced mite just like her mother, and another is
coming.'

" 'She knows nothing of this affair?'

" 'Not a blamed thing. She is the kind of woman who is good because
she can't help herself. She enjoys it. I never did. My mother is different
too. She would die if other people knew of this; my wife would die if
she knew of it herself. Well, I got tired, and I wanted money, so I left
her and went to Dublin. I changed my name and got a clerkship in a
shipping-office. My wife thinks I went to America to get work, and if

she never hears of me she'll probably think no worse. I did intend going to America, but somehow I didn't. I got in with a man who signed somebody's name to a cheque and got me to present it. Then we quarrelled about the money; the man threw the job on me, and the affair came out. But before they arrested me, I ran him down and shot him. I was ridding the world of a damned traitor.'

"He raised the shade with a nervous hand; but the sun flashed into his eyes, and he lowered it.

" 'I suppose I'd hang for it,' he said. 'There isn't much doubt of that. If I waited, I'd hang for it, but I am not going to wait. I am going to die.'

" 'And how?'

" 'Before this train reaches London,' he replied. 'I am a dead man. There are two ways. I might say three, except that a pitch from the carriage might mean only a broken leg. But there is this—' He drew a vial from his pocket and held it to the light. It contained an ounce or so of carbolic acid.

" 'One of the most corrosive of irritants,' I observed.

" 'And there is—your package.'

"My first impulse was to force the vial from him. He was a slight man, and I could have overcome him with but little exertion. But the exertion I did not make. I should as soon have thought, when my rational humour reasserted itself, of knocking a man down and robbing him of his watch. The acid was as exclusively his property as the clothes he wore, and equally his life was his own. Had he declared his intention to hurl himself from the window, I might not have made way for him, but I should certainly not have obstructed his passage.

"But the morphine was mine, and that I should assist him was another matter, so I said:

" 'The package belongs to me.'

" 'And you will not exchange?'

" 'Certainly not.'

"He answered, almost angrily:

" 'Why not be reasonable? You admit that I am in a mess of it?'

" 'Readily.'

" 'You also admit that my life is morally my own?'

" 'Equally.'

" 'That its continuance could in no wise prove to be of benefit to society?'

" 'I do.'

" 'That for all connected with me it is better that I should die unknown and under an assumed name?'

" 'Yes.'

" 'Then you admit also that the best I can do is to kill myself before reaching London?'

" 'Perhaps.'

" 'So you will leave me the morphine when you get off at Leicester?'

" 'No.'

"He struck the window-sill impatiently with the palm of his hand.

" 'And why not?'

"I hesitated an instant.

" 'Because, upon the whole, I do not care to be the instrument of your self-destruction.'

" 'Don't be a fool!' he retorted. 'Speak honestly, and say that because of a little moral shrinking on your part, you prefer to leave a human being to a death of agony. I don't like physical pain. I am like a woman about it, but it is better than hanging, or life-imprisonment, or any jury finding.'

"I became exhortatory.

" 'Why not face it like a man and take your chances? Who knows——'

" 'I have had my chances,' he returned. 'I have squandered more chances than most men ever lay eyes on, and I don't care. If I had the opportunity, I'd squander them again. It is the only thing chances are made for.'

" 'What a scoundrel you are!' I exclaimed.

" 'Well, I don't know,' he answered; 'there have been worse men. I never said a harsh word to a woman, and I never hit a man when he was down——'

"I blushed. 'Oh, I didn't mean to hit you,' I responded.

"He took no notice.

" 'I like my wife,' he said. 'She is a good woman, and I'd do a good deal to keep her and the children from knowing the truth. Perhaps I'd kill myself even if I didn't want to. I don't know, but I am tired— damned tired.'

" 'And yet you deserted her.'

" 'I did. I tried not to, but I couldn't help it. If I were free to go back to her to-morrow, unless I was ill and wanted nursing, I'd see that she had grown shapeless, and that her hands were coarse.' He stretched out his own, which were singularly white and delicate. 'I believe I'd leave her in a week,' he said.

"Then with an eager movement he pointed to my bag.

" 'That is the ending of the difficulty,' he added. 'Otherwise I swear that before the train gets to London, I will swallow this stuff and die like a rat.'

" 'I admit your right to die in any manner you choose; but I don't see that it is my place to assist you. It is an ugly job.'

" 'So am I,' he retorted, grimly. 'At any rate, if you leave the train with that package in your bag it will be cowardice—sheer cowardice. And for the sake of your cowardice you will damn me to this.' He touched the vial.

" 'It won't be pleasant,' I said, and we were silent.

"I knew that the man had spoken the truth. I was accustomed to lies, and had learned to detect them. I knew, also, that the world would be well rid of him and his kind. Why I should preserve him for death upon the gallows I did not see. The majesty of the law would be in no way ruffled by his premature departure; and if I could trust that part of his story, the lives of innocent women and children would, in the other case, suffer considerably. And, even if I and my unopened bag alighted at Leicester, I was sure that he would never reach London alive. He was a desperate man, this I read in his set face, his dazed eyes, his nervous hands. He was a poor devil, and I was sorry for him. Why, then, should I contribute, by my refusal to comply with his request, an additional hour of agony to his existence? Could I, with my pretence of philosophic freedom, alight at my station, leaving him to swallow the acid and die like a rat in a cage before the journey was over? I remembered that I had once seen a guinea-pig die from the effects of carbolic acid, and the remembrance sickened me.

"As I sat there listening to the noise of the slackening train, which was nearing Leicester, I thought of a hundred things. I thought of Schopenhauer and Von Hartmann. I thought of the dying guinea-pig. I thought of the broad-faced Irish wife and the two children.

"Then 'Leicester' flashed before me, and the train stopped. I rose, gathered my coat and rug, and lifted the volume of Von Hartmann from the seat. The man remained motionless in the corner of the compartment, but his eyes followed me.

"I stooped, opened my bag, and laid the chemist's package on the seat. Then I stepped out, closing the door after me."

As the speaker finished, he reached forward, selected an almond from the stand of nuts, fitted it carefully between the crackers, and cracked it slowly.

The young woman in the white dress started up with a shudder.

"What a horrible story!" she exclaimed; "for it is a story, after all, and not a fact."

"A point, rather," suggested the Englishman; "but is that all?"

"All of the point," returned the alienist. "The next day I saw in the

Times that a man, supposed to be James Morganson, who was wanted for murder, was found dead in a first-class smoking-compartment of the Midland Railway. Coroner's verdict, 'Death resulting from an overdose of opium, taken with suicidal intent.'"

The journalist dropped a lump of sugar in his cup and watched it attentively.

"I don't think I could have done it," he said. "I might have left him with his carbolic. But I couldn't have deliberately given him his death-potion."

"But as long as he was going to die," responded the girl in black, "it was better to let him die painlessly."

The Englishman smiled. "Can a woman ever consider the ethical side of a question when the sympathetic one is visible?" he asked.

The alienist cracked another almond. "I was sincere," he said. "Of that there is no doubt. I thought I did right. The question is—did I do right?"

"It would have been wiser," began the lawyer, argumentatively, "since you were the stronger, to take the vial from him and leave him to the care of the law."

"But the wife and children," replied the girl in black. "And hanging is so horrible!"

"So is murder," responded the lawyer, dryly.

The young woman on the Captain's right laid her napkin on the table and rose. "I don't know what was right," she said, "but I do know that in your place I should have felt like a murderer."

The alienist smiled half cynically. "So I did," he answered; "but there is such a thing, my dear young lady, as a conscientious murderer."

Editor's Note

Miss Glasgow's second published story appeared in May, 1899, in *Harper's Magazine*. It, too, has an ocean liner setting and was probably inspired by her summer voyage to England in 1896. The earliest story to be included in *The Shadowy Third* collection, it has been greatly improved by revision. A good deal of characterization and description has been removed to make the story a purer dialogue, without personal distractions. Lengthy editorial comments are reduced to epigrams. Details of the dinner table have been removed. Costumes have been simplified; a girl in a yachting cap becomes a girl in black; a young lady in a pink blouse becomes a young woman in white. Some of the melodramatic phrasing of the intended suicide's speech is toned down. Here, as elsewhere, Miss Glasgow has altered American spellings to English spellings: labour, cravat, cheque, etc.

The result of the revision is a much tighter story, with the emphasis more closely focused on the moral problem than on physical details. The phrasing is more sophisticated and ironic. The presentation of viewpoints is more balanced; Miss Glasgow has avoided stabbing any of her characters mortally.

IV

The Shadowy Third

᚛ WHEN THE call came I remember that I turned from the telephone in a romantic flutter. Though I had spoken only once to the great surgeon, Roland Maradick, I felt on that December afternoon that to speak to him only once—to watch him in the operating-room for a single hour—was an adventure which drained the colour and the excitement from the rest of life. After all these years of work on typhoid and pneumonia cases, I can still feel the delicious tremor of my young pulses; I can still see the winter sunshine slanting through the hospital windows over the white uniforms of the nurses.

"He didn't mention me by name. Can there be a mistake?" I stood, incredulous yet ecstatic, before the superintendent of the hospital.

"No, there isn't a mistake. I was talking to him before you came down." Miss Hemphill's strong face softened while she looked at me. She was a big, resolute woman, a distant Canadian relative of my mother's, and the kind of nurse I had discovered in the month since I had come up from Richmond, that Northern hospital boards, if not Northern patients, appear instinctively to select. From the first, in spite of her hardness, she had taken a liking—I hesitate to use the word "fancy" for a preference so impersonal—to her Virginia cousin. After all, it isn't every Southern nurse, just out of training, who can boast a kinswoman in the superintendent of a New York hospital.

"And he made you understand positively that he meant me?" The thing was so wonderful that I simply couldn't believe it.

"He asked particularly for the nurse who was with Miss Hudson last week when he operated. I think he didn't even remember that you had a name. When I asked if he meant Miss Randolph, he repeated that he wanted the nurse who had been with Miss Hudson. She was small, he said, and cheerful-looking. This, of course, might apply to one or two of the others, but none of these was with Miss Hudson."

"Then I suppose it is really true?" My pulses were tingling. "And I am to be there at six o'clock?"

"Not a minute later. The day nurse goes off duty at that hour, and Mrs. Maradick is never left by herself for an instant."

"It is her mind, isn't it? And that makes it all the stranger that he should select me, for I have had so few mental cases."

"So few cases of any kind," Miss Hemphill was smiling, and when she smiled I wondered if the other nurses would know her. "By the time you have gone through the treadmill in New York, Margaret, you will have lost a good many things besides your inexperience. I wonder how long you will keep your sympathy and your imagination? After all, wouldn't you have made a better novelist than a nurse?"

"I can't help putting myself into my cases. I suppose one ought not to?"

"It isn't a question of what one ought to do, but of what one must. When you are drained of every bit of sympathy and enthusiasm, and have got nothing in return for it, not even thanks, you will understand why I try to keep you from wasting yourself."

"But surely in a case like this—for Doctor Maradick?"

"Oh, well, of course—for Doctor Maradick." She must have seen that I implored her confidence, for, after a minute, she let fall carelessly a gleam of light on the situation: "It is a very sad case when you think what a charming man and a great surgeon Doctor Maradick is."

Above the starched collar of my uniform I felt the blood leap in bounds to my cheeks. "I have spoken to him only once," I murmured, "but he is charming, and so kind and handsome, isn't he?"

"His patients adore him."

"Oh, yes, I've seen that. Everyone hangs on his visits." Like the patients and the other nurses, I also had come by delightful, if imperceptible, degrees to hang on the daily visits of Doctor Maradick. He was, I suppose, born to be a hero to women. From my first day in his hospital, from the moment when I watched, through closed shutters, while he stepped out of his car, I have never doubted that he was assigned to the great part in the play. If I had been ignorant of his spell—of the charm he exercised over his hospital—I should have felt it in the waiting hush, like a dawn breath, which followed his ring at the door and preceded his imperious footstep on the stairs. My first impression of him, even after the terrible events of the next year, records a memory that is both careless and splendid. At that moment, when, gazing through the chinks in the shutters, I watched him, in his coat of dark fur, cross the pavement over the pale streaks of sunshine, I knew beyond any doubt— I knew with a sort of infallible prescience—that my fate was irretrievably

bound up with his in the future. I knew this, I repeat, though Miss
Hemphill would still insist that my foreknowledge was merely a sentimental gleaning from indiscriminate novels. But it wasn't only first love,
impressionable as my kinswoman believed me to be. It wasn't only the
way he looked. Even more than his appearance—more than the shining
dark of his eyes, the silvery brown of his hair, the dusky glow in his face
—even more than his charm and his magnificence, I think, the beauty
and sympathy in his voice won my heart. It was a voice, I heard someone say afterwards, that ought always to speak poetry.

So you will see why—if you do not understand at the beginning, I can
never hope to make you believe impossible things!—so you will see why
I accepted the call when it came as an imperative summons. I couldn't
have stayed away after he sent for me. However much I may have tried
not to go, I know that in the end I must have gone. In those days, while
I was still hoping to write novels, I used to talk a great deal about
"destiny" (I have learned since then how silly all such talk is), and I
suppose it was my "destiny" to be caught in the web of Roland Maradick's
personality. But I am not the first nurse to grow love-sick about a doctor
who never gave her a thought.

"I am glad you got the call, Margaret. It may mean a great deal to
you. Only try not to be too emotional." I remember that Miss Hemphill
was holding a bit of rose-geranium in her hand while she spoke—one
of the patients had given it to her from a pot she kept in her room, and
the scent of the flower is still in my nostrils—or my memory. Since
then—oh, long since then—I have wondered if she also had been caught
in the web.

"I wish I knew more about the case." I was pressing for light. "Have
you ever seen Mrs. Maradick?"

"Oh, dear, yes. They have been married only a little over a year, and
in the beginning she used to come sometimes to the hospital and wait
outside while the doctor made his visits. She was a very sweet-looking
woman then—not exactly pretty, but fair and slight, with the loveliest
smile, I think, I have ever seen. In those first months she was so much
in love that we used to laugh about it among ourselves. To see her face
light up when the doctor came out of the hospital and crossed the pavement to his car, was as good as a play. We never tired of watching her—
I wasn't superintendent then, so I had more time to look out of the
window while I was on day duty. Once or twice she brought her little
girl in to see one of the patients. The child was so much like her that you
would have known them anywhere for mother and daughter."

I had heard that Mrs. Maradick was a widow, with one child, when she first met the doctor, and I asked now, still seeking an illumination I had not found, "There was a great deal of money, wasn't there?"

"A great fortune. If she hadn't been so attractive, people would have said, I suppose, that Doctor Maradick married her for her money. Only," she appeared to make an effort of memory, "I believe I've heard somehow that it was all left in trust away from Mrs. Maradick if she married again. I can't, to save my life, remember just how it was; but it was a queer will, I know, and Mrs. Maradick wasn't to come into the money unless the child didn't live to grow up. The pity of it——"

A young nurse came into the office to ask for something—the keys, I think, of the operating-room, and Miss Hemphill broke off inconclusively as she hurried out of the door. I was sorry that she left off just when she did. Poor Mrs. Maradick! Perhaps I was too emotional, but even before I saw her I had begun to feel her pathos and her strangeness.

My preparations took only a few minutes. In those days I always kept a suitcase packed and ready for sudden calls; and it was not yet six o'clock when I turned from Tenth Street into Fifth Avenue, and stopped for a minute, before ascending the steps, to look at the house in which Doctor Maradick lived. A fine rain was falling, and I remember thinking, as I turned the corner, how depressing the weather must be for Mrs. Maradick. It was an old house, with damp-looking walls (though that may have been because of the rain) and a spindle-shaped iron railing which ran up the stone steps to the black door, where I noticed a dim flicker through the old-fashioned fanlight. Afterwards I discovered that Mrs. Maradick had been born in the house—her maiden name was Calloran—and that she had never wanted to live anywhere else. She was a woman—this I found out when I knew her better—of strong attachments to both persons and places; and though Doctor Maradick had tried to persuade her to move uptown after her marriage, she had clung, against his wishes, to the old house in lower Fifth Avenue. I dare say she was obstinate about it in spite of her gentleness and her passion for the doctor. Those sweet, soft women, especially when they have always been rich, are sometimes amazingly obstinate. I have nursed so many of them since—women with strong affections and weak intellects—that I have come to recognize the type as soon as I set eyes upon it.

My ring at the bell was answered after a little delay, and when I entered the house I saw that the hall was quite dark except for the waning glow from an open fire which burned in the library. When I gave my name, and added that I was the night nurse, the servant appeared to

think my humble presence unworthy of illumination. He was an old negro butler, inherited perhaps from Mrs. Maradick's mother, who, I
learned afterwards, was from South Carolina; and while he passed me
on his way up the staircase, I heard him vaguely muttering that he
"wa'n't gwinter tu'n on dem lights twel de chile had done playin'."

To the right of the hall, the soft glow drew me into the library, and
crossing the threshold timidly, I stooped to dry my wet coat by the fire.
As I bent there, meaning to start up at the first sound of a footstep, I
thought how cosy the room was after the damp walls outside to which
some bared creepers were clinging; and I was watching the strange
shapes and patterns the firelight made on the old Persian rug, when
the lamps of a slowly turning motor flashed on me through the white
shades at the window. Still dazzled by the glare, I looked round in the
dimness and saw a child's ball of red and blue rubber roll towards me
out of the gloom of the adjoining room. A moment later, while I made
a vain attempt to capture the toy as it spun past me, a little girl darted
airily, with peculiar lightness and grace, through the doorway, and
stopped quickly, as if in surprise at the sight of a stranger. She was a
small child—so small and slight that her footsteps made no sound on the
polished floor of the threshold; and I remember thinking while I looked
at her that she had the gravest and sweetest face I had ever seen. She
couldn't—I decided this afterwards—have been more than six or seven
years old, yet she stood there with a curious prim dignity, like the dignity
of an elderly person, and gazed up at me with enigmatical eyes. She was
dressed in Scotch plaid, with a bit of red ribbon in her hair, which was
cut in a fringe over her forehead and hung very straight to her shoulders.
Charming as she was, from her uncurled brown hair to the white socks
and black slippers on her little feet, I recall most vividly the singular
look in her eyes, which appeared in the shifting light to be of an
indeterminate colour. For the odd thing about this look was that it was
not the look of childhood at all. It was the look of profound experience,
of bitter knowledge.

"Have you come for your ball?" I asked; but while the friendly question was still on my lips, I heard the servant returning. In my confusion
I made a second ineffectual grasp at the plaything, which had rolled
away from me into the dusk of the drawing-room. Then, as I raised my
head, I saw that the child also had slipped from the room; and without
looking after her I followed the old negro into the pleasant study above,
where the great surgeon awaited me.

Ten years ago, before hard nursing had taken so much out of me, I
blushed very easily, and I was aware at the moment when I crossed

Doctor Maradick's study that my cheeks were the colour of peonies. Of course, I was a fool—no one knows this better than I do—but I had never been alone, even for an instant, with him before, and the man was more than a hero to me, he was—there isn't any reason now why I should blush over the confession—almost a god. At that age I was mad about the wonders of surgery, and Roland Maradick in the operating-room was magician enough to have turned an older and more sensible head than mine. Added to his great reputation and his marvelous skill, he was, I am sure of this, the most splendid-looking man, even at forty-five, that one could imagine. Had he been ungracious—had he been positively rude to me, I should still have adored him; but when he held out his hand, and greeted me in the charming way he had with women, I felt that I would have died for him. It is no wonder that a saying went about the hospital that every woman he operated on fell in love with him. As for the nurses—well, there wasn't a single one of them who had escaped his spell—not even Miss Hemphill, who could have been scarcely a day under fifty.

"I am glad you could come, Miss Randolph. You were with Miss Hudson last week when I operated?"

I bowed. To save my life I couldn't have spoken without blushing the redder.

"I noticed your bright face at the time. Brightness, I think, is what Mrs. Maradick needs. She finds her day nurse depressing." His eyes rested so kindly upon me that I have suspected since that he was not entirely unaware of my worship. It was a small thing, heaven knows, to flatter his vanity—a nurse just out of a training-school—but to some men no tribute is too insignificant to give pleasure.

"You will do your best, I am sure." He hesitated an instant—just long enough for me to perceive the anxiety beneath the genial smile on his face—and then added gravely, "We wish to avoid, if possible, having to send her away."

I could only murmur in response, and after a few carefully chosen words about his wife's illness, he rang the bell and directed the maid to take me upstairs to my room. Not until I was ascending the stairs to the third storey did it occur to me that he had really told me nothing. I was as perplexed about the nature of Mrs. Maradick's malady as I had been when I entered the house.

I found my room pleasant enough. It had been arranged—at Doctor Maradick's request, I think—that I was to sleep in the house, and after my austere little bed at the hospital, I was agreeably surprised by the cheerful look at the apartment into which the maid led me. The walls were papered in roses, and there were curtains of flowered chintz at the window, which looked down on a small formal garden at the rear of the house. This the maid told me, for it was too dark for me to distinguish more than a marble fountain and a fir-tree, which looked old, though I afterwards learned that it was replanted almost every season.

In ten minutes I had slipped into my uniform and was ready to go to my patient; but for some reason—to this day I have never found out what it was that turned her against me at the start—Mrs. Maradick refused to receive me. While I stood outside her door I heard the day nurse trying to persuade her to let me come in. It wasn't any use, however, and in the end I was obliged to go back to my room and wait until the poor lady got over her whim and consented to see me. That was long after dinner—it must have been nearer eleven than ten o'clock—and Miss Peterson was quite worn out by the time she came for me.

"I'm afraid you'll have a bad night," she said as we went downstairs together. That was her way, I soon saw, to expect the worst of everything and everybody.

"Does she often keep you up like this?"

"Oh, no, she is usually very considerate. I never knew a sweeter character. But she still has this hallucination——"

Here again, as in the scene with Doctor Maradick, I felt that the explanation had only deepened the mystery. Mrs. Maradick's hallucination, whatever form it assumed, was evidently a subject for evasion and subterfuge in the household. It was on the tip of my tongue to ask, "What is her hallucination?"—but before I could get the words past my lips we had reached Mrs. Maradick's door, and Miss Peterson motioned me to be silent. As the door opened a little way to admit me, I saw that Mrs. Maradick was already in bed, and that the lights were out except for a night-lamp burning on a candle-stand beside a book and a carafe of water.

"I won't go in with you," said Miss Peterson in a whisper; and I was on the point of stepping over the threshold when I saw the little girl, in the dress of Scotch plaid, slip by me from the dusk of the room into the electric light of the hall. She held a doll in her arms, and as she went by she dropped a doll's work-basket in the doorway. Miss Peterson must have picked up the toy, for when I turned in a minute to look for it I found that it was gone. I remember thinking that it was late for a child to be up—she looked delicate, too—but, after all, it was no business of mine, and four years in a hospital had taught me never to meddle in things that do not concern me. There is nothing a nurse learns quicker than not to try to put the world to rights in a day.

When I crossed the floor to the chair by Mrs. Maradick's bed, she turned over on her side and looked at me with the sweetest and saddest smile.

"You are the night nurse," she said in a gentle voice; and from the moment she spoke I knew that there was nothing hysterical or violent about her mania—or hallucination, as they called it. "They told me your name, but I have forgotten it."

"Randolph—Margaret Randolph." I liked her from the start, and I think she must have seen it.

"You look very young, Miss Randolph."

"I am twenty-two, but I suppose I don't look quite my age. People usually think I am younger."

For a minute she was silent, and while I settled myself in the chair by the bed, I thought how strikingly she resembled the little girl I had seen first in the afternoon, and then leaving her room a few moments before. They had the same small, heart-shaped faces, coloured ever so faintly; the same straight, soft hair, between brown and flaxen; and the same large, grave eyes, set very far apart under arched eyebrows. What surprised me most, however, was that they both looked at me with that enigmatical and vaguely wondering expression—only in Mrs. Maradick's face the vagueness seemed to change now and then to a definite fear—a flash, I had almost said, of startled horror.

I sat quite still in my chair, and until the time came for Mrs. Maradick to take her medicine not a word passed between us. Then, when I bent over her with the glass in my hand, she raised her head from the pillow and said in a whisper of suppressed intensity:

"You look kind. I wonder if you could have seen my little girl?"

As I slipped my arm under the pillow I tried to smile cheerfully down on her. "Yes, I've seen her twice. I'd know her anywhere by her likeness to you."

A glow shone in her eyes, and I thought how pretty she must have been before illness took the life and animation out of her features. "Then I know you're good." Her voice was so strained and low that I could barely hear it. "If you weren't good you couldn't have seen her."

I thought this queer enough, but all I answered was, "She looked delicate to be sitting up so late."

A quiver passed over her thin features, and for a minute I thought she was going to burst into tears. As she had taken the medicine, I put the glass back on the candle-stand, and bending over the bed, smoothed the straight brown hair, which was as fine and soft as spun silk, back from her forehead. There was something about her—I don't know what it was—that made you love her as soon as she looked at you.

"She always had that light and airy way, though she was never sick a day in her life," she answered calmly after a pause. Then, groping for my hand, she whispered passionately, "You must not tell him—you must not tell any one that you have seen her!"

"I must not tell any one?" Again I had the impression that had come to me first in Doctor Maradick's study, and afterwards with Miss Peterson on the staircase, that I was seeking a gleam of light in the midst of obscurity.

"Are you sure there isn't any one listening—that there isn't any one at the door?" she asked, pushing aside my arm and raising herself on the pillows.

"Quite, quite sure. They have put out the lights in the hall."

"And you will not tell him? Promise me that you will not tell him." The startled horror flashed from the vague wonder of her expression. "He doesn't like her to come back, because he killed her."

"Because he killed her!" Then it was that light burst on me in a blaze. So this was Mrs. Maradick's hallucination! She believed that her child was dead—the little girl I had seen with my own eyes leaving her room; and she believed that her husband—the great surgeon we worshipped in the hospital—had murdered her. No wonder they veiled the dreadful obsession in mystery! No wonder that even Miss Peterson had not dared to drag the horrid thing out into the light! It was the kind of hallucination one simply couldn't stand having to face.

"There is no use telling people things that nobody believes," she resumed slowly, still holding my hand in a grasp that would have hurt me if her fingers had not been so fragile. "Nobody believes that he killed her. Nobody believes that she comes back every day to the house. Nobody believes—and yet you saw her——"

"Yes, I saw her—but why should your husband have killed her?" I spoke soothingly, as one would speak to a person who was quite mad. Yet she was not mad, I could have sworn this while I looked at her.

For a moment she moaned inarticulately, as if the horror of her thoughts were too great to pass into speech. Then she flung out her thin, bare arm with a wild gesture.

"Because he never loved me!" she said. "He never loved me!"

"But he married you," I urged gently while I stroked her hair. "If he hadn't loved you, why should he have married you?"

"He wanted the money—my little girl's money. It all goes to him when I die."

"But he is rich himself. He must make a fortune from his profession."

"It isn't enough. He wanted millions." She had grown stern and tragic. "No, he never loved me. He loved someone else from the beginning—before I knew him."

It was quite useless, I saw, to reason with her. If she wasn't mad, she was in a state of terror and despondency so black that it had almost crossed the border-line into madness. I thought once that I would go upstairs and bring the child down from her nursery; but, after a moment's hesitation, I realized that Miss Peterson and Doctor Maradick must have long ago tried all these measures. Clearly, there was nothing to do except soothe and quiet her as much as I could; and this I did until she dropped into a light sleep which lasted well into the morning.

By seven o'clock I was worn out—not from work but from the strain on my sympathy—and I was glad, indeed, when one of the maids came in to bring me an early cup of coffee. Mrs. Maradick was still sleeping— it was a mixture of bromide and chloral I had given her—and she did not wake until Miss Peterson came on duty an hour or two later. Then, when I went downstairs, I found the dining-room deserted except for the old housekeeper, who was looking over the silver. Doctor Maradick, she explained to me presently, had his breakfast served in the morning-room on the other side of the house.

"And the little girl? Does she take her meals in the nursery?"

She threw me a startled glance. Was it, I questioned afterwards, one of distrust or apprehension?

"There isn't any little girl. Haven't you heard?"

"Heard? No. Why, I saw her only yesterday."

The look she gave me—I was sure of it now—was full of alarm.

"The little girl—she was the sweetest child I ever saw—died just two months ago of pneumonia."

"But she couldn't have died." I was a fool to let this out, but the shock had completely unnerved me. "I tell you I saw her yesterday."

The alarm in her face deepened. "That is Mrs. Maradick's trouble. She believes that she still sees her."

"But don't you see her?" I drove the question home bluntly.

"No." She set her lips tightly. "I never see anything."

So I had been wrong, after all, and the explanation, when it came, only accentuated the terror. The child was dead—she had died of pneumonia two months ago—and yet I had seen her, with my own eyes, playing ball in the library; I had seen her slipping out of her mother's room, with her doll in her arms.

"Is there another child in the house? Could there be a child belonging to one of the servants?" A gleam had shot through the fog in which I was groping.

"No, there isn't any other. The doctors tried bringing one once, but it threw the poor lady into such a state she almost died of it. Besides, there wouldn't be any other child as quiet and sweet-looking as Dorothea. To

see her skipping along in her dress of Scotch plaid used to make me think
of a fairy, though they say that fairies wear nothing but white or green."

"Has any one else seen her—the child, I mean—any of the servants?"

"Only old Gabriel, the coloured butler, who came with Mrs. Maradick's mother from South Carolina. I've heard that negroes often have
a kind of second sight—though I don't know that that is just what you
would call it. But they seem to believe in the supernatural by instinct, and
Gabriel is so old and doty—he does no work except answer the door-bell
and clean the silver—that nobody pays much attention to anything that
he sees——"

"Is the child's nursery kept as it used to be?"

"Oh, no. The doctor had all the toys sent to the children's hospital.
That was a great grief to Mrs. Maradick; but Doctor Brandon thought,
and all the nurses agreed with him, that it was best for her not to be
allowed to keep the room as it was when Dorothea was living."

"Dorothea? Was that the child's name?"

"Yes, it means the gift of God, doesn't it? She was named after the
mother of Mrs. Maradick's first husband, Mr. Ballard. He was the grave,
quiet kind—not the least like the doctor."

I wondered if the other dreadful obsession of Mrs. Maradick's had
drifted down through the nurses or the servants to the housekeeper; but
she said nothing about it, and since she was, I suspected, a garrulous
person, I thought it wiser to assume that the gossip had not reached her.

A little later, when breakfast was over and I had not yet gone upstairs
to my room, I had my first interview with Doctor Brandon, the famous
alienist who was in charge of the case. I had never seen him before, but
from the first moment that I looked at him I took his measure almost
by intuition. He was, I suppose, honest enough—I have always granted
him that, bitterly as I have felt towards him. It wasn't his fault that he
lacked red blood in his brain, or that he had formed the habit, from
long association with abnormal phenomena, of regarding all life as a disease. He was the sort of physician—every nurse will understand what I
mean—who deals instinctively with groups instead of with individuals.
He was long and solemn and very round in the face; and I hadn't talked
to him ten minutes before I knew he had been educated in Germany,
and that he had learned over there to treat every emotion as a pathologi-
cal manifestation. I used to wonder what he got out of life—what any
one got out of life who had analyzed away everything except the bare
structure.

When I reached my room at last, I was so tired that I could barely
remember either the questions Doctor Brandon had asked or the direc-

tions he had given me. I fell asleep, I know, almost as soon as my head touched the pillow; and the maid who came to inquire if I wanted luncheon decided to let me finish my nap. In the afternoon, when she returned with a cup of tea, she found me still heavy and drowsy. Though I was used to night nursing, I felt as if I had danced from sunset to daybreak. It was fortunate, I reflected, while I drank my tea, that every case didn't wear on one's sympathies as acutely as Mrs. Maradick's hallucination had worn on mine.

Through the day I did not see Doctor Maradick; but at seven o'clock when I came up from my early dinner on my way to take the place of Miss Peterson, who had kept on duty an hour later than usual, he met me in the hall and asked me to come into his study. I thought him handsomer than ever in his evening clothes, with a white flower in his buttonhole. He was going to some public dinner, the housekeeper told me, but, then, he was always going somewhere. I believe he didn't dine at home a single evening that winter.

"Did Mrs. Maradick have a good night?" He had closed the door after us, and turning now with the question, he smiled kindly, as if he wished to put me at ease in the beginning.

"She slept very well after she took the medicine. I gave her that at eleven o'clock."

For a minute he regarded me silently, and I was aware that his personality—his charm—was focussed upon me. It was almost as if I stood in the centre of converging rays of light, so vivid was my impression of him.

"Did she allude in any way to her—to her hallucination?" he asked.

How the warning reached me—what invisible waves of sense-perception transmitted the message—I have never known; but while I stood there, facing the splendour of the doctor's presence, every intuition cautioned me that the time had come when I must take sides in the household. While I stayed there I must stand either with Mrs. Maradick or against her.

"She talked quite rationally," I replied after a moment.

"What did she say?"

"She told me how she was feeling, that she missed her child, and that she walked a little every day about her room."

His face changed—how I could not at first determine.

"Have you seen Doctor Brandon?"

"He came this morning to give me his directions."

"He thought her less well to-day. He has advised me to send her to Rosedale."

I have never, even in secret, tried to account for Doctor Maradick. He may have been sincere. I tell you only what I know—not what I believe or imagine—and the human is sometimes as inscrutable, as inexplicable, as the supernatural.

While he watched me I was conscious of an inner struggle, as if opposing angels warred somewhere in the depths of my being. When at last I made my decision, I was acting less from reason, I knew, than in obedience to the pressure of some secret current of thought. Heaven knows, even then, the man held me captive while I defied him.

"Doctor Maradick," I lifted my eyes for the first time frankly to his, "I believe that your wife is as sane as I am—or as you are."

He started. "Then she did not talk freely to you?"

"She may be mistaken, unstrung, piteously distressed in mind"— I brought this out with emphasis—"but she is not—I am willing to stake my future on it—a fit subject for an asylum. It would be foolish—it would be cruel to send her to Rosedale."

"Cruel, you say?" A troubled look crossed his face, and his voice grew very gentle. "You do not imagine that I could be cruel to her?"

"No, I do not think that." My voice also had softened.

"We will let things go on as they are. Perhaps Doctor Brandon may have some other suggestion to make." He drew out his watch and compared it with the clock—nervously, I observed, as if his action were a screen for his discomfiture or perplexity. "I must be going now. We will speak of this again in the morning."

But in the morning we did not speak of it, and during the month that I nursed Mrs. Maradick I was not called again into her husband's study. When I met him in the hall or on the staircase, which was seldom, he was as charming as ever; yet, in spite of his courtesy, I had a persistent feeling that he had taken my measure on that evening, and that he had no further use for me.

As the days went by Mrs. Maradick seemed to grow stronger. Never, after our first night together, had she mentioned the child to me; never had she alluded by so much as a word to her dreadful charge against her husband. She was like any woman recovering from a great sorrow, except that she was sweeter and gentler. It is no wonder that everyone who came near her loved her; for there was a mysterious loveliness about her like the mystery of light, not of darkness. She was, I have always thought, as much of an angel as it is possible for a woman to be on this earth. And yet, angelic as she was, there were times when it seemed to me that she both hated and feared her husband. Though he never entered her room while I was there, and I never heard his name on her lips until an hour before the end, still I could tell by the look of terror in her face whenever his step passed down the hall that her very soul shivered at his approach.

During the whole month I did not see the child again, though one night, when I came suddenly into Mrs. Maradick's room, I found a little garden, such as children make out of pebbles and bits of box, on the window-sill. I did not mention it to Mrs. Maradick, and a little later, as the maid lowered the shades, I noticed that the garden had vanished. Since then I have often wondered if the child were invisible only to the rest of us, and if her mother still saw her. But there was no way of finding out except by questioning, and Mrs. Maradick was so well and patient that I hadn't the heart to question. Things couldn't have been better with her than they were, and I was beginning to tell myself that she might soon go out for an airing, when the end came so suddenly.

It was a mild January day—the kind of day that brings the foretaste of spring in the middle of winter, and when I came downstairs in the afternoon, I stopped a minute by the window at the end of the hall to look down on the box maze in the garden. There was an old fountain, bearing two laughing boys in marble, in the centre of the gravelled walk, and the water, which had been turned on that morning for Mrs. Maradick's pleasure, sparkled now like silver as the sunlight splashed over it. I had never before felt the air quite so soft and springlike in January; and I thought, as I gazed down on the garden, that it would be a good idea for Mrs. Maradick to go out and bask for an hour or so in the sunshine. It seemed strange to me that she was never allowed to get any fresh air except the air that came through her windows.

When I went into her room, however, I found that she had no wish to go out. She was sitting, wrapped in shawls, by the open window, which looked down on the fountain; and as I entered she glanced up from a little book she was reading. A pot of daffodils stood on the window-sill —she was very fond of flowers and we tried always to keep some growing in her room.

"Do you know what I am reading, Miss Randolph?" she asked in her soft voice; and she read aloud a verse while I went over to the candle-stand to measure out a dose of medicine.

" 'If thou hast two loaves of bread, sell one and buy daffodils, for bread nourisheth the body, but daffodils delight the soul.' That is very beautiful, don't you think so?"

I said "Yes," that it was beautiful; and then I asked her if she wouldn't go downstairs and walk about in the garden.

"He wouldn't like it," she answered; and it was the first time she had mentioned her husband to me since the night I came to her. "He doesn't want me to go out."

I tried to laugh her out of the idea; but it was no use, and after a few minutes I gave up and began talking of other things. Even then it did not occur to me that her fear of Doctor Maradick was anything but a fancy. I could see, of course, that she wasn't out of her head; but sane persons, I knew, sometimes have unaccountable prejudices, and I accepted her dislike as a mere whim or aversion. I did not understand then and—I may as well confess this before the end comes—I do not understand any better to-day. I am writing down the things I actually saw, and I repeat that I have never had the slightest twist in the direction of the miraculous.

The afternoon slipped away while we talked—she talked brightly when any subject came up that interested her—and it was the last hour of day —that grave, still hour when the movement of life seems to droop and falter for a few precious minutes—that brought us the thing I had dreaded silently since my first night in the house. I remember that I had risen to close the window, and was leaning out for a breath of the mild air, when there was the sound of steps, consciously softened, in the hall outside, and Doctor Brandon's usual knock fell on my ears. Then, before I could cross the room, the door opened, and the doctor entered with Miss Peterson. The day nurse, I knew, was a stupid woman; but she had never appeared to me so stupid, so armoured and encased in her professional manner, as she did at that moment.

"I am glad to see that you are taking the air." As Doctor Brandon came over to the window, I wondered maliciously what devil of contradictions had made him a distinguished specialist in nervous diseases.

"Who was the other doctor you brought this morning?" asked Mrs. Maradick gravely; and that was all I ever heard about the visit of the second alienist.

"Someone who is anxious to cure you." He dropped into a chair beside her and patted her hand with his long, pale fingers. "We are so anxious to cure you that we want to send you away to the country for a fortnight or so. Miss Peterson has come to help you to get ready, and I've kept my car waiting for you. There couldn't be a nicer day for a trip, could there?"

The moment had come at last. I knew at once what he meant, and so did Mrs. Maradick. A wave of colour flowed and ebbed in her thin cheeks, and I felt her body quiver when I moved from the window and put my arms on her shoulders. I was aware again, as I had been aware that evening in Doctor Maradick's study, of a current of thought that beat from the air around into my brain. Though it cost me my career as a nurse and my reputation for sanity, I knew that I must obey that invisible warning.

"You are going to take me to an asylum," said Mrs. Maradick.

He made some foolish denial or evasion; but before he had finished I turned from Mrs. Maradick and faced him impulsively. In a nurse this was flagrant rebellion, and I realized that the act wrecked my professional future. Yet I did not care—I did not hesitate. Something stronger than I was driving me on.

"Doctor Brandon," I said, "I beg you—I implore you to wait until tomorrow. There are things I must tell you."

A queer look came into his face, and I understood, even in my excitement, that he was mentally deciding in which group he should place me —to which class of morbid manifestations I must belong.

"Very well, very well, we will hear everything," he replied soothingly; but I saw him glance at Miss Peterson, and she went over to the wardrobe for Mrs. Maradick's fur coat and hat.

Suddenly, without warning, Mrs. Maradick threw the shawls away from her, and stood up. "If you send me away," she said, "I shall never come back. I shall never live to come back."

The grey of twilight was just beginning, and while she stood there, in the dusk of the room, her face shone out as pale and flower-like as the daffodils on the window-sill. "I cannot go away!" she cried in a sharper voice. "I cannot go away from my child!"

I saw her face clearly; I heard her voice; and then—the horror of the scene sweeps back over me!—I saw the door open slowly and the little girl run across the room to her mother. I saw the child lift her little arms, and I saw the mother stoop and gather her to her bosom. So closely locked were they in that passionate embrace that their forms seemed to mingle in the gloom that enveloped them.

"After this can you doubt?" I threw out the words almost savagely— and then, when I turned from the mother and child to Doctor Brandon and Miss Peterson, I knew breathlessly—oh, there was a shock in the discovery!—that they were blind to the child. Their blank faces revealed the consternation of ignorance, not of conviction. They had seen nothing except the vacant arms of the mother and the swift, erratic gesture with which she stooped to embrace some invisible presence. Only my vision— and I have asked myself since if the power of sympathy enabled me to penetrate the web of material fact and see the spiritual form of the child —only my vision was not blinded by the clay through which I looked.

"After this can you doubt?" Doctor Brandon had flung my words back
to me. Was it his fault, poor man, if life had granted him only the eyes
of flesh? Was it his fault if he could see only half of the thing there before him?

But they couldn't see, and since they couldn't see I realized that it was
useless to tell them. Within an hour they took Mrs. Maradick to the asylum; and she went quietly, though when the time came for parting from
me she showed some faint trace of feeling. I remember that at the last,
while we stood on the pavement, she lifted her black veil, which she
wore for the child, and said: "Stay with her, Miss Randolph, as long as
you can. I shall never come back."

Then she got into the car and was driven off, while I stood looking
after her with a sob in my throat. Dreadful as I felt it to be, I didn't, of
course, realize the full horror of it, or I couldn't have stood there quietly
on the pavement. I didn't realize it, indeed, until several months afterwards when word came that she had died in the asylum. I never knew
what her illness was, though I vaguely recall that something was said
about "heart failure"—a loose enough term. My own belief is that she
died simply of the terror of life.

To my surprise Doctor Maradick asked me to stay on as his office nurse
after his wife went to Rosedale; and when the news of her death came
there was no suggestion of my leaving. I don't know to this day why he
wanted me in the house. Perhaps he thought I should have less opportunity to gossip if I stayed under his roof; perhaps he still wished to test
the power of his charm over me. His vanity was incredible in so great
a man. I have seen him flush with pleasure when people turned to look
at him in the street, and I know that he was not above playing on the
sentimental weakness of his patients. But he was magnificent, heaven
knows! Few men, I imagine, have been the objects of so many foolish
infatuations.

The next summer Doctor Maradick went abroad for two months, and
while he was away I took my vacation in Virginia. When we came back
the work was heavier than ever—his reputation by this time was tremendous—and my days were so crowded with appointments, and hurried flittings to emergency cases, that I had scarcely a minute left in
which to remember poor Mrs. Maradick. Since the afternoon when she
went to the asylum the child had not been in the house; and at last I
was beginning to persuade myself that the little figure had been an
optical illusion—the effect of shifting lights in the gloom of the old
rooms—not the apparition I had once believed it to be. It does not take
long for a phantom to fade from the memory—especially when one leads

the active and methodical life I was forced into that winter. Perhaps—who knows?—(I remember telling myself) the doctors may have been right, after all, and the poor lady may have actually been out of her mind. With this view of the past, my judgment of Doctor Maradick insensibly altered. It ended, I think, in my acquitting him altogether. And then, just as he stood clear and splendid in my verdict of him, the reversal came so precipitately that I grow breathless now whenever I try to live it over again. The violence of the next turn in affairs left me, I often fancy, with a perpetual dizziness of the imagination.

It was in May that we heard of Mrs. Maradick's death, and exactly a year later, on a mild and fragrant afternoon, when the daffodils were blooming in patches around the old fountain in the garden, the housekeeper came into the office, where I lingered over some accounts, to bring me news of the doctor's approaching marriage.

"It is no more than we might have expected," she concluded rationally. "The house must be lonely for him—he is such a sociable man. But I can't help feeling," she brought out slowly after a pause in which I felt a shiver pass over me, "I can't help feeling that it is hard for that other woman to have all the money poor Mrs. Maradick's first husband left her."

"There is a great deal of money, then?" I asked curiously.

"A great deal." She waved her hand, as if words were futile to express the sum. "Millions and millions!"

"They will give up this house, of course?"

"That's done already, my dear. There won't be a brick left of it by this time next year. It's to be pulled down and an apartment-house built on the ground."

Again the shiver passed over me. I couldn't bear to think of Mrs. Maradick's old home falling to pieces.

"You didn't tell me the name of the bride," I said. "Is she someone he met while he was in Europe?"

"Dear me, no! She is the very lady he was engaged to before he married Mrs. Maradick, only she threw him over, so people said, because he wasn't rich enough. Then she married some lord or prince from over the water; but there was a divorce, and now she has turned again to her old lover. He is rich enough now, I guess, even for her!"

It was all perfectly true, I suppose; it sounded as plausible as a story out of a newspaper; and yet while she told me I felt, or dreamed that I felt, a sinister, an impalpable hush in the air. I was nervous, no doubt; I was shaken by the suddenness with which the housekeeper had sprung her news on me; but as I sat there I had quite vividly an impression that the old house was listening—that there was a real, if invisible, presence somewhere in the room or the garden. Yet, when an instant afterwards I glanced through the long window which opened down to the brick terrace, I saw only the faint sunshine over the deserted garden, with its maze of box, its marble fountain, and its patches of daffodils.

The housekeeper had gone—one of the servants, I think, came for her —and I was sitting at my desk when the words of Mrs. Maradick on that last evening floated into my mind. The daffodils brought her back to me; for I thought, as I watched them growing, so still and golden in the sunshine, how she would have enjoyed them. Almost unconsciously I repeated the verse she had read to me:

"If thou hast two loaves of bread, sell one and buy daffodils"—and it was at this very instant, while the words were still on my lips, that I turned my eyes to the box maze, and saw the child skipping rope along the gravelled path to the fountain. Quite distinctly, as clear as day, I saw her come, with what children call the dancing step, between the low box borders to the place where the daffodils bloomed by the fountain. From her straight brown hair to her frock of Scotch plaid and her little feet, which twinkled in white socks and black slippers over the turning rope, she was as real to me as the ground on which she trod or the laughing marble boys under the splashing water. Starting up from my chair, I made a single step to the terrace. If I could only reach her—only speak to her—I felt that I might at last solve the mystery. But with the first flutter of my dress on the terrace, the airy little form melted into the quiet dusk of the maze. Not a breath stirred the daffodils, not a shadow passed over the sparkling flow of the water; yet, weak and shaken in every nerve, I sat down on the brick step of the terrace and burst into tears. I must have known that something terrible would happen before they pulled down Mrs. Maradick's home.

The doctor dined out that night. He was with the lady he was going to marry, the housekeeper told me; and it must have been almost midnight when I heard him come in and go upstairs to his room. I was downstairs because I had been unable to sleep, and the book I wanted to finish I had left that afternoon in the office. The book—I can't remember what it was—had seemed to me very exciting when I began it in the morning; but after the visit of the child I found the romantic novel as dull as a treatise on nursing. It was impossible for me to follow the lines, and I was on the point of giving up and going to bed, when Doctor Maradick opened the front door with his latch-key and went up the staircase. "There can't be a bit of truth in it." I thought over and over again as I listened to his even step ascending the stairs. "There can't be a bit of truth in it." And yet, though I assured myself that "there couldn't be a bit of truth in it," I shrank, with a creepy sensation, from going through the house to my room in the third storey. I was tired out after a hard day, and my nerves must have reacted morbidly to the silence and the darkness. For the first time in my life I knew what it was to be afraid of the unknown, of the unseen; and while I bent over my book, in the glare of the electric light, I became conscious presently that I was straining my senses for some sound in the spacious emptiness of the rooms overhead. The noise of a passing motor-car in the street jerked me back from the intense hush of expectancy; and I can recall the wave of relief that swept over me as I turned to my book again and tried to fix my distracted mind on its pages.

I was still sitting there when the telephone on my desk rang, with what seemed to my overwrought nerves a startling abruptness, and the voice of the superintendent told me hurriedly that Doctor Maradick was needed at the hospital. I had become so accustomed to these emergency calls in the night that I felt reassured when I had rung up the doctor in his room and had heard the hearty sound of his response. He had not yet undressed, he said, and would come down immediately while I ordered back his car, which must just have reached the garage.

"I'll be with you in five minutes!" he called as cheerfully as if I had summoned him to his wedding.

I heard him cross the floor of his room; and before he could reach the head of the staircase, I opened the door and went out into the hall in order that I might turn on the light and have his hat and coat waiting. The electric button was at the end of the hall, and as I moved towards it, guided by the glimmer that fell from the landing above, I lifted my eyes to the staircase, which climbed dimly, with its slender mahogany balustrade, as far as the third storey. Then it was, at the very moment when the doctor, humming gaily, began his quick descent of the steps, that I distinctly saw—I will swear to this on my deathbed—a child's skipping rope lying loosely coiled, as if it had dropped from a careless little hand, in the bend of the staircase. With a spring I had reached the electric button, flooding the hall with light; but as I did so, while my arm was still outstretched behind me, I heard the humming voice change to a cry of surprise or terror, and the figure on the staircase tripped heavily and stumbled with groping hands into emptiness. The scream of warning died in my throat while I watched him pitch forward down the long flight of stairs to the floor at my feet. Even before I bent over him, before I wiped the blood from his brow and felt for his silent heart, I knew that he was dead.

Something—it may have been, as the world believes, a misstep in the dimness, or it may have been, as I am ready to bear witness, an invisible judgment—something had killed him at the very moment when he most wanted to live.

Editor's Note

This title story of the 1923 collection was first published in *Scribner's Magazine* for December, 1916. It has also been reprinted in *Beware after Dark,* edited by T. E. Harré, and the *Panorama of Modern Literature,* edited by Christopher Morley. This is the original of her ghost stories; its success encouraged her to write three more and to group them at the beginning of her short story collection.

Miss Glasgow revised the magazine version of this story more carefully than any of the others; she made thirty-five changes in phrasing, spelling, and punctuation. She pruned out such thorns as, "This isn't the South, you know, where people still regard nurses as human, not as automata," from the speech of the superintendent of nurses. She also removed this arch comment about Dr. Maradick: "Fate had selected him for the role, and it would have been sheer impudence for a mortal to cross wills with the invisible Powers." Over half of the changes are, as usual, from American to English spellings.

V

Thinking Makes It So

᠑ "I WONDER how it feels to be young and pretty," said Margaret French wistfully as she pushed the soft faded hair back from her forehead and settled the pile of books in the hollow of her arm. She had stopped on her way from the little circulating library where she worked to enquire after Mrs. Mills' sciatica, and she stood now—a tired, faded-looking woman in an old-fashioned dress—and watched her niece Dora trip lightly, in her best spring frock, over the pavement of Franklin Street.

"Well, you must know how it feels to be young anyhow." Mrs. Mills was tentative rather than emphatic, for, though she had known Margaret French all her life, she could think of her only as worn and repressed and overworked and middle-aged. To be sure, there were women who were still young at forty-three, but poor Margaret, she reflected compassionately, was not one of them. There is nothing, she concluded presently, that takes the youth out of one so soon as the habit of self-effacement, and Margaret French had effaced herself consistently ever since Mrs. Mills could remember.

Of course when one is born plain and poetic in a family of commonplace beauties, there isn't anything for one to do except efface oneself speedily; and Margaret's sisters, like the three bouncing nieces she supported by her modest pen, had been as lovely as they were foolish. They had, one and all, married brilliantly, only to be widowed disastrously; and the charming fruits of their conventional folly had fallen presently to the devoted care of their "plain" sister Margaret.

"It isn't as if she had ever had any romance of her own," thought Mrs. Mills, watching sympathetically the lean sallow face of her friend, with its look of haggard stoicism. "When one comes to look at it fairly, I suppose working so hard for Fanny and the girls has given her something to think about, but all the same it's a pity she has had to write so many silly stories when she wanted to be a poet. She had the gift, too. If she hadn't had to slave so making money for other people, she might one day have been as great as Mrs. Browning."

"No, I've never been young," said Margaret suddenly, and her voice, which was charming in quality, held a note of suppressed bitterness, "and of course I've never been pretty."

"Well, you don't know what you might have been, Margaret, if you hadn't been obliged to work your fingers to the bone for other people." It was the best, in the circumstances, that Mrs. Mills could do, and she felt rather proud of herself. "Those girls have sucked the blood out of you; I was telling Harriet so yesterday. You have given your life to them, and they don't half appreciate it. That is exactly what I said." Her round, cheerful face hardened. "They don't half appreciate it. They are among the best-dressed girls in town, too, and I don't believe you've had anything new to wear for years."

"Oh, it doesn't matter about me. Anything will do for me. Nobody notices what I have on." She glanced scornfully down at her ugly blouse and skirt of gray silk which had been turned since autumn.

For the first time, while she looked at her, it occurred to Mrs. Mills that there was a touch of grimness in Margaret's self-sacrifice—a fierce determination to fulfil her martyrdom to the utmost. Why, for instance, had she chosen that atrocious iron-gray garment in which to immolate her rapidly waning youth? Standing there in the pale light of the April afternoon, which was closing mournfully over the city, she reminded her friend of a blighted flower that had withered before it dropped from the stem. She was all colorless and wan and monotonous like the stuff of her gown. "She looks like a woman who has given up hope," thought Mrs. Mills pityingly, adding the next moment, with a gleam of ironic insight, "and yet if the preachers and the philosophers were right, she ought to be happy, for she has never thought of herself. But that's the way life serves a saint, in spite of all the moralizing under the sun, and if you don't help yourself, there isn't anybody on this earth that is going to help you."

"I must be going," said Margaret, "the cook left today without warning, and I shall have to fix Fanny's supper. All the girls are dining out." Gathering the books under her arm, she smiled pensively at her friend and passed on—a listless little figure—in the warm April dusk.

"There is something sweet about her, too," thought Mrs. Mills as she looked after her. "She isn't really so plain when you separate her from her clothes, and she has lovely eyes. But she's right in one thing; she has never been young in her life."

The old French home, with it sallow walls and its bulging portico, stood at the end of the next block, and as Margaret reached the steps, the door opened, and her second niece, Isabel, came out on the porch.

"I sat with mother until I saw you coming, Aunt Margaret. Now, I'll run over to the Campbells. Fred has brought some friends down from the university, and we are going to dance after dinner."

"Very well, dear." Almost unconsciously Margaret's voice softened, for happiness had always seemed to her to belong by rights to the young, and Isabel was both young and lovely. "How is your mother? Has the doctor been to see her?"

"Yes, he says there is nothing serious the matter—only a headache from lack of circulation. Do you know, Aunt Margaret, he told me this morning that mother would be perfectly well if we could only get her off that sofa. He says the sofa is killing her—that she ought to be made to get up and stir about—do housework or something—"

"I know," said Margaret wearily, "I know." She had heard it all so often before—the gruff old doctor's name for Mrs. Buford's malady, which he bluntly diagnosed as "ingrowing selfishness"—that she had ceased to argue about it. For ten years, ever since her tragic divorce, poor Fanny had been too unhappy to do anything except lie on a sofa and read novels—very light ones. Even to order meals gave her a headache.

Smiling happily, Isabel ran down the steps, while Margaret entered the hall and groped for the box of matches she kept behind the jar of flowers on the table. The matches were not there, and she was was still searching for them when her name was called in a gay young voice from the staircase.

"Is that you, Aunt Margaret?"

"Yes, Janet. I thought you were spending the night with Lizzie Pleasants?"

"I am all ready to go, but I waited a minute to speak to you. Oh, Aunt Margaret, Lizzie is going to have a birthday-party next week, and I am dying for a new dress to wear to it. I haven't had a new evening dress for ever so long, and there is a heavenly blue taffeta at Daly's. Do you think you can possibly let me have it?"

The girl's fresh young lips were against her cheek, and Margaret felt that she could refuse her nothing. To be sure, she had meant to buy a new suit for herself, but, after all, what did it matter when nobody noticed her? It was natural for Janet, with her blue eyes and her rosy cheeks, to want things, and even if the girls were grasping, as Mrs. Mills had said, still in their selfish way she knew that they loved her.

"Yes, darling, you may have it. I got a check for a poem this morning."

"Oh, Aunt Margaret, you are an angel! I don't know what in the world I should do without you. Now I must be going." That was always the way. As soon as Janet got what she wanted, she must be going.

With a hasty kiss the girl had gone, and while Margaret struck a match and turned on the gas, she looked wistfully after her flying figure. "I wonder how it feels to be young and pretty like that," she said again, and there was a tinge of bitterness in the question. It was impossible even for a saint, as Mrs. Mills would have said, not to reflect occasionally, among higher meditations, on the particular lot in which her lines had happened to fall.

"Margaret, have you come back?" Mrs. Buford's voice issued in a plaintive wail from the open door of the library.

"Yes, Fanny. I hope your headache is better."

"The doctor says it won't be better until I am able to take more nourishment. Did you get the books from the library?"

"I brought some, but they aren't new. Nothing new had come in today, and I'm afraid you've read all these old ones."

As Margaret turned to gather up the books from the table, she saw that there was a letter lying on the card-tray—a letter addressed in a strange hand which lent a commanding dash to her name. "Who can be writing to me?" she thought as she picked it up, for her work was not the kind to allure the roving correspondent. Then, while she unfolded the letter, a pang, half pain, half bitter sweetness, shot through her heart. "There must be a mistake," she said in a whisper. "He can not possibly be writing to me." For the strangest part of this strange letter was its beginning, "My Poet, I have read your poems, and I love you because of them."

"Margaret!" Mrs. Buford's voice floated fretfully out to her. "Margaret, why don't you light the gas in here? What on earth are you doing?"

"Just a minute, Fanny, I am coming." Again the letter shook in her hand as she turned back to read the words, which danced wildly under the flickering gas.

My Poet,

I have read your poems, and I love you because of them. Out here in Colorado, where I am building a railroad, I stumbled by accident on your book of verse—your adorable book—and last night, before going to sleep, I read it from beginning to end. Then when I went to sleep it was in the moonlight, and they say that sleeping in moonlight will make any man mad. Mad or not I dreamed of you—of you Margaret French—until I woke in the morning. I dreamed of you just as I know you are in reality—brave and strong, pure and beautiful, and I dreamed that you were wearing rose-color, the flaming rose of the sunrise. It will break my heart, Margaret, for I, too, am a poet—

or at least I have always wanted to be a poet—if you are not what you were in my dream—rare and pale and all in rose-colored silk.

I wonder if you will answer this letter. If you are really the Margaret French that I dreamed of—the Margaret French of your poems—you will answer it; and if you are not—well, it will not matter whether you write or keep silent. If you are my Margaret French you will understand; if you are not, you will think me mad and forget my letter as soon as you have read it. If I waited until daylight, I suppose I should not send it—for in the day I am commonplace and sensible and worldly-wise and all the other foolish things that go into the making of an ordinary mortal whom the moon has not touched. Tonight I am courageous enough to do the thing that every man dreams of; when the day comes, I shall be merely the conventional coward with the conventional name of—

JOHN BROWN.

"Margaret, what in the world are you doing?"

"I'm coming in a minute, Fanny. I couldn't remember where I put the matches."

As she folded the letter and slipped it back into the envelop, a laugh broke from her lips. "He must be out of his mind. It is ridiculous," she said aloud.

"What did you say, Margaret?"

"I was just asking if you could eat any supper. Marthy left this morning, you know, without warning, but I can fix anything you fancy in a few minutes."

"What are you going to have?"

"I ordered some chops for you—they are easy to cook—but perhaps you would like an egg better?"

On a faded sofa in the midst of the faded library that had once belonged to Margaret's father, Mrs. Buford was lying with a paper-knife and a magazine in her hands. Though it was too dark to read, she had been cutting the pages by the electric light that fell through the windows.

"I didn't feel able to read, but this dimness is very depressing," she said as Margaret entered.

She was a long pale woman, who had once been queenly and imposing. Her features were still small and pretty, but her skin, once rose-leaf in texture, had withered and grown yellow, and her expression was one of resentful and embittered helplessness. The world had used her badly, and she had thought so long and so deeply about her grievances that every line in her face revealed the tragedy of her life.

"I am sorry I was so late, Fanny." Margaret's voice was almost gay as she watched the gas-light flicker over the desiccated belle and beauty on the sofa, "but I stopped to speak to Mrs. Mills."

While she spoke, a sense of strangeness, of unreality, swept over her, and she found herself thinking, "So that is what it is like to love—so that is what it is like!" Though she knew it was ridiculous, that he was probably out of his mind, that "things like that didn't happen," though she told herself over and over that this absurd letter could make no difference in the monotonous course of her life, still she felt these waves of unreality flowing through her consciousness and suffusing with warmth and softness the melancholy stoicism of her mind. In a minute, as if by magic, she understood that everything was different from what it had been before she entered the house and found that strange, that improbable letter—the kind of letter a man didn't write—on the table. For the first time in her dull and narrow life something had happened to her—something had happened, not through others, not indirectly, but to her, Margaret French. It was as if the merely secondary and impersonal existence she had lived had crumbled at a touch while the saving grace of a righteous egoism stirred within her.

"After all, that's life—that's what it means to be alive and human," she thought, forgetting that a moment before she had called the letter ridiculous and improbable, the kind of thing that did not happen. "If I had only been what he imagines me!"

"I declare, Margaret, you look as if you had a fever!" The paper cutter slipped from Mrs. Buford's hand, and she raised herself on the sofa-pillows while she stared up at her sister. "I never saw you with so much color."

"I walked rapidly, that is all."

An old gilt-framed mirror hung over the mantelpiece, and Margaret's features looked strangely young and innocent as they flashed back at her from the depths of the greenish glass. "He would never have written that letter if he had seen me," she thought, and then, with a thrust of pain sharp as a knife, "Oh, if I could only be what he thinks me!" As the light from the chandelier fell over the mirror, her large sad eyes, of a faded brown like the ashen shade of her hair, stared back at her wonderingly. "I am just what I always was, I haven't changed much," she went on sternly. "I can't even pretend that I was pretty as a girl, because nobody would believe it. Yes, I am just what I always was, and I don't even look very much older. That's the only advantage of being plain, nobody ever tells you you have broken."

"I've read every one of these books, Margaret. Couldn't you find me anything else?"

"I didn't have time to look, Fanny. Suppose you go to the library tomorrow. Doctor Glover says you would be better if you exerted yourself." It was the first revolt of her enslaved and suppressed egoism, the first result in her life of that strange love-letter, and after she had spoken, a dart of self-reproach pierced her heart. "Poor Fanny, I was wrong to speak to her like that. She has had such a hard time," she murmured, but she was not thinking of Fanny and Fanny's "hard time" at all. Something deep within her was saying over and over, "Oh, if I could only be what he thinks me!"

Late that night when she sat down as usual at her desk, she unfolded the strange letter again and read it slowly, word for word, several times. A longing to answer it, to write for once to a living man the love-letter that she had so often written in her dreams, rushed over her. "After all, why shouldn't I pretend to be what he thinks I am?" she asked defiantly of destiny. "Why shouldn't I pretend? What harm can it do him or me? He will never know. He will never see me—and it isn't real, anyhow. It is only make-believe." Then, while the letter lay open before her, she took up her pen, the pen with which she had drudged for a living for so many years, and wrote as if she were the Margaret French—the woman, courageous and strong, pure and beautiful—that he believed her to be.

Dear Lover of my Poems,

If I had known that my verse was for you, I think I should have made only songs of joy, never of sadness. The letter you sent to the strange poet—the poet whom you dreamed of as courageous and strong, pure and beautiful—came to me yesterday; and oh, man of vision! it found me wearing rose-color, the flaming rose of the sunrise. Your poet may be none of the wonderful things you imagine, but she is dark and pale, and she wears the color she wore in your dream.

You say you are an ordinary mortal, you dreamer of dreams, but does an ordinary mortal dream true even when he sleeps in moonlight? So sleep again, and dream again of your poet who is also your

MARGARET FRENCH.

When the note was sealed and stamped, she went down-stairs and out-doors to post it in the box at the corner. If she kept it until tomorrow, she knew that she would lack the courage to send it, and for once, before life was over, she resolved that she would be brave enough to follow the wild sweet spirit of adventure. "I am courageous and strong, pure and beautiful," she said to herself as she dropped off to sleep. "I am really the Margaret French he believes me to be."

In the morning she awoke with a start of surprise and expectancy as she used to awake on Christmas mornings in her childhood. "Something has happened," she thought as she raised her head from the pillow and looked out into the April sunshine, where the sparrows were flitting in and out of the ivy on the wall. "Some thing has happened to me at last—

to me, Margaret French—not to Fanny or Dora or Isabel." Then, as she got out of bed, she remembered the letter and her answer. "Of course it is only make-believe, not real," she said seriously after a minute, "but a beautiful make-believe is better than nothing. If I can't be courageous and strong, pure and beautiful in reality, I can in my thoughts. All day I shall think of myself not as I am, but as he dreams of me."

Fresh from her bath, she sat down before the mirror and brushed her hair until it looked as fine and silky as Dora's. Then stealing across the hall to Isabel's bedroom, she heated the girl's curling-irons and made large loose waves over her forehead and ears. "I wonder how I should look if I were to take more pains?" she said, dusting a little of Isabel's powder over her face. "I suppose I'd have been less hopeless if Fanny and Lizzie had not been pink and white beauties. The way one does one's hair makes a difference."

At breakfast, while she poured the coffee, she felt the eyes of her nieces upon her. They were good girls, and generous, and she knew that they were thinking nothing even tinged with unkindness.

"I wish you'd fix your hair like that every day, Aunt Margaret," said Dora pleasantly. "It makes you look years younger."

"I always told her she ought to wave it," remarked Isabel, helping herself to sugar. "So few people can stand straight hair. It makes mother look plain, and you know what pretty features she has."

Mrs. Buford glanced up with an amiable simper from her breakfast-tray. Though she never felt well enough to come to the table, she woke early and preferred to have her breakfast in the dining-room because, as she said, it was "more sociable."

"Poor mother used to say that some women get better looking as they get older," she observed, "and I believe Margaret is one of them. I never saw her look so well as she did last night when she came in from the library. She had quite a color."

"Nobody ever looks at me when you are by, Fanny," said Margaret truthfully. "I might have taken more pains about myself if you and Lizzie hadn't been beauties."

"It must have been hard," remarked Isabel, who had more sympathy than sense, "but I never thought you plain, Aunt Margaret. I am sure you have a very sweet smile, and Doctor Glover says a sweet smile makes up for everything."

"Well, I am much obliged to him," rejoined Margaret, with a laugh. Her heart felt extraordinarily light, and as she rose from the table and prepared to start to the little circulating library where she worked, she told herself cheerfully, "Thinking so helps anyhow." Then added, "even if it isn't real, it can't do any harm." And then, in a flash as swift as a divine visitation, she discerned one of the profoundest truths of philosophy: "After all, isn't thought the only real thing that there is? There is a Margaret French somewhere who is courageous and strong, pure and beautiful, because he thinks her so. Even if she is only in his mind, still she is real. She exists just as much as I exist to Fanny, or Fanny exists to me. He creates her while he thinks of her."

At the end of the week, on a showery afternoon when her spirits were flagging, the answer came to her letter. As she entered the hall, even before she struck a light, her eyes fell on the big white envelop on the table, and seizing it eagerly, she ran up-stairs to her bedroom. There, behind a locked door, she tore open the envelop and unfolded the pages.

Dear Poet and Woman,
    So for once in the history of this sad old world the dream has come true! You are you, and I have found you. When I wrote to you, half in jest, half in earnest, I never imagined that you would answer. That you should have answered just as you did is almost too good to be real. I feel like pinching myself to prove that I am awake, and that the sunshine is not moonlight. That you should be the Margaret French I dreamed of—my lady, rare and pale and dressed all in flaming rose color—brings the heaven I once believed in down on the earth.
    I have lived hard in rough places, but I have always kept my dreams hidden away somewhere. Deep down in every man there is the eternal dream, I suppose—the dream that is crowded out in the day, but comes back to him sometimes now and then when he falls asleep in the moonlight. Once long ago, before I began to build railroads, I also wrote verses. In those days I wanted to be a poet—such a poet as you are and I could never have been—

It was a long letter, grave at times, gay at times, earnest and humorous. He told her about his life, carelessly as if his life were hardly more than a game he was playing. He had been ill, and he was lonely; he was bored and he needed her—he needed her as no man had ever needed her in her life—not even in her girlhood. He needed, she saw, not the woman, but the thought of her—the ideal that he had created.

"Write to me again, for your letter has given me back my youth," he wrote. "It has brought back all the things I thought dead in me. I feel a boy again since I read it."

As the pages slipped from her hands, she glanced up and met her eyes in the mirror, and for an instant it seemed to her that she gazed at the shining eyes and the flushed face of a girl. "I never looked like that even when I was young," she thought. "Mother always said that my expression was bitter. It must be the way the light falls on the glass." Then she stood

up and turned the gas higher. "No, it is not the light, it is the Margaret
he thinks me. That is the expression she wears, and it is not bitter. She
is the woman who dresses in rose color." With the thought in her mind
it seemed to her that the very essence of life rushed through her veins.
"That is how I must think of myself," she added.

Through the long summer, while Margaret worked in the city, the
letters came every week, and by autumn even the people she saw daily,
even the dull eyes of her little world, had begun to notice the miracle.

"She looks as if she'd got her second wind," remarked old Doctor
Glover jocosely to Mrs. Mills. "I was afraid for awhile that Fanny would
break her pace, but she's coming out ahead, after all; you just watch her."

"I am glad of it," replied Mrs. Mills emphatically. "I always liked Margaret, and I can't abide Fanny."

"Well, you won't deny," the doctor winked, "that Fanny has the features?"

"Oh, if features are all you want! But she hasn't a particle of sense. I
suppose even you woudn't accuse Fanny of that?"

"It wouldn't have been good for the features. Margaret has the sense,
I admit, but it isn't sense that gives a woman new life when she is past
forty. It takes a lover, generally."

"A lover!" Mrs. Mills snapped her fingers. "I don't believe Margaret
ever looked at a man in her life, and I am sure no man ever looked at
her."

"Then what has she done to herself, and why has she done it?"

"Well, she has taken to waving her hair for one thing, and she has
bought a new dress—at least three of them—and they aren't gray."

"I knew there was something." He pondered a moment. "But it goes
deeper than that. Externals can't do it, dear lady, with apologies to your
superior intelligence. It isn't on the surface, you know. It is the idea
working out. Whatever has happened to Margaret French has happened
to her soul. That is the way life works its miracles—from the soul outward, never from the body inward to the soul—"

"Why, doctor, you are talking like a preacher, and I thought you'd
given up church long ago—" Then she broke off abruptly. "Here comes
Margaret now, and in spite of all you say, I maintain that the blue suit
has done most of it. I believe it has changed her expression. You know,
Margaret used to have such a very forbidding expression."

"Well, she certainly gets better looking as she gets older. I've known
a good many women to do that, and sometimes the plain ones leave the
faded beauties like Fanny miles behind them."

"Oh, I don't know about that—" Mrs. Mills was not easily convinced, for she had been the pretty Miss Gage in her youth, and she flattered herself that she was still as attractive as ever even if she had lost her figure.

As Margaret passed she smiled brightly and pressed her letter—the nicest letter she had ever had—more closely in her hand. For the last few months she had lived so intensely in her dream that a veil of unreality had fallen over the world that surrounded her, and the robust figures of Mrs. Mills and the old doctor appeared scarcely more solid than shadows. Even the gradual changes in herself had passed almost unnoticed. Though she felt younger and happier than she had ever felt in her life, and the aching bitterness had faded out of her heart, she still thought of herself as sad and colorless on the surface—as the Margaret French of the dull eyes and the forbidding mouth.

Months after that first letter she had resolved that she would live and die without seeing the writer—without seeing the man she had begun to call in her heart her lover. She had lied to him, and on that lie she had staked her one chance of happiness—the happiness of a dream. For the sake of this dream, which was more vivid to her than the actuality, she had woven a spirit woman, a creature of lights and shadows, of gaiety and mystery, and she had clothed her in the flaming rose of the sunrise. "It would kill me if he were ever to see me," she thought. "The moment that he sees me it will all be over. How could any man care about me when he might care for Dora or Isabel or Janet?" And because she knew that she would never see him, she had poured the wealth of her nature into her letters—the vivid splendor of her imagination, the poetry and tenderness of her feeling, the mirth and richness of her humor. She had given herself as only a poet could give—so abundantly that there were times when she trembled lest he should tire of her generosity. She had given back to him the woman whom his thought had created, and in giving so lavishly she had found herself growing, not poorer, but richer. It was as if she drew inspiration from some inexhaustible source of hope and joy—from that very essence of life which she had felt in her veins.

On the afternoon when she smiled so brightly at Mrs. Mills and the old doctor, she had committed the most reckless act of her life—she had bought a rose-colored gown. "Not an old rose, either," little Miss Smith, who had sold Margaret her gray gowns at Daly's for twenty years, said to her parents at supper. "It wasn't the soft pale shade that anybody might wear. No, it was so bright you wouldn't have believed she would do it—though she was bent on it. She wanted it flaming, she said—she wanted the kind of rose that was in the sunrise."

"I can't make out to save my life what has come over Miss Margaret," observed little Miss Smith's mother, who had done dressmaking for the Frenches ever since she could remember. "It doesn't seem natural, the way she's burst out. I wouldn't have belived it if you had told me. She ain't the same person she used to be, and when all's said and done, it don't seem natural for anybody to change so."

"It's the truth, mother, she ain't the same person," assented little Miss Smith. "I said those very words to her while I was trying on that dress —you can't imagine how well it looked on her. 'I never saw anybody pick up as you've done, Miss Margaret,' I told her. 'You don't look like the same person,' and what do you reckon she answered? 'You're right, Miss Smith, I'm not the same person. I've come to think differently.' What do you suppose she could have meant by that; 'I've come to think differently'?"

"I don't know, my dear, that plain, quiet sort is sometimes the deepest. But you say the rose-colored dress was becoming to her?"

"It made her look real young—that and the way she'd fixed her hair and the look she had got in her eyes, the kind of soft and happy look a girl has when she is trying on the dress for her first party. But I can't help wondering what she meant by, 'I've come to think differently.' I wish I could come to think differently if it would change my expression like that."

"She can't be in love, can she?"

"In love? Miss Margaret? Well, I'd like to know where she's found anybody to be in love with?"

In her room at home, Margaret was trying on the rose-colored dress before the long mirror. Down-stairs supper was waiting, and already Janet had been to knock at the door and ask why she didn't hurry, but still she stood there, transfixed and wondering, with her rapt gaze on her reflection. "Of course I'm a fool," she said. "You can't really make yourself over by taking thought—the Bible says so—yet it does seem less of a lie when I am really wearing rose color. I'm just as plain, I know, as I ever was, but I feel different somehow, just because I've got in the habit of thinking myself attractive. I suppose Doctor Glover was right when he said to Fanny that happiness is a habit of thought."

A second knock came at the door, and Dora fluttered into the room. "What is the matter, Aunt Margaret? Are you never coming?" Then her voice broke in a gasp of astonishment. "Why, Aunt Margaret, are you out of your mind?"

It was the hardest moment of all—harder than the one in which she

had demanded the rose-colored dress of little Miss Smith—but Margaret
met it as bravely as if she had been in reality the woman John Brown
imagined her.

"Of course I know it is a great deal too young for me, Dora, but those
dull colors had begun to depress me. Doctor Glover was telling me only
yesterday about the psychological effect of clothes."

"Well, I shouldn't have believed it if I hadn't seen it with my own eyes,
but it really is becoming to you. I never saw you look so sweet as you do
tonight. Mrs. Mills says it's because you never had any youth when you
were a girl, and that nature is trying not to let you be cheated. Nobody
would ever think that you are older than mother."

"It's nice of you not to laugh at me, dear. Of course I know it is ridiculous for a middle-aged woman to try to look young." Margaret's eyes
filled with tears while she raised her hand to lower the gas.

In spite of her selfishness Dora's nature was sound at the core. She was
modern, too, to her finger tips, and Margaret's ardent prolongation of
youth fitted in with her theories. When all was said, she had far more
sympathy with her aunt's point of view than with her mother's. She de-
spised submission, even submission to the inevitable, with all her soul.

"There isn't anything to laugh at, Aunt Margaret." She was perfectly
serious as she bent over and kissed her. "You look ten years younger and
twenty years happier than you did six months ago. If wearing rose-color
helps you to do it, then wear it every day. I've always said, you remember, that there wasn't a bit of sense in the way you neglected yourself."

"I remember," Margaret was grateful, and she showed it, "but it never
seemed to matter about me, dear, Fanny and Lizzie were so lovely."

"Oh, I don't know." Dora was a philosopher. "It was just your thinking the difference that made it so hard, I suspect. I was reading somewhere the other day that any woman who tries can be attractive. Of
course, that doesn't mean beautiful like mother, but then what has mother's beauty ever done for her? Just look at what she is today. Perhaps,
after all, Mrs. Mills is right, and it is nature's way of equalizing things."

"Of course I haven't really changed, Dora." Margaret's voice faltered.
"It isn't, for instance, as if any man would give me a thought after he
had seen one of you girls."

"Oh, men are such fools," responded Dora sweepingly, "when it comes
to what they think about women."

It was cold comfort at best, and Margaret told herself, while she followed Dora downstairs, that whatever happened she would never, never
consent to a meeting. In his last letter he had asked her to let him come

to her on his next visit to New York, and she had written almost frantically that it would be impossible, that it was out of the question, that she lived like a recluse and saw no one. "I couldn't stand it, it would kill me to have him see me as I really am," she repeated as she followed Dora into the dining-room.

"What on earth have you been doing, Margaret?" Mrs. Buford's peevish voice greeted her. "You haven't been near me all the afternoon. You used to be so sympathetic, and now you appear never to think of anybody except yourself." Lifting her head feebly from the pillows, she caught sight of the rose-colored dress. "I declare I believe you've got clothes on the brain."

It was a bitterer moment even than the one that had revealed her indiscretion to Dora.

"Well, I don't care if she has. It is only fair." Dora was valiant. "You said yourself, mother, that Aunt Margaret had never had any youth."

"She had all she wanted." Mrs. Buford's tone had become spiteful, for she felt that she had been neglected, and the novels from the circulating library had not been returned for two days. "Of course men never admired her, but I am sure we girls were all just as nice to her as we could be. It wasn't our fault if she wasn't taken to dances and plays. Margaret knows as well as I do that she isn't the sort of woman a man ever looks at twice."

"Stop, mother, you are hurting her feelings. I am sure she is a great deal more attractive than a good many of the rest of you—and who cares about men, anyway? I am sure I don't!" It was the triumphant spirit of the twentieth century, but Margaret, victim of a more sentimental period, shrank from the consolation it offered. How she could despise men when John Brown was a man?

"Well, I'm obliged to speak my mind, anyhow," rejoined Mrs. Buford, as she sank back on the sofa, and it was at that very instant—the very last instant in the world that Margaret would have selected for the tremendous event—that Janet brought in a telegram.

"The boy has gone, Aunt Margaret. I signed for him at the door."

The curious eyes were upon her while she unfolded the paper with trembling hands, and read the five words inside.

Arrive at eight this evening. John Brown.

So the blow had fallen at last! The thing she dreaded had happened, and he was coming—he was already on the way to her. He was coming, and there was no way that she could escape. For a wild minute the thought of flight seized her—but where could she go, and what good would come of her going? Flight was not only cowardly; it was ridiculous, since it was impossible to fly from the lie she had created. He thinks me young and lovely, and he will find me middle-aged and plain, she thought; that is the whole of it—that is everything that there is. He will despise me because I have deceived him, and the dream will be over—it is over already, the dream I have lived on. After tonight I must stop thinking myself what he believes me to be—I must stop wearing rose color. After tonight I shall become again the real Margaret French, dull, plain, and quiet, that I have been all my life. It isn't the miracle that I believed it. It is merely one of the mistakes that a man never forgives.

Looking up she found Dora's watchful eyes fixed on her. "I can't eat any supper, dear. I am a little tired. I think I'll go up-stairs and change back into my other dress." Then while the mute questioning in their faces still followed her, she went out of the room, in her fluttering rose-colored draperies, and slowly ascended the steps. "I must put on one of the old gray gowns," she thought wildly. "I must not let him see me in this ridiculous thing." She felt suddenly as if life were ebbing away, the radiant life of the dream she had lived on. After all, how unreal it had been, this bread and wine of her spirit! A thought—nothing more. A thought that could evaporate in an instant, and leave the bare structure of life what it had been from the beginning—the structure of hope and disappointment, of struggle and failure. What a fool she had been to imagine that thinking could alter a single material fact.

She had reached her room and was unfastening the hooks of her gown, when the door opened hurriedly and Janet rushed in.

"Don't undress, Aunt Margaret. There is a strange man down-stairs —a publisher, I suppose—waiting to see you. Marthy asked him into the drawing-room, and I sent her back to make up the fire, for it was almost out. I didn't think there was any use lighting the lamps—he looks awfully dry and uninteresting. The gas will do, won't it?"

"Yes, the gas will do." So he didn't look interesting, either, her lover? A wild hope shot up, and then died quickly down again. He didn't look interesting to Janet, but Janet saw him through the merciless eyes of youth. It is all, she reflected, in the way one happens to see a thing.

"Well, I'll come down in a minute. Hadn't I better change my dress, Janet?" Though her voice was calm, Margaret realized as she spoke that she was asking of Janet—of Janet, with her flower-like face, and her girlish ignorance—the crucial question of her forty-three years. Had the new Margaret triumphed over the old even in the eyes of her niece, or was the rose-colored dress merely a pitiful pretense? Was she only ridiculous when she grasped at happiness, or had thinking differently really changed her from the soul outward as the old doctor had said? Was she still in spite of the miraculous flowering of her soul, just the same dull Margaret French that she had always been on the surface?

For a swift instant Janet glanced carelessly over her. "Oh, I wouldn't trouble to change," she replied indifferently. "He will never know any better."

"Well, run down, then. I'll come in a minute."

After all, she could not shirk the test—she could not even evade the results of her folly. The end had come, she felt, come more disastrously than she had ever foreseen it; and while she stood there, pale and trembling, with the telegram open before her on the bureau, she was conscious of a passionate anger against life, against destiny. "Why couldn't I have been what he believes me?" she demanded of the inscrutable force that had shaped her soul as well as her body. "Why couldn't I have been like Fanny or Lizzie? Why had I, who care so much more than they could ever have cared, to be the only plain one among us?" Then, while the passion of her resentment still gave her courage, she opened the door and went quickly down-stairs and into the drawing-room. If she waited, if she hesitated, she felt that her strength would be unequal to the meeting. Her one chance of fortitude was to act before she had yielded even for an instant to the weakness of self-pity.

He was standing by the table, and as she entered, she noticed that he put down a photograph of Fanny in her youth at which he had been looking. Her first impression was that he was just as Janet had described him—lean and middle-aged, and not in the least remarkable in any way. Then he smiled as she crossed the room toward him, and she saw him, not through Janet's eyes, but enkindled and ennobled by the flame which her imagination had created. It is all, she thought again afterward, in the way one happens to look at a person.

"I knew you would refuse me if I gave you the chance; so I came anyway. I couldn't wait another day, Margaret, without seeing you."

She had paused under the chandelier, and the flickering light from the crystal pendants flashed over her pale face and over the bright rose of her gown. "He sees the truth, and he will never forgive me," she heard a voice saying somewhere. "How could he ever forgive me?"

For that instant, while she stood there, she felt his gaze sweeping over her. She felt it scorching through her superficial stoicism to the secret shame in her heart. "If I could only die," she thought bitterly. "If I could only die before he speaks to me."

Then, while the wish was still in her mind, she saw his smile break like light over his face, and his arms were held out to her.

"My beautiful, I should have known you among a hundred women," he said softly, "for you are just as I dreamed of you!"

Editor's Note

This story was first published in *Good Housekeeping* for February, 1917. Its most distinguished feature is its title, from Hamlet's speech to Rosencrantz and Guildenstern: ". . . there is nothing either good or bad but thinking makes it so." Miss Glasgow has changed Hamlet's Renaissance Platonism into an argument for the power of the imagination. Margaret French almost imagines her suitor into existence. Both she and "John Brown" wish themselves into a romance by mail. The transforming power of the imagination—and the power of Margaret's poetry—works a miracle on two plain people.

It is hard to take this modern Cinderella story seriously, especially when it is drawn out to such length, unless we use it biographically. It is as revealing an example of wish-fulfillment as Miss Glasgow's first fiction, "Only a Daisy." Behind the frustrated poet who is obliged to write silly stories to support her family, we can easily detect Miss Glasgow, also forty-three, who found herself in 1916 in charge of the big gray house in Richmond when her father died.

VI

Dare's Gift

⟜ A year has passed, and I am beginning to ask myself if the thing actually happened? The whole episode, seen in clear perspective, is obviously incredible. There are, of course, no haunted houses in this age of science; there are merely hallucinations, neurotic symptoms, and optical illusions. Any one of these practical diagnoses would, no doubt, cover the impossible occurrence, from my first view of that dusky sunset on James River to the erratic behaviour of Mildred during the spring we spent in Virginia. There is—I admit it readily!—a perfectly rational explanation of every mystery. Yet, while I assure myself that the supernatural has been banished, in the evil company of devils, black plagues, and witches, from this sanitary century, a vision of Dare's Gift, amid its clustering cedars under the shadowy arch of the sunset, rises before me, and my feeble scepticism surrenders to that invincible spirit of darkness. For once in my life—the ordinary life of a corporation lawyer in Washington—the impossible really happened.

It was the year after Mildred's first nervous breakdown, and Drayton, the great specialist in whose care she had been for some months, advised me to take her away from Washington until she recovered her health. As a busy man I couldn't spend the whole week out of town; but if we could find a place near enough—somewhere in Virginia! we both exclaimed, I remember—it would be easy for me to run down once a fortnight. The thought was with me when Harrison asked me to join him for a week's hunting on James River; and it was still in my mind, though less distinctly, on the evening when I stumbled alone, and for the first time, on Dare's Gift.

I had hunted all day—a divine day in October—and at sunset, with a bag full of partridges, I was returning for the night to Chericoke, where Harrison kept his bachelor's house. The sunset had been wonderful;

and I had paused for a moment with my back to the bronze sweep of the land, when I had a swift impression that the memories of the old river gathered around me. It was at this instant—I recall even the trivial detail that my foot caught in a brier as I wheeled quickly about—that I looked past the sunken wharf on my right, and saw the garden of Dare's Gift falling gently from its almost obliterated terraces to the scalloped edge of the river. Following the steep road, which ran in curves through a stretch of pines and across an abandoned pasture or two, I came at last to an iron gate and a grassy walk leading, between walls of box, to the open lawn planted in elms. With that first glimpse the Old World charm of the scene held me captive. From the warm red of its brick walls to the pure Colonial lines of its doorway, and its curving wings mantled in roses and ivy, the house stood there, splendid and solitary. The rows of darkened windows sucked in without giving back the last flare of daylight; the heavy cedars crowding thick up the short avenue did not stir as the wind blew from the river; and above the carved pineapple on the roof, a lonely bat was wheeling high against the red disc of the sun. While I had climbed the rough road, and passed more slowly between the marvelous walls of the box, I had told myself that the place must be Mildred's and mine at any cost. On the upper terrace, before several crude modern additions to the wings, my enthusiasm gradually ebbed, though I still asked myself incredulously, "Why have I never heard of it? To whom does it belong? Has it a name as well known in Virginia as Shirley or Brandon?" The house was of great age, I knew, and yet from obvious signs I discovered that it was not too old to be lived in. Nowhere could I detect a hint of decay or dilapidation. The sound of cattle bells floated up from a pasture somewhere in the distance. Through the long grass on the lawn little twisted paths, like sheep tracks, wound back and forth under the fine old elms, from which a rain of bronze leaves fell slowly and ceaselessly in the wind. Nearer at hand, on the upper terrace, a few roses were blooming; and when I passed between two marble urns on the right of the house, my feet crushed a garden of "simples" such as our grandmothers used to grow.

As I stepped on the porch I heard a child's voice on the lawn, and a moment afterwards a small boy, driving a cow, appeared under the two cedars at the end of the avenue. At sight of me he flicked the cow with the hickory switch he held, and bawled, "Ma! thar's a stranger out here, an' I don't know what he wants."

At his call the front door opened, and a woman in a calico dress, with a sunbonnet pushed back from her forehead, came out on the porch.

"Hush yo' fuss, Eddy!" she remarked authoritatively. "He don't want nothin'." Then, turning to me, she added civilly, "Good evenin', suh. You must be the gentleman who is visitin' over at Chericoke?"

"Yes, I am staying with Mr. Harrison. You know him, of course?"

"Oh, Lordy, yes. Everybody aroun' here knows Mr. Harrison. His folks have been here goin' on mighty near forever. I don't know what me and my children would come to if it wa'n't for him. He is gettin' me my divorce now. It's been three years and mo' sence Tom deserted me."

"Divorce?" I had not expected to find this innovation on James River.

"Of course it ain't the sort of thing anybody would want to come to. But if a woman in the State ought to have one easy, I reckon it's me. Tom went off with another woman—and she my own sister—from this very house——"

"From this house—and, by the way, what is the name of it?"

"Name of what? This place? Why, it's Dare's Gift. Didn't you know it? Yes, suh, it happened right here in this very house, and that, too, when we hadn't been livin' over here mo' than three months. After Mr. Duncan got tired and went away he left us as caretakers, Tom and me, and I asked Tilly to come and stay with us and help me look after the children. It came like a lightning stroke to me, for Tom and Tilly had known each other all their lives, and he'd never taken any particular notice of her till they moved over here and began to tend the cows together. She wa'n't much for beauty, either. I was always the handsome one of the family—though you mightn't think it now, to look at me— and Tom was the sort that never could abide red hair——"

"And you've lived at Dare's Gift ever since?" I was more interested in the house than in the tenant.

"I didn't have nowhere else to go, and the house has got to have a caretaker till it is sold. It ain't likely that anybody will want to rent an out-of-the-way place like this—though now that automobiles have come to stay that don't make so much difference."

"Does it still belong to the Dares?"

"Naw, suh; they had to sell it at auction right after the war on account of mortgages and debts—old Colonel Dare died the very year Lee surrendered, and Miss Lucy she went off somewhere to strange parts. Sence their day it has belonged to so many different folks that you can't keep account of it. Right now it's owned by a Mr. Duncan, who lives out in California. I don't know that he'll ever come back here—he couldn't get on with the neighbours—and he is trying to sell it. No wonder, too, a great big place like this, and he ain't even a Virginian——"

"I wonder if he would let it for a season?" It was then, while I stood there in the brooding dusk of the doorway, that the idea of the spring at Dare's Gift first occurred to me.

"If you want it, you can have it for 'most nothing, I reckon. Would you like to step inside and go over the rooms?"

That evening at supper I asked Harrison about Dare's Gift, and gleaned the salient facts of its history.

"Strange to say, the place, charming as it is, has never been well known in Virginia. There's historical luck, you know, as well as other kinds, and the Dares—after that first Sir Roderick, who came over in time to take a stirring part in Bacon's Rebellion, and, tradition says, to betray his leader—have never distinguished themselves in the records of the State. The place itself, by the way, is about a fifth of the original plantation of three thousand acres, which was given—though I imagine there was more in that than appears in history—by some Indian chief of forgotten name to this notorious Sir Roderick. The old chap—Sir Roderick, I mean—seems to have been something of a fascinator in his day. Even Governor Berkeley, who hanged half the colony, relented, I believe, in the case of Sir Roderick, and that unusual clemency gave rise, I suppose, to the legend of the betrayal. But, however that may be, Sir Roderick had more miraculous escapes than John Smith himself, and died at last in his bed at the age of eighty from overeating cherry-pie."

"And now the place has passed away from the family?"

"Oh, long ago—though not so long, after all, when one comes to think of it. When the old Colonel died the year after the war, it was discovered that he had mortgaged the farm up to the last acre. At that time real estate on James River wasn't regarded as a particularly profitable investment, and under the hammer Dare's Gift went for a song."

"Was the Colonel the last of his name?"

"He left a daughter—a belle, too, in her youth, my mother says—but she died—at least I think she did—only a few months after her father."

Coffee was served on the veranda, and while I smoked my cigar and sipped my brandy—Harrison had an excellent wine-cellar—I watched the full moon shining like a yellow lantern through the diaphanous mist on the river. Downshore, in the sparkling reach of the water, an immense cloud hung low over the horizon, and between the cloud and the river a band of silver light quivered faintly, as if it would go out in an instant.

"It is over there, isn't it?"—I pointed to the silver light—"Dare's Gift, I mean."

"Yes, it's somewhere over yonder—five miles away by the river, and nearly seven by the road."

"It is the dream of a house, Harrison, and there isn't too much history attached to it—nothing that would make a modern beggar ashamed to live in it."

"By Jove! so you are thinking of buying it?" Harrison was beaming. "It is downright ridiculous, I declare, the attraction that place has for strangers. I never knew a Virginian who wanted it; but you are the third Yankee of my acquaintance—and I don't know many—who has fallen in love with it. I searched the title and drew up the deed for John Duncan exactly six years ago—though I'd better not boast of that transaction, I reckon."

"He still owns it, doesn't he?"

"He still owns it, and it looks as if he would continue to own it unless you can be persuaded to buy it. It is hard to find purchasers for these old places, especially when the roads are uncertain and they happen to be situated on the James River. We live too rapidly in these days to want to depend on a river, even on a placid old fellow like the James."

"Duncan never really lived here, did he?"

"At first he did. He began on quite a royal scale; but, somehow, from the very start things appeared to go wrong with him. At the outset he prejudiced the neighbours against him—I never knew exactly why—by putting on airs, I imagine, and boasting about his money. There is something in the Virginia blood that resents boasting about money. However that may be, he hadn't been here six months before he was at odds with every living thing in the county, white, black, and spotted—for even the dogs snarled at him. Then his secretary—a chap he had picked up starving in London, and had trusted absolutely for years—made off with a lot of cash and securities, and that seemed the last straw in poor Duncan's ill luck. I believe he didn't mind the loss half so much—he refused to prosecute the fellow—as he minded the betrayal of confidence. He told me, I remember, before he went away, that it had spoiled Dare's Gift for him. He said he had a feeling that the place had come too high; it had cost him his belief in human nature."

"Then I imagine he'd be disposed to consider an offer?"

"Oh, there isn't a doubt of it. But, if I were you, I shouldn't be too hasty. Why not rent the place for the spring months? It's beautiful here in the spring, and Duncan has left furniture enough to make the house fairly comfortable."

"Well, I'll ask Mildred. Of course Mildred must have the final word in the matter."

"As if Mildred's final word would be anything but a repetition of yours!" Harrison laughed slyly—for the perfect harmony in which we lived had been for ten years a pleasant jest among our friends. Harrison had once classified wives as belonging to two distinct groups—the group of those who talked and knew nothing about their husbands' affairs, and the group of those who knew everything and kept silent. Mildred, he had added politely, had chosen to belong to the latter division.

The next day I went back to Washington, and Mildred's first words to me in the station were,

"Why, Harold, you look as if you had bagged all the game in Virginia!"

"I look as if I had found just the place for you!"

When I told her about my discovery, her charming face sparkled with interest. Never once, not even during her illness, had she failed to share a single one of my enthusiasms; never once, in all the years of our marriage, had there been so much as a shadow between us. To understand the story of Dare's Gift, it is necessary to realize at the beginning all that Mildred meant and means in my life.

Well, to hasten my slow narrative, the negotiations dragged through most of the winter. At first, Harrison wrote me, Duncan couldn't be found, and a little later that he was found, but that he was opposed, from some inscrutable motive, to the plan of renting Dare's Gift. He wanted to sell it outright, and he'd be hanged if he'd do anything less than get the place clean off his hands. "As sure as I let it"—Harrison sent me his letter—"there is going to be trouble, and somebody will come down on me for damages. The damned place has cost me already twice as much as I paid for it."

In the end, however—Harrison has a persuasive way—the arrangements were concluded. "Of course," Duncan wrote after a long silence, "Dare's Gift may be as healthy as heaven. I may quite as easily have contracted this confounded rheumatism, which makes life a burden, either in Italy or from too many cocktails. I've no reason whatever for my dislike for the place; none, that is, except the incivility of my neighbours—where, by the way, did you Virginians manufacture your reputation for manners?—and my unfortunate episode with Paul Grymes. That, as you remark, might, no doubt, have occurred anywhere else, and if a man is going to steal he could have found all the opportunities he wanted in New York or London. But the fact remains that one can't help harbouring associations, pleasant or unpleasant, with the house in which one has lived, and from start to finish my associations with Dare's Gift are frankly unpleasant. If, after all, however, your friend wants the place, and can afford to pay for his whims—let him have it! I hope to Heaven he'll be ready to buy it when his lease has run out. Since he wants it for a hobby, I suppose one place is as good as another; and I can assure him that by the time he has owned it for a few years—especially if he undertakes to improve the motor road up to Richmond—he will regard a taste for Chinese porcelain as an inexpensive diversion." Then, as if impelled by a twist of ironic humour, he added, "He will find the shooting good anyhow."

By early spring Dare's Gift was turned over to us—Mildred was satisfied, if Duncan wasn't—and on a showery day in April, when drifting clouds cast faint gauzy shadows over the river, our boat touched at the old wharf, where carpenters were working, and rested a minute before steaming on to Chericoke Landing five miles away. The spring was early that year—or perhaps the spring is always early on James River. I remember the song of birds in the trees; the veil of bright green over the distant forests; the broad reach of the river scalloped with silver; the dappled sunlight on the steep road which climbed from the wharf to the iron gates; the roving fragrance from lilacs on the lower terrace; and, surmounting all, the two giant cedars which rose like black crags against the changeable blue of the sky—I remember these things as distinctly as if I had seen them this morning.

We entered the wall of box through a living door, and strolled up the grassy walk from the lawn to the terraced garden. Within the garden the air was perfumed with a thousand scents—with lilacs, with young box, with flags and violets and lilies, with aromatic odours from the garden of "simples," and with the sharp sweetness of sheep-mint from the mown grass on the lawn.

"This spring is fine, isn't it?" As I turned to Mildred with the question, I saw for the first time that she looked pale and tired—or was it merely the green light from the box wall that fell over her features? "The trip has been too much for you. Next time we'll come by motor."

"Oh, no, I had a sudden feeling of faintness. It will pass in a minute. What an adorable place, Harold!"

She was smiling again with her usual brightness, and as we passed from the box wall to the clear sunshine on the terrace her face quickly resumed its natural colour. To this day—for Mildred has been strangely reticent about Dare's Gift—I do not know whether her pallor was due to the shade in which we walked or whether, at the instant when I turned to her, she was visited by some intuitive warning against the house we were approaching. Even after a year the events of Dare's Gift are not things I can talk over with Mildred; and, for my part, the occurrence remains, like the house in its grove of cedars, wrapped in an impenetrable mystery. I don't in the least pretend to know how or why

the thing happened. I only know that it did happen—that it happened,
word for word as I record it. Mildred's share in it will, I think, never
become clear to me. What she felt, what she imagined, what she believed, I have never asked her. Whether the doctor's explanation is history or fiction, I do not attempt to decide. He is an old man, and old
men, since Biblical times, have seen visions. There were places in his
story where it seemed to me that he got historical data a little mixed—or
it may be that his memory failed him. Yet, in spite of his liking for
romance and his French education, he is without constructive imagination—at least he says that he is without it—and the secret of Dare's Gift,
if it is not fact, could have sprung only from the ultimate chaos of imagination.

But I think of these things a year afterwards, and on that April morning the house stood there in the sunlight, presiding over its grassy terraces with an air of gracious and intimate hospitality. From the symbolic
pineapple on its sloping roof to the twittering sparrows that flew in and
out of its ivied wings, it reaffirmed that first flawless impression. Flaws,
of course, there were in the fact, yet the recollection of it to-day—the
garnered impression of age, of formal beauty, of clustering memories—is
one of exquisite harmony. We found later, as Mildred pointed out, architectural absurdities—wanton excrescences in the modern additions, which
had been designed apparently with the purpose of providing space at
the least possible cost of material and labour. The rooms, when we passed
through the fine old doorway, appeared cramped and poorly lighted;
broken pieces of the queer mullioned window, where the tracery was
of wood, not stone, had been badly repaired, and much of the original
detail work of the mantels and cornices had been blurred by recent dis-
figurements. But these discoveries came afterwards. The first view of
the place worked like a magic spell—like an intoxicating perfume—on
our senses.

"It is just as if we had stepped into another world," said Mildred,
looking up at the row of windows, from which the ivy had been carefully clipped. "I feel as if I had ceased to be myself since I left Washington." Then she turned to meet Harrison, who had ridden over to welcome us.

We spent a charming fortnight together at Dare's Gift—Mildred
happy as a child in her garden, and I satisfied to lie in the shadow of the
box wall and watch her bloom back to health. At the end of the fortnight I was summoned to an urgent conference in Washington. Some
philanthropic busybody, employed to nose out corruption, had scented
legal game in the affairs of the Atlantic & Eastern Railroad, and I had

been retained as special counsel by that corporation. The fight would be long, I knew—I had already thought of it as one of my great cases—and the evidence was giving me no little anxiety. "It is my last big battle," I told Mildred, as I kissed her good-by on the steps. "If I win, Dare's Gift shall be your share of the spoils; if I lose—well, I'll be like any other general who has met a better man in the field."

"Don't hurry back, and don't worry about me. I am quite happy here."

"I shan't worry, but all the same I don't like leaving you. Remember, if you need advice or help about anything, Harrison is always at hand."

"Yes, I'll remember."

With this assurance I left her standing in the sunshine, with the windows of the house staring vacantly down on her.

When I try now to recall the next month, I can bring back merely a turmoil of legal wrangles. I contrived in the midst of it all to spend two Sundays with Mildred, but I remember nothing of them except the blessed wave of rest that swept over me as I lay on the grass under the elms. On my second visit I saw that she was looking badly, though when I commented on her pallor and the darkened circles under her eyes, she laughed and put my anxious questions aside.

"Oh, I've lost sleep, that's all," she answered, vaguely, with a swift glance at the house. "Did you ever think how many sounds there are in the country that keep one awake?"

As the day went on I noticed, too, that she had grown restless, and once or twice while I was going over my case with her—I always talked over my cases with Mildred because it helped to clarify my opinions— she returned with irritation to some obscure legal point I had passed over. The flutter of her movements—so unlike my calm Mildred—disturbed me more than I confessed to her, and I made up my mind before night that I would consult Drayton when I went back to Washington. Though she had always been sensitive and impressionable, I had never seen her until that second Sunday in a condition of feverish excitability.

In the morning she was so much better that by the time I reached Washington I forgot my determination to call on her physician. My work was heavy that week—the case was developing into a a direct attack upon the management of the road—and in seeking evidence to rebut the charges of illegal rebates to the American Steel Company, I stumbled by accident upon a mass of damaging records. It was a clear case of somebody having blundered—or the records would not have been left for me to discover—and with disturbed thoughts I went down for my third visit to Dare's Gift. It was in my mind to draw out of the case, if an honourable way could be found, and I could barely wait until dinner was over before I unburdened my conscience to Mildred.

"The question has come to one of personal honesty." I remember that I was emphatic. "I've nosed out something real enough this time. There is material for a dozen investigations in Dowling's transactions alone."

The exposure of the Atlantic & Eastern Railroad is public property by this time, and I needn't resurrect the dry bones of that deplorable scandal. I lost the case, as everyone knows; but all that concerns me in it to-day is the talk I had with Mildred on the darkening terrace at Dare's Gift. It was a reckless talk, when one comes to think of it. I said, I know, a great deal that I ought to have kept to myself; but, after all, she is my wife; I had learned in ten years that I could trust her discretion, and there was more than a river between us and the Atlantic & Eastern Railroad.

Well, the sum of it is that I talked foolishly, and went to bed feeling justified in my folly. Afterwards I recalled that Mildred had been very quiet, though whenever I paused she questioned me closely, with a flash of irritation as if she were impatient of my slowness or my lack of lucidity. At the end she flared out for a moment into the excitement I had noticed the week before; but at the time I was so engrossed in my own affairs that this scarcely struck me as unnatural. Not until the blow fell did I recall the hectic flush in her face and the quivering sound of her voice, as if she were trying not to break down and weep.

It was long before either of us got to sleep that night, and Mildred moaned a little under her breath as she sank into unconsciousness. She was not well, I knew, and I resolved again that I would see Drayton as soon as I reached Washington. Then, just before falling asleep, I became acutely aware of all the noises of the country which Mildred said had kept her awake—of the chirping of the crickets in the fireplace, of the fluttering of swallows in the chimney, of the sawing of innumerable insects in the night outside, of the croaking of frogs in the marshes, of the distant solitary hooting of an owl, of the whispering sound of wind in the leaves, of the stealthy movement of a myriad creeping lives in the ivy. Through the open window the moonlight fell in a milk-white flood, and in the darkness the old house seemed to speak with a thousand voices. As I dropped off I had a confused sensation—less a perception than an apprehension—that all these voices were urging me to something—somewhere——

The next day I was busy with a mass of evidence—dull stuff, I remember. Harrison rode over for luncheon, and not until late afternoon, when I strolled out, with my hands full of papers, for a cup of tea on the terrace, did I have a chance to see Mildred alone. Then I noticed that she was breathing quickly, as if from a hurried walk.

"Did you go to meet the boat, Mildred?"

"No, I've been nowhere—nowhere. I've been on the lawn all day," she answered sharply—so sharply that I looked at her in surprise.

In the ten years that I had lived with her I had never before seen her irritated without cause—Mildred's disposition, I had once said, was as flawless as her profile—and I had for the first time in my life that baffled sensation which comes to men whose perfectly normal wives reveal flashes of abnormal psychology. Mildred wasn't Mildred, that was the upshot of my conclusions; and, hang it all! I didn't know any more than Adam what was the matter with her. There were lines around her eyes, and her sweet mouth had taken an edge of bitterness.

"Aren't you well, dear?" I asked.

"Oh, I'm perfectly well," she replied, in a shaking voice, "only I wish you would leave me alone!" And then she burst into tears.

While I was trying to comfort her the servant came with the tea things, and she kept him about some trivial orders until the big touring-car of one of our neighbours rushed up the drive and halted under the terrace.

In the morning Harrison motored up to Richmond with me, and on the way he spoke gravely of Mildred.

"Your wife isn't looking well, Beckwith. I shouldn't wonder if she were a bit seedy—and if I were you I'd get a doctor to look at her. There is a good man down at Chericoke Landing—old Pelham Lakeby. I don't care if he did get his training in France half a century ago; he knows more than your half-baked modern scientists."

"I'll speak to Drayton this very day," I answered, ignoring his suggestion of the physician. "You have seen more of Mildred this last month than I have. How long have you noticed that she isn't herself?"

"A couple of weeks. She is usually so jolly, you know." Harrison had played with Mildred in his childhood. "Yes, I shouldn't lose any time over the doctor. Though, of course, it may be only the spring," he added, reassuringly.

"I'll drop by Drayton's office on my way uptown," I replied, more alarmed by Harrison's manner than I had been by Mildred's condition.

But Drayton was not in his office, and his assistant told me that the great specialist would not return to town until the end of the week. It was impossible for me to discuss Mildred with the earnest young man who discoursed so eloquently of the experiments in the Neurological Institute, and I left without mentioning her, after making an appointment for Saturday morning. Even if the consultation delayed my return to Dare's Gift until the afternoon, I was determined to see Drayton, and, if possible, take him back with me. Mildred's last nervous breakdown had been too serious for me to neglect this warning.

I was still worrying over that case—wondering if I could find a way to draw out of it—when the catastrophe overtook me. It was on Saturday morning, I remember, and after a reassuring talk with Drayton, who had promised to run down to Dare's Gift for the coming week-end, I was hurrying to catch the noon train for Richmond. As I passed through the station, one of the *Observer's* sensational "war extras" caught my eye, and I stopped for an instant to buy the paper before I hastened through the gate to the train. Not until we had started, and I had gone back to the dining-car, did I unfold the pink sheets and spread them out on the table before me. Then, while the waiter hung over me for the order, I felt the headlines on the front page slowly burn themselves into my brain—for, instead of the news of the great French drive I was expecting, there flashed back at me, in large type, the name of the opposing counsel in the case against the Atlantic & Eastern. The *Observer's* "extra" battened not on the war this time, but on the gross scandal of the railroad; and the front page of the paper was devoted to a personal interview with Herbert Tremaine, the great Tremaine, that philanthropic busybody who had first scented corruption. It was all there, every ugly detail—every secret proof of the illegal transactions on which I had stumbled. It was all there, phrase for pharse, as I alone could have told it—as I alone, in my folly, had told it to Mildred. The Atlantic & Eastern had been betrayed, not privately, not secretly, but in large type in the public print of a sensational newspaper. And not only the road! I also had been betrayed —betrayed so wantonly, so irrationally, that it was like an incident out of melodrama. It was conceivable that the simple facts might have leaked out through other channels, but the phrases, the very words of Tremaine's interview, were mine.

The train had started; I couldn't have turned back even if I had wanted to do so. I was bound to go on, and some intuition told me that the mystery lay at the end of my journey. Mildred had talked indiscreetly to someone, but to whom? Not to Harrison, surely! Harrison, I knew, I could count on, and yet whom had she seen except Harrison? After my first shock the absurdity of the thing made me laugh aloud. It was all as ridiculous, I realized, as it was disastrous! It might so easily not have happened. If only I hadn't stumbled on those accursed records! If only I had kept my mouth shut about them! If only Mildred had not talked unwisely to someone! But I wonder if there was ever a tragedy so inevitable that the victim, in looking back, could not see a hundred ways, great or small, of avoiding or preventing it?—a hundred trivial incidents which, falling differently, might have transformed the event into pure comedy?

The journey was unmitigated torment. In Richmond the car did not meet me, and I wasted half an hour in looking for a motor to take me to Dare's Gift. When at last I got off, the road was rougher than ever, plowed into heavy furrows after the recent rains, and filled with mudholes from which it seemed we should never emerge. By the time we puffed exhaustedly up the rocky road from the river's edge, and ran into the avenue, I had worked myself into a state of nervous apprehension bordering on panic. I don't know what I expected, but I think I shouldn't have been surprised if Dare's Gift had lain in ruins before me. Had I found the house levelled to ashes by a divine visitation, I believe I should have accepted the occurrence as within the bounds of natural phenomena.

But everything—even the young peacocks on the lawn—was just as I had left it. The sun, setting in a golden ball over the pineapple on the roof, appeared as unchangeable, while it hung there in the glittering sky, as if it were made of metal. From the somber dusk of the wings, where the ivy lay like a black shadow, the clear front of the house, with its formal doorway and its mullioned windows, shone with an intense brightness, the last beams of sunshine lingering there before they faded into the profound gloom of the cedars. The same scents of roses and sage and mown grass and sheep-mint hung about me; the same sounds—the croaking of frogs and the sawing of katydids—floated up from the low grounds; the very books I had been reading lay on one of the tables on the terrace, and the front door still stood ajar as if it had not closed since I passed through it.

I dashed up the steps, and in the hall Mildred's maid met me. "Mrs. Beckwith was so bad that we sent for the doctor—the one Mr. Harrison recommended. I don't know what it is, sir, but she doesn't seem like herself. She talks as if she were quite out of her head."

"What does the doctor say?"

"He didn't tell me. Mr. Harrison saw him. He—the doctor, I mean—has sent a nurse, and he is coming again in the morning. But she isn't herself, Mr. Beckwith. She says she doesn't want you to come to her——"

"Mildred!" I had already sprung past the woman, calling the beloved name aloud as I ran up the stairs.

In her chamber, standing very straight, with hard eyes, Mildred met me. "I had to do it, Harold," she said coldly—so coldly that my outstretched arms fell to my sides. "I had to tell all I knew."

"You mean you told Tremaine—you wrote to him—you, Mildred?"

"I wrote to him—I had to write. I couldn't keep it back any longer. No, don't touch me. You must not touch me. I had to do it. I would do it again."

Then it was, while she stood there, straight and hard, and rejoiced because she had betrayed me—then it was that I knew that Mildred's mind was unhinged.

"I had to do it. I would do it again," she repeated, pushing me from her.

II

All night I sat by Mildred's bedside, and in the morning, without having slept, I went downstairs to meet Harrison and the doctor.

"You must get her away, Beckwith," began Harrison with a curious, suppressed excitement. "Dr. Lakeby says she will be all right again as soon as she gets back to Washington."

"But I brought her away from Washington because Drayton said it was not good for her."

"I know, I know." His tone was sharp, "But it's different now. Dr. Lakeby wants you to take her back as soon as you can."

The old doctor was silent while Harrison spoke, and it was only after I had agreed to take Mildred away to-morrow that he murmured something about "bromide and chloral," and vanished up the staircase. He impressed me then as a very old man—old not so much in years as in experience, as if, living there in that flat and remote country, he had exhausted all human desires. A leg was missing, I saw, and Harrison explained that the doctor had been dangerously wounded in the battle of Seven Pines, and had been obliged after that to leave the army and take up again the practice of medicine.

"You had better get some rest," Harrison said, as he parted from me. "It is all right about Mildred, and nothing else matters. The doctor will see you in the afternoon, when you have had some sleep, and have a talk with you. He can explain things better than I can."

Some hours later, after a profound slumber, which lasted well into the afternoon, I waited for the doctor by the tea-table, which had been laid out on the upper terrace. It was a perfect afternoon—a serene and cloudless afternoon in early summer. All the brightness of the day gathered on the white porch and the red walls, while the clustering shadows slipped slowly over the box garden to the lawn and the river.

I was sitting there, with a book I had not even attempted to read, when the doctor joined me; and while I rose to shake hands with him I received again the impression of weariness, of pathos and disappoint-

ment, which his face had given me in the morning. He was like sun-
dried fruit, I thought, fruit that has ripened and dried under the open
sky, not withered in tissue paper.

Declining my offer of tea, he sat down in one of the wicker chairs, selecting, I noticed, the least comfortable among them, and filled his pipe
from a worn leather pouch.

"She will sleep all night," he said; "I am giving her bromide every
three hours, and to-morrow you will be able to take her away. In a week
she will be herself again. These nervous natures yield quickest to the influence, but they recover quickest also. In a little while this illness, as you
choose to call it, will have left no mark upon her. She may even have
forgotten it. I have known this to happen."

"You have known this to happen?" I edged my chair nearer.

"They all succumb to it—the neurotic temperament soonest, the phleg-
matic one later—but they all succumb to it in the end. The spirit of the
place is too strong for them. They surrender to the thought of the house
—to the psychic force of its memories——"

"There are memories, then? Things have happened here?"

"All old houses have memories, I suppose. Did you ever stop to wonder about the thoughts that must have gathered within walls like these?
—to wonder about the impressions that must have lodged in the bricks,
in the crevices, in the timber and the masonry? Have you ever stopped
to think that these multiplied impressions might create a current of
thought—a mental atmosphere—an inscrutable power of suggestion?"

"Even when one is ignorant? When one does not know the story?"

"She may have heard scraps of it from the servants—who knows? One
can never tell how traditions are kept alive. Many things have been
whispered about Dare's Gift; some of these whispers may have reached
her. Even without her knowledge she may have absorbed the suggestion;
and some day, with that suggestion in her mind, she may have gazed too
long at the sunshine on these marble urns before she turned back into
the haunted rooms where she lived. After all, we know so little, so
pitifully little about these things. We have only touched, we physicians,
the outer edges of psychology. The rest lies in darkness——"

I jerked him up sharply. "The house, then, is haunted?"

For a moment he hesitated. "The house is saturated with a thought.
It is haunted by treachery."

"You mean something happened here?"

"I mean——" He bent forward, groping for the right word, while his
gaze sought the river, where a golden web of mist hung midway between sky and water. "I am an old man, and I have lived long enough

to see every act merely as the husk of an idea. The act dies; it decays like the body, but the idea is immortal. The thing that happened at Dare's Gift was over fifty years ago, but the thought of it still lives— still utters its profound and terrible message. The house is a shell, and if one listens long enough one can hear in its heart the low murmur of the past—of that past which is but a single wave of the great sea of human experience——"

"But the story?" I was becoming impatient of his theories. After all, if Mildred was the victim of some phantasmal hypnosis, I was anxious to meet the ghost who had hypnotized her. Even Drayton, I reflected, keen as he was about the fact of mental suggestion, would never have re- garded seriously the suggestion of a phantom. And the house looked so peaceful—so hospitable in the afternoon light.

"The story? Oh, I am coming to that—but of late the story has meant so little to me beside the idea. I like to stop by the way. I am getting old, and an amble suits me better than too brisk a trot—particularly in this weather——"

Yes, he was getting old. I lit a fresh cigarette and waited impatiently. After all, this ghost that he rambled about was real enough to destroy me, and my nerves were quivering like harp-strings.

"Well, I came into the story—I was in the very thick of it, by acci- dent, if there is such a thing as accident in this world of incomprehensi- ble laws. The Incomprehensible! That has always seemed to me the supreme fact of life, the one truth overshadowing all others—the truth that we know nothing. We nibble at the edges of the mystery, and the great Reality—the Incomprehensible—is still untouched, undiscovered. It unfolds hour by hour, day by day, creating, enslaving, killing us, while we painfully gnaw off—what? A crumb or two, a grain from that vast- ness which envelops us, which remains impenetrable——"

Again he broke off, and again I jerked him back from his reverie.

"As I have said, I was placed, by an act of Providence, or of chance, in the very heart of the tragedy. I was with Lucy Dare on the day, the un- forgettable day, when she made her choice—her heroic or devilish choice, according to the way one has been educated. In Europe a thousand years ago such an act committed for the sake of religion would have made her a saint; in New England, a few centuries past, it would have en- titled her to a respectable position in history—the little history of New England. But Lucy Dare was a Virginian, and in Virginia—except in the brief, exalted Virginia of the Confederacy—the personal loyalties have always been esteemed beyond the impersonal. I cannot imagine us as a people canonizing a woman who sacrificed the human ties for the superhuman—even for the divine. I cannot imagine it, I repeat; and so Lucy Dare—though she rose to greatness in that one instant of sacrifice—has not even a name among us to-day. I doubt if you can find a child in the State who has ever heard of her—or a grown man, outside of this neighbourhood, who could give you a single fact of her history. She is as completely forgotten as Sir Roderick, who betrayed Bacon—she is forgotten because the thing she did, though it might have made a Greek tragedy, was alien to the temperament of the people among whom she lived. Her tremendous sacrifice failed to arrest the imagination of her time. After all, the sublime cannot touch us unless it is akin to our ideal; and though Lucy Dare was sublime, according to the moral code of the Romans, she was a stranger to the racial soul of the South. Her memory died because it was the bloom of an hour—because there was nothing in the soil of her age for it to thrive on. She missed her time; she is one of the mute inglorious heroines of history; and yet, born in another century, she might have stood side by side with Antigone——" For an instant he paused. "But she has always seemed to me diabolical," he added.

"What she did, then, was so terrible that it has haunted the house ever since?" I asked again, for, wrapped in memories, he had lost the thread of his story.

"What she did was so terrible that the house has never forgotten. The thought in Lucy Dare's mind during those hours while she made her choice has left an ineffaceable impression on the things that surrounded her. She created in the horror of that hour an unseen environment more real, because more spiritual, than the material fact of the house. You won't believe this, of course—if people believed in the unseen as in the seen, would life be what it is?"

The afternoon light slept on the river; the birds were mute in the elm-trees; from the garden of herbs at the end of the terrace an aromatic fragrance rose like invisible incense.

"To understand it all, you must remember that the South was dominated, was possessed by an idea—the idea of the Confederacy. It was an exalted idea—supremely vivid, supremely romantic—but, after all, it was only an idea. It existed nowhere within the bounds of the actual unless the souls of its devoted people may be regarded as actual. But it is the dream, not the actuality, that commands the noblest devotion, the completest self-sacrifice. It is the dream, the ideal, that has ruled mankind from the beginning.

"I saw a great deal of the Dares that year. It was a lonely life I led after I lost my leg at Seven Pines, and dropped out of the army, and, as you may imagine, a country doctor's practice in wartimes was far from lucrative. Our one comfort was that we were all poor, that we were all starving together; and the Dares—there were only two of them, father and daughter—were as poor as the rest of us. They had given their last coin to the government—had poured their last bushel of meal into the sacks of the army. I can imagine the superb gesture with which Lucy Dare flung her dearest heirloom—her one remaining brooch or pin—into the bare coffers of the Confederacy. She was a small woman, pretty rather than beautiful—not the least heroic in build—yet I wager that she was heroic enough on that occasion. She was a strange soul, though I never so much as suspected her strangeness while I knew her—while she moved among us with her small oval face, her gentle blue eyes, her smoothly banded hair, which shone like satin in the sunlight. Beauty she must have had in a way, though I confess a natural preference for queenly women; I dare say I should have preferred Octavia to Cleopatra, who, they tell me, was small and slight. But Lucy Dare wasn't the sort to blind your eyes when you first looked at her. Her charm was like a fragrance rather than a colour—a subtle fragrance that steals into the senses and is the last thing a man ever forgets. I knew half a dozen men who would have died for her—and yet she gave them nothing, nothing, barely a smile. She appeared cold—she who was destined to flame to life in an act. I can see her distinctly as she looked then, in that last year—grave, still, with the curious, unearthly loveliness that comes to pretty women who are underfed—who are slowly starving for bread and meat, for bodily nourishment. She had the look of one dedicated—as ethereal as a saint, and yet I never saw it at the time; I only remember it now, after fifty years, when I think of her. Starvation, when it is slow, not quick—when it means, not acute hunger, but merely lack of the right food, of the blood-making, nerve-building elements—starvation like this often plays strange pranks with one. The visions of the saints, the glories of martyrdom, come to the underfed, the anæmic. Can you recall one of the saints—the genuine sort—whose regular diet was roast beef and ale?

"Well, I have said that Lucy Dare was a strange soul, and she was, though to this day I don't know how much of her strangeness was the result of improper nourishment, of too little blood to the brain. Be that as it may, she seems to me when I look back on her to have been one of those women whose characters are shaped entirely by external events—who are the playthings of circumstance. There are many such women. They move among us in obscurity—reserved, passive, commonplace—and we never suspect the spark of fire in their natures until it flares up at the touch of the unexpected. In ordinary circumstances Lucy Dare would have been ordinary, submissive, feminine, domestic; she adored children. That she possessed a stronger will than the average Southern girl, brought up in the conventional manner, none of us—least of all I, myself—ever imagined. She was, of course, intoxicated, obsessed, with the idea of the Confederacy; but, then, so were all of us. There wasn't anything unusual or abnormal in that exalted illusion. It was the common property of our generation. . . .

"Like most non-combatants, the Dares were extremists, and I, who had got rid of a little of my bad blood when I lost my leg, used to regret sometimes that the Colonel—I never knew where he got his title—was too old to do a share of the actual fighting. There is nothing that takes the fever out of one so quickly as a fight; and in the army I had never met a hint of this concentrated, vitriolic bitterness towards the enemy. Why, I've seen the Colonel, sitting here on this terrace, and crippled to the knees with gout, grow purple in the face if I spoke so much as a good word for the climate of the North. For him, and for the girl, too, the Lord had drawn a divine circle round the Confederacy. Everything inside of that circle was perfection; everything outside of it was evil. Well, that was fifty years ago, and his hate is all dust now; yet I can sit here, where he used to brood on this terrace, sipping his blackberry wine—I can sit here and remember it all as if it were yesterday. The place has changed so little, except for Duncan's grotesque additions to the wings, that one can scarcely believe all these years have passed over it. Many an afternoon just like this I've sat here, while the Colonel nodded and Lucy knitted for the soldiers, and watched these same shadows creep down the terrace and that mist of light—it looks just as it used to—hang there over the James. Even the smell from those herbs hasn't changed. Lucy used to keep her little garden at the end of the terrace, for she was fond of making essences and beauty lotions. I used to give her all the prescriptions I could find in old books I read—and I've heard people say that she owed her wonderful white skin to the concoctions she brewed from shrubs and herbs. I couldn't convince them that lack of meat, not lotions, was responsible for the pallor—pallor was all the fashion then—that they admired and envied."

He stopped a minute, just long enough to refill his pipe, while I glanced with fresh interest at the garden of herbs.

"It was a March day when it happened," he went on presently; "cloudless, mild, with the taste and smell of spring in the air. I had been at Dare's Gift almost every day for a year. We had suffered together, hoped, feared, and wept together, hungered and sacrificed together. We had felt together the divine, invincible sway of an idea.

"Stop for a minute and picture to yourself what it is to be of a war and yet not in it; to live in imagination until the mind becomes inflamed with the vision; to have no outlet for the passion that consumes one except the outlet of thought. Add to this the fact that we really knew nothing. We were as far away from the truth, stranded here on our river, as if we had been anchored in a canal on Mars. Two men—one crippled, one too old to fight—and a girl—and the three living for a country which in a few weeks would be nothing—would be nowhere not on any map of the world. . . .

"When I look back now it seems to me incredible that at that time any persons in the Confederacy should have been ignorant of its want of resources. Yet remember we lived apart, remote, unvisited, out of touch with realities, thinking the one thought. We believed in the ultimate triumph of the South with that indomitable belief which is rooted not in reason, but in emotion. To believe had become an act of religion; to doubt was rank infidelity. So we sat there in our little world, the world of unrealities, bounded by the river and the garden, and talked from noon till sunset about our illusion—not daring to look a single naked fact in the face—talking of plenty when there were no crops in the ground and no flour in the storeroom, prophesying victory while the Confederacy was in her death struggle. Folly! All folly, and yet I am sure even now that we were sincere, that we believed the nonsense we were uttering. We believed, I have said, because to doubt would have been far too horrible. Hemmed in by the river and the garden, there wasn't anything left for us to do—since we couldn't fight—but believe. Someone has said, or ought to have said, that faith is the last refuge of the inefficient. The twin devils of famine and despair were at work in the country, and we sat there—we three, on this damned terrace—and prophesied about the second president of the Confederacy. We agreed, I remember, that Lee would be the next president. And all the time, a few miles away, the demoralization of defeat was abroad, was around us, was in the air. . . .

"It was a March afternoon when Lucy sent for me, and while I walked up the drive—there was not a horse left among us, and I made all my rounds on foot—I noticed that patches of spring flowers were blooming in the long grass on the lawn. The air was as soft as May, and in the woods at the back of the house buds of maple-trees ran like a flame. There were, I remember, leaves—dead leaves, last year's leaves—everywhere, as if, in the demoralization of panic, the place had been forgotten, had been untouched since autumn. I remember rotting leaves that gave like moss underfoot; dried leaves that stirred and murmured as one walked over them; black leaves, brown leaves, wine-coloured leaves, and the still glossy leaves of the evergreens. But they were everywhere—in the road, over the grass on the lawn, beside the steps, piled in wind-drifts against the walls of the house.

"On the terrace, wrapped in shawls, the old Colonel was sitting; and he called out excitedly, 'Are you bringing news of a victory?' Victory! when the whole country had been scraped with a fine-tooth comb for provisions.

"'No, I bring no news except that Mrs. Morson has just heard of the death of her youngest son in Petersburg. Gangrene, they say. The truth is the men are so ill-nourished that the smallest scratch turns to gangrene——'

"'Well, it won't be for long—not for long. Let Lee and Johnston get together and things will go our way with a rush. A victory or two, and the enemy will be asking for terms of peace before the summer is over.'

"A lock of his silver-white hair had fallen over his forehead, and pushing it back with his clawlike hand, he peered up at me with his little nearsighted eyes, which were of a peculiar burning blackness, like the eyes of some small enraged animal. I can see him now as vividly as if I had left him only an hour ago, and yet it is fifty years since then—fifty years filled with memories and with forgetfulness. Behind him the warm red of the bricks glowed as the sunshine fell, sprinkled with shadows, through the elm boughs. Even the soft wind was too much for him, for he shivered occasionally in his blanket shawls, and coughed the dry, hacking cough which had troubled him for a year. He was a shell of a man—a shell vitalized and animated by an immense, an indestructible illusion. While he sat there, sipping his blackberry wine, with his little fiery dark eyes searching the river in hope of something that would end his interminable expectancy, there was about him a fitful sombre gleam of romance. For him the external world, the actual truth of things, had vanished—all of it, that is, except the shawl that wrapped him and the glass of blackberry wine he sipped. He had died already to the material fact, but he lived intensely, vividly, profoundly, in the idea. It was the idea that nourished him, that gave him his one hold on reality.

"'It was Lucy who sent for you,' said the old man presently. 'She has been on the upper veranda all day overlooking something—the sunning of winter clothes, I think. She wants to see you about one of the servants—a sick child, Nancy's child, in the quarters.'

"'Then I'll find her,' I answered readily, for I had, I confess, a mild curiosity to find out why Lucy had sent for me.

"She was alone on the upper veranda, and I noticed that she closed her Bible and laid it aside as I stepped through the long window that opened from the end of the hall. Her face, usually so pale, glowed now with a wan illumination, like ivory before the flame of a lamp. In this illumination her eyes, beneath delicately pencilled eyebrows, looked unnaturally large and brilliant, and so deeply, so angelically blue that they made me think of the Biblical heaven of my childhood. Her beauty, which had never struck me sharply before, pierced through me. But it was her fate —her misfortune perhaps—to appear commonplace, to pass unrecognized, until the fire shot from her soul.

" 'No, I want to see you about myself, not about one of the servants.'

"At my first question she had risen and held out her hand—a white, thin hand, small and frail as a child's.

" 'You are not well, then?' I had known from the first that her starved look meant something.

" 'It isn't that; I am quite well.' She paused a moment, and then looked at me with a clear shining gaze. 'I have had a letter,' she said.

" 'A letter?' I have realized since how dull I must have seemed to her in that moment of excitement, of exaltation.

" 'You didn't know. I forgot that you didn't know that I was once engaged—long ago—before the beginning of the war. I cared a great deal —we both cared a great deal, but he was not one of us; he was on the other side—and when the war came, of course there was no question. We broke it off; we had to break it off. How could it have been possible to do otherwise?'

" 'How, indeed!' I murmured; and I had a vision of the old man downstairs on the terrace, of the intrepid and absurd old man.

" 'My first duty is to my country,' she went on after a minute, and the words might have been spoken by her father. 'There has been no thought of anything else in my mind since the beginning of the war. Even if peace comes I can never feel the same again—I can never forget that he has been a part of all we have suffered—of the thing that has made us suffer. I could never forget—I can never forgive.'

"Her words sound strange now, you think, after fifty years; but on that day, in this house surrounded by dead leaves, inhabited by an inextinguishable ideal—in this country, where the spirit had fed on the body until the impoverished brain reacted to transcendent visions—in this place, at that time, they were natural enough. Scarcely a woman of the South but would have uttered them from her soul. In every age one ideal enthralls the imagination of mankind; it is in the air; it subjugates the will; it enchants the emotions. Well, in the South fifty years ago this ideal was patriotism; and the passion of patriotism, which bloomed like some red flower, the flower of carnage, over the land, had grown in Lucy Dare's soul into an exotic blossom.

"Yet even to-day, after fifty years, I cannot get over the impression she made upon me of a woman who was, in the essence of her nature, thin and colourless. I may have been wrong. Perhaps I never knew her. It is not easy to judge people, especially women, who wear a mask by instinct. What I thought lack of character, of personality, may have been merely reticence; but again and again there comes back to me the thought that she never said or did a thing—except the one terrible thing—that one could remember. There was nothing remarkable that one could point to about her. I cannot recall either her smile or her voice, though both were sweet, no doubt, as the smile and the voice of a Southern woman would be. Until that morning on the upper veranda I had not noticed that her eyes were wonderful. She was like a shadow, a phantom, that attains in one supreme instant, by one immortal gesture, union with reality. Even I remember her only by that one lurid flash.

" 'And you say you have had a letter?'

" 'It was brought by one of the old servants—Jacob, the one who used to wait on him when he stayed here. He was a prisoner. A few days ago he escaped. He asked me to see him—and I told him to come. He wishes to see me once again before he goes North—for ever——' She spoke in gasps in a dry voice. Never once did she mention his name. Long afterwards I remembered that I had never heard his name spoken. Even to-day I do not know it. He also was a shadow, a phantom—a part of the encompassing unreality.

" 'And he will come here?'

"For a moment she hesitated; then she spoke quite simply, knowing that she could trust me.

" 'He is here. He is in the chamber beyond.' She pointed to one of the long windows that gave on the veranda. 'The blue chamber at the front.'

"I remember that I made a step towards the window when her voice arrested me. 'Don't go in. He is resting. He is very tired and hungry.'

" 'You didn't send for me, then, to see him?'

" 'I sent for you to be with father. I knew you would help me—that you would keep him from suspecting. He must not know, of course. He must be kept quiet.'

" 'I will stay with him,' I answered, and then, 'Is that all you wish to say to me?'

" 'That is all. It is only for a day or two. He will go on in a little while, and I can never see him again. I do not wish to see him again.'

"I turned away, across the veranda, entered the hall, walked the length of it, and descended the staircase. The sun was going down in a ball—just as it will begin to go down in a few minutes—and as I descended the stairs I saw it through the mullioned window over the door—huge and red and round above the black cloud of the cedars.

"The old man was still on the terrace. I wondered vaguely why the servants had not brought him indoors; and then, as I stepped over the threshold, I saw that a company of soldiers—Confederates—had crossed the lawn and were already gathering about the house. The commanding officer—I was shaking hands with him presently—was a Dare, a distant cousin of the Colonel's, one of those excitable, nervous, and slightly theatrical natures who become utterly demoralized under the spell of any violent emotion. He had been wounded at least a dozen times, and his lean, sallow, still handsome features had the greenish look which I had learned to associate with chronic malaria.

"When I look back now I can see it all as a part of the general disorganization—of the fever, the malnutrition, the complete demoralization of panic. I know now that each man of us was facing in his soul defeat and despair; and that we—each one of us—had gone mad with the thought of it. In a little while, after the certainty of failure had come to us, we met it quietly—we braced our souls for the issue; but in those last weeks defeat had all the horror, all the insane terror of a nightmare, and all the vividness. The thought was like a delusion from which we fled, and which no flight could put farther away from us.

"Have you ever lived, I wonder, from day to day in that ever-present and unchanging sense of unreality, as if the moment before you were but an imaginary experience which must dissolve and evaporate before the touch of an actual event? Well, that was the sensation I had felt for days, weeks, months, and it swept over me again while I stood there, shaking hands with the Colonel's cousin, on the terrace. The soldiers, in their ragged uniforms, appeared as visionary as the world in which we had been living. I think now that they were as ignorant as we were of the things that had happened—that were happening day by day to the army. The truth is that it was impossible for a single one of us to believe that our heroic army could be beaten even by unseen powers—even by hunger and death.

"'And you say he was a prisoner?' It was the old man's quavering voice, and it sounded avid for news, for certainty.

"'Caught in disguise. Then he slipped through our fingers.' The cousin's tone was querulous, as if he were irritated by loss of sleep or of food. 'Nobody knows how it happened. Nobody ever knows. But he has found out things that will ruin us. He has plans. He has learned things that mean the fall of Richmond if he escapes.'

"Since then I have wondered how much they sincerely believed—how much was simply the hallucination of fever, of desperation? Were they trying to bully themselves by violence into hoping? Or had they honestly convinced themselves that victory was still possible? If one only repeats a phrase often and emphatically enough one comes in time to believe it; and they had talked so long of that coming triumph, of the established Confederacy, that it had ceased to be, for them at least, merely a phrase. It wasn't the first occasion in life when I had seen words bullied—yes, literally bullied into beliefs.

"Well, looking back now after fifty years, you see, of course, the weakness of it all, the futility. At that instant, when all was lost, how could any plans, any plotting have ruined us? It seems irrational enough now— a dream, a shadow, that belief—and yet not one of us but would have given our lives for it. In order to understand you must remember that we were, one and all, victims of an idea—of a divine frenzy.

" 'And we are lost—the Confederacy is lost, you say, if he escapes?'

"It was Lucy's voice; and turning quickly, I saw that she was standing in the doorway. She must have followed me closely. It was possible that she had overheard every word of the conversation.

" 'If Lucy knows anything, she will tell you. There is no need to search the house,' quavered the old man, 'she is my daughter.'

" 'Of course we wouldn't search the house—not Dare's Gift,' said the cousin. He was excited, famished, malarial, but he was a gentleman, every inch of him.

"He talked on rapidly, giving details of the capture, the escape, the pursuit. It was all rather confused. I think he must have frightfully exaggerated the incident. Nothing could have been more unreal than it sounded. And he was just out of a hospital—was suffering still, I could see, from malaria. While he drank his blackberry wine—the best the house had to offer—I remember wishing that I had a good dose of quinine and whiskey to give him.

"The narrative lasted a long time; I think he was glad of a rest and of the blackberry wine and biscuits. Lucy had gone to fetch food for the soldiers; but after she had brought it she sat down in her accustomed chair by the old man's side and bent her head over her knitting. She was a wonderful knitter. During all the years of the war I seldom saw her without her ball of yarn and her needles—the long wooden kind that the women used at that time. Even after the dusk fell in the evenings the click of her needles sounded in the darkness.

" 'And if he escapes it will mean the capture of Richmond?' she asked once again when the story was finished. There was no hint of excitement in her manner. Her voice was perfectly toneless. To this day I have no idea what she felt—what she was thinking.

" 'If he gets away it is the ruin of us—but he won't get away. We'll find him before morning.'

"Rising from his chair, he turned to shake hands with the old man before descending the steps. 'We've got to go on now. I shouldn't have stopped if we hadn't been half starved. You've done us a world of good, Cousin Lucy. I reckon you'd give your last crust to the soldiers?'

" 'She'd give more than that,' quavered the old man. 'You'd give more than that, wouldn't you, Lucy?'

" 'Yes, I'd give more than that,' repeated the girl quietly, so quietly that it came as a shock to me—like a throb of actual pain in the midst of a nightmare—when she rose to her feet and added, without a movement, without a gesture, 'You must not go, Cousin George. He is upstairs in the blue chamber at the front of the house.'

"For an instant surprise held me speechless, transfixed, incredulous; and in that instant I saw a face—a white face of horror and disbelief—look down on us from one of the side-windows of the blue chamber. Then, in a rush it seemed to me the soldiers were everywhere, swarming over the terrace, into the hall, surrounding the house. I had never imagined that a small body of men in uniforms, even ragged uniforms, could so possess and obscure one's surroundings. The three of us waited there—Lucy had sat down again and taken up her knitting—for what seemed hours, or an eternity. We were still waiting—though, for once, I noticed, the needles did not click in her fingers—when a single shot, followed by a volley, rang out from the rear of the house, from the veranda that looked down on the grove of oaks and the kitchen.

"Rising, I left them—the old man and the girl—and passed from the terrace down the little walk which led to the back. As I reached the lower veranda one of the soldiers ran into me.

" 'I was coming after you,' he said, and I observed that his excitement had left him. 'We brought him down while he was trying to jump from the veranda. He is there now on the grass.'

"The man on the grass was quite dead, shot through the heart; and while I bent over to wipe the blood from his lips, I saw him for the first time distinctly. A young face, hardly more than a boy—twenty-five at the most. Handsome, too, in a poetic and dreamy way; just the face, I thought, that a woman might have fallen in love with. He had dark hair, I remember, though his features have long ago faded from my memory. What will never fade, what I shall never forget, is the look he wore—the look he was still wearing when we laid him in the old graveyard next day—a look of mingled surprise, disbelief, terror, and indignation.

"I had done all that I could, which was nothing, and rising to my feet, I saw for the first time that Lucy had joined me. She was standing perfectly motionless. Her knitting was still in her hands, but the light had

gone from her face, and she looked old—old and gray—beside the glowing youth of her lover. For a moment her eyes held me while she spoke
as quietly as she had spoken to the soldiers on the terrace.

" 'I had to do it,' she said. 'I would do it again.' "

Suddenly, like the cessation of running water, or of wind in the tree-
tops, the doctor's voice ceased. For a long pause we stared in silence at
the sunset; then, without looking at me, he added slowly:

"Three weeks later Lee surrendered and the Confederacy was over."

The sun had slipped, as if by magic, behind the tops of the cedars, and
dusk fell quickly, like a heavy shadow, over the terrace. In the dimness
a piercing sweetness floated up from the garden of herbs, and it seemed
to me that in a minute the twilight was saturated with fragrance. Then
I heard the cry of a solitary whippoorwill in the graveyard, and it
sounded so near that I started.

"So she died of the futility, and her unhappy ghost haunts the house?"

"No, she is not dead. It is not her ghost; it is the memory of her act
that has haunted the house. Lucy Dare is still living. I saw her a few
months ago."

"You saw her? You spoke to her after all these years?"

He had refilled his pipe, and the smell of it gave me a comfortable assurance that I was living here, now, in the present. A moment ago I had
shivered as if the hand of the past, reaching from the open door at my
back, had touched my shoulder.

"I was in Richmond. My friend Beverly, an old classmate, had asked
me up for a week-end, and on Saturday afternoon, before motoring into
the country for supper, we started out to make a few calls which had
been left over from the morning. For a doctor, a busy doctor, he had
always seemed to me to possess unlimited leisure, so I was not surprised
when a single visit sometimes stretched over twenty-five minutes. We
had stopped several times, and I confess that I was getting a little impatient when he remarked abruptly while he turned his car into a shady
street,

" 'There is only one more. If you don't mind, I'd like you to see her.
She is a friend of yours, I believe.'

"Before us, as the car stopped, I saw a red-brick house, very large, with
green shutters, and over the wide door, which stood open, a sign reading
'St. Luke's Church Home.' Several old ladies sat, half asleep, on the long
veranda; a clergyman, with a prayer-book in his hand, was just leaving;
a few pots of red geraniums stood on little green-wicker stands; and
from the hall, through which floated the smell of freshly baked bread,

there came the music of a victrola—sacred music, I remember. Not one of these details escaped me. It was as if every trivial impression was stamped indelibly in my memory by the shock of the next instant.

"In the centre of the large, smoothly shaven lawn an old woman was sitting on a wooden bench under an ailantus-tree which was in blossom. As we approached her, I saw that her figure was shapeless, and that her eyes, of a faded blue, had the vacant and listless expression of the old who have ceased to think, who have ceased even to wonder or regret. So unlike was she to anything I had ever imagined Lucy Dare could become, that not until my friend called her name and she glanced up from the muffler she was knitting—the omnipresent dun-coloured muffler for the war relief associations—not until then did I recognize her.

" 'I have brought an old friend to see you, Miss Lucy.'

"She looked up, smiled slightly, and after greeting me pleasantly, relapsed into silence. I remembered that the Lucy Dare I had known was never much of a talker.

"Dropping on the bench at her side, my friend began asking her about her sciatica, and, to my surprise, she became almost animated. Yes, the pain in her hip was better—far better than it had been for weeks. The new medicine had done her a great deal of good; but her fingers were getting rheumatic. She found trouble holding her needles. She couldn't knit as fast as she used to.

"Unfolding the end of the muffler, she held it out to us. 'I have managed to do twenty of these since Christmas. I've promised fifty to the War Relief Association by autumn, and if my fingers don't get stiff I can easily do them.'

"The sunshine falling through the ailantus-tree powdered with dusty gold her shapeless, relaxed figure and the dun-coloured wool of the muffler. While she talked her fingers flew with the click of the needles— older fingers than they had been at Dare's Gift, heavier, stiffer, a little knotted in the joints. As I watched her the old familiar sense of strangeness, of encompassing and hostile mystery, stole over me.

"When we rose to go she looked up, and, without pausing for an instant in her knitting, said, gravely, 'It gives me something to do, this work for the Allies. It helps to pass the time, and in an Old Ladies' Home one has so much time on one's hands.'

"Then, as we parted from her, she dropped her eyes again to her needles. Looking back at the gate, I saw that she still sat there in the faint sunshine—knittting—knitting——"

"And you think she has forgotten?"

He hesitated, as if gathering his thoughts. "I was with her when she came back from the shock—from the illness that followed—and she had forgotten. Yes, she has forgotten, but the house has remembered."

Pushing back his chair, he rose unsteadily on his crutch, and stood staring across the twilight which was spangled with fireflies. While I waited I heard again the loud cry of the whippoorwill.

"Well, what could one expect?" he asked, presently. "She had drained the whole of experience in an instant, and there was left to her only the empty and withered husks of the hours. She had felt too much ever to feel again. After all," he added slowly, "it is the high moments that make a life, and the flat ones that fill the years."

Editor's Note

"Dare's Gift" appeared as a two-part story in the February and March issues of *Harper's Magazine* in 1917. In *The Shadowy Third,* this structure makes apparent a cause-and-effect study. In the revision, Miss Glasgow removed two glaring pieces of editorial comment. She said in the magazine version, ". . . but I may as well confess that this narrative is written for the intrepid few who dare believe in the incredible." This disappeared in the collected edition along with the following meditation at the end of the story: "What was life after all? Was the essence of it drained fifty years ago by Lucy Dare or was there a profounder significance in this old woman knitting her interminable mufflers for another army?" Miss Glasgow considered either the answer to this question too obvious, or the question itself too pompous.

The story is flawed by such earnest analysis of the Southern code. However, Miss Glasgow's spokesman, Dr. Lakeby, does more than illustrate the dominance of beliefs over the facts of life. His allusion to the dilemma of Antigone is appropriate. Lucy Dare must choose between personal loyalty (the Southern code) and loyalty to the State. Dr. Lakeby, like most Southerners, applauds Antigone but pities Lucy.

VII

The Past

I HAD no sooner entered the house than I knew something was wrong. Though I had never been in so splendid a place before —it was one of those big houses just off Fifth Avenue—I had a suspicion from the first that the magnificence covered a secret disturbance. I was always quick to receive impressions, and when the black iron doors swung together behind me, I felt as if I were shut inside a prison.

When I gave my name and explained that I was the new secretary, I was delivered into the charge of an elderly lady's-maid, who looked as if she had been crying. Without speaking a word, though she nodded kindly enough, she led me down the hall, and then up a flight of stairs at the back of the house to a pleasant bedroom in the third storey. There was a great deal of sunshine, and the walls, which were painted a soft yellow, made the room very cheerful. It would be a comfortable place to sit in when I was not working, I thought, while the sad-faced maid stood watching me remove my wraps and hat.

"If you are not tired, Mrs. Vanderbridge would like to dictate a few letters," she said presently, and they were the first words she had spoken.

"I am not a bit tired. Will you take me to her?" One of the reasons, I knew, which had decided Mrs. Vanderbridge to engage me was the remarkable similarity of our handwriting. We were both Southerners, and though she was now famous on two continents for her beauty, I couldn't forget that she had got her early education at the little academy for young ladies in Fredericksburg. This was a bond of sympathy in my thoughts at least, and, heaven knows, I needed to remember it while I followed the maid down the narrow stairs and along the wide hall to the front of the house.

In looking back after a year, I can recall every detail of that first meeting. Though it was barely four o'clock, the electric lamps were turned

on in the hall, and I can still see the mellow light that shone over the
staircase and lay in pools on the old pink rugs, which were so soft and
fine that I felt as if I were walking on flowers. I remember the sound
of music from a room somewhere on the first floor, and the scent of
lilies and hyacinths that drifted from the conservatory. I remember it all,
every note of music, every whiff of fragrance; but most vividly I remember Mrs. Vanderbridge as she looked round, when the door opened,
from the wood fire into which she had been gazing. Her eyes caught me
first. They were so wonderful that for a moment I couldn't see anything
else; then I took in slowly the dark red of her hair, the clear pallor of
her skin, and the long, flowing lines of her figure in a tea-gown of blue
silk. There was a white bearskin rug under her feet, and while she stood
there before the wood fire, she looked as if she had absorbed the beauty
and colour of the house as a crystal vase absorbs the light. Only when
she spoke to me, and I went nearer, did I detect the heaviness beneath
her eyes and the nervous quiver of her mouth, which drooped a little at
the corners. Tired and worn as she was, I never saw her afterwards—
not even when she was dressed for the opera—look quite so lovely, so
much like an exquisite flower, as she did on that first afternoon. When
I knew her better, I discovered that she was a changeable beauty; there
were days when all the colour seemed to go out of her, and she looked
dull and haggard; but at her best no one I've ever seen could compare
with her.

She asked me a few questions, and though she was pleasant and kind,
I knew that she scarcely listened to my responses. While I sat down at
the desk and dipped my pen into the ink, she flung herself on the
couch before the fire with a movement which struck me as hopeless. I
saw her feet tap the white fur rug, while she plucked nervously at the
lace on the end of one of the gold-coloured sofa pillows. For an instant the
thought flashed through my mind that she had been taking something—a
drug of some sort—and that she was suffering now from the effects of it.
Then she looked at me steadily, almost as if she were reading my thoughts,
and I knew that I was wrong. Her large radiant eyes were as innocent as a
child's.

She dictated a few notes—all declining invitations—and then, while
I still waited pen in hand, she sat up on the couch with one of her quick
movements, and said in a low voice, "I am not dining out to-night, Miss
Wrenn. I am not well enough."

"I am sorry for that." It was all I could think of to say, for I did not
understand why she should have told me.

"If you don't mind, I should like you to come down to dinner. There will be only Mr. Vanderbridge and myself."

"Of course I will come if you wish it." I couldn't very well refuse to do what she asked me, yet I told myself, while I answered, that if I had known she expected me to make one of the family, I should never, not even at twice the salary, have taken the place. It didn't take me a minute to go over my slender wardrobe in my mind and realize that I had nothing to wear that would look well enough.

"I can see you don't like it," she added after a moment, almost wistfully, "but it won't be often. It is only when we are dining alone."

This, I thought, was even queerer than the request—or command—for I knew from her tone, just as plainly as if she had told me in words, that she did not wish to dine alone with her husband.

"I am ready to help you in any way—in any way that I can," I replied, and I was so deeply moved by her appeal that my voice broke in spite of my effort to control it. After my lonely life I dare say I should have loved any one who really needed me, and from the first moment that I read the appeal in Mrs. Vanderbridge's face I felt that I was willing to work my fingers to the bone for her. Nothing that she asked of me was too much when she asked it in that voice, with that look.

"I am glad you are nice," she said, and for the first time she smiled— a charming, girlish smile with a hint of archness. "We shall get on beautifully, I know, because I can talk to you. My last secretary was English, and I frightened her almost to death whenever I tried to talk to her." Then her tone grew serious. "You won't mind dining with us. Roger—Mr. Vanderbridge—is the most charming man in the world."

"Is that his picture?"

"Yes, the one in the Florentine frame. The other is my brother. Do you think we are alike?"

"Since you've told me, I notice a likeness." Already I had picked up the Florentine frame from the desk, and was eagerly searching the features of Mr. Vanderbridge. It was an arresting face, dark, thoughtful, strangely appealing, and picturesque—though this may have been due, of course, to the photographer. The more I looked at it, the more there grew upon me an uncanny feeling of familiarity; but not until the next day, while I was still trying to account for the impression that I had seen the picture before, did there flash into my mind the memory of an old portrait of a Florentine nobleman in a loan collection last winter. I can't remember the name of the painter—I am not sure that it was known—but this photograph might have been taken from the painting.

There was the same imaginative sadness in both faces, the same haunt-ing beauty of feature, and one surmised that there must be the same rich darkness of colouring. The only striking difference was that the man in the photograph looked much older than the original of the portrait, and I remembered that the lady who had engaged me was the second wife of Mr. Vanderbridge and some ten or fifteen years younger, I had heard, than her husband.

"Have you ever seen a more wonderful face?" asked Mrs. Vander-bridge. "Doesn't he look as if he might have been painted by Titian?"

"Is he really so handsome as that?"

"He is a little older and sadder, that is all. When we were married it was exactly like him." For an instant she hesitated and then broke out almost bitterly, "Isn't that a face any woman might fall in love with, a face any woman—living or dead—would not be willing to give up?"

Poor child, I could see that she was overwrought and needed some-one to talk to, but it seemed queer to me that she should speak so frankly to a stranger. I wondered why any one so rich and so beautiful should ever be unhappy—for I had been schooled by poverty to believe that money is the first essential of happiness—and yet her unhappiness was as evident as her beauty, or the luxury that enveloped her. At that instant I felt that I hated Mr. Vanderbridge, for whatever the secret tragedy of their marriage might be, I instinctively knew that the fault was not on the side of the wife. She was as sweet and winning as if she were still the reigning beauty in the academy for young ladies. I knew with a knowledge deeper than any conviction that she was not to blame, and if she wasn't to blame, then who under heaven could be at fault ex-cept her husband?

In a few minutes a friend came in to tea, and I went upstairs to my room, and unpacked the blue taffeta dress I had bought for my sister's wedding. I was still doubtfully regarding it when there was a knock at my door, and the maid with the sad face came in to bring me a pot of tea. After she had placed the tray on the table, she stood nervously twist-ing a napkin in her hands while she waited for me to leave my unpack-ing and sit down in the easy chair she had drawn up under the lamp.

"How do you think Mrs. Vanderbridge is looking?" she asked abruptly in a voice that held a breathless note of suspense. Her nervous-ness and the queer look in her face made me stare at her sharply. This was a house, I was beginning to feel, where everybody, from the mistress down, wanted to question me. Even the silent maid had found voice for interrogation.

"I think her the loveliest person I've ever seen," I answered after a moment's hesitation. There couldn't be any harm in telling her how much I admired her mistress.

"Yes, she is lovely—everyone thinks so—and her nature is as sweet as her face." She was becoming loquacious. "I have never had a lady who was so sweet and kind. She hasn't always been rich, and that may be the reason she never seems to grow hard and selfish, the reason she spends so much of her life thinking of other people. It's been six years now, ever since her marriage, that I've lived with her, and in all that time I've never had a cross word from her."

"One can see that. With everything she has she ought to be as happy as the day is long."

"She ought to be." Her voice dropped, and I saw her glance suspiciously at the door, which she had closed when she entered. "She ought to be, but she isn't. I have never seen any one so unhappy as she has been of late—ever since last summer. I suppose I oughtn't to talk about it, but I've kept it to myself so long that I feel as if it was killing me. If she was my own sister, I couldn't be any fonder of her, and yet I have to see her suffer day after day, and not say a word—not even to her. She isn't the sort of lady you could speak to about a thing like that."

She broke down, and dropping on the rug at my feet, hid her face in her hands. It was plain that she was suffering acutely, and while I patted her shoulder, I thought what a wonderful mistress Mrs. Vanderbridge must be to have attached a servant to her so strongly.

"You must remember that I am a stranger in the house, that I scarcely know her, that I've never so much as laid eyes on her husband," I said warningly, for I've always avoided, as far as possible, the confidences of servants.

"But you look as if you could be trusted." The maid's nerves, as well as the mistress's, were on edge, I could see. "And she needs somebody who can help her. She needs a real friend—somebody who will stand by her no matter what happens."

Again, as in the room downstairs, there flashed through my mind the suspicion that I had got into a place where people took drugs or drink —or were all out of their minds. I had heard of such houses.

"How can I help her? She won't confide in me, and even if she did, what could I do for her?"

"You can stand by and watch. You can come between her and harm —if you see it." She had risen from the floor and stood wiping her reddened eyes on the napkin. "I don't know what it is, but I know it is there. I feel it even when I can't see it."

Yes, they were all out of their minds; there couldn't be any other ex-

planation. The whole episode was incredible. It was the kind of thing,
I kept telling myself, that did not happen. Even in a book nobody could
believe it.

"But her husband? He is the one who must protect her."

She gave me a blighting look. "He would if he could. He isn't to
blame—you mustn't think that. He is one of the best men in the world,
but he can't help her. He can't help her because he doesn't know. He
doesn't see it."

A bell rang somewhere, and catching up the tea-tray, she paused just
long enough to throw me a pleading word, "Stand between her and
harm, if you see it."

When she had gone I locked the door after her, and turned on all the
lights in the room. Was there really a tragic mystery in the house, or
were they all mad, as I had first imagined? The feeling of apprehension,
of vague uneasiness, which had come to me when I entered the iron
doors, swept over me in a wave while I sat there in the soft glow of the
shaded electric light. Something was wrong. Somebody was making
that lovely woman unhappy, and who, in the name of reason, could this
somebody be except her husband? Yet the maid had spoken of him as
"one of the best men in the world," and it was impossible to doubt the
tearful sincerity of her voice. Well, the riddle was too much for me. I
gave it up at last with a sigh—dreading the hour that would call me
downstairs to meet Mr. Vanderbridge. I felt in every nerve and fibre of
my body that I should hate him the moment I looked at him.

But at eight o'clock, when I went reluctantly downstairs, I had a surprise. Nothing could have been kinder than the way Mr. Vanderbridge
greeted me, and I could tell as soon as I met his eyes that there wasn't
anything vicious or violent in his nature. He reminded me more than
ever of the portrait in the loan collection, and though he was so much
older than the Florentine nobleman, he had the same thoughtful look.
Of course I am not an artist, but I have always tried, in my way, to be a
reader of personality; and it didn't take a particularly keen observer
to discern the character and intellect in Mr. Vanderbridge's face. Even
now I remember it as the noblest face I have ever seen; and unless I had
possessed at least a shade of penetration, I doubt if I should have detected the melancholy. For it was only when he was thinking deeply
that this sadness seemed to spread like a veil over his features. At other
times he was cheerful and even gay in his manner; and his rich dark
eyes would light up now and then with irrepressible humour. From the
way he looked at his wife I could tell that there was no lack of love or
tenderness on his side any more than there was on hers. It was obvious

that he was still as much in love with her as he had been before his marriage, and my immediate perception of this only deepened the mystery that enveloped them. If the fault wasn't his and wasn't hers, then who was responsible for the shadow that hung over the house?

For the shadow was there. I could feel it, vague and dark, while we talked about the war and the remote possibilities of peace in the spring. Mrs. Vanderbridge looked young and lovely in her gown of white satin with pearls on her bosom, but her violet eyes were almost black in the candlelight, and I had a curious feeling that this blackness was the colour of thought. Something troubled her to despair, yet I was as positive as I could be of anything I had ever been told that she had breathed no word of this anxiety or distress to her husband. Devoted as they were, a nameless dread, fear, or apprehension divided them. It was the thing I had felt from the moment I entered the house; the thing I had heard in the tearful voice of the maid. One could scarcely call it horror, because it was too vague, too impalpable, for so vivid a name; yet, after all these quiet months, horror is the only word I can think of that in any way expresses the emotion which pervaded the house.

I had never seen so beautiful a dinner table, and I was gazing with pleasure at the damask and glass and silver—there was a silver basket of chrysanthemums, I remember, in the centre of the table—when I noticed a nervous movement of Mrs. Vanderbridge's head, and saw her glance hastily towards the door and the staircase beyond. We had been talking animatedly, and as Mrs. Vanderbridge turned away, I had just made a remark to her husband, who appeared to have fallen into a sudden fit of abstraction, and was gazing thoughtfully over his soup-plate at the white and yellow chrysanthemums. It occurred to me, while I watched him, that he was probably absorbed in some financial problem, and I regretted that I had been so careless as to speak to him. To my surprise, however, he replied immediately in a natural tone, and I saw, or imagined that I saw, Mrs. Vanderbridge throw me a glance of gratitude and relief. I can't remember what we were talking about, but I recall perfectly that the conversation kept up pleasantly, without a break, until dinner was almost half over. The roast had been served, and I was in the act of helping myself to potatoes, when I became aware that Mr. Vanderbridge had again fallen into his reverie. This time he scarcely seemed to hear his wife's voice when she spoke to him, and I watched the sadness cloud his face while he continued to stare straight ahead of him with a look that was almost yearning in its intensity.

Again I saw Mrs. Vanderbridge, with her nervous gesture, glance in the direction of the hall, and to my amazement, as she did so, a woman's figure glided noiselessly over the old Persian rug at the door, and entered the dining-room. I was wondering why no one spoke to her, why she spoke to no one, when I saw her sink into a chair on the other side of Mr. Vanderbridge and unfold her napkin. She was quite young, younger even than Mrs. Vanderbridge, and though she was not really beautiful, she was the most graceful creature I had ever imagined. Her dress was of grey stuff, softer and more clinging than silk, and of a peculiar misty texture and colour, and her parted hair lay like twilight on either side of her forehead. She was not like any one I had ever seen before—she appeared so much frailer, so much more elusive, as if she would vanish if you touched her. I can't describe, even months afterwards, the singular way in which she attracted and repelled me.

At first I glanced inquiringly at Mrs. Vanderbridge, hoping that she would introduce me, but she went on talking rapidly in an intense, quivering voice, without noticing the presence of her guest by so much as the lifting of her eyelashes. Mr. Vanderbridge still sat there, silent and detached, and all the time the eyes of the stranger—starry eyes with a mist over them—looked straight through me at the tapestried wall at my back. I knew she didn't see me and that it wouldn't have made the slightest difference to her if she had seen me. In spite of her grace and her girlishness I did not like her, and I felt that this aversion was not on my side alone. I do not know how I received the impression that she hated Mrs. Vanderbridge—never once had she glanced in her direction—yet I was aware, from the moment of her entrance, that she was bristling with animosity, though animosity is too strong a word for the resentful spite, like the jealous rage of a spoiled child, which gleamed now and then in her eyes. I couldn't think of her as wicked any more than I could think of a bad child as wicked. She was merely wilful and undisciplined and—I hardly know how to convey what I mean—elfish.

After her entrance the dinner dragged on heavily. Mrs. Vanderbridge still kept up her nervous chatter, but nobody listened, for I was too embarrassed to pay any attention to what she said, and Mr. Vanderbridge had never recovered from his abstraction. He was like a man in a dream, not observing a thing that happened before him, while the strange woman sat there in the candlelight with her curious look of vagueness and unreality. To my astonishment not even the servants appeared to notice her, and though she had unfolded her napkin when she sat down, she wasn't served with either the roast or the salad. Once or twice, particularly when a new course was served, I glanced at Mrs. Vanderbridge to see if she would rectify the mistake, but she kept her gaze fixed on her plate. It was just as if there were a conspiracy to ignore the presence of the stranger, though she had been, from the moment of her entrance, the dominant figure at the table. You tried to pretend she wasn't there, and yet you knew—you knew vividly that she was gazing insolently straight through you.

The dinner lasted, it seemed, for hours, and you may imagine my relief when at last Mrs. Vanderbridge rose and led the way back into the drawing-room. At first I thought the stranger would follow us, but when I glanced round from the hall she was still sitting there beside Mr. Vanderbridge, who was smoking a cigar with his coffee.

"Usually he takes his coffee with me," said Mrs. Vanderbridge, "but to-night he has things to think over."

"I thought he seemed absent-minded."

"You noticed it, then?" She turned to me with her straightforward glance. "I always wonder how much strangers notice. He hasn't been well of late, and he has these spells of depression. Nerves are dreadful things, aren't they?"

I laughed. "So I've heard, but I've never been able to afford them."

"Well, they do cost a great deal, don't they?" She had a trick of ending her sentences with a question. "I hope your room is comfortable, and that you don't feel timid about being alone on that floor. If you haven't nerves, you can't get nervous, can you?"

"No, I can't get nervous." Yet while I spoke, I was conscious of a shiver deep down in me, as if my senses reacted again to the dread that permeated the atmosphere.

As soon as I could, I escaped to my room, and I was sitting there over a book, when the maid—her name was Hopkins, I had discovered—came in on the pretext of inquiring if I had everything I needed. One of the innumerable servants had already turned down my bed, so when Hopkins appeared at the door, I suspected at once that there was a hidden motive underlying her ostensible purpose.

"Mrs. Vanderbridge told me to look after you," she began. "She is afraid you will be lonely until you learn the way of things."

"No, I'm not lonely," I answered. "I've never had time to be lonely."

"I used to be like that; but time hangs heavy on my hands now. That's why I've taken to knitting." She held out a grey yarn muffler. "I had an operation a year ago, and since then Mrs. Vanderbridge has had another maid—a French one—to sit up for her at night and undress her. She is always so fearful of overtaxing us, though there isn't really enough work for two lady's-maids, because she is so thoughtful that she never gives any trouble if she can help it."

"It must be nice to be rich," I said idly, as I turned a page of my book.

Then I added almost before I realized what I was saying, "The other lady doesn't look as if she had so much money."

Her face turned paler if that were possible, and for a minute I thought she was going to faint. "The other lady?"

"I mean the one who came down late to dinner—the one in the grey dress. She wore no jewels, and her dress wasn't low in the neck."

"Then you saw her?" There was a curious flicker in her face as if her pallor came and went.

"We were at the table when she came in. Has Mr. Vanderbridge a secretary who lives in the house?"

"No, he hasn't a secretary except at his office. When he wants one at the house, he telephones to his office."

"I wondered why she came, for she didn't eat any dinner, and nobody spoke to her—not even Mr. Vanderbridge."

"Oh, he never speaks to her. Thank God, it hasn't come to that yet."

"Then why does she come? It must be dreadful to be treated like that, and before the servants, too. Does she come often?"

"There are months and months when she doesn't. I can always tell by the way Mrs. Vanderbridge picks up. You wouldn't know her, she is so full of life—the very picture of happiness. Then one evening she—the Other One, I mean—comes back again, just as she did to-night, just as she did last summer, and it all begins over from the beginning."

"But can't they keep her out—the Other One? Why do they let her in?"

"Mrs. Vanderbridge tries hard. She tries all she can every minute. You saw her to-night?"

"And Mr. Vanderbridge? Can't he help her?"

She shook her head with an ominous gesture. "He doesn't know."

"He doesn't know she is there? Why, she was close by him. She never took her eyes off him except when she was staring through me at the wall."

"Oh, he knows she is there, but not in that way. He doesn't know that any one else knows."

I gave it up, and after a minute she said in a suppressed voice, "It seems strange that you should have seen her. I never have."

"But you know all about her."

"I know and I don't know. Mrs. Vanderbridge lets things drop some-times—she gets ill and feverish very easily—but she never tells me any-thing outright. She isn't that sort."

"Haven't the servants told you about her—the Other One?"

At this, I thought, she seemed startled. "Oh, they don't know anything to tell. They feel that something is wrong; that is why they never stay longer than a week or two—we've had eight butlers since autumn —but they never see what it is."

She stooped to pick up the ball of yarn which had rolled under my chair. "If the time ever comes when you can stand between them, you will do it?" she asked.

"Between Mrs. Vanderbridge and the Other One?"

Her look answered me.

"You think, then, that she means harm to her?"

"I don't know. Nobody knows—but she is killing her."

The clock struck ten, and I returned to my book with a yawn, while Hopkins gathered up her work and went out, after wishing me a formal good-night. The odd part about our secret conferences was that as soon as they were over, we began to pretend so elaborately to each other that they had never been.

"I'll tell Mrs. Vanderbridge that you are very comfortable," was the last remark Hopkins made before she sidled out of the door and left me alone with the mystery. It was one of those situations—I am obliged to repeat this over and over—that was too preposterous for me to believe in even while I was surrounded and overwhelmed by its reality. I didn't dare face what I thought, I didn't dare face even what I felt; but I went to bed shivering in a warm room, while I resolved passionately that if the chance ever came to me I would stand between Mrs. Vanderbridge and this unknown evil that threatened her.

In the morning Mrs. Vanderbridge went out shopping, and I did not see her until the evening, when she passed me on the staircase as she was going out to dinner and the opera. She was radiant in blue velvet, with diamonds in her hair and at her throat, and I wondered again how any one so lovely could ever be troubled.

"I hope you had a pleasant day, Miss Wrenn," she said kindly. "I have been too busy to get off any letters, but to-morrow we shall begin early." Then, as if from an afterthought, she looked back and added, "There are some new novels in my sitting-room. You might care to look over them."

When she had gone, I went upstairs to the sitting-room and turned over the books, but I couldn't, to save my life, force an interest in printed romances after meeting Mrs. Vanderbridge and remembering the mystery that surrounded her. I wondered if "the Other One," as Hopkins called her, lived in the house, and I was still wondering this when the maid came in and began putting the table to rights.

"Do they dine out often?" I asked.

"They used to, but since Mr. Vanderbridge hasn't been so well, Mrs.

Vanderbridge doesn't like to go without him. She only went to-night because he begged her to."

She had barely finished speaking when the door opened, and Mr. Vanderbridge came in and sat down in one of the big velvet chairs before the wood fire. He had not noticed us, for one of his moods was upon him, and I was about to slip out as noiselessly as I could when I saw that the Other One was standing in the patch of firelight on the hearthrug. I had not seen her come in, and Hopkins evidently was still unaware of her presence, for while I was watching, I saw the maid turn towards her with a fresh log for the fire. At the moment it occurred to me that Hopkins must be either blind or drunk, for without hesitating in her advance, she moved on the stranger, holding the huge hickory log out in front of her. Then, before I could utter a sound or stretch out a hand to stop her, I saw her walk straight through the grey figure and carefully place the log on the andirons.

So she isn't real, after all, she is merely a phantom, I found myself thinking, as I fled from the room, and hurried along the hall to the staircase. She is only a ghost, and nobody believes in ghosts any longer. She is something that I know doesn't exist, yet even, though she can't possibly be, I can swear that I have seen her. My nerves were so shaken by the discovery that as soon as I reached my room I sank in a heap on the rug, and it was here that Hopkins found me a little later when she came to bring me an extra blanket.

"You looked so upset I thought you might have seen something," she said. "Did anything happen while you were in the room?"

"She was there all the time—every blessed minute. You walked right through her when you put the log on the fire. Is it possible that you didn't see her?"

"No, I didn't see anything out of the way." She was plainly frightened. "Where was she standing?"

"On the hearthrug in front of Mr. Vanderbridge. To reach the fire you had to walk straight through her, for she didn't move. She didn't give way an inch."

"Oh, she never gives way. She never gives way living or dead."

This was more than human nature could stand. "In heaven's name," I cried irritably, "who is she?"

"Don't you know?" She appeared genuinely surprised. "Why, she is the other Mrs. Vanderbridge. She died fifteen years ago, just a year after they were married, and people say a scandal was hushed up about her, which he never knew. She isn't a good sort, that's what I think of her, though they say he almost worshipped her."

"And she still has this hold on him?"

"He can't shake it off, that's what's the matter with him, and if it goes on, he will end his days in an asylum. You see, she was very young, scarcely more than a girl, and he got the idea in his head that it was marrying him that killed her. If you want to know what I think, I believe she puts it there for a purpose."

"You mean——?" I was so completely at sea that I couldn't frame a rational question.

"I mean she haunts him purposely in order to drive him out of his mind. She was always that sort, jealous and exacting, the kind that clutches and strangles a man, and I've often thought, though I've no head for speculation, that we carry into the next world the traits and feelings that have got the better of us in this one. It seems to me only common sense to believe that we're obliged to work them off somewhere until we are free of them. That is the way my first lady used to talk, anyhow, and I've never found anybody that could give me a more sensible idea."

"And isn't there any way to stop it? What has Mrs. Vanderbridge done?"

"Oh, she can't do anything now. It has got beyond her, though she has had doctor after doctor, and tried everything she could think of. But, you see, she is handicapped because she can't mention it to her husband. He doesn't know that she knows."

"And she won't tell him?"

"She is the sort that would die first—just the opposite from the Other One—for she leaves him free, she never clutches and strangles. It isn't her way." For a moment she hesitated, and then added grimly—"I've wondered if you could do anything?"

"If I could? Why, I am a perfect stranger to them all."

"That's why I've been thinking it. Now, if you could corner her some day—the Other One—and tell her up and down to her face what you think of her."

The idea was so ludicrous that it made me laugh in spite of my shaken nerves. "They would fancy me out of my wits! Imagine stopping an apparition and telling it what you think of it!"

"Then you might try talking it over with Mrs. Vanderbridge. It would help her to know that you see her also."

But the next morning, when I went down to Mrs. Vanderbridge's room, I found that she was too ill to see me. At noon a trained nurse came on the case, and for a week we took our meals together in the morning-room upstairs. She appeared competent enough, but I am sure that she didn't so much as suspect that there was anything wrong in the house except the influenza which had attacked Mrs. Vanderbridge the night of the opera. Never once during that week did I catch a glimpse of the Other One, though I felt her presence whenever I left my room and passed through the hall below. I knew all the time as well as if I had seen her that she was hidden there, watching, watching——

At the end of the week Mrs. Vanderbridge sent for me to write some letters, and when I went into her room, I found her lying on the couch with a tea-table in front of her. She asked me to make the tea because she was still so weak, and I saw that she looked flushed and feverish, and that her eyes were unnaturally large and bright. I hoped she wouldn't talk to me, because people in that state are apt to talk too much and then to blame the listener; but I had hardly taken my seat at the tea-table before she said in a hoarse voice—the cold had settled on her chest:

"Miss Wrenn, I have wanted to ask you ever since the other evening —did you—did you see anything unusual at dinner? From your face when you came out I thought—I thought——"

I met this squarely. "That I might have? Yes, I did see something."

"You saw her?"

"I saw a woman come in and sit down at the table, and I wondered why no one served her. I saw her quite distinctly."

"A small woman, thin and pale, in a grey dress?"

"She was so vague and—and misty, you know what I mean, that it is hard to describe her; but I should know her again anywhere. She wore her hair parted and drawn down over her ears. It was very dark and fine —as fine as spun silk."

We were speaking in low voices, and unconsciously we had moved closer together while my idle hands left the tea things.

"Then you know," she said earnestly, "that she really comes—that I am not out of my mind—that it is not an hallucination?"

"I know that I saw her. I would swear to it. But doesn't Mr. Vanderbridge see her also?"

"Not as we see her. He thinks that she is in his mind only." Then, after an uncomfortable silence, she added suddenly, "She is really a thought, you know. She is his thought of her—but he doesn't know that she is visible to the rest of us."

"And he brings her back by thinking of her?"

She leaned nearer while a quiver passed over her features and the flush deepened in her cheeks. "That is the only way she comes back—the only way she has the power to come back—as a thought. There are months and months when she leaves us in peace because he is thinking of other things, but of late, since his illness, she has been with him almost constantly." A sob broke from her, and she buried her face in her hands. "I suppose she is always trying to come—only she is too vague—and hasn't any form that we can see except when he thinks of her as she used to look when she was alive. His thought of her is like that, hurt and tragic and revengeful. You see, he feels that he ruined her life because she died when the child was coming—a month before it would have been born."

"And if he were to see her differently, would she change? Would she cease to be revengeful if he stopped thinking her so?"

"God only knows. I've wondered and wondered how I might move her to pity."

"Then you feel that she is really there? That she exists outside of his mind?"

"How can I tell? What do any of us know of the world beyond? She exists as much as I exist to you or you to me. Isn't thought all that there is—all that we know?"

This was deeper than I could follow; but in order not to appear stupid, I murmured sympathetically,

"And does she make him unhappy when she comes?"

"She is killing him—and me. I believe that is why she does it."

"Are you sure that she could stay away? When he thinks of her isn't she obliged to come back?"

"Oh, I've asked that question over and over! In spite of his calling her so unconsciously, I believe she comes of her own will. I have always the feeling—it has never left me for an instant—that she could appear differently if she would. I have studied her for years until I know her like a book, and though she is only an apparition, I am perfectly positive that she wills evil to us both. Don't you think he would change that if he could? Don't you think he would make her kind instead of vindictive if he had the power?"

"But if he could remember her as loving and tender?"

"I don't know. I give it up—but it is killing me."

It *was* killing her. As the days passed I began to realize that she had spoken the truth. I watched her bloom fade slowly and her lovely features grow pinched and thin like the features of a starved person. The harder she fought the apparition, the more I saw that the battle was a losing one, and that she was only wasting her strength. So impalpable yet so pervasive was the enemy that it was like fighting a poisonous odour. There was nothing to wrestle with, and yet there was everything. The struggle was wearing her out—was, as she had said, actually "killing her"; but the physician who dosed her daily with drugs—there was need now of a physician—had not the faintest idea of the malady he was treating. In those dreadful days I think that even Mr. Vanderbridge hadn't a suspicion of the truth. The past was with him so constantly—he was so steeped in the memories of it—that the present was scarcely more than a dream to him. It was, you see, a reversal of the natural order of things; the thought had become more vivid to his perceptions than any object. The phantom had been victorious so far, and he was like a man recovering from the effects of a narcotic. He was only half awake, only half alive to the events through which he lived and the people who surrounded him. Oh, I realize that I am telling my story badly!—that I am slurring over the significant interludes! My mind has dealt so long with external details that I have almost forgotten the words that express invisible things. Though the phantom in the house was more real to me than the bread I ate or the floor on which I trod, I can give you no impression of the atmosphere in which we lived day after day—of the suspense, of the dread of something we could not define, of the brooding horror that seemed to lurk in the shadows of the firelight, of the feeling always, day and night, that some unseen person was watching us. How Mrs. Vanderbridge stood it without losing her mind, I have never known; and even now I am not sure that she could have kept her reason if the end had not come when it did. That I accidentally brought it about is one of the things in my life I am most thankful to remember.

It was an afternoon in late winter, and I had just come up from luncheon, when Mrs. Vanderbridge asked me to empty an old desk in one of the upstairs rooms. "I am sending all the furniture in that room away," she said; "it was bought in a bad period, and I want to clear it out and make room for the lovely things we picked up in Italy. There is nothing in the desk worth saving except some old letters from Mr. Vanderbridge's mother before her marriage."

I was glad that she could think of anything so practical as furniture, and it was with relief that I followed her into the dim, rather musty room over the library, where the windows were all tightly closed. Years ago, Hopkins had once told me, the first Mrs. Vanderbridge had used this room for a while, and after her death her husband had been in the habit of shutting himself up alone here in the evenings. This, I inferred, was the secret reason why my employer was sending the furniture away. She had resolved to clear the house of every association with the past.

For a few minutes we sorted the letters in the drawers of the desk, and then, as I expected, Mrs. Vanderbridge became suddenly bored by the task she had undertaken. She was subject to these nervous reactions, and I was prepared for them even when they seized her so spasmodically. I

remember that she was in the very act of glancing over an old letter
when she rose impatiently, tossed it into the fire unread, and picked up
a magazine she had thrown down on a chair.

"Go over them by yourself, Miss Wrenn," she said, and it was characteristic of her nature that she should assume my trustworthiness. "If
anything seems worth saving you can file it—but I'd rather die than have
to wade through all this."

They were mostly personal letters, and while I went on, carefully filing
them, I thought how absurd it was of people to preserve so many papers
that were entirely without value. Mr. Vanderbridge I had imagined to
be a methodical man, and yet the disorder of the desk produced a painful effect on my systematic temperament. The drawers were filled with
letters evidently unsorted, for now and then I came upon a mass of business receipts and acknowledgments crammed in among wedding invitations or letters from some elderly lady, who wrote interminable pale
epistles in the finest and most feminine of Italian hands. That a man of
Mr. Vanderbridge's wealth and position should have been so careless
about his correspondence amazed me until I recalled the dark hints
Hopkins had dropped in some of her midnight conversations. Was it
possible that he had actually lost his reason for months after the death
of his first wife, during that year when he had shut himself alone with
her memory? The question was still in my mind when my eyes fell on
the envelope in my hand, and I saw that it was addressed to Mrs. Roger
Vanderbridge. So this explained, in a measure at least, the carelessness
and the disorder! The desk was not his, but hers, and after her death
he had used it only during those desperate months when he barely
opened a letter. What he had done in those long evenings when he sat
alone here it was beyond me to imagine. Was it any wonder that the
brooding should have permanently unbalanced his mind?

At the end of an hour I had sorted and filed the papers, with the intention of asking Mrs. Vanderbridge if she wished me to destroy the
ones that seemed to be unimportant. The letters she had instructed me
to keep had not come to my hand, and I was about to give up the search
for them, when, in shaking the lock of one of the drawers, the door of a
secret compartment fell open, and I discovered a dark object, which
crumbled and dropped apart when I touched it. Bending nearer, I saw that
the crumbled mass had once been a bunch of flowers, and that a streamer
of purple ribbon still held together the frail structure of wire and stems.
In this drawer someone had hidden a sacred treasure, and moved by a
sense of romance and adventure, I gathered the dust tenderly in tissue
paper, and prepared to take it downstairs to Mrs. Vanderbridge. It was

not until then that some letters tied loosely together with a silver cord
caught my eye, and while I picked them up, I remember thinking that
they must be the ones for which I had been looking so long. Then, as
the cord broke in my grasp and I gathered the letters from the lid of the
desk, a word or two flashed back at me through the torn edges of the
envelopes, and I realized that they were love letters written, I surmised,
some fifteen years ago, by Mr. Vanderbridge to his first wife.

"It may hurt her to see them," I thought, "but I don't dare destroy
them. There is nothing I can do except give them to her."

As I left the room, carrying the letters and the ashes of the flowers, the
idea of taking them to the husband instead of to the wife flashed through
my mind. Then—I think it was some jealous feeling about the phantom
that decided me—I quickened my steps to a run down the staircase.

"They would bring her back. He would think of her more than ever,"
I told myself, "so he shall never see them. He shall never see them if I
can prevent it." I believe it occurred to me that Mrs. Vanderbridge would
be generous enough to give them to him—she was capable of rising above
her jealousy, I knew—but I determined that she shouldn't do it until I
had reasoned it out with her. "If anything on earth would bring back
the Other One for good, it would be his seeing these old letters," I repeated as I hastened down the hall.

Mrs. Vanderbridge was lying on the couch before the fire, and I
noticed at once that she had been crying. The drawn look in her sweet
face went to my heart, and I felt that I would do anything in the world
to comfort her. Though she had a book in her hand, I could see that she
had not been reading. The electric lamp on the table by her side was
already lighted, leaving the rest of the room in shadow, for it was a grey
day with a biting edge of snow in the air. It was all very charming in the
soft light; but as soon as I entered I had a feeling of oppression that made
me want to run out into the wind. If you have ever lived in a haunted
house—a house pervaded by an unforgettable past—you will understand
the sensation of melancholy that crept over me the minute the shadows
began to fall. It was not in myself—of this I am sure, for I have naturally
a cheerful temperament—it was in the space that surrounded us and the
air we breathed.

I explained to her about the letters, and then, kneeling on the rug in
front of her, I emptied the dust of the flowers into the fire. There was,
though I hate to confess it, a vindictive pleasure in watching it melt into
the flames; and at the moment I believe I could have burned the apparition as thankfully. The more I saw of the Other One, the more I found

myself accepting Hopkins's judgment of her. Yes, her behaviour, living and dead, proved that she was not "a good sort."

My eyes were still on the flames when a sound from Mrs. Vanderbridge—half a sigh, half a sob—made me turn quickly and look up at her.

"But this isn't his handwriting," she said in a puzzled tone. "They are love letters, and they are to her—but they are not from him." For a moment or two she was silent, and I heard the pages rustle in her hands as she turned them impatiently. "They are not from him," she repeated presently, with an exultant ring in her voice. "They are written after her marriage, but they are from another man." She was as sternly tragic as an avenging fate. "She wasn't faithful to him while she lived. She wasn't faithful to him even while he was hers——"

With a spring I had risen from my knees and was bending over her.

"Then you can save him from her. You can win him back! You have only to show him the letters, and he will believe."

"Yes, I have only to show him the letters." She was looking beyond me into the dusky shadows of the firelight, as if she saw the Other One standing there before her. "I have only to show him the letters," I knew now that she was not speaking to me, "and he will believe."

"Her power over him will be broken," I cried out. "He will think of her differently. Oh, don't you see? Can't you see? It is the only way to make him think of her differently. It is the only way to break for ever the thought that draws her back to him."

"Yes, I see, it is the only way," she said slowly; and the words were still on her lips when the door opened and Mr. Vanderbridge entered.

"I came for a cup of tea," he began, and added with playful tenderness, "What is the only way?"

It was the crucial moment, I realized—it was the hour of destiny for these two—and while he sank wearily into a chair, I looked imploringly at his wife and then at the letters lying scattered loosely about her. If I had had my will I should have flung them at him with a violence which would have startled him out of his lethargy. Violence, I felt, was what he needed—violence, a storm, tears, reproaches—all the things he would never get from his wife.

For a minute or two she sat there, with the letters before her, and watched him with her thoughtful and tender gaze. I knew from her face, so lovely and yet so sad, that she was looking again at invisible things—at the soul of the man she loved, not at the body. She saw him, detached and spiritualized, and she saw also the Other One—for while we waited I became slowly aware of the apparition in the firelight—of the white face and the cloudy hair and the look of animosity and bitterness in the eyes. Never before had I been so profoundly convinced of the malignant will veiled by that thin figure. It was as if the visible form were only a spiral of grey smoke covering a sinister purpose.

"The only way," said Mrs. Vanderbridge, "is to fight fairly even when one fights evil." Her voice was like a bell, and as she spoke, she rose from the couch and stood there in her glowing beauty confronting the pale ghost of the past. There was a light about her that was almost unearthly —the light of triumph. The radiance of it blinded me for an instant. It was like a flame, clearing the atmosphere of all that was evil, of all that was poisonous and deadly. She was looking directly at the phantom, and there was no hate in her voice—there was only a great pity, a great sorrow and sweetness.

"I can't fight you that way," she said, and I knew that for the first time she had swept aside subterfuge and evasion, and was speaking straight to the presence before her. "After all, you are dead and I am living, and I cannot fight you that way. I give up everything. I give him back to you. Nothing is mine that I cannot win and keep fairly. Nothing is mine that belongs really to you."

Then, while Mr. Vanderbridge rose, with a start of fear, and came towards her, she bent quickly, and flung the letters into the fire. When he would have stooped to gather the unburned pages, her lovely flowing body curved between his hands and the flames; and so transparent, so ethereal she looked, that I saw—or imagined that I saw—the firelight shine through her. "The only way, my dear, is the right way," she said softly.

The next instant—I don't know to this day how or when it began— I was aware that the apparition had drawn nearer, and that the dread and fear, the evil purpose, were no longer a part of her. I saw her clearly for a moment—saw her as I had never seen her before—young and gentle and—yes, this is the only word for it—loving. It was just as if a curse had turned into a blessing, for, while she stood there, I had a curious sensation of being enfolded in a kind of spiritual glow and comfort—only words are useless to describe the feeling because it wasn't in the least like anything else I had ever known in my life. It was light without heat, glow without light—and yet it was none of these things. The nearest I can come to it is to call it a sense of blessedness—of blessedness that made you at peace with everything you had once hated.

Not until afterwards did I realize that it was the victory of good over evil. Not until afterwards did I discover that Mrs. Vanderbridge had triumphed over the past in the only way that she could triumph. She had won, not by resisting, but by accepting; not by violence, but by gentleness; not by grasping, but by renouncing. Oh, long, long afterwards, I knew that she had robbed the phantom of power over her by robbing it of hatred. She had changed the thought of the past, in that lay her victory.

At the moment I did not understand this. I did not understand it even when I looked again for the apparition in the firelight, and saw that it had vanished. There was nothing there—nothing except the pleasant flicker of light and shadow on the old Persian rug.

Editor's Note

"The Past" appeared in *Good Housekeeping* for October, 1920. Its similarity in technique and theme to "The Shadowy Third" is obvious. Its symbolism is all too obvious, but Miss Glasgow probably included it in the 1923 collection to reinforce the ghost stories.

There are fewer changes in this story than in any other that the author revised. She merely removed two unnecessary hyphens and added one necessary apostrophe.

The popularity of this story is proved by its inclusion in *Best Short Stories of 1921* and the *Fireside Book of Short Stories,* edited by Edward Wagenknecht.

VIII

Whispering Leaves

IT WAS fifteen years ago to-day; yet I can still see that road stretching through vinelike shadows into the spring landscape.

Though I was never in Virginia before, I had been brought up on the traditions of my mother's old home on the Rappahannock; and when the invitation came to spend a week with my unknown cousins, the Blantons, at Whispering Leaves, I was filled with a delightful sense of expectancy and adventure. None of my family had ever seen the present owner of the place—one Pelham Blanton, a man of middle age, who was, as far as we were aware, without a history. All I knew of him was that his first wife had died at the birth of a child about seven years before, and that immediately afterward he had married one of his neighbours, a common person, my mother insisted, though she had heard nothing of the second wife except that her name before her marriage was Twine. Whether the child of the first wife had lived or not we did not know, for the letters from the family had stopped, and we had no further news of the place until I wrote from Richmond asking permission to visit the house in which my mother and so many of my grandmothers were born.

The spring came early that year. When I descended from the train into the green and gold of the afternoon, I felt almost as if I were stepping back into some old summer. An ancient family carriage, drawn by two drowsy black horses with flowing tails, was waiting for me under a blossoming locust tree; and as soon as my foot touched the ground I was greeted affectionately by the coloured driver, who still called my mother "Miss Effie." He was an imposing, ceremonious old man, very nearly as black as the horses, with a mass of white hair, which is unusual in a negro, and a gay bandanna handkerchief crossed over his chest. After an unconscionable wait for the mail, he brought the dilapidated leather pouch from the office, and tossed it on the floor of the carriage. A minute later, as he mounted over the wheel to his seat, he glanced back at me and remarked in an encouraging tone, "dar ain' nuttin' to hinder us now."

"How far is it to Whispering Leaves, Uncle Moab?"

The old negro pondered the question while he flicked the reins over the broad swaying backs of the horses. He was so long in replying that, thinking he had forgotten to answer, I repeated the words more distinctly.

"Can you tell me how far it is to Whispering Leaves?"

At this he turned and looked back at me over his shoulder. "I reckon hit's sum un like ten miles, or mebbe hit's gwine on twelve," he responded.

"When did you leave there?"

Again there was a long silence while we jogged sleepily out of the deeply shaded streets of the little village. "I ain' been dar dis mawnin', Miss Effie," he answered at last.

"Why, I thought you lived there?"

I was so accustomed by this time to the slowness of his responses that I waited patiently until he brought out with hesitation, "I use' ter."

"Then you are no longer the family coachman?"

He shook his head above the bandanna handkerchief, and I could see his deep perplexity written in the brown creases of his neck. "Yas'm. I'se still de driver."

"But how can you be if you don't live on the place?"

"One er dem w'ite sarvants brungs de car'ige down ter de creek, en I tecks en drives hit along de road," he replied. "I goes dar in de daytime," he added impressively after a minute. "Dar's some un um ain' never set foot dar sence we all moved off, but I ain' skeered er nuttin', sweet Jesus, in de daytime."

"Do you mean that all the old servants moved off together?"

"Yas'm. Ev'y last one un um. Dey's all w'ite folks dar now."

"When did that happen?"

But, as I was beginning to discover, time and space are the flimsiest abstractions in the imagination of the negro. "Hit wuz a long time ago, Miss Effie," replied Uncle Moab. "Pell, he wa'n much mo'n a baby den. He wuz jes' in dresses, en he's done been in breeches now fur a pa'cel er Christmas times."

"Pell? It that the child of the first Mrs. Blanton?"

"Yas'm. He's Miss Clarissa's chile. Miss Hannah Twine, she's got a heap er chillun; dar's two pa'cel er twins en den de baby dat wuz bo'n las' winter. But Pell, he ain' 'er chile."

I was beginning to see light. "Then Pell must be about seven years old, and you moved off the place while he was still in short dresses. That must have been just four or five years ago."

"Dat's hit, honey, dat's hit."

"And all the coloured servants moved away at the same time?"

"De same day. Dar wa'nt er one un um lef dar by sundown."

"And they've had to have white servants ever since?"

"Dey's all w'ite ones dat stays on atter sundown. De coloured folks dey goes back in de daytime, but dey don't stay on twell supper. Naw'm, dar ain' noner dem but de w'ite folks dat stays on ter git supper."

While I questioned him the drowsy horses trotted slowly through the sun and shadow on the dun-coloured road. The air was fragrant with mingled wood scents and honeysuckle. A sky of flowerlike blue shone overhead. Now and then a redbird, flying low, darted across the road, and far off in the trees there was the sound of a joyous chorus.

"I never saw so many redbirds, Uncle Moab."

"Yas'm. Dar sutney is er plenty er dem dis yeah. Hit's a bird yeah, sho nuff. Hit pears ter me like I cyarn' put my foot outside er my do' dat I don't moughty near step on er robin, en I ain' never hearn tell er sech er number uv blue jays. De blue jay he's de meanest bird dat ever wuz, but he sutney is got er heap er sense. He knows jes ez well on w'ich side his bread is buttered ez ef'n he wuz sho nuff folks. Hi! Don' you begin ter study 'bout birds twel you git to W'isperin' Leaves. Hit seems dat ar place wuz jes made ter drive folks bird crazy. Dey's ev'rywhar' dose birds. De wrens en de pheobes dey's in de po'ch, en de swallows dey's in de chimleys, en de res' un um is calling ter you en pesterin' de life outer you in de trees."

Well, I liked birds! If there were nothing more dangerous than birds at Whispering Leaves, I could be happy there.

While we jogged on there crept over me the feeling of restlessness, of wistful yet indefinable desire, which is the very essence of spring. My thoughts had been brushed for an instant by that magic spirit of beauty; and I saw the wide landscape, with its flushed meadows sinking into the grapelike bloom of the distance, as if it were a part, not of the actual world, but of a universe painted on air, as transparent as the faintly coloured shadows across the road. In the thick woods on the left delicate green appeared to rise and fall like the foam of the sea. Accustomed as I was to the late northern season, there was an intoxication in this spring which was as flowery as June. A bird year, the old coachman had called it; but a miraculous spring it seemed to me, with its bright soft winds, as sweet as honey, and its far, serene sky. And from the fragrant woods and rosy meadows there floated always the joyous piping of invisible birds; of birds hidden in low thickets; of birds high in the misty woods; of birds by the silver stream in the pasture; of birds flying swiftly into the impalpable shadows.

"I thought birds were quiet in the afternoon, Uncle Moab?"

"Dey ain' never quiet heah, honey. Dey chatters even in de night time. Dey don' hol' dere tongues fur nuttin', not even w'en de snow is on de groun'."

Gradually, after what seemed to me to be hours of that monotonous pace, the light on the road faded slowly to a delicate primrose. The sun was setting beyond the rich woods on the horizon, and a thin clear veil, like silver tissue, was dropping over the spring landscape. Presently, as we came under the gloom of arching boughs, the old negro turned the heads of the horses and scrambled down from the coachman's seat.

"I ain' gwine no furder den dis, Miss Effie," he explained; and then, as the gate swung open, I saw that a young white man had run forward to unfasten it. When the old negro, with a pull at his front lock, had shuffled off in the direction of the sunset, the young man made a bound into the driver's seat and jerked up the reins.

"Does Uncle Moab live near here?" I inquired.

"About a mile up the road, miss. Mr. Blanton gave him the cabin at the fork when he moved away."

"I wonder why he moved?"

The young man broke into a cheery laugh. "When a darkey once gets a notion in his head, the only way to get it out is with an ax," he retorted; and a minute later he added: "I reckon you don't know much about the darkeys up North?"

"Very little," I conceded, and we drove on in silence.

The road into which we had turned was a narrow private way, very steep and rocky, which led between rotting "worm" fences and neglected fields to a dense avenue of cedars on the brow of the hill. As we went on, I wondered why the fields so near the house should be abandoned. The remains of last year's harvest still strewed the ragged furrows, and against the skyline on the top of the hill there was a desolate row of corn stubble. Presently, as the carriage jolted over the rocky road, I heard the sound of barking, or, as it seemed to me at that sombre hour, the kind of baying to which hounds give voice on moonlit nights. Then, when we reached the high ground at last, I found that two black and yellow hounds were sitting amid the naked cornstalks and barking at our approach.

"Won't these fields be planted this year?" I asked in surprise.

"We can't get any of the darkeys to work here," replied the driver. "They are too near the house."

As we came to the brow of the hill the dogs ran to meet us, and then, after a few barks of welcome, turned and padded on noiselessly beside the horses. Between us and the beginning of the cedar avenue there was a clear space of road, and when we reached this the veil over the sunset parted suddenly like a curtain, and a glow, which I can compare to nothing except clouded amber, suffused the horizon and the abandoned cornfields. In this glow I discerned the gigantic shape of an old mulberry tree near the avenue; and the next instant I made out, amid the foliage on the high boughs, the lightly poised figure of a little boy in a blue cotton suit, with a mass of streaming ruddy curls.

"Why, he might slip and fall," I thought; and the words had scarcely formed themselves in my mind, when the little figure turned sharply, as if in terror, and uttered a cry of alarm.

"Mammy, I am falling!" he called out, as his feet slipped from the bough.

I had already made a spring from the carriage, with the sunset dazzling my eyes, when an old negro woman emerged swiftly from the underbrush by the fence, and caught the child in her arms. In that instant of terror, while my eyes were still filled with the sunset, I observed only that the woman was tall and straight like an Indian, and that her face, framed in a red turban, was as brown and wrinkled as a November leaf. Then, as she placed the child on his feet, I saw that her features were irradiated by a passion of tenderness which gave it a strange glow like the burning light of the sunset.

"You saved his life!" I started to cry; but before I could utter the words she vanished into the shadow of the mulberry tree, and left the boy standing alone in the road.

"You might have been killed," I said sternly as I reached him, for I was still trembling from the fright he had given me.

The boy looked up with a strange elfin glee—there is no other word for it—in his face. "I knew Mammy would catch me," he responded defiantly.

"Suppose she hadn't been here?" As I spoke I looked about me for the old negress.

At this the child laughed shrilly, with a sound that was like the ironic mirth of an old man. "She is always where I am," he replied.

He was a queer child, I thought as I gazed at him, ugly and pinched, and yet with a charm which I felt from the first moment my eyes fell on him. There was a defiant shyness in his manner, and his little face, under the flaming curls, was too thin and pale for healthy childhood. But, in spite of his strangeness, I had never in my life been so strongly attracted, so completely drawn, to a child.

"You must be Pell!" I exclaimed, after a pause in which I had watched him in silence.

He stared at me critically. "Yes, I am Pell. How did you know?"

"Oh, I've heard about you. Uncle Moab told me on the way over."

At the name of Uncle Moab his face grew less blank and hard. "Where is he?" he asked, turning to the driver. "I was going down to the gate to meet him. I want him to mend my kite."

"Uncle Moab went on to his cabin," answered the young man, and I noticed that he subdued his tone as he might have done to an ill person or a startled colt.

"Then I'll go after him," replied the child. "I am not afraid."

With a bound he started down the steep road, running in restless leaps, with his bright curls blown out like an aureole round his head. The two black and yellow hounds, jumping up from the stubble, followed, as noiseless as shadows, on his trail; and in a few minutes the three shapes melted into the obscurity of the fields.

When I was in the carriage again I remarked inquiringly to the driver: "For a delicate child he does not appear to be timid."

"Not out of doors. He is never afraid out of doors. In the house they have a good deal of trouble with him."

"Do the other children look so thin and pale?"

"Oh, no, ma'am. The other children are healthy enough. They don't get on well with this one, and that's why he stays out of the house whenever they'll let him, even when it is raining. Pell is the child of the first Mrs. Blanton."

"Yes, I know. Were you here in her time?"

"No, I came afterward. The year the darkeys moved away. But anybody can see how different she must have been from this one, who is the daughter of old Mr. Twine, the miller. She kept house for Mr. Blanton after his first wife died." This was news to me, for I was absolutely ignorant of the family circumstances. I was eager to learn more of the story; but I could not gossip about my relatives with a stranger, so I said merely,

"Then she brought up the child—Pell, I mean?"

Though the driver's back was turned to me, I could see by the stubborn shake of his head that my question had aroused an unpleasant train of reflections. "No, Pell's mammy took care of him until he was five years old. She had nursed his mother before him. I reckon she belonged to the family of the first Mrs. Blanton and came to Whispering Leaves with the bride. I never saw her. She died before my time here; but they say that as long as the old woman lived Pell never knew what it was to miss his mother. Mammy Rhody—that was her name—had promised the first Mrs. Blanton when she was dying that she would never let the child out of her sight; and they say she kept her promise to the dead as long as she lived. Whenever you saw Pell there was Mammy Rhody, sure enough, with her eyes on him. She slept in the room with him, and she always stood behind his high chair when they had him down to the table. Darkeys are like that, I reckon. A vow's a vow. When she swore she'd never take her eyes off him, she meant just what she said."

"The child must miss her terribly?"

Again I saw that stubborn shake of his head. "The queer part is that the boy insists she ain't dead. Nothing they can do to him—Mrs. Blanton has talked to him by the hour—will make him admit that Mammy Rhody is dead. He says she plays with him just as she used to, and that all these birds you hear about Whispering Leaves are the ones that she tamed for him. Birds! Well, there never was, they say, such a hand with birds as Mammy Rhody. She could tame anything going from an eagle to a wren, I've heard, and some of the darkeys have got the notion that the woods about here are still full of the ghosts of Mammy Rhody's pets. They say it ain't natural for birds to call in and out of season as they do around Whispering Leaves."

"And does Pell believe this also?"

"Nobody knows, ma'am, just how much Pell believes. They've tried to stop all that foolishness because it turns the heads of the darkeys. You can't get one of them to stay on the place after sunset, not for love or money. It all started with the way Pell goes about talking to himself. Holy Moses! I ain't skeery myself, ma'am, for a big fellow like me, but it gives me the creeps sometimes when I watch that child playing by himself in the shrubbery and hear him talking to somebody that ain't there. He does the queerest things, too, just like climbing out on that high limb and calling out to his mammy that he was going to fall."

"He might have been badly hurt if somebody hadn't caught him," I said.

The driver laughed politely, as if I had made a poor joke which he accepted on faith though he missed the humour. "He goes on pretending like that all the time," he returned.

"But the old coloured woman, the one who caught him? Who is she?" I asked.

At this the man turned sharply, letting the reins fall on the backs of the horses. "The old coloured woman?" he repeated inquiringly.

"I mean the tall one in the black dress, with the white apron and the red turban on her head." There was a slight asperity in my tone, for it seemed to me the man was incredibly stupid.

The blankness—or was it suspicion?—in his face deepened. "I don't know. I didn't see anybody," he answered presently.

Turning his head away from me again, he gathered up the reins and urged the horses with a clucking noise into the long avenue of cedars.

Dusk, dusk, dusk. As we drove on rapidly beneath the high, closely woven arch of the cedars, I was conscious again of a deep intuitive feeling that the world in which I moved was as unreal as the surroundings in a dream. Dreamlike, too, were my own sensations as I passed into that greenish twilight which shut out the light of the afterglow. Feathery branches edged with brighter green brushed my cheeks like the wings of a bird; and though I knew it must be only my fancy, I seemed to hear a hundred jubilant notes in the enchanted gloom of the trees.

Presently, as if the thought were suggested by that imaginary music, I found myself returning to the old negress. Surely, if she had merely hastened on in front of us, we must overtake her before we reached the end of the avenue. Wherever the shadows crowded more thickly, wherever there was a sudden stir in the underbrush, I peered eagerly into the obscurity, hoping that we had at last come up with the old woman, and that I might offer her a place in the carriage. Though I had had only the briefest glimpse of her, I had found her serene leaf-brown face strangely attractive, almost, I thought oddly enough, as if her mysterious black eyes, under the heavy brows, had penetrated to some secret chamber of my memory. I had never seen her before, and yet I felt as if I had known her all my life, particularly in some half-forgotten childhood which haunted me like a dream. Could it be that she had nursed my mother and my grandmother, and that she saw a resemblance to the children she had trained in her youth? Stranger still, I felt not only that she recognized me, but that she possessed some secret which she wished to confide to me, that she was charged with a profoundly significant message which, sooner or later, she would find an opportunity to deliver.

As we went on, the hope that we should overtake her increased with every foot of the road. I stared into the mass of shadows. I started at every rustle on the scented ground. But still I caught no further glimpse of her; and at last, while I was gazing breathlessly beneath the cedars, we came out of the avenue on the edge of an open lawn, which was sown with small star-shaped flowers of palest blue. In front of me there were other ancient cedars, seven in number; and farther off, beyond the row of cedars, there was a long white house standing against the pomegranate-coloured afterglow, where a little horned moon was sailing.

I can shut my eyes now, after all these years, and summon back the scene as vividly as I saw it when we emerged from the long stretch of twilight. I can still see the blue glimmer of the flowers in the grass; the low house, with deep wings, where the stucco was peeling from the red brick beneath a delicate tracery of Virginia creeper; the seven pyramidal cedars guarding the hooded roof of gray shingles; and the clear afterglow in which the little moon sailed like a ship. Fifteen years ago! And I have not forgotten so much as the spiral pattern the Virginia creeper made on the pinkish white of the wall.

"Are there no trees," I asked, "except cedars?"

The driver lifted his whip and pointed over the roof. "You never saw such elms. I reckon there ain't any finer trees in the country, but they're all at the back, every last one of 'em. Mr. Blanton's grandfather had a notion that cedars didn't mix, and he wouldn't have any other trees planted in front."

I understood as I looked, in the flushed evening air, at the dark trees presiding over the approach to the house, with its Ionic columns and its quaint wings, added, one could see, long after the original walls were built. The drooping eaves, I knew, sheltered a multitude of wrens and phœbes, and the whole place was alive with swallows, which dipped and wheeled under the glowing sky.

We turned briskly into the circular drive, and a few minutes later, when we stopped before the walk of sunken flagstones, the driver jumped down and assisted me to descend. As I reached the porch, the door opened in a leisurely manner, and my cousin Pelham, a tall, relaxed, indolent-looking man of middle age, with gray hair, brilliant dark eyes and an air of pensive resignation, came out to receive me. I had heard, or had formed some vague idea, that the family had "run to seed," as they say in the South, and my first view of Cousin Pelham helped to fix this impression more firmly in my mind. He looked, I thought, a man who had ceased to desire anything intensely except physical comfort.

"So this is Cousin Effie's daughter," he remarked by way of greeting, as he stooped and placed a perfunctory kiss on my cheek.

Beyond him I saw a large angular woman, with massive features and hair of ambiguous brown, and I inferred, from the baby in her arms and four sturdy children at her skirts, that she was the "Miss Hannah," for whom Uncle Moab had prepared me. She appeared to me then and afterward to be a woman who was proficient in the art of making a man comfortable, and who hadn't, as the phrase goes, "a nerve in her body."

After greeting me cordially enough in her dry fashion, she directed the driver to take my bag upstairs to "the red room."

"I hope you can do without your trunk until to-morrow," she added. "All the teams have been ploughing to-day, and we couldn't send over to the station."

I replied that I could do very well without it since I had brought my travelling bag. Then, after a few questions from Cousin Pelham about my mother, whom he had not seen since they were both children at Whispering Leaves, Mrs. Blanton led me into the wide hall, where I saw a picture, framed in the open back door, of clustering elms and a flagged walk which ran down into a sunken garden. A minute later, while we ascended the circular staircase, with its beautifully carved balustrade, I found my eyes turning toward that vision of spring which I had seen through the open door.

"How white it looks out there in the garden," I said. "It seems carpeted with moonlight."

She bent her head indifferently to glance over the balustrade. "That's narcissus. It's in full bloom now," she answered. "The first Mrs. Blanton" (she might have been speaking of some one she had just left on the porch) "planted the whole garden in those flowers, and we have never got rid of them. The poet's narcissus, Mr. Blanton calls it."

"There are lilacs, too," I responded, for the cool dim hall was filled with the fragrance which seemed to me to be the secret of spring.

"Oh, yes, there are a great many lilacs about the wings, but they are thickest out by the kitchen."

The upstairs hall, like the one below, was large and dim, and while we crossed it, my companion called my attention to a loosened board or two in the floor. "The rats are bad," she observed. "I hope they won't bother you. They make a good deal of noise at night." And then almost immediately: "I don't know how you'll manage without a bathroom, but Mr. Blanton would never have water put in the house."

As she spoke, she opened a door at the front and ushered me into an immense bedroom, which was hung in a last-century fashion with faded calico. So far as I could distinguish in the dim light, there was not so much as a touch of red in the room. The furniture was all of rich old mahogany, made in too heavy a style for the taste that has been formed on Chippendale or Sheraton, and much of it looked as if it were dropping to pieces for lack of proper care. There was a high-tester bed, hung with the dingy calico; there was an elaborately carved bureau, with a greenish mirror which reflected my features in a fog; and there was a huge screen, papered in a design of castles and peacocks, which concealed an old-fashioned washstand. Yes, it was primitive. The touch about the water belonged to the dark ages; and yet the place possessed, for me at least, an inexpressible charm.

When Mrs. Blanton had left me alone, after telling me that supper would be served in half an hour, I made a few hurried preparations, while I tried in vain to get a glimpse of myself in the mirror, where my reflection floated like a leaf in a lily pond. Then, stealing cautiously from the room and across the deserted hall, with its musty smell of old spices, I crept down the staircase and out of the open back door. Here that provocative fragrance, the aroma of vanished springs, seized me again; and running down the worn steps of the porch, I passed the bower of lilacs beside the whitewashed kitchen wall, and followed the flagged walk to the sunken garden.

At the end of the walk a primitive wooden stile, like an illustration in *Mother Goose,* led into the garden; and when I passed it, I found myself in a flowery space, which was surrounded by banks of honeysuckle instead of a wall. A few old fruit trees, now well past blooming, stood in the centre; and edging the grassy paths, there were all the shrubs with quaint-sounding names of which I had dreamed in my childhood —guelder rose, bridal wreath, mock orange, flowering quince, and caly-canthus. Over all there hung a mist which had floated up from the low ground by the river; and it seemed to me that this moisture released the scents of a hundred springs. Never until that moment had I known what the rapture of smell could be. And the starry profusion of the narcissi! From bank to bank of honeysuckle the garden looked as if the Milky Way had fallen over it and been caught in the high grass.

Suddenly, in that enchanted silence, I heard the sound of a bell. In a house where there were no bathrooms, I surmised that bells were prob-ably still rung for meals; and turning reluctantly, I started back to the stile. I had gone but a step or two when a light flashing through the windows of the house arrested my gaze; and the next instant, when I glanced round again, I saw the figure of the old negress, in her white apron and red turban, standing motionless under the boughs of a pear-tree. In the twilight I saw her eyes fixed upon me, as I had seen them at sunset, with a look of entreaty like the inarticulate appeal in the eyes of the dumb. While I returned her gaze I felt, as I had felt at our first meeting, that she was speaking to me in some inaudible language which I did not yet understand, that she bore a message to me which, sooner or later, she would find a way to deliver. What could she mean? Why had she sought out me, a stranger, when she appeared to avoid the family and even the servants? Quickening my steps, I hastened toward her with a question on my lips; but before I reached her the bell rang again with a chiming sound, and when I withdrew my eyes from the old woman's face, I noticed that the little boy was running down the flagged walk to the stile. Bitterly I regretted the moment's inadvertence, for when I looked back, the negress had slipped beyond some of the flowering shrubs, and the garden appeared to be deserted. Well, next time I would be more careful, I resolved. And with this resolution in my mind, I hurried to meet Pell at the stile.

"She says you must come to supper," began the boy as soon as I came within reach of his voice. It was the first time I had heard him allude to his stepmother, and never, during the week I spent at Whispering Leaves, did he speak of her, in my presence, by any more intimate name.

I held out my arms, and he came to me shyly but trustingly. Though I could see that he was a nervous and sensitive child, the victim, I fancied, of an excitable imagination, I felt that it would not be difficult to win his confidence, if only one started about it in the right way. For the first time in my life I was drawn to a child, and I knew that the boy returned my liking in spite of his reserved manner.

"It is so beautiful I hate to go in," I said, with my arm about him.

"I wish I could never go in," he answered, turning back to the garden. "It is so lonely inside the house."

"Lonely?" I repeated, for the word struck me as a queer one for a child to use. "Aren't your little brothers and sisters there to play with you?"

He shook his head impatiently. "But they don't like Mammy to come in."

As I glanced down at his grave little face I wondered if he could be not quite right in his mind? Beneath his vivid hair, his wide-set greenish-blue eyes held a burning ardour that was unusual in so young a child. I could see that he was delicate in frame, and I inferred that his intelligence was dangerously advanced for his years.

"Do you come to the table?" I asked.

He nodded with uncanny glee. "Ever since I was four years old. I had a high chair then. Bobbie uses it now."

"Is Bobbie one of the twins?"

"One of the littlest twins. Janie is the other. Jack and Gerty, they are the big ones." Then he laughed slyly. "I'm glad I'm not a twin! I'd hate to have a girl tagging round after me."

We had reached the back steps, and I turned, before going in, to have a last look at the garden.

The twilight was the colour of white grapes, and the wisp of moon was scarcely more than a thread in the paling sky. Above the kitchen roof there was a flight of bats. An instant later I asked myself if I were dreaming, or if I actually saw the glimmer of the old negress's apron by the stile. Then the boy waved his arm in an affectionate good-night, and I knew that my imagination had not played a trick on me.

"Who is it, Pell?" I asked.

He glanced at me with his unchildish mirth. "Don't you see her at the stile over yonder?"

"The old coloured woman? Yes. I've seen her twice before. Who is she?"

Again he laughed. For some indefinable reason the laugh grated on my nerves. "If I tell you, will you promise not to let them know?"

I pressed his thin little body to my heart. "I'll never repeat anything you ask me not to, Pell."

His hand, so like a bird's claw, went up to my cheek with a caress; and he was on the point of replying when a step sounded in the hall, and one of the white servants came out on the porch to remind us that Mr. Blanton was waiting. To keep Cousin Pelham waiting for his meals was, I soon discovered, an unforgivable offence.

II

In the dining room, which was lighted by tallow candles, I found an obviously exasperated host and hostess. When I entered Cousin Pelham was fussing about a mahogany cellaret, while Mrs. Blanton was pinning a bib of checked gingham round the neck of a little girl in a high chair. With my English ideas of bringing up children, I thought it an odd custom to have the row of high chairs and trays at the table, and to allow such mere babies to appear at the evening meal.

"This is Gertrude," said Mrs. Blanton, after my apologies had been contritely offered and graciously accepted by Cousin Pelham, "and that," nodding to a little boy of the same age, "is John. The other two are Robert and Jane." They were robust, healthy-looking children, with dark hair and high colour, as unlike their delicate half-brother as one could well imagine.

At supper there was little conversation, for Cousin Pelham, who, I surmised, could talk delightfully when he made the effort, appeared to be absorbed in the food that was placed before him. This was of excellent quality. Evidently, I decided, the second Mrs. Blanton was the right wife for him. Vain, spoiled, selfish, amiable as long as he was given everything that he wanted, and still good-looking in an obvious and somewhat flashing style, he had long ago passed into that tranquil state of mind which follows a complete surrender to the habits of life. I wondered how that first wife, Clarissa of the romantic name and the flaming hair, had endured existence in this lonely neighbourhood with the companionship of a man who thought of nothing but food and drink. Perhaps he was different then; and yet was it possible for such abnormal egoism to develop in the years since her death? He ate immoderately, I observed, and even before he left the table I could see that the drowsiness which afflicts the overfed was descending upon him.

"The garden is charming," I said. "I have never seen one like it, so irregular and apparently neglected, and yet with a formal soul of its own."

Cousin Pelham stared at me over the dish of fried chicken from which he was carefully selecting the brownest and tenderest piece. "The garden? Oh, yes, we've had to let that go. It was kept up as long as Clarissa lived. She had a passion for flowers; but we can't get any of the darkeys to work it now." Then he appealed directly to his wife, who was engaged in teaching Gertrude how to hold her fork properly. "There hasn't been a spade stuck in the garden this spring, has there, Hannah?"

Mrs. Blanton shook her head, without removing her eyes from the little girl. "Nor last spring, nor the one before that," she rejoined. "Nobody sets foot in it now except Pell, and he oughtn't to go there. I tell him there might be snakes in the long grass; but he won't mind what I say. It takes as much work as we can manage to plough the fields and the kitchen beds. We can't spare any for that old garden you have to spade."

"Perhaps that's a part of the charm," I responded. "It expresses itself, not some human being's idea of planting."

She looked at me as if she did not know what I meant, and on my other side Cousin Pelham chuckled softly. "That sounds like Clarissa," he said, and there was no trace of sadness in his voice.

Across the table little Pell was eating delicately, pretending to be a bird. Now and then his stepmother turned away from the younger children to scold him about his fastidious appetite, or his odd manner of using his knife and fork, as if they were a superior kind of chopsticks. Her tone was not harsh. It was no sharper indeed than the one she used to her own children; yet, whenever she spoke to him, I felt rather than saw that he winced and shrank away from her. The child's nerves were overstrung, I could tell that just by watching him with his stepmother; and to her, who could see nothing that was not directly before her eyes, his sensitiveness appeared deliberate perversity. Yet he was an attractive child in spite of his elfin ways. If he could only find the sympathy and understanding he needed so desperately, I felt that he might become very lovable.

Though I was sorry for the child then, I had barely touched the edge of the passion which presently filled my heart. The hardest hour of all, and one of the most trying moments in my life, came when we passed into the library, and Mrs. Blanton summoned the children to bed. The younger children, already nodding, obeyed without protest; but when it came to Pell's turn to kiss his father good-night, he began to shake and whimper with terror. For a minute I did not understand; then turning to Cousin Pelham, I asked, with a sympathy so acute that it stabbed like a knife,

"Is Pell afraid of the dark?"

Cousin Pelham, sunk in the softest old leather chair, was beyond the sound of my voice; but his wife answered immediately in her firm and competent tone.

"We are trying to break him of it. It would be dreadful for his father's son to be a coward."

"Does he sleep in the nursery?"

"He used to, but we had to move his bed across the hall because he kept the other children awake. He gets, or pretends to get, the most ridiculous notions into his head, and he carries on so that the other children don't get any sleep when they are in the room with him."

"Where does he stay now?"

"In the spare room next to yours. We moved him there a few weeks ago, and you would think from the way he behaved that we were sending him to his grave."

"But doesn't that seem the wrong way, to frighten a nervous child into hysterics?"

At this she turned on me the most exasperating force in the universe, impregnable common sense.

"We've got to break him of it," she retorted, "or he will be a baby all his life."

"I think you're wrong," was all I could say feebly in denial; and my words had as little effect as the dash of hail on a window-pane. But, while I answered, I was telling myself that I had found out where the boy slept, and that I would go to his room as soon as I had bidden the family good-night. Cousin Pelham and his wife stayed downstairs, I knew, in what they called "the chamber" behind the drawing room, so I should have to guard against only the stupid-looking nurse who had a room, I supposed, near the children.

Bending over, I pressed the boy to my heart. "I am near you, and I will take care of you," I whispered. Then, releasing him, I stood back and watched him walk, wincing and trembling, after the sturdy children of his stepmother.

It seemed to me that the evening would never end. Every minute I was straining my ears for a sound from the floor above, while Cousin Pelham dozed through the processes of digestion, and Mrs. Blanton and I discussed such concrete facts as wood and stones and preserves and the best way to build a road or to cut down a tree. At last, when I was exhausted beyond belief, though it was only a little after nine o'clock, she laid down her mending, rose from her chair, and, with her hand on her husband's shoulder, wished me good-night.

"You will find a candle in the hall," she said. "We never use lamps in the chambers." Her use of the archaic word struck me at the time as poetic. It was the only poetic touch I ever observed about her.

On a table in the hall I found a row of tallow dips in old brass candlesticks; and after lighting one, I took it in my hand and ascended the circular staircase. Ahead of me the light flitted like a moth up the worn steps, which the feet of generations had hollowed out in the centre as water hollows out a stairway of rock. The hall above was empty —it occurred to me at the moment that I had never seen such empty-looking halls—and was quite dark except for the flickering light of my candle. As I crossed the floor the green mist which I had left in the garden floated in and enveloped me, and that wistful fragrance became intolerably sweet. I had suddenly the feeling that the dim corners and winding recesses of the hall were crowded with intangible shapes.

After glancing through my open door to assure myself that I had not made a mistake, I stole across the hall and hesitated before the threshold of what Mrs. Blanton had pointed out to me as "the spare room." If the child were sleeping, I did not wish to arouse him, but all idea that he slept was banished as I pushed the door wider and heard him talking aloud to himself. Then, while the pointed flame of my candle pierced the obscurity, I saw that he was not, as I had first thought, alone. The old coloured woman in the black alpaca dress, with the white apron and the red turban, was bending over him. When I approached she turned slowly and looked at me; and I felt that her dark, compassionate face was love made manifest to my eyes. So she had looked down on the child, and so, for one miraculous instant, she gazed directly into my heart. For one miraculous instant! Then, while I stood there, transfixed as by an arrow, she passed, with that slow movement, across the room to the door which I had left open. Before I could stir, before I could utter a word to detain her, she had disappeared; and the boy, sitting up in the heavily draped bed, was staring at me with wondering eyes.

"Mammy was telling me a story," he said.

"I didn't know that you had a mammy now." This was the best that I could do at the moment.

"Oh, yes, I have!" He smiled with charming archness, and I noticed that the fear had passed out of his voice.

"When did she come?" I asked.

"She has been here always, ever since," he hesitated, "since before I was."

"Does she look after the other children too?"

He laughed, cuddling down into the middle of the feather bed. "They don't know about her. They have never seen her."

"But how can she come and go in the house without anybody seeing her?"

At this the laughter stopped. "She has a way," he answered enigmatically. "She never comes into the house except when I'm afraid."

I bent over and kissed him. "Well, you're not frightened any longer?"

"Oh, no. I'm all right now," he replied, stroking my hand. "The next time it gets dark Mammy says she will come back and finish her story."

"And I am next door," I said. "Whenever you begin to feel frightened you can come and sleep on the big couch by the window."

"By the window," he repeated eagerly, "where Mammy's wrens are under the eaves. That would be fun."

Then, as I arranged the bedclothes over him, he turned his cheek to the pillow, and settled himself for the night. A moment later, when I went out of the room, I began wondering again about the old negress. Was she a faithful servant who had sacrificed her superstition to her affection for Clarissa's child, and had stayed on at Whispering Leaves when the other negroes had gone away? In the morning I would make some inquiries. Meanwhile I liked to remember the glory—there is no other word to describe it—that I had seen in her dark face when she bent over the boy.

In the morning, when I came out of doors, it was into a world of maize-coloured sunshine. There was new green on the cedars, and the little blue flowers in the grass looked as formal as the blossoms in a Gothic tapestry. Suddenly a harsh scream sounded a little way to the right, and a peacock, with flaunting plumage, marched across the lawn, through the sunlight and shadow. As I stood there, entranced by the colour of the morning, it seemed to me that this circle of sunlight and shadow became alive with the quiver of innumerable gauzy wings, the bright ghosts of all the birds that had ever sung in this place.

When, presently, I turned in the direction of the garden, I saw that Pell was playing in a row of flowering quince near the stile. He was on his knees, building a castle of rocks, which he had brought in a little wagon from the road in the pasture; and while I approached, I observed that he was talking aloud to himself as children talk in their play. Then, before I reached him, I found my gaze arrested by a glimmer of red amid the smoke-gray boughs of a crêpe myrtle tree; and it seemed to my startled fancy that I made out the figure of the old negress. But the next minute a scarlet tanager flashed out of the branches, and the image proved to be one of those grotesque shapes which crêpe myrtle bushes, like ancient olive trees, frequently assume.

The child was playing happily by himself. When my shadow fell over him, he looked up with his expression of secret wisdom. Kneeling there, with his red curls and his blue-green eyes enkindled by the sunshine, he reminded me of some unearthly flower of light.

"It will be a fine castle," I said.

He glanced hastily over his shoulder; and I noticed that his manner was shy and furtive, though it expressed also a childish pleasure that was very appealing.

"I've got something better than a castle," he answered. "I found it yesterday down by the ice pond. Will you promise not to tell if I let you look?"

"I promise," I assured him gravely; and, with another suspicious glance in the direction of the house, he sprang to his feet and caught me by the hand. Leading me round the shrubbery and over the stile, he showed me a hollow he had made in the tall grasses beneath a cluster of lilac bushes. Lying there on a bed of dry fern I saw a black and white mongrel puppy, a delightful, audacious, independent puppy, half terrier and half unknown, with an engaging personality and a waggish black ear that dropped over one sparkling eye. Fastened securely by a strip of red cotton to the shrub, beside a partly gnawed bone and a saucer of water, he sat surveying me with an expectant, inquisitive look.

"Isn't he a beauty?" asked Pell, enraptured, as he went down on his knees and flung his arms about the puppy.

"A beauty," I repeated; and I also went down on my knees to embrace boy and dog.

"He hadn't had anything to eat for ever so long when I found him. Martha gives me scraps for him, and William lets him sleep in the stable." Then he looked straight into my eyes. "You won't tell?" he pleaded. "She wouldn't let him stay if she knew. She doesn't like dogs."

Of course she didn't like dogs. Hadn't I felt from the first that she wouldn't? Why, there wasn't a dog on the place, except the two black and yellow hounds I had seen half a mile away in the cornfield, and they belonged doubtless to one of the negroes.

"No, I won't tell," I promised. "I'll help you take care of him."

His eyes shone. "Can you teach him to do tricks? He knows how to beg already. Mammy taught him."

I released the child quickly and rose to my feet. "Where is your Mammy, Pell?"

His rapid glance flew down the garden walk, and across the narcissi, to the twisted pear tree. "She's just gone," he answered. "She went when she saw you coming."

"Where does she live?"

At this he broke into a laugh. "Oh, she lives away, way over yonder," he responded, with a sweep of his hand.

For the next week Pell and I were cheerful conspirators. When I look back on it now, after so many years, I can still recall those cautious trips to the barn or the little bed of ferns under the lilacs. We fed Wop, that was the name we chose at last, until he grew as round as a ball; and he was just passing into the second stage of his education when Mrs. Blanton discovered his presence, as I was sure that she would be obliged to do sooner or later.

I had been away for the afternoon to visit some relatives at a distance; and as we drove home about sunset, we passed on the road the old coloured woman whom Pell had called Mammy. I could not be mistaken, I told myself. I should have recognized her anywhere, not only by the quaint turban she wore bound about her head, but by that indescribable light which shone in her face.

At the time we were driving through a stretch of burned pines, and when I first noticed her she had stopped to rest and was sitting on a charred stump by the roadside, with the red disc of the sun at her back. The light was in my eyes; but, as I leaned out and smiled at her, she gave me again that long deep look so filled with inarticulate yearning. I knew then, as I had known the first afternoon, that she was trying to make me understand, that she was charged with some message she could not utter. While her eyes met mine I was smitten—that is the only word for the sensation—into silence; but after we had driven on, I recovered myself sufficiently to say to the cousin who was taking me home:

"If she is going a long way, don't you think we might give her a lift?"

My cousin, an obtuse young man, gazed at me vacantly. "If who is going a long way?"

"The old coloured woman by the roadside. Didn't you see her?"

He shook his head. "No, I wasn't looking. I didn't see anybody."

While he was still speaking, I leaned out with an exclamation of surprise. "Why, there she is now in front of us! She must have run ahead of us through the pines. She is waiting by the dead tree at the fork of the road."

My cousin was laughing now. "The sunset makes you see double. There isn't anybody there. Can you see anything except the blasted oak at the fork of the road, Jacob?"

A few minutes later, when we reached the place where the road branched, I saw that it was deserted. The red blaze of the sun could play tricks with one's vision, I knew; but it was odd that on both occasions, at precisely the same hour, I should be visited by this hallucination. That it was an hallucination, I no longer doubted when, looking up a short while afterward, I saw again the old woman's figure ahead of me. This time, however, I kept silent, for the first thing one learns from such visitations is the danger of talking to people of things which they cannot understand. But I drove on with my heart in my throat. In front of me in the blue air was that vision; and in my mind there was a voiceless apprehension. Then, as we reached the lawn, the old woman vanished, and a moment later the sound of a child's crying fell on my ears.

Alone on the front steps, Pell sat weeping inconsolably, with his face hidden in his thin little hands. When I sprang from the carriage, he rushed into my arms.

"She has sent him away! She has sent him away to be drowned!" he cried in a heartbreaking voice.

As I drew him close, the door opened, and Mrs. Blanton looked out.

"Come in, Pell," she called, not unkindly, but unseeingly. "You will fret yourself into a fever. The circus is coming next week, and if you make yourself sick, you won't be able to go to it."

At this Pell turned on her a white and quivering face. "I don't want to go to the circus," he said. "I don't want any supper. I want Wop, and I wish you were dead!"

"Pell, dear!" I cried, but Mrs. Blanton only laughed good-naturedly, a laugh that was as common as her features.

"He's got his mother's temper all right," she remarked to me over the child's head. "If you don't want any supper," she added, dragging him indoors, while he struggled to free himself from the grasp of her large firm hand which seemed as inexorable as her purpose, "you must go straight upstairs to bed."

When we had entered the house the boy broke away from her, and marched, without a tremor of hesitation, across the hall and into the thick dusk of the staircase.

"Let me go after him," I said. "He is so afraid of the dark, and the candles are not lighted upstairs."

Mrs. Blanton detained me by a gesture. "He is the sort of child you have to be firm with," she returned, and then immediately, "Mr. Blanton"—she always addressed her husband as "Mr. Blanton"—"is waiting for us in the dining room. It frets him to be kept waiting."

After this there was nothing to do but follow her, with a heavy heart, into the room, where Cousin Pelham stood, ponderously frowning at the door. I could not this evening meet his annoyance with my usual playful apology; and a little later, when the excellent supper was served, I found that I was unable to swallow a morsel. The fact that I was leaving the next day, that I should, perhaps, not see Pell again for years, had turned my heart to lead.

When supper was over I escaped as soon as I could and ran upstairs to the room where Pell slept. A candle was burning by his bed, and to my amazement the child was sleeping peacefully, with a smile on his face where the traces of tears were scarcely dried. While I looked down on him, he stirred and opened his eyes.

"I thought you were Mammy," he murmured, with a drowsy laugh.

"Has Mammy been here?" I asked.

He was so sleepy that he could barely answer; but, as he nestled down into the middle of the feather bed, he replied without the faintest sign of his recent distress:

"She was here when I came up. She told me it was all right about Wop. Uncle Moab is keeping him for me."

"Uncle Moab is keeping him?" I pressed my hand on his forehead under the vivid hair; but there was no hint of fever.

"She says she gave Wop to Uncle Moab. Mammy wouldn't let anybody hurt him."

Then his eyes closed while the smile quivered on his lips. "Mammy says you must take me with you when you go away," he murmured. His face changed to an almost unearthly loveliness, and before I could answer, before I could even take in the words he had spoken, he had fallen asleep.

For a minute I stood looking down on him. Then leaving the candle still burning, I went out, closing the door softly, and ran against the maid, a young Irish woman, whose face I liked.

"I was just going to see if Pell had fallen asleep," she explained a little nervously. "I have a message for him. You won't tell Mrs. Blanton I brought it?"

"No. I won't tell Mrs. Blanton."

For an instant the girl hesitated. "She is so strict," she blurted out, and then more guardedly, "William wouldn't have drowned the child's puppy. He just took it away and gave it to Uncle Moab who was going along the road."

"I am glad," I said eagerly. "Uncle Moab will look after it?"

"He sent Pell a message not to worry. I was going in to tell him."

"But he knows it already," I replied indiscreetly. "Somebody told him."

A puzzled look came into her face. "But nobody knew. William just came back a minute ago, and there hasn't been another soul on the place this afternoon."

I saw my slip at once and hastened to remedy it. "Then I was mistaken of course. The child must have imagined it."

"Yes, he does imagine things," she responded readily; and after a word of good-night, she turned back to the stairs while I crossed the hall to my room.

There, as soon as I had closed the door, I put down my candle, and turned to the open window to think over what I had heard. There was nothing really strange, I told myself, in the incident of the puppy and Uncle Moab. It was natural enough that William should have refused to obey an order he thought was cruel; it was natural enough also that Uncle Moab should have been going by in the road at that hour. Everything was easily explained except the singular change in the child, and the happy smile on his little tear-stained face when he murmured, "Mammy says you must take me with you when you go away." Over and over again I heard those words as I sat there by the window. So insistent was the repetition that I might have deluded myself into the belief that they were spoken aloud in the darkness outside. How could I take the child away with me? I asked at last, as if I were disputing with some invisible presence at my side. What room was there for a child in my active life? I loved Pell; I hated to leave him; but how could I possibly take him with me when I went away in the morning? Yet, even after I had undressed, climbed into the canopied bed, and blown out my candle, I still heard that phrase again and again in my mind. I was still hearing it hours afterward when I fell asleep and dreamed of the old coloured woman sitting on the charred stump by the roadside.

Dreams. The old coloured woman by the roadside. The song of far-off birds coming nearer. The jade-green mist of the twilight changing suddenly to opal. Light growing out of darkness. Light turning from clear gold to flame colour. Still the song of birds that became so loud it was like the torrent of waters—or of fire. Dreams. Dreams. Nothing more. . . .

Starting awake, I was aware first of that opal-coloured light; then of the fact that I was stifling, that a gray cloud had swept in from the window, or the open door, and enveloped me. The next instant, with a cry, I sprang up and caught at the dressing-gown on a chair by my bed. From outside, mingled with that dream of singing birds and rushing torrents, the sound of voices was reaching me. The words I could not hear, but I needed no words to tell me that these were voices of warning. Whispering Leaves was burning while I dreamed. Whispering Leaves was burning, and I must fight my way to safety through the smoke that rushed in at my open door!

"Pell!" I called in terror, as I ran out into the hall. But there was no answer to my cry, and the next minute, when I looked into the child's room, I saw that the bed was empty. They had saved him and forgotten me. Well, at least they had saved him!

Of the next few minutes, which seemed an eternity of terror, I can recall nothing now except a struggle for air. I must have fought my way through the smoke upstairs. I must have passed that savage light so close that it scorched my face, which was blistered afterward, though I felt no pain at the moment. I must have heard that rush of flames so near that it deafened me; but of this I can remember nothing to-day. Yet I can still feel the air blowing in my face on the lawn outside. I can still see the little green leaves on the cedars standing out illuminated in that terrible glow. I can still hear the cry that rang out:

"Pell! Where is Pell? Didn't you bring Pell with you?"

Fifteen years ago. Fire and ashes, pain and happiness, have passed and are forgotten; but that question, as I heard it then, still sounds in my ears.

"Where is Pell? Didn't you bring Pell with you?"

"I thought he was safe," my voice was so thick that the words were scarcely articulate. "His room was empty."

"He isn't with the other children. We thought he had gone to you." The speaker I have forgotten—Cousin Pelham or his wife, or the nurse, it is no matter—but the words are still living.

"I will go back." This was Cousin Pelham, I knew, for he had turned to enter the burning house.

"It is too late now." This was not one, but several voices together. As they spoke the windows of the house shone like the sunrise while a torrent of flame swept through the hall.

"Oh, Pell! Pell!" I cried out in agony. "Cannot you come to me?"

For a minute—it was scarcely longer—after I called, there was no answer. We stood in that red glare, and round us and beyond us closed the mysterious penumbra of the darkness. Without the circle, where we clung together in our horror, there was the freshness and the sweetness of the spring, and all the little quiet stirs that birds make when they nest at night. And it was out of this bird-hunted darkness that a shape moved suddenly past me into the flames, a shape which as the light edged it round I saw to be that of the old negress.

"She is looking for him," I cried now. "Oh, don't you see her?"

They gathered anxiously round me. "The fire has blinded her," I heard them say. "She is looking straight at the flames."

Yes, I was looking straight at the flames, for beyond the flames, past the unburned wing of the house, from the window of an old storeroom, which was never opened, they had told me, I saw the shape of the old negress pass again like a shadow. The next instant my heart melted with joy, for I saw that she was bringing the child in her arms. The little face was pale as death; the red curls were singed to black; but it was the child that she held. Even the unperceiving eyes about me, though they could see only material things, knew that Pell had come unharmed out of the fire. To them it was merely a shadow, a veil of smoke, which surrounded him. I alone saw the dark arms that enfolded him. I alone, among all those standing there in that awful light, recognized that dark compassionate face.

Her eyes found me at last, and I knew, in that moment of vision, what the message was that she had for me. Without a word I stepped forward, and held out my arms. As I did so, I saw a glory break in the dim features. Then, even while I gave my voiceless answer, the face melted from me into spirals of smoke. Was it a dream, after all? Was the only reality the fact that I held the child safe and unharmed in my arms?

Editor's Note

Miss Glasgow's *annus mirabilis* for short stories was 1923. She published four stories that year, three in magazines and one in her *The*

Shadowy Third collection. This, the first and largest of the group, appeared in the January and February issues of *Harper's Magazine* for 1923. It is another two-part story, but its division is not so appropriate as in "Dare's Gift." The story moves along chronologically from beginning to end. Part I is devoted almost entirely to preliminary exposition; Part II analyzes the situation. Or, to put it another way, we meet all the good people in the first half of the story; in the second half we meet the villains.

Revisions in the collected edition showed greater restraint and more accurate Negro dialect. Miss Glasgow removed this giveaway sentence early in the story: "For the first time it occurred to me that there was an unnatural note in the joyous piping [of the birds]." She replaced Mammy's white kerchief with a red turban. She also substituted discreet commas for the more anxious dashes that punctuated the narrator's observations. The spelling of the story is meticulously British.

The only serious flaw in "Whispering Leaves" is the excessive symbolism of birds, trees, and flowers; there is enough horticultural detail to fill a gardening magazine. Further pruning would have helped.

IX

The Difference

⟡ OUTSIDE, IN the autumn rain, the leaves were falling.

For twenty years, every autumn since her marriage, Margaret Fleming had watched the leaves from this window; and always it had seemed to her that they were a part of her life which she held precious. As they fell she had known that they carried away something she could never recover—youth, beauty, pleasure, or only memories that she wanted to keep. Something gracious, desirable and fleeting; but never until this afternoon had she felt that the wind was sweeping away the illusion of happiness by which she lived. Beyond the panes, against which the rain was beating in gray sheets, she looked out on the naked outlines of the city: bleak houses, drenched grass in squares, and boughs of trees where a few brown or yellow leaves were clinging.

On the hearth rug the letter lay where it had fallen a few minutes—or was it a few hours ago? The flames from the wood fire cast a glow on the white pages; and she imagined that the ugly words leaped out to sting her like scorpions as she moved by them. Not for worlds, she told herself, would she stoop and touch them again. Yet what need had she to touch them when each slanting black line was etched in her memory with acid? Never, though she lived a hundred years, could she forget the way the letters fell on the white paper!

Once, twice, three times, she walked from window to door and back again from door to window. The wood fire burned cheerfully with a whispering sound. As the lights and shadows stirred over the familiar objects she had once loved, her gaze followed them hungrily. She had called this upstairs library George's room, and she realized now that every piece of furniture, every book it contained, had been chosen to please him. He liked the golden brown of the walls, the warm colours in the Persian rugs, the soft depth of the cushioned chairs. He liked, too, the flamboyant red lilies beneath the little Chippendale mirror.

After twenty years of happiness, of comradeship, of mutual dependence, after all that marriage could mean to two equal spirits, was there nothing left except ashes? Could twenty years of happiness be destroyed in an afternoon, in an hour? Stopping abruptly, with a jerk which ran like a spasm through her slender figure, she gazed with hard searching eyes over the red lilies into the mirror. The grave beauty of her face, a beauty less of flesh than of spirit, floated there in the shadows like a flower in a pond.

"I am younger than he is by a year," she thought, "and yet he can begin over again to love, while a new love for me would be desecration."

There was the sound of his step on the stair. An instant later his hand fell on the door, and he entered the room.

Stooping swiftly, she picked up the letter from the rug and hid it in her bosom. Then turning toward him, she received his kiss with a smile. "I didn't wait lunch for you," she said.

"I got it at the club." After kissing her cheek, he moved to the fire and stood warming his hands. "Beastly day. No chance of golf, so I've arranged to see that man from Washington. You won't get out, I suppose?"

She shook her head. "No, I sha'n't get out."

Did he know, she wondered, that this woman had written to her? Did he suspect that the letter lay now in her bosom? He had brought the smell of rain, the taste of dampness, with him into the room; and this air of the outer world enveloped him while he stood there, genial, robust, superbly vital, clothed in his sanguine temperament as in the healthy red and white of his flesh. Still boyish at forty-five, he had that look of perennial innocence which some men carry untarnished through the most enlightening experiences. Even his moustache and his sharply jutting chin could not disguise the softness that hovered always about his mouth, where she noticed now, with her piercing scrutiny, the muscles were growing lax. Strange that she had never seen this until she discovered that George loved another woman! The thought flashed into her mind that she knew him in reality no better than if she had lived with a stranger for twenty years. Yet, until a few hours ago, she would have said, had any one asked her, that their marriage was as perfect as any mating between a man and a woman could be in this imperfect world.

"You're wise. The wind's still in the east, and there is no chance, I'm afraid, of a change." He hesitated an instant, stared approvingly at the red lilies, and remarked abruptly, "Nice colour."

"You always liked red." Her mouth lost its softness. "And I was pale even as a girl."

His genial gaze swept her face. "Oh, well, there's red and red, you know. Some cheeks look best pale."

Without replying to his words, she sat looking up at him while her thoughts, escaping her control, flew from the warm room out into the rough autumn weather. It was as if she felt the beating of the rain in her soul, as if she were torn from her security and whirled downward and onward in the violence of the storm. On the surface of her life nothing had changed. The fire still burned; the lights and shadows still flickered over the Persian rugs; her husband still stood there, looking down on her through the cloudless blue of his eyes. But the real Margaret, the vital part of her, was hidden far away in that deep place where the seeds of mysterious impulses and formless desires lie buried. She knew that there were secrets within herself which she had never acknowledged in her own thoughts; that there were unexpressed longings which had never taken shape even in her imagination. Somewhere beneath the civilization of the ages there was the skeleton of the savage.

The letter in her bosom scorched her as if it were fire. "That was why you used to call me magnolia blossom," she said in a colourless voice, and knew it was only the superficial self that was speaking.

His face softened; yet so perfectly had the note of sentiment come to be understood rather than expressed in their lives that she could feel his embarrassment. The glow lingered in his eyes, but he answered only, "Yes, you were always like that."

An irrepressible laugh broke from her. Oh, the irony, the bitterness! "Perhaps you like them pale!" she tossed back mockingly, and wondered if this Rose Morrison who had written to her was coloured like her name?

He looked puzzled but solicitous. "I'm afraid I must be off. If you are not tired, could you manage to go over these galleys this afternoon? I'd like to read the last chapter aloud to you after the corrections are made." He had written a book on the history of law; and while he drew the roll of proof sheets from his pocket, she remembered, with a pang as sharp as the stab of a knife, all the work of last summer when they had gathered material together. He needed her for his work, she realized, if not for his pleasure. She stood, as she had always done, for the serious things of his life. This book could not have been written without her. Even his success in his profession had been the result of her efforts as well as his own.

"I'm never too tired for that," she responded, and though she smiled up at him, it was a smile that hurt her with its irony.

"Well, my time's up," he said. "By the way, I'll need my heavier golf things if it is fine to-morrow." To-morrow was Sunday, and he played golf with a group of men at the Country Club every Sunday morning.

"They are in the cedar closet. I'll get them out."

"The medium ones, you know. That English tweed."

"Yes, I know. I'll have them ready," Did Rose Morrison play golf? she wondered.

"I'll try to get back early to dinner. There was a button loose on the waistcoat I wore last evening. I forgot to mention it this morning."

"Oh, I'm sorry. I left it to the servants, but I'll look after it myself." Again this perverse humour seized her. Had he ever asked Rose Morrison to sew on a button?

At the door he turned back. "And I forgot to ask you this morning to order flowers for Morton's funeral. It is to be Monday."

The expression on her face felt as stiff as a wax mask, and though she struggled to relax her muscles, they persisted in that smile of inane cheerfulness. "I'll order them at once, before I begin the galleys," she answered.

Rising from the couch on which she had thrown herself at his entrance, she began again her restless pacing from door to window. The library was quiet except for the whispering flames. Outside in the rain the leaves were falling thickly, driven hither and thither by the wind which rocked the dappled boughs of the sycamores. In the gloom of the room the red lilies blazed.

The terror, which had clutched her like a living thing, had its fangs in her heart. Terror of loss, of futility. Terror of the past because it tortured her. Terror of the future because it might be empty even of torture. "He is mine, and I will never give him up," she thought wildly. "I will fight to the end for what is mine."

There was a sound at the door and Winters, the butler, entered. "Mrs. Chambers, Madam. She was quite sure you would be at home."

"Yes, I am at home." She was always at home, even in illness, to Dorothy Chambers. Though they were so different in temperament, they had been friends from girlhood; and much of the gaiety of Margaret's life had been supplied by Dorothy. Now, as her friend entered, she held out her arms. "You come whenever it rains, dear," she said. "It is so good of you." Yet her welcome was hollow, and at the very instant when she returned her friend's kiss she was wishing that she could send her away. That was one of the worst things about suffering; it made one indifferent and insincere.

Dorothy drew off her gloves, unfastened her furs, and after raising her veil over the tip of her small inquisitive nose, held out her hand with a beseeching gesture.

"I've come straight from a committee luncheon. Give me a cigarette."

Reaching for the Florentine box on the desk, Margaret handed it to her. A minute later, while the thin blue flame shot up between them, she asked herself if Dorothy could look into her face and not see the difference?

Small, plain, vivacious, with hair of ashen gold, thin intelligent features, and a smile of mocking brilliance, Dorothy was the kind of woman whom men admire without loving and women love without admiring. As a girl she had been a social success without possessing a single one of the qualities upon which social success is supposed to depend.

Sinking back in her chair, she blew several rings of smoke from her lips and watched them float slowly upward.

"We have decided to give a bridge party. There's simply no other way to raise money. Will you take a table?"

Margaret nodded. "Of course." Suffering outside of herself made no difference to her. Her throbbing wound was the only reality.

"Janet is going to lend us her house." A new note had come into Dorothy's voice. "I haven't seen her since last spring. She had on a new hat, and was looking awfully well. You know Herbert has come back."

Margaret started. At last her wandering attention was fixed on her visitor. "Herbert? And she let him?" There was deep disgust in her tone.

Dorothy paused to inhale placidly before she answered. "Well, what else could she do? He tried to make her get a divorce, and she wouldn't."

A flush stained Margaret's delicate features. "I never understood why she didn't. He made no secret of what he wanted. He showed her plainly that he loved the other woman."

Dorothy's only reply was a shrug; but after a moment, in which she smoked with a luxurious air, she commented briefly, "But man's love isn't one of the eternal verities."

"Well, indifference is, and he proved that he was indifferent to Janet. Yet she has let him come back to her. I can't see what she is to get out of it."

Dorothy laughed cynically. "Oh, she enjoys immensely the attitude of forgiveness, and at last he has permitted her to forgive him. There is a spiritual vanity as well as a physical one, you know, and Janet's weakness is spiritual."

"But to live with a man who doesn't love her? To remember every minute of the day and night that it is another woman he loves?"

"And every time that she remembers it she has the luxury of forgiving again." Keenness flickered like a blade in Dorothy's gray eyes. "You are very lovely, Margaret," she said abruptly. "The years seem only to leave you rarer and finer, but you know nothing about life."

A smile quivered and died on Margaret's lips. "I might retort that you know nothing about love."

With an impatient birdlike gesture Dorothy tossed her burned-out cigarette into the fire. "Whose love?" she inquired as she opened the Florentine box, "Herbert's or yours?"

"It's all the same, isn't it?"

By the flame of the match she had struck Dorothy's expression appeared almost malign. "There, my dear, is where you are wrong," she replied. "When a man and a woman talk of love they speak two different languages. They can never understand each other because women love with their imagination and men with their senses. To you love is a thing in itself, a kind of abstract power like religion; to Herbert it is simply the way he feels."

"But if he loves the other woman, he doesn't love Janet; and yet he wants to return to her."

Leaning back in her chair, Dorothy surveyed her with a look which was at once sympathetic and mocking. Her gaze swept the pure grave features; the shining dusk of the hair; the narrow nose with its slight arch in the middle; the straight red lips with their resolute pressure; the skin so like a fading rose-leaf. Yes, there was beauty in Margaret's face if one were only artist or saint enough to perceive it.

"There is so much more in marriage than either love or indifference," she remarked casually. "There is, for instance, comfort."

"Comfort?" repeated Margaret scornfully. She rose, in her clinging draperies of chiffon, to place a fresh log on the fire. "If he really loves the other woman, Janet ought to give him up," she said.

At this Dorothy turned on her. "Would you, if it were George?" she demanded.

For an instant, while she stood there in front of the fire, it seemed to Margaret that the room whirled before her gaze like the changing colours in a kaleidoscope. Then a gray cloud fell over the brightness, and out of this cloud there emerged only the blaze of the red lilies. A pain struck her in the breast, and she remembered the letter she had hidden there.

"Yes," she answered presently. "I should do it if it were George."

A minute afterward she became conscious that while she spoke, a miracle occurred within her soul.

The tumult of sorrow, of anger, of bitterness, of despair, was drifting farther and farther away. Even the terror, which was worse than any tumult, had vanished. In that instant of renunciation she had reached some spiritual haven. What she had found, she understood presently, was the knowledge that there is no support so strong as the strength that enables one to stand alone.

"I should do it if it were George," she said again, very slowly.

"Well, I think you would be very foolish." Dorothy had risen and was lowering her veil. "For when George ceases to be desirable for senti- mental reasons, he will still have his value as a good provider." Her mocking laugh grated on Margaret's ears. "Now, I must run away. I only looked in for an instant. I've a tea on hand, and I must go home and dress."

When she had gone, Margaret stood for a minute, thinking deeply. For a minute only, but in that space of time her decision was made. Crossing to the desk, she telephoned for the flowers. Then she left the library and went into the cedar closet at the end of the hall. When she had found the golf clothes George wanted, she looked over them care- fully and hung them in his dressing room. Her next task was to lay out his dinner clothes and to sew the loose button on the waistcoat he had worn last evening. She did these things deliberately, automatically, re- peating as if it were a formula, "I must forget nothing"; and when at last she had finished, she stood upright, with a sigh of relief, as if a burden had rolled from her shoulders. Now that she had attended to the details of existence, she would have time for the problem of living.

Slipping out of her gray dress, she changed into a walking suit of blue homespun. Then, searching among the shoes in her closet, she selected a pair of heavy boots she had worn in Maine last summer. As she put on a close little hat and tied a veil of blue chiffon over her face, she re- flected, with bitter mirth, that only in novels could one hide one's identity behind a veil.

In the hall downstairs she met Winters, who stared at her discreetly but disapprovingly.

"Shall I order the car, madam?"

She shook her head, reading his thoughts as plainly as if he had ut- tered them. "No, it has stopped raining. I want to walk."

The door closed sharply on her life of happiness, and she passed out into the rain-soaked world where the mist caught her like damp smoke. So this was what it meant to be deserted, to be alone on the earth! The smell of rain, the smell that George had brought with him into the warm room upstairs, oppressed her as if it were the odour of melancholy.

As the chill pierced her coat, she drew her furs closely about her neck, and walked briskly in the direction of the street car. The address on the letter she carried was burned into her memory not in numbers, but in the thought that it was a villa George owned in an unfashionable suburb named Locust Park. Though she had never been there, she knew that, with the uncertain trolley service she must expect, it would take at least two hours to make the trip and return. Half an hour for Rose Morrison; and even then it would be night, and Winters at least would be anxious, before she reached home. Well, that was the best she could do.

The street car came, and she got in and found a seat behind a man who had been shooting and carried a string of partridges. All the other seats were filled with the usual afternoon crowd for the suburbs—women holding bundles or baskets and workmen returning from the factories. A sense of isolation like spiritual darkness descended upon her; and she closed her eyes and tried to bring back the serenity she had felt in the thought of relinquishment. But she could remember only a phrase of Dorothy's which floated like a wisp of thistledown through her thoughts, "Spiritual vanity. With some women it is stronger than physical vanity." Was that her weakness, vanity, not of the body, but of the spirit?

Thoughts blew in and out of her mind like dead leaves, now whirling, now drifting, now stirring faintly in her consciousness with a moaning sound. Twenty years. Nothing but that. Love and nothing else in her whole life. . . . The summer of their engagement. A rose garden in bloom. The way he looked. The smell of roses. Or was it only the smell of dead leaves rotting to earth? . . . All the long, long years of their marriage. Little things that one never forgot. The way he laughed. The way he smiled. The look of his hair when it was damp on his forehead. The smell of cigars in his clothes. The three lumps of sugar in his coffee. The sleepy look in his face when he stood ready to put out the lights while she went up the stairs. Oh, the little things that tore at one's heart!

The street car stopped with a jerk, and she got out and walked through the drenched grass in the direction one of the women had pointed out to her.

"The Laurels? That low yellow house at the end of this lane, farther on where the piles of dead leaves are. You can't see the house now, the lane turns, but it's just a stone's throw farther on."

Thanking her, Margaret walked on steadily toward the turn in the lane. Outside of the city the wind blew stronger, and the coloured leaves, bronze, yellow, crimson, lay in a thick carpet over the muddy road. In the west a thin line of gold shone beneath a range of heavy, smoke-coloured clouds. From the trees rain still dripped slowly; and between the road and the line of gold in the west there stretched the desolate autumn landscape.

"Oh, the little things!" her heart cried in despair. "The little things that make happiness!"

Entering the sagging gate of The Laurels, she passed among mounds of sodden leaves which reminded her of graves, and followed the neglected walk between rows of leafless shrubs which must have looked gay in summer. The house was one of many cheap suburban villas (George had bought it, she remembered, at an auction) and she surmised that, until this newest tenant came, it must have stood long unoccupied. The whole place wore, she reflected as she rang the loosened bell, a furtive and insecure appearance.

After the third ring the door was hurriedly opened by a dishevelled maid, who replied that her mistress was not at home.

"Then I shall wait," said Margaret firmly. "Tell your mistress, when she comes in, that Mrs. Fleming is waiting to see her." With a step as resolute as her words, she entered the house and crossed the hall to the living room where a bright coal fire was burning.

The room was empty, but a canary in a gilded cage at the window broke into song as she entered. On a table stood a tray containing the remains of tea; and beside it there was a half-burned cigarette in a bronze Turkish bowl. A book—she saw instantly that it was a volume of the newest plays—lay face downward beneath a pair of eyeglasses, and a rug, which had fallen from the couch, was in a crumpled pile on the floor.

"So she isn't out," Margaret reflected; and turning at a sound, she confronted Rose Morrison.

For an instant it seemed to the older woman that beauty like a lamp blinded her eyes. Then, as the cloud passed, she realized that it was only a blaze, that it was the loveliness of dead leaves when they are burning.

"So you came?" said Rose Morrison, while she gazed at her with the clear and competent eyes of youth. Her voice, though it was low and clear, had no softness; it rang like a bell. Yes, she had youth, she had her flamboyant loveliness; but stronger than youth and loveliness, it seemed to Margaret, surveying her over the reserves and discriminations of the centuries, was the security of one who had never doubted her own judgment. Her power lay where power usually lies in an infallible self-esteem.

"I came to talk it over with you," began Margaret quietly; and though she tried to make her voice insolent, the deep instinct of good manners was greater than her effort. "You tell me that my husband loves you."

The glow, the flame, in Rose Morrison's face made Margaret think again of leaves burning. There was no embarrassment, there was no evasion even, in the girl's look. Candid and unashamed, she appeared to glory in this infatuation, which Margaret regarded as worse than sinful, since it was vulgar.

"Oh, I am so glad that you did," Rose Morrison's sincerity was disarming. "I hated to hurt you. You can never know what it cost me to write that letter; but I felt that I owed it to you to tell you the truth. I believe that we always owe people the truth."

"And did George feel this way also?"

"George?" The flame mounted until it enveloped her. "Oh, he doesn't know. I tried to spare him. He would rather do anything than hurt you, and I thought it would be so much better if we could talk it over and find a solution just between ourselves. I knew if you cared for George, you would feel as I do about sparing him."

About sparing him! As if she had done anything for the last twenty years, Margaret reflected, except think out new and different ways of sparing George!

"I don't know," she answered, as she sat down in obedience to the other's persuasive gesture. "I shall have to think a minute. You see this has been—well, rather—sudden."

"I know, I know." The girl looked as if she did. "May I give you a cup of tea? You must be chilled."

"No, thank you. I am quite comfortable."

"Not even a cigarette? Oh, I wonder what you Victorian women did for a solace when you weren't allowed even a cigarette!"

You Victorian women! In spite of her tragic mood, a smile hovered on Margaret's lips. So that was how this girl classified her. Yet Rose Morrison had fallen in love with a Victorian man.

"Then I may?" said the younger woman with her full-throated laugh. From her bright red hair, which was brushed straight back from her forehead, to her splendid figure, where her hips swung free like a boy's, she was a picture of barbaric beauty. There was a glittering hardness about her, as if she had been washed in some indestructible glaze; but it was the glaze of youth, not of experience. She reminded Margaret of a gilded statue she had seen once in a museum; and the girl's eyes, like the eyes of the statue, were gleaming, remote and impassive—eyes that had never looked on reality. The dress she wore was made of some strange "art cloth," dyed in brilliant hues, fashioned like a kimono, and girdled at the hips with what Margaret mistook for a queer piece of rope. Nothing, not even her crude and confident youth, revealed Rose Morrison to her visitor so completely as this end of rope.

"You are an artist?" she asked, for she was sure of her ground. Only an artist, she decided, could be at once so arrogant with destiny and so ignorant of life.

"How did you know? Has George spoken of me?"

Margaret shook her head. "Oh, I knew without any one's telling me."

"I have a studio in Greenwich Village, but George and I met last summer at Ogunquit. I go there every summer to paint."

"I didn't know." How easily, how possessively, this other woman spoke her husband's name.

"It began at once." To Margaret, with her inherited delicacy and reticence, there was something repellent in this barbaric simplicity of emotion.

"But you must have known that he was married," she observed coldly.

"Yes, I knew, but I could see, of course, that you did not understand him."

"And you think that you do?" If it were not tragic, how amusing it would be to think of her simple George as a problem!

"Oh, I realize that it appears very sudden to you; but in the emotions time counts for so little. Just living with a person for twenty years doesn't enable one to understand him, do you think?"

"I suppose not. But do you really imagine," she asked in what struck her as a singularly impersonal tone for so intimate a question, "that George is complex?"

The flame, which was revealed now as the illumination of some secret happiness, flooded Rose Morrison's features. As she leaned forward, with clasped hands, Margaret noticed that the girl was careless about those feminine details by which George declared so often that he judged a woman. Her hair was carelessly arranged; her finger nails needed attention; and beneath the kimonolike garment, a frayed place showed at the back of her stocking. Even her red morocco slippers were run down at the heels; and it seemed to Margaret that this physical negligence had extended to the girl's habit of thought.

"He is so big, so strong and silent, that it would take an artist to understand him," answered Rose Morrison passionately. Was this really, Margaret wondered, the way George appeared to the romantic vision?

"Yes, he is not a great talker," she admitted. "Perhaps if he talked more, you might find him less difficult." Then before the other could reply, she inquired sharply, "Did George tell you that he was misunderstood?"

"How you misjudge him!" The girl had flown to his defense; and though Margaret had been, as she would have said "a devoted wife," she felt that all this vehemence was wasted. After all, George, with his easy, prosaic temperament, was only made uncomfortable by vehemence. "He never speaks of you except in the most beautiful way," Rose Morrison was insisting. "He realizes perfectly what you have been to him, and he would rather suffer in silence all his life than make you unhappy."

"Then what is all this about?" Though she felt that it was unfair, Margaret could not help putting the question.

Actually there were tears in Rose Morrison's eyes. "I could not bear to see his life ruined," she answered. "I hated to write to you; but how else could I make you realize that you were standing in the way of his happiness? If it were just myself, I could have borne it in silence. I would never have hurt you just for my own sake; but, the subterfuge, the dishonesty, is spoiling his life. He does not say so, but, oh, I see it every day because I love him!" As she bent over, the firelight caught her hair, and it blazed out triumphantly like the red lilies in Margaret's library.

"What is it that you want me to do?" asked Margaret in her dispassionate voice.

"I felt that we owed you the truth," responded the girl, "and I hoped that you would take what I wrote you in the right spirit."

"You are sure that my husband loves you?"

"Shall I show you his letters?" The girl smiled as she answered, and her full red lips reminded Margaret suddenly of raw flesh. Was raw flesh, after all, what men wanted?

"No!" The single word was spoken indignantly.

"I thought perhaps they would make you see what it means," explained Rose Morrison simply. "Oh, I wish I could do this without causing you pain!"

"Pain doesn't matter. I can stand pain."

"Well, I'm glad you aren't resentful. After all, why should we be enemies? George's happiness means more than anything else to us both."

"And you are sure you know best what is for George's happiness?"

"I know that subterfuge and lies and dishonesty cannot bring happiness." Rose Morrison flung out her arms with a superb gesture. "Oh, I realize that it is a big thing, a great thing, I am asking of you. But in your place, if I stood in his way, I should so gladly sacrifice myself for his sake I should give him his freedom. I should acknowledge his right to happiness, to self-development."

A bitter laugh broke from Margaret's lips. What a jumble of sounds these catchwords of the new freedom made! What was this self-development which could develop only through the sacrifice of others? How would these immature theories survive the compromises and concessions, and adjustments which made marriage permanent?

"I cannot feel that our marriage has interfered with his development," she rejoined presently.

"You may be right," Rose Morrison conceded the point. "But to-day he needs new inspiration, new opportunities. He needs the companionship of a modern mind."

"Yes, he has kept young at my cost," thought the older woman. "I have helped by a thousand little sacrifices, by a thousand little cares and worries, to preserve this unnatural youth which is destroying me. I have taken over the burden of details in order that he might be free for the larger interests of life. If he is young to-day, it is at the cost of my youth."

For the second time that day, as she sat there in silence, with her eyes on the blooming face of Rose Morrison, a wave of peace, the peace of one who has been shipwrecked and then swept far off into some serene haven, enveloped her. Something to hold by, that at least she had found. The law of sacrifice, the ideal of self-surrender, which she had learned in the past. For twenty years she had given freely, abundantly, of her best; and to-day she could still prove to him that she was not beggared. She could still give the supreme gift of her happiness. "How he must love you!" she exclaimed. "How he must love you to have hurt me so much for your sake! Nothing but a great love could make him so cruel."

"He does love me," answered Rose Morrison, and her voice was like the song of a bird.

"He must." Margaret's eyes were burning, but no tears came. Her lips felt cracked with the effort she made to keep them from trembling. "I think if he had done this thing with any other motive than a great love, I should hate him until I died." Then she rose and held out her hand. "I shall not stand in your way," she added.

Joy flashed into the girl's eyes. "You are very noble," she answered. "I am sorry if I have hurt you. I am sorry, too, that I called you old-fashioned."

Margaret laughed. "Oh, I am old-fashioned. I am so old-fashioned that I should have died rather than ruin the happiness of another woman."

The joy faded from Rose Morrison's face. "It was not I," she answered. "It was life. We cannot stand in the way of life."

"Life to-day, God yesterday, what does it matter? It is a generation that has grasped everything except personal responsibility." Oh, if one could only keep the humour! A thought struck her, and she asked abruptly, "When your turn comes, if it ever does, will you give way as I do?"

"That will be understood. We shall not hold each other back."

"But you are young. You will tire first. Then he must give way?" Why, in twenty years George would be sixty-five and Rose Morrison still a young woman!

Calm, resolute, uncompromising, Rose Morrison held open the door. "Whatever happens, he would never wish to hold me back."

Then Margaret passed out, the door closed behind her, and she stood breathing deep draughts of the chill, invigorating air. Well, that was over.

The lawn, with its grave-like mounds of leaves, looked as mournful as a cemetery. Beyond the bare shrubs the road glimmered; the wind still blew in gusts, now rising, now dying away with a plaintive sound; in the west the thread of gold had faded to a pale greenish light. Veiled in the monotonous fall of the leaves, it seemed to Margaret that the desolate evening awaited her.

"How he must love her," she thought, not resentfully, but with tragic resignation. "How he must love her to have sacrificed me as he has done."

This idea, she found as she walked on presently in the direction of the street car, had taken complete possession of her point of view. Through its crystal lucidity she was able to attain some sympathy with her husband's suffering. What agony of mind he must have endured in these past months, these months when they had worked so quietly side by side on his book! What days of gnawing remorse! What nights of devastating anguish! How this newer love must have rent his heart asunder before he could stoop to the baseness of such a betrayal! Tears, which had not come for her own pain, stung her eyelids. She knew that he must have fought it hour by hour, day by day, night by night. Conventional as he was, how violent this emotion must have been to have conquered him so completely. "Terrible as an army with banners," she repeated softly, while a pang of jealously shot through her heart. Was there in George, she asked now, profounder depths of feeling than she had ever reached; was there some secret garden of romance where she had never entered? Was George larger, wilder, more adventurous in imagination, than she had dreamed? Had the perfect lover lain hidden in his nature, awaiting only the call of youth?

The street car returned almost empty; and she found restfulness in the monotonous jolting, as if it were swinging her into some world beyond space and time, where mental pain yielded to the sense of physical discomfort. After the agony of mind, the aching of body was strangely soothing.

Here and there, the lights of a house flashed among the trees, and she thought, with an impersonal interest, of the neglected villa, surrounded by mounds of rotting leaves, where that girl waited alone for happiness. Other standards. This was how the newer generation appeared to Margaret—other standards, other morals. Facing life stripped bare of every safeguard, of every restraining tradition, with only the courage of ignorance, of defiant inexperience, to protect one. That girl was not wilfully cruel. She was simply greedy for emotion; she was gasping at the pretense of happiness like all the rest of her undisciplined generation. She was caught by life because she had never learned to give up, to do without, to stand alone.

Her corner had come, and she stepped with a sensation of relief on the wet pavement. The rain was dripping steadily in a monotonous drizzle. While she walked the few blocks to her door, she forced herself by an effort of will to go on, step by step, not to drop down in the street and lose consciousness.

The tinkle of the bell and the sight of Winters's face restored her to her senses.

"Shall I bring you tea, madam?"

"No, it is too late."

Going upstairs to her bedroom, she took off her wet clothes and slipped into her prettiest tea gown, a trailing thing of blue satin and chiffon. While she ran the comb through her damp hair and touched her pale lips with colour, she reflected that even renunciation was easier when one looked desirable. "But it is like painting the cheeks of the dead," she thought, as she turned away from the mirror and walked with a dragging step to the library. Never, she realized suddenly, had she loved George so much as in this hour when she had discovered him only to lose him.

As she entered, George hurried to meet her with an anxious air. "I didn't hear you come in, Margaret. I have been very uneasy. Has anything happened?"

By artificial light he looked younger even than he had seemed in the afternoon; and this boyishness of aspect struck her as strangely pathetic. It was all a part, she told herself, of that fulfilment which had come too late, of that perilous second blooming, not of youth, but of Indian Summer. The longing to spare him, to save him from the suffering she had endured, pervaded her heart.

"Yes, something has happened," she answered gently. "I have been to see Rose Morrison."

As she spoke the name, she turned away from him, and walking with unsteady steps across the room, stood looking down into the fire. The knowledge of all that she must see when she turned, of the humiliation, the anguish, the remorse in his eyes, oppressed her heart with a passion of shame and pity. How could she turn and look on his wounded soul which she had stripped bare?

"Rose Morrison?" he repeated in an expressionless voice. "What do you know of Rose Morrison?"

At his question she turned quickly, and faced not anguish, not humiliation, but emptiness. There was nothing in his look except the blankness of complete surprise. For an instant the shock made her dizzy; and in the midst of the dizziness there flashed through her mind the memory of an evening in her childhood, when she had run bravely into a dark room where they told her an ogre was hiding, and had found that it was empty.

"She wrote to me." Her legs gave way as she replied, and, sinking into the nearest chair, she sat gazing up at him with an immobile face.

A frown gathered his eyebrows, and a purplish flush (he flushed so easily of late) mounted slowly to the smooth line of his hair. She watched the quiver that ran through his under lip (strange that she had not noticed how it had thickened) while his teeth pressed it sharply. Everything about him was acutely vivid to her, as if she were looking at him closely for the first time. She saw the furrow between his eyebrows, the bloodshot stain on one eyeball, the folds of flesh beneath his jutting chin, the crease in his black tie, the place where his shirt gave a little because it had grown too tight—all these insignificant details would exist indelibly in her brain.

"She wrote to you?" His voice sounded strained and husky, and he coughed abruptly as if he were trying to hide his embarrassment. "What the devil! But you don't know her."

"I saw her this afternoon. She told me everything."

"Everything?" Never had she imagined that he could appear so helpless, so lacking in the support of any conventional theory. A hysterical laugh broke from her, a laugh as utterly beyond her control as a spasm, and at the sound he flushed as if she had struck him. While she sat there she realized that she had no part or place in the scene before her. Never could she speak the words that she longed to utter. Never could she make him understand the real self behind the marionette at which he was looking. She longed with all her heart to say: "There were possibilities in me that you never suspected. I also am capable of a great love. In my heart I also am a creature of romance, of adventure. If you had only known it, you might have found in marriage all that you have sought elsewhere . . ." This was what she longed to cry out, but instead she said merely,

"She told me of your love. She asked me to give you up."

"She asked you to give me up?" His mouth fell open as he finished, and while he stared at her he forgot to shut it. It occurred to her that he had lost the power of inventing a phrase, that he could only echo the ones she had spoken. How like a foolish boy he looked as he stood there, in front of the sinking fire, trying to hide behind that hollow echo!

"She said that I stood in your way." The phrase sounded so grotesque as she uttered it that she found herself laughing again. She had not wished to speak these ugly things. Her heart was filled with noble words, with beautiful sentiments, but she could not make her lips pronounce them in spite of all the efforts she made. And she recalled suddenly the princess in the fairy tale who, when she opened her mouth, found that toads and lizards escaped from it instead of pearls and rubies.

At first he did not reply, and it seemed to her that only mechanical force could jerk his jaw back into place and close the eyelids over his vacant blue eyes. When at last he made a sound it was only the empty echo again, "stood in my way!"

"She is desperately in earnest." Justice wrung this admission from her. "She feels that this subterfuge is unfair to us all. Your happiness, she thinks, is what we should consider first, and she is convinced that I should be sacrificed to your future. She was perfectly frank. She suppressed nothing."

For the first time George Fleming uttered an original sound. "O Lord!" he exclaimed devoutly.

"I told her that I did not wish to stand in your way," resumed Margaret, as if the exclamation had not interrupted the flow of her thoughts. "I told her I would give you up."

Suddenly, without warning, he exploded. "What, in the name of heaven, has it got to do with you?" he demanded.

"To do with me?" It was her turn to echo. "But isn't that girl—" she corrected herself painfully—"isn't she living in your house at this minute?"

He cast about helplessly for an argument. When at last he discovered one, he advanced it with a sheepish air, as if he recognized its weakness. "Well, nobody else would take it, would they?"

"She says that you love her."

He shifted his ground nervously. "I can't help what she says, can I?"

"She offered to show me your letters."

"Compliments, nothing more."

"But you must love her, or you couldn't—you wouldn't——" A burning flush scorched Margaret's body.

"I never said that I . . ." Even with her he had always treated the word love as if it were a dangerous explosive, and he avoided touching it now, "that I cared for her in that way."

"Then you do in another way?"

He glanced about like a trapped animal. "I am not a fool, am I? Why, I am old enough to be her father! Besides, I am not the only one anyway. She was living with a man when I met her, and he wasn't the first. She isn't bad, you know. It's a kind of philosophy with her. She calls it self . . ."

"I know." Margaret cut the phrase short. "I have heard what she calls it." So it was all wasted! Nothing that she could do could lift the situation above the level of the commonplace, the merely vulgar. She was defrauded not only of happiness, but even of the opportunity to be generous. Her sacrifice was as futile as that girl's passion. "But she is in love with you now," she said.

"I suppose she is." His tone had grown stubborn. "But how long would it last? In six months she would be leaving me for somebody else. Of course, I won't see her again," he added, with the manner of one who is conceding a reasonable point. Then, after a pause in which she made no response, his stubbornness changed into resentment. "Anybody would think that you are angry because I am not in love with her!" he exclaimed. "Anybody would think—but I don't understand women!"

"Then you will not—you do not mean to leave me?" she asked; and her manner was as impersonal, she was aware, as if Winters had just given her notice.

"Leave you?" He glanced appreciatively round the room. "Where on earth could I go?"

For an instant Margaret looked at him in silence. Then she insisted coldly, "To her, perhaps. She thinks that you are in love with her."

"Well, I suppose I've been a fool," he confessed, after a struggle, "but you are making too much of it."

Yes, she was making too much of it; she realized this more poignantly than he would ever be able to do. She felt like an actress who has endowed a comic part with the gesture of high tragedy. It was not, she saw clearly now, that she had misunderstood George, but that she had overplayed life.

"We met last summer at Ogunquit." She became aware presently that he was still making excuses and explanations about nothing. "You couldn't go about much, you know, and we went swimming and played golf together. I liked her, and I could see that she liked me. When we came away I thought we'd break it off, but somehow we didn't. I saw her several times in New York. Then she came here unexpectedly, and I offered her that old villa nobody would rent. You don't understand such things, Margaret. It hadn't any more to do with you than— than——" He hesitated, fished in the stagnant waters of his mind, and flung out abruptly, "than golf has. It was just a sort of—well, sort of— recreation."

Recreation! The memory of Rose Morrison's extravagant passion smote her sharply. How glorified the incident had appeared in the girl's imagination, how cheap and tawdry it was in reality. A continual compromise with the second best, an inevitable surrender to the average, was this the history of all romantic emotion? For an instant, such is the perversity of fate, it seemed to the wife that she and this strange girl were united by some secret bond which George could not share—by the bond of woman's immemorial disillusionment.

"I wouldn't have had you hurt for worlds, Margaret," said George, bending over her. The old gentle voice, the old possessive and complacent look in his sleepy blue eyes, recalled her wandering senses. "If I could only make you see that there wasn't anything in it."

She gazed up at him wearily. The excitement of discovery, the exaltation, the anguish, had ebbed away, leaving only gray emptiness. She had lost more than love, more than happiness, for she had lost her belief in life.

"If there had been anything in it, I might be able to understand," she replied.

He surveyed her with gloomy severity. "Hang it all! You act as if you wanted me to be in love with her." Then his face cleared as if by magic. "You're tired out, Margaret and you're nervous. There's Winters now. You must try to eat a good dinner."

Anxious, caressing, impatient to have the discussion end and dinner begin, he stooped and lifted her in his arms. For an instant she lay there without moving, and in that instant her gaze passed from his face to the red lilies and the uncurtained window beyond.

Outside the leaves were falling.

Editor's Note

With this story, Miss Glasgow returns to her favorite theme: man's moral inferiority to woman. "The Difference" is her second *Harper's Magazine* story for 1923; this appeared in the June issue.

The magazine version contains many melodramatic dashes and even new paragraphs within the same speech to stress emotional high points. In the revision, Miss Glasgow replaced the dashes with periods and paragraphed the speeches more conventionally.

X

The Artless Age

∽ "I FELT that Richard ought to be thrown with at least one nice girl," remarked Mrs. Askew, with her usual precision. "That is why I invited her." We were seated in my neighbor's pleasant drawing-room in Richmond, with our watchful eyes turned toward the pansies in the window boxes, while we waited for the car to bring Mary Louise Littleton from the station. Outside the trees were in leaf, the scent of lilacs floated in from the garden, and the Easter sunshine sparkled over the singing kettle on the tea table.

"And a nice boy like Richard ought to prefer nice girls," was my comment.

"He does," Richard's mother assented emphatically; and she added in a less positive tone, "I suppose she expected me to meet her; but there wasn't a minute to spare from that committee on eugenics."

She was a small, dark, very thin woman, with thick black eyebrows which curved like bands of fur over her long sallow face. Her features expressed great intelligence and sagacity, and there was a gleam of ironic humor in her smile. She was the kind of woman to whom one resorted in any difficulty, from the failure of the mayonnaise to a sudden funeral in the house. By instinct she was a public benefactor, and by accident she had become a wife and mother, and was now a widow with a comfortable fortune. Though she was president of innumerable societies for social welfare, it was as chairman of the National Committee on Eugenics that she had recently come into prominence. Earnest, untiring, and driven by her passion for improvement as if it were a disease, Richard had once, in a burst of undisciplined humor, described her as a conscientious objector to joy.

"Perhaps she would just as soon see Richard," I suggested mildly.

Never, I felt, had my neighbor's resourcefulness been more evident

than in the adroit ease with which she had designed the destiny of her
son. Richard must marry only a nice girl; she was so determined on this
point that when none of the daughters of her friends appeared to meet
her requirements, she had tracked a distant half-forgotten cousin to her
retreat in the Virginia mountains, and snatched her child from a French
convent. Mary Louise Littleton had spent all her life, with the exception
of her cloistered years, in a village at the foot of the Blue Ridge, where
she cultivated roses for an occupation and played croquet for exercise.
"Just as I did in my girlhood," observed Mrs. Askew complacently.
Though the girl was just twenty, the Victorian aura still surrounded her,
if her mother's letters were to be trusted. The possibility that Mary Louise
might have been drawn from her seclusion by the temptation, not of a
Prince Charming, but of a great catch for a poor girl, had never crossed
the firm but thin mind of Richard's mother.

"Is she pretty?" I inquired after a pause.

It was absurd, of course, to imagine that Richard, a superb blond giant
of two and twenty, with the jutting eyebrows, straight features and
square shoulders of the star performer in a moving picture, would fancy
any girl who was not beautiful.

"Lovely," replied Mrs. Askew, with sparkling enthusiasm. "She is the
living image of a Raphael Madonna—the thinnest of them," she amended
decisively.

This was promising, I admitted. It occurred to me that a Madonna by
Raphael might hold her own even in a collection of futurists, and the
modern young girl impressed me as decidedly futurist in style.

"She will be a wonderful influence for Richard," Mrs. Askew was mur-
muring. When she spoke her son's name her metallic voice softened with
suppressed feeling. "I don't like to say anything against my half-sister's
child," she continued after a minute, "but Geraldine is impossible."

I breathed an inarticulate protest, though at the moment I could think
of no better description of my friend's niece, Geraldine Plummer, than
that elastic epithet. Poor Mrs. Askew, as so often happens in the careers
of great reformers, had encountered an immediate reaction to her public
virtues in her own household. The girl had just flitted through on her
way upstairs, spinning round on the threshold to make an impudent
grimace with her flat little features, which were painted chalk-white,
cherry-red and bluish-black, like the face of a geisha on a Japanese fan.
She was small, dark and lithe, with eyes like sloes, hair of burnished
dusk that was just long enough after bobbing to twist up again, and a
manner of piquant audacity. Wit she had, I suppose, or at least that
effrontery which passes for wit in a conversational desert.

"Perhaps Mary Louise may have a good influence on her too," I remarked satirically as the girl disappeared up the staircase.

Mrs. Askew shook her head.

"She scoffs at the idea of her coming. When I told her that Mary Louise reminded me of a violet, she inquired if I had provided a mossy stone. Yes," she repeated sorrowfully, "I'm afraid Geraldine is impossible."

"It seems so strange, with her bringing up," was all that I could answer.

For, typical as she was of her age, the girl appeared a moral changeling when one considered the advantages she possessed in the matter of heredity. As the niece of a successful philanthropist and the daughter of a distinguished professor of archaeology, she was little less than an enigma in eugenics. For her father I had a curiously impersonal sentiment, as if he were an institution that I respected. Mr. Plummer was an imposing, scholarly looking man of middle age, with clear-cut, slightly impassive features, and the dark hair and eyes of his daughter. He was not only a famous archaeologist but he had been as well the faithful widower of a single wife for twenty years, a personal distinction which excelled scientific achievement in the feminine judgment.

"I hear the car!" exclaimed Mrs. Askew nervously; and lifting the kettle, she poured boiling water on the leaves of China tea in the Wedgwood teapot.

The door opened as if blown by a wind, and they came in together, laughing in the meaningless fashion of youth. First there was Mary Louise, a slim, lovely figure in navy-blue serge, a wide white collar, and a straw hat trimmed with a wreath of daisies and cornflowers; then Geraldine, who had run upstairs to change into a dress of apple green crepe; and after her, Mr. Plummer, walking sedately, with the air of some wise, handsome and very dignified prehistoric bird. In the rear Richard loomed, large, blond, immaculate. Oh, there wasn't any flaw that one could pick in Richard's appearance! He was magnificent, but somehow he did not seem real. Of course, he was just the type to admire Mary Louise. I saw him flash one startled glance at her as Mrs. Askew took off the girl's hat; and then a mask—I assumed it was of admiration—closed over his conventional features.

"Come and have tea, dear," said Mrs. Askew when she had embraced her guest and inquired solicitously after her parents. "Was the trip a very bad one?"

"I didn't mind it at all, thank you," replied Mary Louise in a low sweet voice which was soothing to my ears after Geraldine's shrill fluting. "The wild flowers were so pretty."

She sat down modestly and crossed her slender feet in their gray stockings with black slippers. "A Raphael, indeed!" I exclaimed in a whisper as I tried in vain to catch Richard's glance. Who could resist this perfect oval, those delicate features, that pure pale skin, innocent even of rice powder, and those exquisitely penciled eyebrows over the shining brown of her eyes? So enraptured was I by her loveliness that I had forgotten to notice the way she wore her clothes until I detected the malicious smile on Geraldine's lips. Yes, Mary Louise's dress was old-fashioned; there was no dash, no smartness about her; but what did such artificial things matter? No wonder, I thought, that Mr. Plummer and Richard stared at her as if in a trance.

The next instant I saw that Mary Louise had turned away from her hostess and was gazing up at the two men with an expression of eager deference, as if she were waiting to drink in wisdom from their lips. Yet when they spoke they said nothing remarkable, nothing that either Mrs. Askew or I might not have evolved from the common processes of intelligence. Mr. Plummer asked her if she was fond of flowers; she replied sweetly but firmly that she adored them; and when Richard remarked that his favorite flower was the rose she clasped her hands and exclaimed softly, "How very strange! The rose is my favorite flower too!" This coincidence appeared strange to Richard also, for his trancelike expression deepened, while his fine eyes seemed held by an invisible wire to the features of Mary Louise.

I glanced hastily at Geraldine, and, before the secret I surprised in her face, I looked as quickly away again. For an instant the Japanese mask that she wore, the expression of impish mockery, the chalk-white, the cherry-red and the bluish-black, became as transparent as gauze, and her pitiful little soul, so flamelike in its thinness and its intensity, flickered there in mortal anguish before my eyes. Until that moment of betrayal I had never suspected Geraldine's interest in Richard. Well, it was hopeless, of course; she must have realized that even before the intrusion of Mary Louise, with her mid-Victorian atmosphere and her disastrous beauty. And if Geraldine did not realize the hopelessness of her passion, surely she was using the worst possible tactics. Yet in spite of my disapprobation, I felt sorry for her. Even the flimsiest emotion can scorch if one comes too near the edge of it.

"My favorite flower is the violet," she exclaimed pertly, and the elfin look she cast at Mrs. Askew made me laugh inwardly while I began to sip my tea.

Mrs. Askew, with a lump of sugar poised in the tongs and her keen gray eyes on the teapot, shook her head disapprovingly. While I watched the aunt I discovered the source of her niece's Japanese look. The woman and the girl had the same accentuated eyebrows, the same narrow eyes with slightly slanting corners; and I wondered if the real difference between them was one not so much of inherited tendencies as of acquired characteristics. If Mrs. Askew had been born in an age when the only psychological vice appeared to be self-control, would she also have developed the indomitable egoism of Geraldine?

"I love violets too," Mary Louise acquiesced gently—almost too gently. I had already discerned that she had little conversation, and that the little she had was spoken in the sentimental idiom of another century. While she talked I had a vision of the scenery of Sweet Lavender assuming form and substance about her. When I glanced again at the two men I saw the syllables of an immortal poem shaping themselves on the lips of Mr. Plummer, and I knew as well as if he had told me the thought in the mind of that eminent archaeologist. With Richard I felt that my intuitions were far from infallible. Men of the Victorian age expected— or at least accepted—triteness as the penalty one paid for the combination of beauty and virtue; but would the rising generation conform submissively to the same standard of values? I couldn't answer. I gave up the problem, because I had been born twenty-odd years before Richard, and I had lived long enough to know that nothing passes so completely as an outworn ideal.

But if Mary Louise was conventional, Geraldine was becoming frankly outrageous. Something had happened to offend her, and she reminded me of a golden bee preparing to sting. I suspected that she was engaged in revenging herself on her aunt for the invitation to Mary Louise.

"It was such a pity you couldn't come in time for the dance in the country Saturday night," she said in a tone that was barbed with bitterness. "Richard would have adored taking you, for he couldn't keep up with the rest of us. Nice old thing, he isn't gay enough for the set I go with. But, I tell you, aunty, we went the pace Saturday night!" She went on exultantly in the sprightly slang of her group. "I danced a hole in my best slippers, and whenever my spirits began to flag we slipped out on the porch, and one of the boys gave me a sip of corn whisky out of his flask."

"Geraldine!" exclaimed Mrs. Askew. Her face was scarlet as she turned on her niece, and the heightened color made her look almost artificial. "Horace," she added peremptorily to her brother-in-law, "if you won't take your daughter in hand I am going to begin!"

The threat jerked Mr. Plummer back from what may have been, from the rapt expression of his face, a dream of prehistoric flora. I noticed that he looked younger, and yet at the same time more distinguished, as if a sudden rosy light had fallen over him, or he was presented from a new and becoming angle of vision.

"You will have more than my permission, Edmonia; you will have my gratitude," he rejoined mildly.

"Do you admit, my dear Horace, that you cannot manage your own child?"

He met this squarely.

"I do, my dear Edmonia," he affirmed.

With a gesture which implied that she washed her hands of him, Mrs. Askew concentrated her moral force and her piercing gaze upon her niece.

"Geraldine," she said sternly, "as long as you live in my house I exact that you shall try to behave like a lady."

I hated to look at Geraldine while she was admonished; but her piquant face, brimming over with vivacity, attracted my eyes like a blaze.

"Oh, aunty," she protested, "you wouldn't want me to do anything so horrid as that! It would be as much as my reputation is worth. Why, people might begin to call me a nice girl, and then where would my popularity be?"

Through this scene Mary Louise sat perfectly motionless, with her eyes on her teacup and a soft flush in her cheeks. My admiration for her beauty was increased by my approval of her manners. Surely no period could have produced a more ladylike deportment.

I rose to go, for I felt it was quite time that the gathering broke up; but Mrs. Askew, who fell back on Mary Louise much as an intrepid soldier might sink on a bed of down after defeat, begged me to run in and see the girls dressed for their Easter german.

"Mary Louise is going to wear white chiffon," she said enthusiastically, "and Richard has sent her the loveliest orchids. He is going to take her, you know."

"I'll trade flowers but not dancers with you, Mary Louise," mocked Geraldine. "I've got violets and they suit your style better than mine."

"Oh, I couldn't change," replied Mary Louise gravely, while her cousin made a provoking face at Richard over her father's shoulder.

Geraldine was the only girl I ever saw who could look fascinating in a grimace—perhaps because she was so airy and spritelike; but Richard only stared at her blankly, as he might have done at a naughty child. What he really thought of her I had never discovered, though he teased her unmercifully and she scratched back with all her claws. However, he usually got the better in these fights, and I have seen her fly in tears of rage from the room.

"The trouble with you, Jerry Boy"—that was his nickname for her—he remarked in the most amiable tone, "is that you were not spanked enough. I'd like to start a society for the revival of spanking."

"And I am ready to lend a hand," Mrs. Askew declared heartily.

On this note of not too agreeable hilarity I left with the promise that I should run over again after dinner. But when I reached my home, which was next door, I found that my husband had returned from a business trip a day sooner than I expected him. I did not keep my promise to see Mary Louise dressed for the dance, and not until breakfast was over next morning could I find an opportunity to ask my neighbor if the country visitor had been the belle of the evening. When I went down into my garden to gather flowers for the table, Mrs. Askew was inspecting a border of tulips on the other side of the hedge, and as soon as she caught sight of me she motioned with a beaming smile for me to come nearer.

"You ought to have seen her," she breathed in the rapturous tone of a young lover. "She was a vision."

"And, of course, it was the happiest time of her life?"

"She doesn't say much. I suppose you noticed that she is not a great talker. But she must have enjoyed it. Richard said everyone thought her a beauty."

"And what about Geraldine?" I inquired lightly.

Mrs. Askew raised her eyebrows until their exaggerated arch disappeared under the gray fringe on her forehead.

"Geraldine is worse than ever," she answered. "I don't know what has got into her except that Richard always rubs her the wrong way. I sometimes believe that she hates him."

"What did she wear?" I asked, for I had no wish to betray Geraldine's secret.

"That spangled green thing that makes her look exactly like a fish. I wonder she didn't slip out of Johnny Preston's arms when he danced with her."

"And what did she say about Mary Louise?"

On this point, I confess, I was really curious.

Mrs. Askew laughed shortly.

"She said, 'Of course, everybody wanted to dance with her once.' Isn't that like Geraldine?"

Yes, I recognized the sting. It was like Geraldine. Then Mrs. Askew was summoned to the telephone and I turned back to my flowers.

After this there were dances every night for a week, and I watched the airy figures flit out of the house next door and heard the cars roll back again in the small hours of the morning. I knew that Richard was with Mary Louise a great deal. Mrs. Askew was doing her best to throw them together; and they appeared, from my not too close observation, to need little assistance. I had seen them go out in the evening, and for a spin in his car every afternoon, so I assumed that my friend's matchmaking scheme was progressing according to her design.

Then, quite suddenly one morning, she told me over the garden hedge that Mary Louise had twisted her ankle and could not dance any more until it was well. The news seemed to me so distressing that I was duly compassionate.

"How did it happen?" I asked.

"It was night before last at the dance the Caldwells gave. Richard brought her home just after supper. She said she couldn't stand without pain, but she was very sweet and brave about it. Mary Louise is a wonderful girl, Julia."

"Wonderful," I assented; "but what does the doctor think?"

"She hasn't let me have a doctor; she hates so to give trouble. Of course, I wanted to at once; but she insists her ankle is only strained inside, that it isn't swollen or bruised, and that the doctor would tell her to give it a rest. She won't let me send her meals upstairs, and she limps down to the dining room without a single complaint. Late yesterday she managed to get as far as Richard's car, and they went for a little drive. All the afternoon she lay on the sofa in the drawing-room."

"And does Richard sit with her in the drawing-room?" I asked.

"He was there yesterday; but he is going to play golf with Geraldine this afternoon. She is simply making him go. You know Geraldine's way. I'm afraid she has been teasing him—ragging, she calls it. Isn't their vocabulary dreadful beyond words?"

"I shouldn't mind it so much," I returned, "if I could understand what it means." After a minute I added impulsively, "I'll come over this afternoon and take Mary Louise off your hands for a while before tea."

She accepted my offer with an eagerness that surprised me.

"Oh, do!" There was a yearning sound in her voice which I couldn't explain. "Mary Louise is the sweetest girl in the world," she added, as she turned away; "but I don't find her always easy to talk to." Then, as if her conscience were pricking her for the confession, she tossed back gayly, "Of course, Richard would be perfectly satisfied if only Geraldine would let him alone. They quarreled all through breakfast about his going with her. She'd rather have anybody else in the world, she told him frankly; but he is the only man she knows who has the whole afternoon free. I did all I could for Richard, of course; but I am no match for Geraldine when there is anything that she wants."

No, I had begun to wonder if even Richard—if any man, for that matter—was a match for Geraldine.

When I entered Mrs. Askew's delightful room that afternoon I caught my breath at the vision of loveliness on the Sheraton sofa. Arrayed in chiffon of an angelic blue, Mary Louise sat enthroned in the midst of a twittering group of Geraldine's friends. A beam of sunlight was falling over the Madonna head, and I thought how it would have enraptured any artist whose taste had not been corrupted by the jazz art of the period.

I told her how distressed I had been to hear of her accident, and she lifted her poetic eyes to my face, and responded appealingly that it did not hurt her except when she tried to walk.

"But you've had to give up the dances?"

"Oh, yes, that was a disappointment, of course," she replied, with a strangely stoical philosophy for one so young.

She loved dancing, she added, but people had been so kind to her, and had sent her so many lovely flowers that she had not had time to remember the parties she had missed. Richard, she rippled on like a shallow brook, had sent her the most beautiful roses because the rose was her favorite flower, and Mr. Plummer had brought her a copy of *Sesame and Lilies,* bound in blue and gold. She was so fond of it. They had read a part of it aloud that afternoon.

During this gentle flow of words, the other girls, all lean and supple and slangy, kept up an incessant twitter, like so many noisy sparrows in the spring grass. They behaved to Mary Louise exactly as if she were a distinguished foreigner whose language they did not understand, while she gazed at them, in their startling sports clothes, with a detached and serene wonder. When tea was almost over Richard and Geraldine were heard quarrelling on the front steps, and a minute later they rushed in breathlessly and demanded something to eat in a hurry.

"Golf makes you simply ravenous," declared Geraldine; and then, while they devoured all the sandwiches that were left, the dispute began again more shrilly than ever. Geraldine was in knickerbockers—they had ridden out—and a peaked cap, which made her look like an impudent little boy. Exercise or the warm day had washed the chalky white from her face. Her cheeks were glowing with natural color, and I had never seen her look so attractive. There was a witchery about the girl, I couldn't deny it.

"Beaten me?" jeered Richard. "Why, you were never in sight of me!
Where would you have been, Jerry Boy, without that handicap?"

"Well, at the ninth hole, anyhow——"

It kept up vehemently for some time, the other girls breaking in
hilariously whenever an opening occurred, which was not often. At the
end, Mrs. Askew was obliged to call them to order.

"Mary Louise does not play golf," she said firmly. "This discussion
cannot be amusing to her."

"I beg your pardon. I forgot," replied Richard, polite and amiable;
"but Geraldine is such a monkey."

"Monkey yourself, old thing!" sang out Geraldine pertly.

Richard turned his square shoulders on her with the classic gesture
of the cave man in a moving picture. For the first time since he had
entered the room he looked directly at Mary Louise on her sofa; and I
watched the startled admiration, as of one who is dazzled by too bright a
light, leap again into his eyes. While he gazed at her, she held him
fast without lifting her finger and he had the manner of brushing the
impertinence of Geraldine away as if they had been the light stings of a
bee.

"I am sorry you couldn't go with us," he said. "You would have liked
the ride anyway. I hope you haven't been too awfully bored."

Mary Louise responded, with her adorable smile, "Oh, I wasn't bored
at all. Mr. Plummer gave me the most beautiful Ruskin. I am so fond
of Ruskin."

But Geraldine had been ignored too long.

"What's a Ruskin?" she demanded with sardonic mirth. "Do you
make it with gin?"

As usual she gained her point by her rudeness, for Richard turned at
her indecorous outburst and shook her soundly by the shoulders, while
she got a firm grip on his hair and gave it a vicious tug. Of course, they
were near cousins, but even then——

In the midst of the squabble the callers floated casually to the door, and
I went down the steps into the yard, with Mrs. Askew calling wearily
after me, "Don't you find the younger generation very exhausting?"

Over the garden hedge, several days afterward, I replied to her question.

"How they keep it up is a mystery."

"Could we ever have been like that?" she asked wonderingly. There
was a frown between her arched eyebrows.

"No; but things were different then."

"Were we like Mary Louise?" she persisted, lowering her voice.

"I think so, don't you? Though some of us—you, for instance—were more lively. It seems like a different century, and of course it is——"

She interrupted me impatiently.

"I am going to tell you something, Julia, that I don't wish you to repeat even to your husband." She paused long enough for me to absorb this admonition, and then continued relentlessly, "I have discovered that Mary Louise is sly."

"Sly?" I jumped, not with surprise but with amusement. "Well, we were, too, weren't we?"

She shook her head.

"If we were, it is so long ago that I have forgotten."

"Are you sure that you can't be mistaken about her?"

"I am perfectly positive."

"Well, how did you discover it?"

Our heads were close together, over the hedge, like two gossips on the comic page of a Sunday newspaper.

"Quite by accident. I've found out that she did not really hurt her ankle. She pretended it all the time."

I was unprepared, I confess, for this startling disclosure.

"Do you mean she never even twisted it?"

"Not a twist, not a twinge. She forgot all about it yesterday and ran upstairs as easily as Geraldine. I caught her at the top of the steps just five minutes after Horace and Richard had almost carried her down. 'Why, Mary Louise!' I exclaimed, and she stood there, blushing like a peony, and murmured 'Oh, I forgot!' There isn't any use trying to evade the truth, Julia. Mary Louise is sly."

"But what was her purpose?"

"Purpose? Why, she didn't have a bit of attention after that first german. Geraldine let that out to me, and I must say for her that she was glad enough of the opportunity. The men were all wild about Mary Louise when they first saw her, she said. They all danced with her once, but nobody asked her a second time, and at her last dance she would have been almost a wallflower if she hadn't decided to sprain her ankle."

I pondered this for a minute.

"Well, you can't blame her. No girl wants to be a wallflower if she can help it. It's exactly, you know, the sort of thing we should have done in her place. She is using the only weapons she knows by instinct—those of another day. I suppose," I added compassionately, "it is all on Richard's account."

"Yes, I believe she is sincerely interested in Richard." My friend paused to sigh softly. "I wish I hadn't brought her here, but I did it for the best. She is a good girl as girls go in these days, though she hasn't been a success. Do you know, I've discovered something else too. Beauty isn't the power it used to be in our generation."

"I thought that never changed."

"I used to think so, but I've found out that I was mistaken. Everything changes. It used to be enough for a man just to sit still and look at a beautiful face; but today, as Richard says, there is so much else to do. Nobody wants to sit still, even with beauty, any longer. The age has a jazz temperament. I suppose that is the trouble. If young people stare at a picture, Richard says, it must be a moving one or they get restless. They are so easily bored, you know. That is why the really popular girl today is not the beauty like Mary Louise, but the comedienne like Geraldine. They are the same age, yet they are symbols of two different periods."

"And which do you dislike most?"

Mrs. Askew looked at me with an enigmatic expression.

"Both," she rejoined concisely. Stooping down, she snipped the head from a withered tulip. Then she straightened herself with a sigh. "It isn't the time; it isn't even the war," she said, with the philosophy of complete exhaustion; "it is youth. Don't talk to me of the designing selfishness of age! Why, nothing that has ever inhabited this planet is as designing or as selfish as youth. Our youth had illusions, and the youth of today has lost them; that is the only difference. Mary Louise and Geraldine are both fighting for what they want, and both are fighting unscrupulously whenever it serves their purpose. I can see no difference between the youth of yesterday and the youth of today except that we were ignorant, and the things that Geraldine knows"—she finished with a wail—"make me shudder!"

Her wail was answered by a shrill cry from the house.

"Aunt Edmonia! Aunt Edmonia, I am waiting for you!"

"There!" Mrs. Askew waved her garden shears in the direction of the sound. "Waiting is the one thing they have never wanted to do!" She had moved a step away, when she looked back and said dryly, "I am having a party, you know, for Mary Louise tomorrow evening, and nothing will satisfy Geraldine except that the guests shall be made to come in fancy dress. She simply adores making herself up like an actress."

"I suppose it is because she is such a good mimic," I answered; "but what will Mary Louise wear?"

"The robes of an angel, with gauze wings and a harp."

My friend lingered to perceive the effect of her reply.

"Well, she will look the part; and Geraldine?" I added as an after-thought.

A laugh broke from Mrs. Askew's prim lips.

"She is getting herself up as a devil. Of course, it is to spite Mary Louise; but she has been working for days over her costume of red satin. You must not fail me, remember. My strength has almost given out."

"Oh, I'll be there!" I tossed back gayly. "And I dare say Richard will appear as the squire of dames."

If my patience with the rising generation was greater than Mrs. Askew's, it was probably, I reflected, due to the fact that my experience was more limited and less evenly sustained. To live in the house with modern love must have been trying to a mind that was firmly fixed on one's duty to the race.

It was late the next evening when I went over to my neighbor's, and the two long drawing-rooms were already filled with dancers, who whirled before my gaze like the changing colors in a kaleidoscope. As I entered, Mary Louise drifted toward me, attired in flowing robes of white chiffon, with wings at her shoulders and a harp of gilded paste-board in her hands. She was dancing tonight for the first time since her accident, and I noticed that she moved with a prim, old-fashioned step, and kept her partner, a bold blond youth, at arm's length. From a distance, at least, she presented the appearance of a reigning belle, though I surmised that this was due as much to the diligent attention of Richard and Mr. Plummer as to her own unaided charms. She was by far the loveliest girl in the rooms; but I overheard the bold blond youth complain when his dance was over that you couldn't get a thrill out of toddling with an Easter card.

Geraldine, in red satin tights, which gave the impression of extending from her slim feet to her sleek dark head, was, as usual, the life of the party. Though she was not the beauty that Mary Louise was, she possessed a fascination which made Mary Louise appear almost negative. Perhaps Mrs. Askew was right, and beauty alone, beauty "icily regular, splendidly null," was no longer the thing that men ran after.

As Geraldine darted like a slender flame among the dancers, my gaze followed her in spite of the disapprobation she aroused. Eager youths, with the blank faces and the glossy hair of the fashion, crowded about her. Swift, gay, defiant, a scarlet embodiment of magic, she ignored Richard completely.

They had quarreled again, I inferred, with greater bitterness; for when he asked her for a dance, I heard her reply with airy insolence, "You'd better ask Mary Louise. She needs you more than I do."

"She doesn't need me at all," he retorted, uncompromisingly loyal.

Geraldine tossed her head in its peaked hood.

"Then do you imagine that I do?"

"I was thinking of my pleasure, not of your necessity," he returned with distant gallantry.

But she flitted off with an elfin laugh.

"Sorry, old thing, but my pleasure comes first tonight. There are no substitutes in this war!"

He glowered after her for a moment; then, turning quickly on his heel, he went back to Mary Louise. Richard could stand as little as Geraldine not getting the thing that he wanted. He did not speak to her again, I observed, until the guests were leaving, and she tripped up to him saucily in the deserted library and spun round on one scarlet toe. I was standing in the doorway, waiting to say good night to Mrs. Askew, and I watched the little comedy unobserved by the actors.

"He wants to be an angel," she piped in a shrill treble, "and with the angels stand!"

For an instant he stood regarding her with a stormy expression. Then, picking her up as easily as if she had been a doll, he strode across the room, still holding her in his arms, and placed her on top of the high rosewood bookcase in one corner.

"There you stay till you mend your manners," he said.

While she scolded fiercely from her perch, he turned away to meet Mary Louise, who was coming in from the hall.

"Why, what in the world are you doing in here all by yourself?" she inquired, with her sweetest expression.

"Disciplining a bad child," he replied, smiling tenderly down into her eyes.

Well, I was thankful that one person knew how to get the better of Geraldine, I reflected, as I went home.

For two days after this I did not see Mrs. Askew; and then, on the third morning, just as I had finished breakfast, there came an imperative summons.

"Come over at once, Julia," said a trembling voice over the telephone. "Something dreadful has happened."

She did not wait for a response, and the impression I received, as she cut me off, was that my philosophic friend had burst into tears. The thought of her mysterious distress was too much for me. While my maids stared after me in astonishment, I ran breathlessly down the steps and across the strip of lawn to the house next door. When I rushed into my friend's room I found her sitting up in bed, with a handkerchief to her eyes and a lace cap awry over her long, sallow face.

As I appeared she removed the handkerchief and gasped weakly, "Oh, Julia, he has married her!"

"Married her?" I sat down panting beside the bed. "Do you mean Mary Louise?"

"Worse than that!" She waved the handkerchief feebly before her. "I mean Geraldine. Oh, Richard! Oh, my son!" she concluded in the Shakesperean manner.

For a moment I could do nothing but stare at her.

Then I asked bluntly, "Did you never suspect it?"

"Suspect it? Of course, I knew she had her eye on him. She had it on every man. That was the reason I asked Mary Louise to visit us. But I had such confidence in Richard. I believed he had too much sense, too much feeling of responsibility to the race," she added, lifting her head in that fantastic cap as if she were addressing the committee on eugenics. "It wasn't more than a week ago that he told me Geraldine would ruin any man who married her."

"Well, they have said that before and then gone and married them," I reminded her cynically. "When did they do it?"

"They went to Washington yesterday. Geraldine pretended she was spending the night with Lizzie Brandon." A sob broke from her lips. "If it had only been Mary Louise! At least you know where you are with her."

"That, I fancy, is exactly what he objected to. He liked the feeling of being at sea. Some men do."

"Oh, he told me he knew Mary Louise would make a perfect wife, but he said perfection wasn't amusing. Imagine marrying for the sake of being amused!"

"And what does he say now—about Geraldine, I mean? Has he told you why he did it so suddenly?"

"He has given no reason. He doesn't seem to have any. All he says is that it was time somebody took her in hand. He added, too, that he liked her because she was unafraid."

"Unafraid?" I laughed in spite of my effort to appear sympathetic. "It seems that her single virtue captured him, after all."

Mrs. Askew sank back wearily among her pillows.

"I shan't get up today," she said. "I don't want them to come near me.

But I wish on your way out you would speak to Geraldine and tell me what she says. Richard has gone down to see about tickets, and she is in her room packing. They are going away on the noon train."

"And what about Mary Louise?" I inquired, for it seemed to me that she was the one who needed attention.

"It is hard on her, of course, because she must have known why I asked her here; but I must say she has shown a great deal of pride. Horace and I both think that she is a girl of much character, and that she would be good for Geraldine if they could be thrown together. I wish it could be arranged." A pucker of anxiety appeared suddenly in my friend's forehead, and I knew that the ruling principle of her nature was already beginning to recover from its defeat. "But Mary Louise," she continued, "lives in such an out-of-the-way place."

I comforted her as best I could in the circumstances; and then, with the promise that I would return as soon as I had finished my housekeeping for the day, I left her room and crossed the hall to Geraldine's open door. Here I found three large trunks standing in the center of the floor, and around them the bed, the couch and every available chair held a litter of dresses. In the midst of the confusion Geraldine was moving about in a composed and capable manner. She was wearing a kimono of rose-colored crepe, her short dark hair hung in a cloud round her head, and her eyes were shining with happiness. She had the air of a woman who has attained the ambition of her life, the end for which she has suffered and striven, and who is satisfied with the reward. It appeared to me while I watched her that the child had grown up in a day. Smiling, serene, competent, she was wearing the crown of victory, and it rested like a rosy wreath on her brow.

"Well, Geraldine," I said as I kissed her, "you have certainly surprised us."

She made an ecstatic little face, like a child over a sugarplum.

"But I thought you knew all along."

"Oh, I saw there was something between you, but I thought you were going the wrong way to get what you wanted."

With a laugh she shook her head over the dress she was folding.

"How else on earth could I ever have got it?" she asked.

"Then you did it deliberately for a purpose?"

She looked at me with a flicker of Mrs. Askew's ironic humor.

"You don't imagine that I went to all that trouble just for fun, do you?" she demanded. Throwing herself back on a pile of clothes, she clasped her hands above her pretty head and surveyed me meditatively, as if I were an inanimate object which helped her to think clearly. "Do you really think any of us would be like that if we weren't obliged to?" she inquired at last.

"Obliged to? But nobody makes you. Nobody likes that kind of behavior. Richard simply detested it."

She smiled with inscrutable wisdom.

"Oh, he did, did he? Then why did he marry me instead of Mary Louise? Of course, he thinks he doesn't like it," she pursued slowly; "but until he began thinking he didn't like me, he had never thought of me at all, not for a single minute in his life. I had always liked Richard, you know," she confessed; "but he had never even looked at me until I made myself so conspicuous that he couldn't avoid it. You can't make a man fall in love with you," she explained sagely, "until you have first arrested his attention, and the only way to be absolutely sure of arresting his attention is by a shock. In this age," she concluded, while I stared at her incredulously, "if you aren't conspicuous, you might just as well lie down and die, or become another Mary Louise."

"Well, there are worse fates than that," I rejoined placidly.

For a few minutes she gazed at herself in the mirror as if she were alone. Then, without acknowledging my comment, she took up the tangled thread of her discourse.

"Beauty used to be enough," she said, "but it isn't any longer. Mary Louise is a real movie star as far as looks go; but what good did that do her when it came to being popular at a dance? If a girl wants to be a perfect lady, nobody is trying to prevent her; but she has got to realize just what she loses—and that is all the fun. Nobody is hunting timid bunnies these days. You've got to be bold game if you want any attention. Why, there's scarcely one of us who doesn't hate the smell of cigarettes on her fingers, and who wouldn't rather have the taste of rose water in her mouth any day than whisky. We get so tired of it sometimes that we'd like to have a vacation in an old ladies' home as a change; but it's as much as our popularity is worth to drop out of the rush." She yawned, stretched her arms, and added in a burst of confidence: "Do you think if the men really wanted the nice girl like Mary Louise; if they would rush her at a dance or keep her busy at the telephone, that the rest of us, every last one, wouldn't begin wearing dresses to our ankles and shying off when we toddled? But they don't want her, or they have a precious way of showing it." For a moment after this revelation she was silent; then she said abruptly, "Of course, with the older generation it is different. Now there is papa——"

But she was wandering from the point, I thought, and I recalled her.

"Then it all comes back to the men, my dear?"

"Doesn't everything come back to the men?" she gibed mockingly. "Why, as long as swooning brought every man in sight to our sides, didn't swooning come to us as naturally as the one-step? Then just as soon as swooning ceased to do the trick, and the men left us to old ladies with *sal volatile,* we began to sit up and take notice. The fashion changes, that is all," she said with startling seriousness, "and I hope it will change to something else before I have a daughter." Sitting erect, she shook her finger warningly in my face. "If ever I have a daughter," she declared, "I am going to spank her till it hurts."

I laughed and rose to my feet. After all, did the eternal feminine ever vary?

"And what will you do now?" I asked.

Her figure drooped again, and she fell back with a gesture of exhaustion that reminded me of Mrs. Askew.

"I'd like to get a little rest," she answered, "for the Lord knows I need it! It takes work to be a success these days. It takes what Mammy Rhody calls elbow grease to put it over, and I did put it over," she boasted, with a sly wink at the mirror.

"If it is any satisfaction to you, and I hope it is," I echoed her lively slang, "you put it over completely."

She sighed, but it was the sigh of a weary conqueror.

"Then I hope marriage will be a little less strenuous," she said. "I think I'll try to take things easily until I see some other perfect lady beginning to make golliwog eyes at Richard."

"That's not fair to Marry Louise," I reprimanded her, while I laughed. "After all, it is hard on Mary Louise."

"Well, she got what was coming to her," Geraldine retorted, with imperturbable sagacity. "With the older generation her methods are infallible; and, of course, all the time it was papa she was after."

"Papa?"

The faithful widower of a single wife for twenty years toppled with a crash from his pedestal. Another idol was shattered.

"Why, it didn't take young eyes to see that," remarked Geraldine sweetly.

"But he is old enough to be her father!" I cried in horror. "Would she marry him?"

Geraldine shrugged her shoulders.

"Well, he's the only archaeologist she knows, isn't he? And I warned Aunt Edmonia in the beginning that she would have to provide a mossy stone."

Editor's Note

Ellen Glasgow's third story published in 1923 appeared in the *Saturday Evening Post* for August 25. It is the most frivolous of all her stories, anticipating the domestic comedies of the late twenties. Here she is making a determined effort to laugh at the follies of courtship. The story has a bitter edge, however, for all of its witty comment on young people. Justice does not triumph in Miss Glasgow's world.

This makes a painful story, because Miss Glasgow is trying to bend her vein of iron, but it was no longer malleable. *Barren Ground* two years later shows that her spirit was still firmly rooted in the timeless verities, not in passing fashions.

XI

Jordan's End

AT THE fork of the road there was the dead tree where buzzards were roosting, and through its boughs I saw the last flare of the sunset. On either side the November woods were flung in broken masses against the sky. When I stopped they appeared to move closer and surround me with vague, glimmering shapes. It seemed to me that I had been driving for hours; yet the ancient negro who brought the message had told me to follow the Old Stage Road till I came to Buzzard's Tree at the fork. "F'om dar on hit's moughty nigh ter Marse Jur'dn's place," the old man had assured me, adding tremulously, "en young Miss she sez you mus' come jes' ez quick ez you kin." I was young then (that was more than thirty years ago), and I was just beginning the practice of medicine in one of the more remote counties of Virginia.

My mare stopped, and leaning out, I gazed down each winding road, where it branched off, under half bared boughs, into the autumnal haze of the distance. In a little while the red would fade from the sky, and the chill night would find me still hesitating between those dubious ways which seemed to stretch into an immense solitude. While I waited uncertainly there was a stir in the boughs overhead, and a buzzard's feather floated down and settled slowly on the robe over my knees. In the effort to drive off depression, I laughed aloud and addressed my mare in a jocular tone:

"We'll choose the most God-forsaken of the two, and see where it leads us."

To my surprise the words brought an answer from the trees at my back. "If you're goin' to Isham's store, keep on the Old Stage Road," piped a voice from the underbrush.

Turning quickly, I saw the dwarfed figure of a very old man, with a hunched back, who was dragging a load of pine knots out of the woods.

Though he was so stooped that his head reached scarcely higher than my wheel, he appeared to possess unusual vigour for one of his age and infirmities. He was dressed in a rough overcoat of some wood brown shade, beneath which I could see his overalls of blue jeans. Under a thatch of grizzled hair his shrewd little eyes twinkled cunningly, and his bristly chin jutted so far forward that it barely escaped the descending curve of his nose. I remember thinking that he could not be far from a hundred; his skin was so wrinkled and weather-beaten that, at a distance, I had mistaken him for a negro.

I bowed politely. "Thank you, but I am going to Jordan's End," I replied.

He cackled softly. "Then you take the bad road. Thar's Jur'dn's turn-out." He pointed to the sunken trail, deep in mud, on the right. "An' if you ain't objectin' to a little comp'ny, I'd be obleeged if you'd give me a lift. I'm bound thar on my own o' count, an' it's a long ways to tote these here lightwood knots."

While I drew back my robe and made room for him, I watched him heave the load of resinous pine into the buggy, and then scramble with agility to his place at my side.

"My name is Peterkin," he remarked by way of introduction. "They call me Father Peterkin along o' the gran'child'en." He was a garrulous soul, I suspected, and would not be averse to imparting the information I wanted.

"There's not much travel this way," I began, as we turned out of the cleared space into the deep tunnel of the trees. Immediately the twilight enveloped us, though now and then the dusky glow in the sky was still visible. The air was sharp with the tang of autumn; with the effluvium of rotting leaves, the drift of wood smoke, the ripe flavour of crushed apples.

"Thar's nary a stranger, thoughten he was a doctor, been to Jur'dn's End as fur back as I kin recollect. Ain't you the new doctor?"

"Yes, I am the doctor." I glanced down at the gnomelike shape in the wood brown overcoat. "Is it much farther?"

"Naw, suh, we're all but thar jest as soon as we come out of Whitten woods."

"If the road is so little travelled, how do you happen to be going there?"

Without turning his head, the old man wagged his crescent shaped profile. "Oh, I live on the place. My son Tony works a slice of the farm on shares, and I manage to lend a hand at the harvest or corn shuckin', and, now-and-agen, with the cider. The old gentleman used to run the place that away afore he went deranged, an' now that the young one is laid up, thar ain't nobody to look arter the farm but Miss Judith. Them old ladies don't count. Thar's three of 'em, but they're all addle-brained an' look as if the buzzards had picked 'em. I reckon that comes from bein' shut up with crazy folks in that thar old tumbledown house. The roof ain't been patched fur so long that the shingles have most rotted away, an' thar's times, Tony says, when you kin skearcely hear yo' years fur the rumpus the wrens an' rats are makin' overhead."

"What is the trouble with them—the Jordans, I mean?"

"Jest run to seed, suh, I reckon."

"Is there no man of the family left?"

For a minute Father Peterkin made no reply. Then he shifted the bundle of pine knots, and responded warily. "Young Alan, he's still livin' on the old place, but I hear he's been took now, an' is goin' the way of all the rest of 'em. 'Tis a hard trial for Miss Judith, po' young thing, an' with a boy nine year old that's the very spit an' image of his pa. Wall, wall, I kin recollect away back yonder when old Mr. Timothy Jur'dn was the proudest man anywhar aroun' in these parts; but arter the War things sorter begun to go down hill with him, and he was obleeged to draw in his horns."

"Is he still living?"

The old man shook his head. "Mebbe he is, an' mebbe he ain't. Nobody knows but the Jur'dn's, an' they ain't tellin' fur the axin'."

"I suppose it was this Miss Judith who sent for me?"

" 'Twould most likely be she, suh. She was one of the Yardlys that lived over yonder at Yardly's Field; an' when young Mr. Alan begun to take notice of her, 'twas the first time sence way back that one of the Jur'dn's had gone courtin' outside the family. That's the reason the blood went bad like it did, I reckon. Thar's a sayin' down aroun' here that Jur'dn an' Jur'dn won't mix." The name was invariably called Jurdin by all classes; but I had already discovered that names are rarely pronounced as they are spelled in Virginia.

"Have they been married long?"

"Ten year or so, suh. I remember as well as if 'twas yestiddy the day young Alan brought her home as a bride, an' thar warn't a soul besides the three daft old ladies to welcome her. They drove over in my son Tony's old buggy, though 'twas spick an' span then. I was goin' to the house on an arrant, an' I was standin' right down thar at the ice pond when they come by. She hadn't been much in these parts, an' none of us had ever seed her afore. When she looked up at young Alan her face was pink all over and her eyes war shinin' bright as the moon. Then the front do' opened an' them old ladies, as black as crows, flocked out on the po'ch. Thar never was anybody as peart-lookin' as Miss Judith was when she come here; but soon arterwards she begun to peak an' pine, though she never lost her sperits an' went mopin' roun' like all the other women folks at Jur'dn's End. They married sudden, an' folks do say she didn't know nothin' about the family, an' young Alan didn't know much mo' than she did. The old ladies had kep' the secret away from him, sorter believin' that what you don't know cyarn' hurt you. Anyways they never let it leak out tell arter his chile was born. Thar ain't never been but that one, an' old Aunt Jerusly declars he was born with a caul over his face, so mebbe things will be all right fur him in the long run."

"But who are the old ladies? Are their husbands living?"

When Father Peterkin answered the question he had dropped his voice to a hoarse murmur. "Deranged. All gone deranged," he replied.

I shivered, for a chill depression seemed to emanate from the November woods. As we drove on, I remembered grim tales of enchanted forests filled with evil faces and whispering voices. The scents of wood earth and rotting leaves invaded my brain like a magic spell. On either side the forest was as still as death. Not a leaf quivered, not a bird moved, not a small wild creature stirred in the underbrush. Only the glossy leaves and the scarlet berries of the holly appeared alive amid the bare interlacing branches of the trees. I began to long for an autumn clearing and the red light of the afterglow.

"Are they living or dead?" I asked presently.

"I've hearn strange tattle," answered the old man nervously, "but nobody kin tell. Folks do say as young Alan's pa is shut up in a padded place, and that his gran'pa died thar arter thirty years. His uncles went crazy too, an' the daftness is beginnin' to crop out in the women. Up tell now it has been mostly the men. One time I remember old Mr. Peter Jur'dn tryin' to burn down the place in the dead of the night. Thar's the end of the wood, suh. If you'll jest let me down here, I'll be gittin' along home across the old-field, an' thanky too."

At last the woods ended abruptly on the edge of an abandoned field which was thickly sown with scrub pine and broomsedge. The glow in the sky had faded now to a thin yellow-green, and a melancholy twilight pervaded the landscape. In this twilight I looked over the few sheep huddled together on the ragged lawn, and saw the old brick house crumbling beneath its rank growth of ivy. As I drew nearer I had the feeling that the surrounding desolation brooded there like some sinister influence.

Forlorn as it appeared at this first approach, I surmised that Jordan's

End must have possessed once charm as well as distinction. The proportions of the Georgian front were impressive, and there was beauty of design in the quaint doorway, and in the steps of rounded stone which were brocaded now with a pattern of emerald moss. But the whole place was badly in need of repair. Looking up, as I stopped, I saw that the eaves were falling away, that crumbled shutters were sagging from loosened hinges, that odd scraps of hemp sacking or oil cloth were stuffed into windows where panes were missing. When I stepped on the floor of the porch, I felt the rotting boards give way under my feet.

After thundering vainly on the door, I descended the steps, and followed the beaten path that led round the west wing of the house. When I had passed an old boxwood tree at the corner, I saw a woman and a boy of nine years or so come out of a shed, which I took to be the smokehouse, and begin to gather chips from the woodpile. The woman carried a basket made of splits on her arm, and while she stooped to fill this, she talked to the child in a soft musical voice. Then, at a sound that I made, she put the basket aside, and rising to her feet, faced me in the pallid light from the sky. Her head was thrown back, and over her dress of some dark calico, a tattered gray shawl clung to her figure. That was thirty years ago; I am not young any longer; I have been in many countries since then, and looked on many women; but her face, with that wan light on it, is the last one I shall forget in my life. Beauty! Why, that woman will be beautiful when she is a skeleton, was the thought that flashed into my mind.

She was very tall, and so thin that her flesh seemed faintly luminous, as if an inward light pierced the transparent substance. It was the beauty, not of earth, but of triumphant spirit. Perfection, I suppose, is the rarest thing we achieve in this world of incessant compromise with inferior forms; yet the woman who stood there in that ruined place appeared to me to have stepped straight out of legend or allegory. The contour of her face was Italian in its pure oval; her hair swept in wings of dusk above her clear forehead; and, from the faintly shadowed hollows beneath her brows, the eyes that looked at me were purple-black, like dark pansies.

"I had given you up," she began in a low voice, as if she were afraid of being overheard. "You are the doctor?"

"Yes, I am the doctor. I took the wrong road and lost my way. Are you Mrs. Jordan?"

She bowed her head. "Mrs. Alan Jordan. There are three Mrs. Jordans besides myself. My husband's grandmother and the wives of his two uncles."

"And it is your husband who is ill?"

"My husband, yes. I wrote a few days ago to Doctor Carstairs." (Thirty years ago Carstairs, of Baltimore, was the leading alienist in the country.) "He is coming to-morrow morning; but last night my husband was so restless that I sent for you to-day." Her rich voice, vibrating with suppressed feeling, made me think of stained glass windows and low organ music.

"Before we go in," I asked, "will you tell me as much as you can?"

Instead of replying to my request, she turned and laid her hand on the boy's shoulder. "Take the chips to Aunt Agatha, Benjamin," she said, "and tell her that the doctor has come."

While the child picked up the basket and ran up the sunken steps to the door, she watched him with breathless anxiety. Not until he had disappeared into the hall did she lift her eyes to my face again. Then, without answering my question, she murmured, with a sigh which was like the voice of that autumn evening, "We were once happy here." She was trying, I realized, to steel her heart against the despair that threatened it.

My gaze swept the obscure horizon, and returned to the mouldering woodpile where we were standing. The yellow-green had faded from the sky, and the only light came from the house where a few scattered lamps were burning. Through the open door I could see the hall, as bare as if the house were empty, and the spiral staircase which crawled to the upper story. A fine old place once, but repulsive now in its abject decay, like some young blood of former days who has grown senile.

"Have you managed to wring a living out of the land?" I asked, because I could think of no words that were less compassionate.

"At first a poor one," she answered slowly. "We worked hard, harder than any negro in the fields, to keep things together, but we were happy. Then three years ago this illness came, and after that everything went against us. In the beginning it was simply brooding, a kind of melancholy, and we tried to ward it off by pretending that it was not real, that we imagined it. Only of late, when it became so much worse, have we admitted the truth, have we faced the reality——"

This passionate murmur, which had almost the effect of a chant rising out of the loneliness, was addressed, not to me, but to some abstract and implacable power. While she uttered it her composure was like the tranquillity of the dead. She did not lift her hand to hold her shawl, which was slipping unnoticed from her shoulders, and her eyes, so like dark flowers in their softness, did not leave my face.

"If you will tell me all, perhaps I may be able to help you," I said.

"But you know our story," she responded. "You must have heard it."

"Then it is true? Heredity, intermarriage, insanity?"

She did not wince at the bluntness of my speech. "My husband's grandfather is in an asylum, still living after almost thirty years. His father—my husband's, I mean—died there a few years ago. Two of his uncles are there. When it began I don't know, or how far back it reaches. We have never talked of it. We have tried always to forget it—— Even now I cannot put the thing into words—— My husband's mother died of a broken heart, but the grandmother and the two others are still living. You will see them when you go into the house. They are old women now, and they feel nothing."

"And there have been other cases?"

"I do not know. Are not four enough?"

"Do you know if it has assumed always the same form?" I was trying to be as brief as I could.

She flinched, and I saw that her unnatural calm was shaken at last. "The same, I believe. In the beginning there is melancholy, moping, Grandmother calls it, and then——" She flung out her arms with a despairing gesture, and I was reminded again of some tragic figure of legend.

"I know, I know," I was young, and in spite of my pride, my voice trembled. "Has there been in any case partial recovery, recurring at intervals?"

"In his grandfather's case, yes. In the others none. With them it has been hopeless from the beginning."

"And Carstairs is coming?"

"In the morning. I should have waited, but last night——" Her voice broke, and she drew the tattered shawl about her with a shiver. "Last night something happened. Something happened," she repeated, and could not go on. Then, collecting her strength with an effort which made her tremble like a blade of grass in the wind, she continued more quietly, "To-day he has been better. For the first time he has slept, and I have been able to leave him. Two of the hands from the fields are in the room." Her tone changed suddenly, and a note of energy passed into it. Some obscure resolution brought a tinge of colour to her pale cheek. "I must know," she added, "if this is as hopeless as all the others."

I took a step toward the house. "Carstairs's opinion is worth as much as that of any man living," I answered.

"But will he tell me the truth?"

I shook my head. "He will tell you what he thinks. No man's judgment is infallible."

Turning away from me, she moved with an energetic step to the house.

As I followed her into the hall the threshold creaked under my tread, and I was visited by an apprehension, or, if you prefer, by a superstitious dread of the floor above. Oh, I got over that kind of thing before I was many years older; though in the end I gave up medicine, you know, and turned to literature as a safer outlet for a suppressed imagination.

But the dread was there at that moment, and it was not lessened by the glimpse I caught, at the foot of the spiral staircase, of a scantily furnished room, where three lean black-robed figures, as impassive as the Fates, were grouped in front of a wood fire. They were doing something with their hands. Knitting, crocheting, or plaiting straw?

At the head of the stairs the woman stopped and looked back at me. The light from the kerosene lamp on the wall fell over her, and I was struck afresh not only by the alien splendour of her beauty, but even more by the look of consecration, of impassioned fidelity that illumined her face.

"He is very strong," she said in a whisper. "Until this trouble came on him he had never had a day's illness in his life. We hoped that hard work, not having time to brood, might save us; but it has only brought the thing we feared sooner."

There was a question in her eyes, and I responded in the same subdued tone. "His health, you say, is good?" What else was there for me to ask when I understood everything?

A shudder ran through her frame. "We used to think that a blessing, but now——" She broke off and then added in a lifeless voice, "We keep two field hands in the room day and night, lest one should forget to watch the fire, or fall asleep."

A sound came from a room at the end of the hall, and, without finishing her sentence, she moved swiftly toward the closed door. The apprehension, the dread, or whatever you choose to call it, was so strong upon me, that I was seized by an impulse to turn and retreat down the spiral staircase. Yes, I know why some men turn cowards in battle.

"I have come back, Alan," she said in a voice that wrung my heart-strings.

The room was dimly lighted; and for a minute after I entered, I could see nothing clearly except the ruddy glow of the wood fire in front of which two negroes were seated on low wooden stools. They had kindly faces, these men; there was a primitive humanity in their features, which might have been modelled out of the dark earth of the fields.

Looking round the next minute, I saw that a young man was sitting away from the fire, huddled over in a cretonne-covered chair with a high back and deep wings. At our entrance the negroes glanced up with surprise; but the man in the winged chair neither lifted his head nor turned his eyes in our direction. He sat there, lost within the impenetrable wilderness of the insane, as remote from us and from the sound of our voices as if he were the inhabitant of an invisible world. His head was sunk forward; his eyes were staring fixedly at some image we could not see; his fingers, moving restlessly, were plaiting and unplaiting the fringe of a plaid shawl. Distraught as he was, he still possessed the dignity of mere physical perfection. At his full height he must have measured not under six feet three; his hair was the colour of ripe wheat, and his eyes, in spite of their fixed gaze, were as blue as the sky after rain. And this was only the beginning, I realized. With that constitution, that physical frame, he might live to be ninety.

"Alan!" breathed his wife again in her pleading murmur.

If he heard her voice, he gave no sign of it. Only when she crossed the room and bent over his chair, he put out his hand, with a gesture of irritation, and pushed her away, as if she were a veil of smoke which came between him and the object at which he was looking. Then his hand fell back to its old place, and he resumed his mechanical plaiting of the fringe.

The woman lifted her eyes to mine. "His father did that for twenty years," she said in a whisper that was scarcely more than a sigh of anguish.

When I had made my brief examination, we left the room as we had come, and descended the stairs together. The three old women were still sitting in front of the wood fire. I do not think they had moved since we went upstairs; but, as we reached the hall below, one of them, the youngest, I imagine, rose from her chair, and came out to join us. She was crocheting something soft and small, an infant's sacque, I perceived as she approached, of pink wool. The ball had rolled from her lap as she stood up, and it trailed after her now, like a woolen rose, on the bare floor. When the skein pulled at her, she turned back and stooped to pick up the ball, which she rewound with caressing fingers. Good God, an infant's sacque in that house!

"Is it the same thing?" she asked.

"Hush!" responded the younger woman kindly. Turning to me she added, "We cannot talk here," and opening the door, passed out on the porch. Not until we had reached the lawn, and walked in silence to where my buggy stood beneath an old locust tree, did she speak again.

Then she said only, "You know now?"

"Yes, I know," I replied, averting my eyes from her face while I gave my directions as briefly as I could. "I will leave an opiate," I said. "To-morrow, if Carstairs should not come, send for me again. If he does come," I added, "I will talk to him and see you afterward."

"Thank you," she answered gently; and taking the bottle from my hand, she turned away and walked quickly back to the house.

I watched her as long as I could; and then getting into my buggy, I turned my mare's head toward the woods, and drove by moonlight, past Buzzard's Tree and over the Old Stage Road, to my home. "I will see Carstairs to-morrow," was my last thought that night before I slept.

But, after all, I saw Carstairs only for a minute as he was taking the train. Life at its beginning and its end had filled my morning; and when at last I reached the little station, Carstairs had paid his visit, and was waiting on the platform for the approaching express. At first he showed a disposition to question me about the shooting, but as soon as I was able to make my errand clear, his jovial face clouded.

"So you've been there?" he said. "They didn't tell me. An interesting case, if it were not for that poor woman. Incurable, I'm afraid, when you consider the predisposing causes. The race is pretty well deteriorated, I suppose. God! what isolation! I've advised her to send him away. There are three others, they tell me, at Staunton."

The train came; he jumped on it, and was whisked away while I gazed after him. After all, I was none the wiser because of the great reputation of Carstairs.

All that day I heard nothing more from Jordan's End; and then, early next morning, the same decrepit negro brought me a message.

"Young Miss, she tole me ter ax you ter come along wid me jes' ez soon ez you kin git ready."

"I'll start at once, Uncle, and I'll take you with me."

My mare and buggy stood at the door. All I needed to do was to put on my overcoat, pick up my hat, and leave word, for a possible patient, that I should return before noon. I knew the road now, and I told myself, as I set out, that I would make as quick a trip as I could. For two nights I had been haunted by the memory of that man in the armchair, plaiting and unplaiting the fringe of the plaid shawl. And his father had done that, the woman had told me, for twenty years!

It was a brown autumn morning, raw, windless, with an overcast sky and a peculiar illusion of nearness about the distance. A high wind had blown all night, but at dawn it had dropped suddenly, and now there was not so much as a ripple in the broomsedge. Over the fields, when we came out of the woods, the thin trails of blue smoke were as motionless as cobwebs. The lawn surrounding the house looked smaller than it had appeared to me in the twilight, as if the barren fields had drawn closer since my last visit. Under the trees, where the few sheep were browsing, the piles of leaves lay in windrifts along the sunken walk and against the wings of the house.

When I knocked the door was opened immediately by one of the old women, who held a streamer of black cloth or rusty crape in her hands.

"You may go straight upstairs," she croaked; and, without waiting for an explanation, I entered the hall quickly, and ran up the stairs.

The door of the room was closed, and I opened it noiselessly, and stepped over the threshold. My first sensation, as I entered, was one of cold. Then I saw that the windows were wide open, and that the room seemed to be full of people, though, as I made out presently, there was no one there except Alan Jordan's wife, her little son, the two old aunts, and an aged crone of a negress. On the bed there was something under a yellowed sheet of fine linen (what the negroes call "a burial sheet," I suppose), which had been handed down from some more affluent generation.

When I went over, after a minute, and turned down one corner of the covering, I saw that my patient of the other evening was dead. Not a line of pain marred his features, not a thread of gray dimmed the wheaten gold of his hair. So he must have looked, I thought, when she first loved him. He had gone from life, not old, enfeebled and repulsive, but enveloped still in the romantic illusion of their passion.

As I entered, the two old women, who had been fussing about the bed, drew back to make way for me, but the witch of a negress did not pause in the weird chant, an incantation of some sort, which she was mumbling. From the rag carpet in front of the empty fireplace, the boy, with his father's hair and his mother's eyes, gazed at me silently, broodingly, as if I were trespassing; and by the open window, with her eyes on the ashen November day, the young wife stood as motionless as a statue. While I looked at her a redbird flew out of the boughs of a cedar, and she followed it with her eyes.

"You sent for me?" I said to her.

She did not turn. She was beyond the reach of my voice, of any voice, I imagine; but one of the palsied old women answered my question.

"He was like this when we found him this morning," she said. "He had a bad night, and Judith and the two hands were up with him until daybreak. Then he seemed to fall asleep, and Judith sent the hands, turn about, to get their breakfast."

While she spoke my eyes were on the bottle I had left there. Two nights ago it had been full, and now it stood empty, without a cork, on

the mantelpiece. They had not even thrown it away. It was typical of
the pervading inertia of the place that the bottle should still be standing
there awaiting my visit.

For an instant the shock held me speechless; when at last I found my
voice it was to ask mechancially.

"When did it happen?"

The old woman who had spoken took up the story. "Nobody knows.
We have not touched him. No one but Judith has gone near him."
Her words trailed off into unintelligible muttering. If she had ever had
her wits about her, I dare-say fifty years at Jordan's End had unsettled
them completely.

I turned to the woman at the window. Against the gray sky and the
black intersecting branches of the cedar, her head, with its austere perfection, was surrounded by that visionary air of legend. So Antigone might
have looked on the day of her sacrifice, I reflected. I had never seen a
creature who appeared so withdrawn, so detached, from all human associations. It was as if some spiritual isolation divided her from her kind.

"I can do nothing," I said.

For the first time she looked at me, and her eyes were unfathomable.
"No, you can do nothing," she answered. "He is safely dead."

The negress was still crooning on; the other old women were fussing
helplessly. It was impossible in their presence, I felt, to put in words the
thing I had to say.

"Will you come downstairs with me?" I asked. "Outside of this
house?"

Turning quietly, she spoke to the boy. "Run out and play, dear. He
would have wished it."

Then, without a glance toward the bed, or the old women gathered
about it, she followed me over the threshold, down the stairs, and out on
the deserted lawn. The ashen day could not touch her, I saw then. She
was either so remote from it, or so completely a part of it, that she was
impervious to its sadness. Her white face did not become more pallid
as the light struck it; her tragic eyes did not grow deeper; her frail
figure under the thin shawl did not shiver in the raw air. She felt nothing, I realized suddenly.

Wrapped in that silence as in a cloak, she walked across the windrifts
of leaves to where my mare was waiting. Her step was so slow, so un-
hurried, that I remember thinking she moved like one who had all
eternity before her. Oh, one has strange impressions, you know, at such
moments!

In the middle of the lawn, where the trees had been stripped bare in the night, and the leaves were piled in long mounds like double graves, she stopped and looked in my face. The air was so still that the whole place might have been in a trance or asleep. Not a branch moved, not a leaf rustled on the ground, not a sparrow twittered in the ivy; and even the few sheep stood motionless, as if they were under a spell. Farther away, beyond the sea of broomsedge, where no wind stirred, I saw the flat desolation of the landscape. Nothing moved on the earth, but high above, under the leaden clouds, a buzzard was sailing.

I moistened my lips before I spoke. "God knows I want to help you!" At the back of my brain a hideous question was drumming. How had it happened? Could she have killed him? Had that delicate creature nerved her will to the unspeakable act? It was incredible. It was inconceivable. And yet. . . .

"The worst is over," she answered quietly, with that tearless agony which is so much more terrible than any outburst of grief. "Whatever happens, I can never go through the worst again. Once in the beginning he wanted to die. His great fear was that he might live too long, until it was too late to save himself. I made him wait then. I held him back by a promise."

So she had killed him, I thought. Then she went on steadily, after a minute, and I doubted again.

"Thank God, it was easier for him than he feared it would be," she murmured.

No, it was not conceivable. He must have bribed one of the negroes. But who had stood by and watched without intercepting? Who had been in the room? Well, either way! "I will do all I can to help you," I said.

Her gaze did not waver. "There is so little that any one can do now," she responded, as if she had not understood what I meant. Suddenly, without the warning of a sob, a cry of despair went out of her, as if it were torn from her breast. "He was my life," she cried, "and I must go on!"

So full of agony was the sound that it seemed to pass like a gust of wind over the broomsedge. I waited until the emptiness had opened and closed over it. Then I asked as quietly as I could:

"What will you do now?"

She collected herself with a shudder of pain. "As long as the old people live, I am tied here. I must bear it out to the end. When they die, I shall go away and find work. I am sending my boy to school. Doctor Carstairs will look after him, and he will help me when the time comes. While my boy needs me, there is no release."

While I listened to her, I knew that the question on my lips would never be uttered. I should always remain ignorant of the truth. The thing I feared most, standing there alone with her, was that some accident might solve the mystery before I could escape. My eyes left her face and wandered over the dead leaves at our feet. No, I had nothing to ask her.

"Shall I come again?" That was all.

She shook her head. "Not unless I send for you. If I need you, I will send for you," she answered; but in my heart I knew that she would never send for me.

I held out my hand, but she did not take it; and I felt that she meant me to understand, by her refusal, that she was beyond all consolation and all companionship. She was nearer to the bleak sky and the deserted fields than she was to her kind.

As she turned away, the shawl slipped from her shoulders to the dead leaves over which she was walking; but she did not stoop to recover it, nor did I make a movement to follow her. Long after she had entered the house I stood there, gazing down on the garment that she had dropped. Then climbing into my buggy, I drove slowly across the field and into the woods.

Editor's Note

According to Louise Collier Willcox, "Jordan's End" appeared for the first time in *The Shadowy Third* in 1923. This is odd, because the story wears better than most of the others; its stark, sharp outlines and freedom from intrusive moralizing would make it a prize for any publisher to capture. Either Miss Glasgow found that its theme was too somber for the popular magazines or, more likely, she was too absorbed in *Barren Ground* and *The Shadowy Third* collection to publish it elsewhere first. Nevertheless, it is the only Glasgow short story to have attracted any critical attention recently.

As in "Dare's Gift" the dilemma of Antigone is re-enacted. Unlike Lucy Dare, however, Lucy Jordan lives up to the Greek and the Southern code by defying the laws of society in order to fulfill her loyalty to her husband.

XII

Romance and Sally Byrd

"NEVER AGAIN," thought Sally Byrd Littlepage, as she opened her eyes. "Never again."

She awoke with the feeling that something delightful was about to happen, just as she used to awake on Christmas mornings in her childhood. Only her Christmas mornings were always disappointing. They had burst like bubbles when she touched them, while this dreamlike expectancy was as real as Stanley.

The name sang in her mind, as if a thrush were imprisoned there and could not get out. And not only the thrush, but the sunshine, the fragrant wind, and the blue sky filled with little clouds like mimosa blossoms—all these made a fairy ring in her thoughts where there was only dull grayness a few weeks ago.

Only three weeks ago what a dreary round life had been! Only three weeks ago she had gone plodding through her days, unaware that Stanley was in the world waiting for her. Awaking in the morning with nothing to expect, falling asleep at night with nothing to dream about. Going out after breakfast to teach in the kindergarten of the public school, coming back after lunch to wait on Grandfather or Grandmother Littlepage. Breakfast, dinner, bed, that was all. Grandfather's worry about money; Grandmother's worry about meals; Aunt Louisa's worry about neuralgia; Aunt Matilda's worry about salvation. Just that and nothing else in her days. Drabness everywhere that she looked. Drabness and poverty and the irksome monotony of things that did not matter. And then, in the midst of the grayness, sunshine had flooded the world. She had met Stanley one day, by the strangest chance, in the library where she had gone to return a book. They had both had to wait for the librarian, and while they were waiting they had begun to talk about

Shakespeare's plays. Afterward she had discovered that he was related to Gerty Cunningham, who taught in the kindergarten with her, and that he wrote plays which were so fine that she had never seen them; but it was really Shakespeare who introduced them. From beginning to end it had all been miraculous. It was one of those accidents which appear, when you look back on them in tender retrospect, to have occurred through some divine intervention in the chaos of circumstances. Nothing, she felt, except a beneficent Providence could have created so perfect an event out of the vast commonplace of existence.

Though she was only nineteen, it seemed to her that she had lived through a lifetime of drudgery before Stanley came. Even as a child she had been cramped and isolated by poverty, as if poverty were a contagious disease. They had never let her play with the other children in the streets; they had always kept her sewing with the elderly aunts in the faded drawing-room, or walking back and forth to the park with Grandfather Littlepage. In the solitude of the once fashionable and now fallen street in which they lived, there were no neighbors of their own class for them to mingle with, and mingling with "the common children" was sternly forbidden by Sally Byrd's grandparents.

Well, it was all over now. In a few minutes she would slip out of bed and bathe in water that sparkled like happiness; she would brush her dark hair, and wind it in a wreath of plaits round her head; she would touch her glowing cheeks with the powder she had bought yesterday; she would put on her green crepe dress and the locket with her mother's miniature; and she would go down to breakfast, with the joy in her heart shining through her gray-green eyes which Stanley once said were the color of April mist. "Why did you put on your Sunday dress?" Aunt Matilda would ask; and, made wise by love, she would lie happily, "Oh, it's May Day, you know. There's to be a celebration in the kindergarten." Then, when breakfast was over, she would run out to meet Stanley in the park, and they would go away to be married. After that her thoughts dissolved in a rosy glow of expectancy. She thought of marriage as her Grandfather thought of great wealth or her Aunt Matilda thought of heaven, as a passive and permanent condition of bliss.

In the dining-room, which looked dark and smelt depressingly, Grandfather, a withered tree of an old man, was facing Grandmother, a withered bush of an old woman. The only difference between them was that Grandfather was very tall and thin and Grandmother was very short and thick. Both were old, tired, embittered, and drained of humanity by self-denial. They had gone so long without pleasure that they had come to regard it, even for the young, as a luxury, not a necessity.

"You are late, Sally Byrd," remarked Grandmother, pouring coffee with her trembling hands. "You will have to hurry to be in time for school."

"I know, Grandmother. I overslept myself."

"Why did you put on your Sunday dress?" inquired Aunt Matilda in her dry, crackling voice. She was a pale, long, narrow woman, whose ideas were embalmed in religion as if it were a preserving fluid. Her features had once been pretty and aristocratic, and there was a legend that she had been in love with an infidel in her youth. She suffered day and night from a sense of sin, and if possible she was a more depressing companion than Aunt Louisa, who suffered day and night from neuralgia.

"Oh, it's May Day. There's to be a celebration in the kindergarten," replied Sally Byrd, just as she had imagined. It was wonderful, she told herself, while she sprinkled sugar on her oatmeal and wished for cream, the way life went on blandly repeating one's imagination.

"Did you put the money in the ginger jar yesterday, Sally Byrd?" asked Aunt Louisa.

"Yes, I put it in." Every month she put her salary in the green ginger jar on the mantelpiece. Aunt Louisa, who attended to the rent and the housekeeping, kept the money there because she imagined it was a place where no burglar would ever think of looking. Aunt Verbena, the ancient maid of all work, having lived in the family for forty years, had proved herself to be perfectly honest. And, besides, since she spent her working hours in dim regions below ground, it was logical to suppose that character in her place was supplemented by lack of opportunity.

"I shan't need any money," Sally Byrd was thinking. "Stanley told me not to bring anything, not even a bag. He will buy clothes for me. Prettier clothes than I have ever had in my life." Her eyes grew softer and greener, more like an April mist than ever, when she thought of the clothes Stanley would buy for her.

"Yes, I put the money in," she answered. "How is your neuralgia, Aunt Louisa?" "Never again!" sang the thrush. "Never again!"

Aunt Louisa, with the resigned smile of the neuralgic or the recently bereaved, replied in chastened tones that she was waiting for her coffee before taking a third dose of aspirin. "Matilda insisted on having air in the room last night," she said, "though she knows that I cannot stand air at night."

"I must hurry away," said the girl gayly, as she finally drew back from the table. Did they hear the excitement in her voice, she wondered, the suppressed joy?

"But you've eaten nothing, Sally Byrd," protested Grandfather, and Grandmother repeated after her habit, "eaten nothing."

"Oh, I took oatmeal, and oatmeal is so very filling, you know," replied Sally Byrd, laughing.

Then, as she turned to leave the room, her heart contracted with a spasm of pity. She saw them all caught together like mice in a trap. Perhaps in their youth, before they grew too old to struggle, they also had tried to escape into freedom.

"Good-by!" she called, waving back from the door; and in spite of the pity through which she looked at them, the thrush in her thoughts sang eagerly, "Never again!"

As soon as she was outside of the house, she felt that she wanted to dance on the pavement. Did prisoners always feel like this on the morning they were released? How beautiful the world, the same world that she had once thought so sordid, looked to-day!

And the people she passed looked at her so pleasantly, as if, one and all, they were sharing her secret joy. That kind old man leaning on his stick at the crossing; the woman with a shawl over her head hurrying to market; the nurse in uniform on the porch of a boarding-house; the milkman swinging himself down from his wagon; the baby in the perambulator thumping the head of his Teddy bear; all these different persons gazed at her with little sympathetic smiles peeping from their eyes and the corners of their lips. Did they suspect that she was going to be married to-day? Oh, if you could only dance with your feet when you danced with your heart!

At the crossing she darted like a sparrow among the vehicles in the street. In the park, by the fountain, she knew Stanley was waiting. As soon as that laundry wagon drawn by the white horse went by, she would be able to see him. Why did it move so slowly? Would it never go on again? Yes, it was passing just as she reached the opposite pavement; and while her eyes searched the walks of the park, she caught her breath and stopped suddenly, rooted by the magic of a thought to the spot on which she was standing. Suppose he should not have come! Suppose something had happened! Suppose he had changed his mind at the last minute! For an instant it seemed to her that her blood ran cold in her veins. Her pulses flagged, and then, with a throb of delight, they began beating a jazz rhapsody. She had caught a glimpse of him by the fountain. When she entered the park, and could look under the young leaves on the trees, she could see him distinctly. He was standing there alone with his hat in his hand, and his arm on the railing. She could see his brown hair, with the gloss catching the light, where it swept back from his forehead; the ruddy tan of his face; the easy, delightful look of his figure in the gray clothes she loved to touch. In a minute she would see his hazel eyes twinkling down on her. As soon as he caught sight of her, she knew that his face would come alive just as a dark room does when you light a lamp in it.

"Stanley!" she called softly, and ran toward him with her hands outstretched and the sunshine in her eyes.

He started as if he were jerked back from a reverie, and glanced swiftly over his shoulder, before he drew her into his arms.

"Sally Byrd, you darling!" he exclaimed as he kissed her.

She laughed with happiness. "Oh, you oughtn't to! Not here in the park."

"But there isn't a soul about. There isn't a blessed thing in sight except the sparrows, and they won't tell on us."

Of course he was right to be merry; but on a morning like this, when they were going away in secret, she felt she should have preferred him to be—well, not grave exactly, but at least serious. After all, when you came to think of it, and she had thought of nothing else for the last three weeks, marriage was a very, very serious thing. And when you married at nineteen you would have such a long time ahead either to enjoy it or to regret it.

"So you really came?"

"Didn't you know I was coming?"

"I hardly dared believe it. Did you look in the glass this morning?"

"When I did my hair. But why? Is my hat on wrong?"

"No, your hat is all right, but you've got a carnation for a face."

She laughed and drew closer to his side. Then a fat man strolled by leisurely, after the habit of the fat, and she slipped away again. "How long have you been waiting?"

"Ten minutes, and every minute was longer than the one before it."

"I know," she agreed. "It was like that all day yesterday." The fat man had sat down on a bench under a locust tree, just where he couldn't help seeing them if he glanced up from his newspaper. Wasn't that like life! she exclaimed inwardly while she looked at him.

"Let's go on the other side," said Stanley, turning away, and she followed him obediently round the fountain. "I'd like to have a picture of you as you look this morning," he said. "I'd call it April."

How lovely of him that was! There came over her suddenly the feeling that she was living not in the actual world, but in some enchanting dream. Life was too beautiful to be real.

"I can't believe that it is going to happen," she said.

His eyes were grave as he looked at her. "It takes courage, dear. Have you courage enough?"

"Courage?" she faltered because she could not understand. "To be happy?"

"To be happy like this. A great many have tried it, and very few have succeeded. The difference is one of courage. Nothing else can take its place, not even love."

She looked at him with the eyes of youth. "I don't think I can ever be afraid of anything with you," she answered.

"Not even of me?" he asked. "I mean afraid that I might some day make you unhappy."

"But you love me."

"That is only another reason why I may hurt you." For a moment he was silent, and then he said very slowly, "Yes, I love you. I am sure that I love you." Just as if love were a thing you had to reason about, she told herself, and not a miracle which you perceived in a flash through some infallible instinct.

"Then I know you will never hurt me," she said.

He had drawn her to his side on a bench, and was holding her hands in his while he spoke. She wished now that he would be less grave, that he would take their happiness more lightly.

"If I could be sure you would never reproach me," he said.

The color ebbed from her face. "Do you mean," she asked in a small cold voice, "that you don't want to take me away with you?"

"No, no, I don't mean that." He was kissing her hands. "I want you more than ever. I am sure I want you; but I am afraid. I am afraid of the future."

"You don't know—you can't feel with all your heart and soul that you want to marry me?" Oh, if only the earth would open and let her sink through it!

He was pressing her hands to his lips. "If it were only that!" he replied, "but you know, dear, we can't be perfectly sure even of that. After all, my wife may refuse to divorce me."

For a minute after he had spoken she sat gazing at him in silence, as if she had been turned to stone by his words. Her look was still fastened to his; her hand was still pressed to his lips; but the color had died so utterly in her face that it might have been the face of a statue. Only her gray-green eyes seemed to open suddenly like a vista in a wood, and something looked out of them that he had never seen there before.

"But—but I don't undrstand. I didn't know you had a wife," she said in a whisper, as if she were afraid of being overheard.

At first she had felt nothing, only the stunned sensation that follows a blow; but while she answered, it seemed to her that her body became full of wires and that along these wires, which crossed and recrossed, quivers of pain, like tiny flames, were passing.

"I thought you knew. Gerty told me that you knew in the beginning. All the time I imagined you avoided speaking to her from some feeling of delicacy. So I went on blindly avoiding too."

"But I didn't understand. I didn't dream," she repeated helplessly.

"Does it make all that difference to you, Sally Byrd?"

His voice was miles away from her; it came out of the dim horizon beyond the young green leaves and the roofs and chimneys of the city. Beyond everything. Out of nothing. Strange that he should have passed so far away from her in a moment. Scarcely a moment even, only a few seconds before she had been quite close to him; and now they were sitting side by side with an immense distance between them.

"No, it doesn't make any difference in my love. It doesn't make any difference at all in that," she heard herself saying in thin, faint tones that sounded like the far off whistle of a train. Then a sudden thought made her glance at him sharply. "Does it make any difference in hers?" she asked.

"In hers? My wife's, you mean? Oh, we got over that sort of thing long ago. We've been separated for years. But I've never asked her for a divorce," he added contritely. "I've never wanted one until now."

She collected her shattered courage with an effort, picking up, one by one, the pieces of her happiness. Then, with a tremulous gesture, she reached for her little beaded bag which she had laid on the bench, and rose to her feet. "I must be going now," she said in that small smothered voice which was so punctiliously polite, just as if she were trying to make conversation with a visitor. "I am late for school already. If I don't hurry, I'll miss the second class."

"You don't mean—you can't mean, Sally Byrd—" He was gazing at her with a distressed look in his face, and through some perverted sense of humor, he reminded her of one of the children in the kindergarten when he was denied a whirligig of colored paper. How dreadful of her to think of such things! And yet the more she tried not to think of it, the more obstinately she thought of it. A nervous feeling came over her that she was going to burst out laughing, not softly like a lady, but in a hysterical scream that would bring a crowd gathering about her.

"It—it is such a joke," she murmured; and the words gave her a shock because she had not meant to say them at all. They might as well have been spoken by the fountain, or by the fat man reading his newspaper under the locust tree, so little did they express anything that she had intended to utter. "I am going to laugh or cry in a minute," she added, "I don't in the least know which it is going to be."

"Sit down again," he said anxiously, drawing her to the bench. "You aren't fit to teach school." The hurt look had spread all over his face, and even his clothes seemed to give way suddenly, as if he had wilted inside of them.

"No," she repeated vacantly, because it was such a relief to have some words provided for her to speak, "I am not fit to teach school."

He put his hand gently over hers. It felt, she told herself, like a hand that was asleep. "You won't let it make any difference, will you, dear?" Why did he persist in asking that question? "You won't stop loving me?"

"Oh, no," she replied, as pleasantly as she could while this confusion between laughter and tears was spinning in her mind. "I shan't stop loving you."

"Then you'll go away with me just the same?" There was a new note in his voice, which she felt rather than heard, as deaf people feel the vibration of sound. Had he grown more eager for her because he suspected that she was slipping away? How alone it made you feel to think that! Couldn't anything in the world, couldn't love even, bring two persons so close that thoughts and sensations could not come in between them?

She drew away very gently, afraid of waking the sleeping hand that covered her own. "Oh, I couldn't do that," she replied under her breath. "Of course I couldn't do that."

"You can, if you love me, Sally Byrd."

"But it has nothing to do with love. It has nothing in the world to do with love." She was eager to make him understand. "It has to do with something entirely different."

What this something was she could not have explained if he had asked her, so she was thankful in her heart that he did not ask her. She longed to go away with him. Every fiber of her being felt tight with longing; yet she knew that she should never be able to go because an instinct stronger than her longing would hold her back. No righteous indignation inspired her. She realized, almost with a shock, that she wasn't indignant at all. She was even glad and grateful that it had happened. But she couldn't go away with him unmarried. That was one of the things you didn't do, no matter how much you wanted to, like getting drunk because you were thirsty, or taking off all your clothes because you were hot. No, you might do a great many other things that were not nice; but those particular things you did not do.

"I must be going back to school," she said again, beginning to walk away. "It is awfully late."

"Then you mean this is good-by?"

Her eyes filled with tears. "You are going away by yourself?"

"I'm obliged to. I can't stay on here forever—and, besides, what is the use?"

"There isn't any use of course, but it is very nice."

"It wouldn't be if I stayed on."

"You mean you'd stop caring?"

"No, I don't mean that. In fact I don't know what I mean. I'm not very jolly myself, and I've made you unhappy."

At this she stopped and held out both hands to him. "You mustn't think that because it isn't true," she said. "You haven't made me unhappy. Compared to what I was before I knew you, I'm as happy as—as a queen. You can't imagine how empty my life was before I knew you."

"But look what I've put into it."

She smiled at him through her tears. "You've put loveliness into it." Then she drew a long breath and spoke with a sob in her voice. "Oh, you can't know how much better it is to have an unhappy love in your life than to have nothing at all."

His face was softer and finer, more adorable, than she had ever seen it. "If I can ever come back to you honestly, I will come back," he promised, moved to the depths of his facile being.

"And I'll never forget you. I'll wait for you always," she answered.

Smothered in summer dust, the days, weeks, months, crawled by like beetles. While school lasted, Sally Byrd taught her kindergarten with passion; when school was over, she devoted herself to her grandfather, who was beginning, as Aunt Matilda observed every morning, "to go down hill very fast." On Sundays, when Grandfather could spare her, she assembled a group of pious-minded infants in the infant class of the Sunday school. Though she was unhappy, it was not, as she often assured herself, the forlorn, weedy, and utterly destitute form of unhappiness that Aunt Louisa, who had nothing but neuralgia to remember, was obliged to endure. No, it was the rich, bracing, romantic sorrow of Aunt Matilda, who had mourned in secret the loss of her infidel lover. Gradually, as the summer advanced, it seemed to Sally Byrd that her tragic love affair had become a tonic in her life. Lying awake through the breathless nights, when the odors of decaying fruits and vegetables crept in on the stagnant air, and the yellow moonlight looked so hot that she felt as if it would scorch her, she found that she could shut her eyes and withdraw into the memory of her hopeless love as into some secret garden of fragrance and bloom. No matter how hot and dusty and evil-smelling the street was outside, she had only to open an imaginary green wicket gate, and she was back, in the twinkle of an eye, among dew-drenched flowers. "No, as long as you have something beautiful to think about, you can't be a beggar," thought Sally Byrd, when she drooped.

Every morning Grandfather said sternly, "We must find a new way in which to economize," and Grandmother piped shrilly after him, "a new way to economize." Every morning Aunt Matilda wailed, "I feel as if I couldn't swallow a mouthful," and Aunt Louisa sighed, "If you had neuralgia, you couldn't go without eating." And every morning Sally Byrd wished for cream while she sprinkled sugar on her oatmeal!

Then, just when it seemed to her that she had got used to the monotony, she met Gerty Cunningham one afternoon in the street. All summer she had avoided Gerty, but it was impossible, she knew, not to run across her sooner or later. After school began they would be thrown together again.

"Sally Byrd, I was just coming to see you," said Gerty, clutching her arm. She was a dramatic girl, who had once yearned to act in motion pictures, and who instinctively clutched everything that came within her reach. "I was just coming to see you, dear. I thought you might not have heard."

"Heard what?" Sally Byrd drew back a step, not that she particularly disliked clutching, but because she wanted to look at Gerty's face. It was not a face, however, when one looked at it, that told one very much except the story of Gerty's temperament.

"About Stanley. You may, of course, have seen it in the paper."

"Seen what?" She sounded awfully stupid, she knew, but why did Gerty always have to work up to situations as if she were playing them on the stage? Was it possible, she asked herself while she waited, that Stanley had got a divorce? In that instant, before Gerty answered, she felt like a drowning man who sees a hundred memories of his former life flash through his mind, only in her case the images were not memories but anticipations. She saw Stanley returning to her; she saw herself Stanley's wife; she saw them going away together; she saw the future stretching ahead, like an avenue of bliss, into a rosy haze. Then the light died as it had come, and the roseate visions faded into obscurity.

Gerty had turned away to toss a word and a smile to a passing acquaintance. "So sorry not to have been at home yesterday. Do come again soon. Yes, my dear," she had wheeled round on Sally Byrd, "I was saying to Mother only this morning that I knew you would be distressed. He always admired you so. And a writer too! Of course, that makes it worse, if anything, as Mother says, could make the worst worse. Poor Stanley! His car was struck by a train at a railroad crossing somewhere in New Jersey, and he was so badly hurt that they don't know yet whether he will live or die. And they say he will lose his eyesight even if he recovers. Think of that, dear!" It was perfectly evident that Gerty was thinking of it with personal sorrow and temperamental satisfaction. "A writer, and blind! I can't help feeling that it would have been better if he had been killed outright, like the friend who was with him."

This time Sally Byrd, not Gerty, was clutching. If she did not hold on to something, she knew that she should not be able to stand, that she should drop straight down to the pavement and lie there without moving a finger. "Yes, I think it would have been better." The echo sounded hollow, but Gerty did not appear to notice it.

"I was sure you would want to write him a word of sympathy. He thinks you so lovely, and of course all his friends must rally about him now."

"Is it the same address? He hasn't moved, has he?"

"No, it is the same place, that beautiful apartment house in Park Avenue. Mother and I had tea with him only three weeks ago when we came down from Ogunquit. You never saw anything so artistic as his apartment, and now just to think that he may never be able to see it again."

"Are you quite, quite sure that he will be blind if he lives?" One must leave a wide margin, she was aware, for Gerty's sensational imagination.

"As soon as we read it in the paper, Mother called up over the telephone, and the nurse answered. She said they were not perfectly positive, but they feared, those were her very words, that he would never recover his sight. She seemed glad to hear that Mother was a relative, for she said he was entirely alone there except for the nurses. If it were not for school, and having spent all our money in Maine last summer, we'd go straight back to New York. But at this season of the year we are always so dreadfully hard up."

This was truth unadorned, and Sally Byrd accepted it in its simplicity. "When you write to him, tell him that I—that I am as distressed as I can be," she faltered.

Won't you write him a note yourself? I am sure he would like to hear from you. Of course I know how shocked you are. Your face is as white as your blouse."

"Yes, I'll write to him, though there doesn't seem anything in the world I can say."

"Oh, it will please him to know you are thinking of him."

Had Gerty ever suspected, she wondered, just how much she thought of him? Well, what did it matter? Gerty and her mother and her own people, Grandfather, Grandmother, and the two aunts, all would know presently. It was not a thing that you could keep secret in your heart like a hopeless love. It was not a thing that she would wish to keep secret now that Stanley needed her more than anyone else in the world needed her.

Even before she parted from Gerty she had made her decision. She was going to him not because she loved him—she could have held out against her love forever, she said to herself—but because he needed her so desperately. Ever since Gerty had told her of the accident, a single picture had stood out vividly in her mind, as if it were flashed there on a blank white sheet by a magic lantern; and this was the picture of herself leading Stanley along a crowded street—oh, a street filled with people! Of course it was dreadful always to see things in pictures; but if your mind worked this way, how on earth could you help it?

Turning home, she walked slowly back again, with her errand forgotten. It was after six o'clock, and she must be ready, with her bag packed and her excuses made up in her mind, to take the night train to New York. "If I had the money with me," she thought "I could get my ticket and my berth before I go in." But she did not have money enough; she had only the seventy-five cents for Grandmother's yarn, which she had not remembered to buy. She would be obliged to take the money for her trip, she realized, out of the green ginger jar when Aunt Louisa was not looking. "I am only taking what is mine," she told herself steadily. Though it felt like stealing, it was not stealing at all.

When she entered the house at half past six o'clock, supper was ready. "Just a cup of tea and a crust of bread in the evening," insisted Grandfather, whose digestion was weaker than his appetite.

"Did you get my yarn, Sally Byrd," piped Grandmother from behind the Rebekah-at-the-Well teapot.

"Oh, I'm so sorry, Grandmother. I forgot it."

"Forgot it? Why, I thought that was what you went out for."

"It was, but I met Gerty Cunningham, and we got to talking and the yarn slipped right out of my mind. I'll get it the first thing to-morrow on my way back from school."

She paused and looked as grave as if she were solving a problem in arithmetic. Then, after a minute or two of what appeared to be the deepest concentration, she said resolutely, "I promised Gerty to spend the night with her. Her mother is away and she doesn't like staying in the house all alone." How easy lying was, easier than speaking the truth! But why did she always have to embroider falsehoods just as she embroidered her plain muslin underclothes?

She walked through the entrance of the apartment house, and from the entrance into the large white hall. Here an attendant in green, just like the footman in a fairy palace, sprang up at her side, and she asked in a voice which sounded stern because she was trying so hard to make it steady, for Mr. Stanley Kenton. The fairy footman waved her to the elevator, but when she sought to enter it, a second attendant in green inquired if she was the nurse? "Orders are that I shall take up nobody but nurses and doctors."

For an instant she hesitated. "Yes, I am the nurse," she replied, after reflection, and stepped past him into the elevator. It was perfectly true. Hadn't she come all this distance to nurse Stanley?

They shot upward so suddenly that she caught at the iron grille for support.

"Is it very far?" she asked while her heart palpitated.

"Tenth floor," responded the attendant, gazing straight upward.

Then they stopped as quickly as they had started, and he had the manner of letting her out of a cage as he opened the door of the elevator. "Apartment on the right," he rapped out like a machine before he shot down again.

She walked to the door he had indicated, and with her hand stretched out to knock, she stood divided between the longing for Stanley and the impulse to turn and run down those white marble stairs which she could see in the distance. While she still hesitated, the sound of the returning elevator reached her, and she rang quickly. To her surprise the door opened immediately, and a maid, in her morning gray and white, stretched out her hand.

"Oh, I beg your pardon," she said the next minute. "I was so sure you were a telegram. They've been coming that thick and fast I've had to stand at the door. We're dreadfully upset this morning because the night nurse was taken ill and had to go home, and we had to try so long before we could get you. You're the nurse of course?" she added, struck by the youthfulness of Sally Byrd's appearance.

"Yes, I'm the nurse." She had got used to the idea. "I'd like to see Mr. Kenton at once."

"Well, come in. You'll want to change into your uniform. I'll see what room you can go to. My, but you're young, Miss," she finished as the girl followed her into the hall. "You don't look old enough to have been through training."

"I look younger than I am."

"That's a nice way to be. Just come into the living-room, and I'll find out at once."

Then, as she disappeared down the hall, Sally Byrd entered the long, bright room, which seemed to her the most beautiful place she had ever seen or imagined. A dampness fell over her spirits while she gazed at it. If only Stanley were not so rich, she would have felt better about coming.

Resting on the edge of a Florentine chair, she stared with fascinated eyes at the Italian furniture, the tapestry on the wall, the pictures, the books in rich and beautiful bindings, the wicker bird cages, the flower-like bowl of Venetian glass in which brightly colored goldfish swam round amid exotic seaweed. Yes, she wished with all her heart that Stanley was—well, not really poor, but less oppressively rich.

Then, in the midst of all this foreign-looking splendor, her eyes, wandering about the room were arrested by an object which appeared as out of place as herself. After she had once looked at it she found that she could not look anywhere else. On a little table near the fireplace there stood a workbasket filled with stockings that needed darning—just an ordinary workbasket made of willow. It was the kind of basket that Aunt Matilda and Aunt Louisa used, only in this case the stockings, she saw, after a minute, were really socks, black and gray, socks of fine, soft silk which had been worn into holes in places. In one of them the darning egg had been dropped, and a needle with a long thread in it was stuck carelessly into the pile, as if it had been thrust there by someone who had been called suddenly away from her work. Poor Stanley! He must have worn out all those socks, such nice ones, too, and flung them aside because there was nobody to mend them. Well, she was thankful now, though she had often complained of it, that she was brought up to be practical.

At the sound of a step in the hall, she withdrew her gaze from the workbasket and stared at the goldfish. A minute later she heard a brisk, composed voice saying, "Why, you can't be the nurse! You are scarcely more than a child, and this is a serious case."

Turning her eyes, which had been fixed on the goldfish, she met the astonished regard of a dark, pleasant-looking woman, whose hair, just sprinkled with gray, was brushed carelessly back from her forehead, and whose large, firm figure was beginning ever so slightly to spread. She wore the serene air of a woman who has passed through the furnace of romance, and has attained the cool judgment and the ample leisure which await those who have finished with love.

"I—I am not the nurse you expected," Sally Byrd tried to explain, while the other's kindly humorous eyes, with their disconcerting expression of taking everything with a tinge of irony, gazed at her wonderingly. "I came because I heard he was all alone and needed somebody to look after him."

"Oh, that is it!" observed the older woman, without surprise, and she asked in a gentle voice, "Won't you sit down?"

Sally Byrd sat down, and then, because she could think of nothing else to do or say, she stared at the workbasket.

"Yes, there are a great many, aren't there?" remarked the other, following the direction of the girl's eyes. "Men are so careless about their things, and these socks cost seven dollars a pair. I thought I might as well go over them while I sit and wait. There is so much time, and I always hate to sit and fold my hands." Her glance went back to Sally Byrd, and she inquired in the same practical tone, "How far did you come?"

"From Virginia." Sally Byrd's voice choked as she answered, though there was nothing to do, she felt, but answer. If this competent-looking woman was a sister or an aunt of Stanley's, she supposed she had the right to question her.

"You knew Stanley in Virginia?"

"We met last spring when he was there. I thought—I thought—"

"Wait a minute," said the other quietly. Rising, she went quickly out of the room, and returned almost immediately with a cup of coffee on a little tray. "You look faint. I'm sorry there isn't any breakfast yet, but we have coffee made early for the nurses. Do you take cream and sugar?" She put the tray down on the table beside the workbasket, and gave the cup to the girl. "Drink it while you talk. It will make you feel better. So you knew Stanley in Virginia?"

Sally Byrd nodded.

"And you fell in love with each other. Well, you're pretty enough, and I suppose he is charming enough, though I never quite understand that part of it."

This time Sally Byrd did not nod. She only stared with tragic eyes over the brim of the cup. The coffee did make a wonderful difference. She felt it go all over her just like happiness, only more staying.

The other woman sat down in the chair by the table, and picking up the sock with the darning egg inside of it, examined the hole, with meticulous attention, through a pair of rimless eyeglasses which she had slipped on her nose. Then she drew the toe of the sock tightly over the egg, and ran her needle in precise stitches round the hole. "That was spring," she remarked, without glancing up, "and this is autumn. A long time for a love affair to last."

"It isn't a love affair," protested Sally Byrd, in anguish. "It is—oh, it is —" She broke down and began to cry softly. A miserable feeling had descended on her out of the clouds. She felt vaguely that her bright, beautiful romance had been pricked like a bubble, and was melting away into soapsuds. Glamour had suddenly departed. Stripped of illusion, she was beginning to see herself simply as a fool who would have to pay for her folly. In an instant, by an act of intelligence, she seemed to grow up, to attain maturity of judgment.

Still the other did not look up from her darning, so intent was she upon filling in the hole perfectly. "I know," she said, "I know, but why did you think he would need you? Didn't you know he had a wife?"

"But they don't love each other. They are separated." Sally Byrd ended in a sob, and hid her face in her hands.

The older woman nodded affirmatively over her work. There was a singular detachment about her, as if all shades of feeling had been absorbed by the ironic point of view. She possessed the dignity which distinguishes the spectator of life from the protagonist. Her unfashionable garments—for she wore an odd blouse and skirt with a courage which had become the better part of discretion—could not make her commonplace. Even Sally Byrd could perceive that this woman had attained a superiority that was independent of clothes, that was independent even of feature.

"Yes, we were separated three years ago, but in those three years he has sent for me three times when he was in trouble. Marriage for some men, you know, is merely a prop to lean against when they need a support, and Stanley is one of these men. He doesn't need a prop often, but when he does he needs it very badly. Once he had pneumonia; once his heart was broken because some woman had thrown him over; and now this dreadful accident. This, of course, is the most serious. Even if he recovers his sight—and we hope to save his eyes—he will not be able to do without me for some little time."

While she talked she went on placidly filling in the hole with her needle. She did not look up, though Sally Byrd was gazing at her as if she were in a trance and incapable of moving so much as a finger.

"You!" cried the girl at last in breathless amazement. "I didn't dream that you were his wife!"

"Well, I suppose I do look older. There is a difference in our ages, but the chief difference is that Stanley has never grown up, and I have. One of us had to."

"But I didn't know, I didn't know," said Sally Byrd, stumbling to her feet.

For the first time Mrs. Kenton let the darning egg drop into the basket and turned her quizzical gaze on the girl.

"Did you think that you were the only one?" she asked softly.

"The only one?" Rooted to the spot, Sally Byrd stared at her, while the tears rolled in pearly drops down her flushed cheeks.

"The only woman Stanley was in love with. There have been so many of them you know, that I wondered," she continued in her dispassionate tone. "The woman in the car with him—the one who was killed, poor thing—was the latest. He had just asked me to get a divorce, so he might marry her." For a minute she hesitated. "Of course he knew I would refuse, or he wouldn't have asked me."

"I must go," cried Sally Byrd wildly, while she groped toward the door. If she did not go at once, if she did not break away before another word was said, she felt she should begin to scream in the way Aunt Verbena had screamed when they told her her husband had been run over. Then Mrs. Kenton's voice, cool, composed, impersonal, arrested her, and she stood still at the door and turned round.

"Are you sure you won't stay to breakfast?"

"Oh, no, I must go. I must go back immediately."

"You will go back to Virginia and forget him?"

Lifting her head with a gallant gesture, Sally Byrd looked into the eyes that were watching her. "Yes, I will go back to Virginia and forget him."

Mrs. Kenton's face softened. "How old are you?"

"Nineteen. Or I was when I came here."

The other smiled. "At nineteen nothing is permanent. You will forget him and be happy."

Sally Byrd shook her head. "I shall forget, but I shall not be happy. It has broken my heart."

A wistful expression crossed the other's face. "No, your heart isn't broken—not so long as it hurts. When your heart is really broken, it lies still and dead like mine. You can't imagine the relief it is," she added simply, "to have your heart break at last."

For an instant Sally Byrd was awed into silence. Then she murmured under her breath, as if she were at church or a funeral with the deeper realities. "I'm so sorry, I'm so sorry. I didn't know." She longed desperately to escape, but she could not go, she could not even move while those eyes, which had seen everything, were fixed on her.

The older woman opened the door. "Don't let it happen again, dear," she said, "but if it ever does, remember the wife. It is worth while to re-member the wife because, when all is said and done, the last word is usually hers."

Then she smiled and turned away while Sally Byrd ran out of the apartment and into the elevator.

Down in the street she walked rapidly away from the building in the aimless, distracted flight with which people run away from a burning home or an earthquake. Not until she was breathless and ready to drop with fatigue did she pause long enough to look up and read the name Lexington Avenue. Well, it did not make any difference. From the way she felt she would as soon be in Lexington Avenue as anywhere else in the world. She was tired and stiff, and the bag was so heavy that she could scarcely carry it. Yet it had seemed very light when she ran with it down into the dining-room at home. "I must go straight back to the station," she thought. "I must take the next train home." For the first time, while she looked helplessly round in search of a policeman, it oc-curred to her that she had only four dollars left of the money she had taken out of the ginger jar. Not enough even to buy a ticket. Why, four dollars wouldn't take her much farther, she supposed, than somewhere in New Jersey. The practical difficulty eased the pain in her heart, after the way of practical difficulties, and she began to worry less about her unhappy love and more about the problem of getting back to Virginia. "If I could only sell my clothes," she thought, "I wonder if there is anybody in New York so poor that they would buy my clothes." Then, while she stooped down to rest her bag on the pavement, a cool, smooth object sliding round her neck reminded her of her mother's miniature. "I shall have to sell the locket," she told herself with a grim determina-tion from which, to her surprise, sentiment was strangely absent. "After an experience like this I suppose you lose your sentiment about every-thing," she concluded.

Her gaze searched the block and dropped like a tired bird on a jeweler's shop tucked in between a green grocer and a flower shop, where the window was ablaze with yellow chrysanthemums.

"I'll go in there," she said aloud; and picking up her bag, walked reso-lutely across the street, and through the small open door. Once inside she realized that it was a place where watches were repaired; but when an elderly man in big spectacles popped out of a box at the back, she held out the locket.

"I wonder if you would be willing to lend me some money on this?"

He looked first at her face and then at the locket, shaking his head all the time, as if he regretted what he had to say. "No, we don't lend money. Our work is repairing watches. I'm sorry."

"Is there any place near?" Her voice trembled. "Could you tell me of any place where they would take it?"

"There's a pawnshop near here. You might try there. Just a little way around the corner."

"Yes, I'll go there." She hesitated and looked at him wistfully. "Would you mind taking the picture out for me? I don't want to leave the picture."

He held out his hand, and when she had given him the locket, opened it and pried out the miniature with a pointed instrument. How lovely the face looked lying there in the palm of his hand:

"It's very like you," said the jeweler, handing it back to her. "That must be your mother?"

"Yes, it is my mother." As she said the words the realization came to her that her mother would have felt disgraced if she had known. Poor, soft, delicate, lovely mother, to be taken out of her case like that in a shop in Lexington Avenue!

Thanking the man hurriedly, she went out, carrying her bag with an effort because her arms ached, and started down the side street in the direction of the pawnshop. Yes, there it was round the corner. She could see the gold balls, and as she drew nearer, the window filled with a queer collection of rusty trinkets. She shrank from leaving her locket among the tawdry looking ornaments; but after all it would be only for a few days. In a week at most, even if she had to take the money out of the ginger jar, she would send back to redeem it.

Within the shop, which was saturated with the odors of beer and stale fish, a grimy old man, with a yellow skin and hooked nose, who reminded her of Shylock fallen on evil days, took the locket in his hand and examined it through a magnifying glass which he wore attached by a black cord to his alpaca coat.

"If you could lend me twenty dollars on this," she said nervously, watching him.

After examining it, he laid it down on a strip of dirty red velvet, and muttered that he would give her ten dollars.

"But that wouldn't buy my ticket." Though she struggled to appear composed, the words burst out in a strangled sob. Oh, was any girl ever placed in such a dreadful situation before? "As soon as I get home, I'll send back to redeem it. Really and truly, I will send back."

In reply to this appeal he merely grumbled that, "they all said that, and he was obliged to make a living." Then, after haggling over the sum, he agreed to lend her fifteen dollars, and crept noiselessly away in his carpet slippers to the back of the shop. When he returned he counted out fifteen greasy one-dollar notes on the strip of velvet. Then he handed her the pawn ticket and one of his cards which was as yellow as his face. Cramming the money and ticket into her purse, she picked up her traveling bag and ran out into the air. In the street she took out her handkerchief and vigorously rubbed her face. Would she ever feel clean again? Would she ever get that horrible smell out of her clothes? Well, at least she could go home. She would walk back to Fifth Avenue and take the bus that had brought her from the station. Only two hours ago! It seemed a lifetime, but it was, in reality, only two hours ago.

At the station she found that there was a train leaving immediately; and after buying her ticket, she went into the day coach because she could not afford to travel in the chair car. She was so tired she felt dazed and numb, and there was what Grandmother described as "a gone feeling" inside of her. By the time the conductor came by she had grown so weak that she asked him if she could get something to eat on the train, and observing her plight, he helped her back to the dining-car. "Be sure to take this sick lady's order at once," he said to the waiter as he went back.

She ordered tea and toast and an egg, because that was what Aunt Louisa took when she was in the worst twinges of neuralgia, and after she had eaten the egg and sipped the tea, she began to feel better. An elderly woman in youthful black sat opposite to her at the beginning of her meal, and when she made an unexpected remark, Sally Byrd jumped as she did when the train jolted. Her courage and self-respect had oozed out of her under the pressure of disappointment. She felt not only tired and faint, but dreadfully humble and inferior, exactly like, she told herself despondently, the poor relation of the world.

Then the elderly woman nodded to her and went out, and a young man with blue eyes came in and took the opposite place. Presently, after he had written his order, he made a remark just as the woman had done, and Sally Byrd jumped again.

"Have you been ill?" he asked in a sympathetic tone. "You look as if you might have toothache—or something."

She shook her head while her eyes brimmed over with tears. To think of looking as if she had toothache! "No, but I'm in great trouble," she answered.

"I'm sorry for that." He looked as if he meant it. "Is there anything I can do? Do you know I had an impression when I came in that I'd seen you somewhere before. You don't act in the movies, do you?"

In a rush her courage returned to her. "Oh, no, but I go to see them whenever I get the chance."

They talked a little while, and she discovered presently that he lived in her city, only a few blocks away from her home. She must have passed him often in the street, if she had only remembered. And he knew Abbie Dance, a teacher in one of the higher grades of the public school. "How very strange!" she exclaimed when he told her. And it seemed strange to him also, strange as well as profoundly original and significant. The kind of thing that had never happened to anyone else.

When she went back to the day coach, he brought her a magazine, and told her that he was stopping at Philadelphia to keep a business appointment. "But we'll be sure to meet again. I'll arrange that," he observed in his boyish way, which she found so attractive. He was really much better looking than Stanley, she reflected after he had gone, and so much younger. For the first time it occurred to her that Stanley was —well, not exactly old, but middle-aged. Yes, certainly, middle-aged. Of course she had been foolish to let her heart be broken by a man who was both married and middle-aged; but since it had happened the only sensible thing was to make the best she could out of what remained to her. Romance, of course, was over forever, but there were many useful virtues in which she might learn in time to excel. All day, while the train was bearing her home, she sat turning the pages of the magazine, and trying to adjust her future to the procession of useful virtues which filed through her mind.

When she reached the city, day had drawn to a close and a mournful twilight filled the street as she descended from the car at the corner of her block. How dejected everything looked! How gloomy and depressed seemed the people who hurried past her on their way home from work! How sad the falling leaves! How ugly and harsh the houses appeared under the yellow-brown in the sky! Well, she had had her adventure, and she would have to spend the rest of her life paying for it, she supposed. Romance was over. Nothing remained to her now except school teaching or church work, until she grew as old and stringy as Aunt Matilda and Aunt Louisa. Then she wondered how she could ever explain to them. They would never, of course, as long as they lived, understand. Looking ahead as she passed, limping with fatigue, down the street, she saw the future as a gray, deserted road strewn with dead leaves, and she saw herself, a small shrunken figure, toiling to the end of it. Yes, she had finished with romance forever. Then suddenly, out of nothing, there flashed into her mind the image of the young man she had met on the train. Would she ever see him again, she wondered. How smooth and glossy his hair was! How blue and sparkling his eyes! Why, he lived in this street, and she might pass him any morning on her way to teach school. The world, which had been so gray the moment before, became faintly suffused with color. In this very street, amid the falling leaves and the dust and the dingy houses, the indestructible illusion was springing up again. Yes, it was quite possible that any day she might meet him.

Her home was reached at last. There were withered leaves on the front porch. A light shone in the window. Well, she had learned her lesson. It seemed to her now that life had nothing more to teach her. "Never again!" she said softly, as she went up the steps and entered the house.

Editor's Note

"Romance and Sally Byrd" was published in *Woman's Home Companion* for December, 1924. It contains a double revelation of the moral selfishness of men and the moral weakness of women. Sally Byrd is a typical twentieth-century girl—sentimental, idealistic, but pretty and resilient enough to avoid getting scarred permanently in her encounters with men.

With this work Ellen Glasgow is entering her major phase. The story is slight and obvious, but there is strength and bitter wisdom in Mrs. Kenton. Sally Byrd, the ingenue, is described with more than usual tolerance, too. There is a certain inevitability in the romantic cycle here, which must end in despair for all but the young or the strong. It was too late for Miss Glasgow to be anything but strong, but that strength is the trademark of all her best writing.

"Romance and Sally Byrd" was reprinted in *World's Best Short Stories*, 1925, edited by William Johnston.

XIII

The Professional Instinct

⌒ AS HE unfolded his napkin and broke his toast with the precise touch of fingers that think, Doctor John Estbridge concluded that holidays were becoming unbearable. Christmas again, he reflected gloomily, and Christmas in New York, with a heavy snowstorm that meant weeks of dirt and slush and [insidious *changed to* back-breaking] [1] epidemics of influenza and pneumonia! Beyond the curtains of rose-colored damask the storm rocked the boughs of an ailantus tree which grew midway of the [desolate *changed to* high-fenced] backyard. Long ago, in the days of his youth and his [fiery enthusiasm *changed to* mania] for reform, [Esterbridge *changed to* Estbridge] remembered that he had once tried to [turn *changed to* convert] the backyard into an Italian garden. For a brief season box had survived, if it had not actually flourished there, and a cypress tree, sent [by an ex-patient *added*] from Northern Italy, had lived through a single summer and had died with the first [smoke *changed to* frost] of winter. That was nearly twenty years ago, for [Esterbridge *changed to* Estbridge] had relinquished his garden with the other dreams of his youth, and to-day the [vigorous *changed to* brawny] ailantus [tree *deleted*] stood [there *added*] as a symbol of the prosperous failure of his career.

"What's to be got out of this business of living anyhow?" he enquired, gazing over his breakfast at a [picture *changed to* portrait] of Savonarola which hung above the French clock on the mantelpiece. With a laugh he recalled it had been his business for twenty years to answer this immemorial question for the satisfaction of the unsound or the dejected. "To have stuffed all those poor devils with sawdust," he added, and a minute later: "By Jove, if happiness were only as cheap as philosophy!"

Within the last few weeks [he had had *deleted*] several cases of

[1] Bracketed comments by the editor indicate Miss Glasgow's longhand revisions of her manuscript.

239

changed [personalities—of men and women, *changed to* personalities had passed through his hands. They concerned men and women,] not far from his own age, who had undergone curious psychological [revolutions *changed to* crises that brought quite new personalities]—and the thought flashed through his mind that he was in something of the same mental state at this moment. "What if I should cut it for good and begin over again?" he asked suddenly. "What if I should take the only way out and cut it for good?"

Over the trivial French clock the eyes of the great [Italian *added*] reformer looked down on him. "You were right, Monk, as far as you went," murmured Estbridge ironically, "but the primal force got beyond you; the trouble was that man wanted his little happiness in Florence just as badly as he wants it here to-day in New York."

For a blank instant, while his gaze still hung on the portrait, he tried to evoke the impression of that day, more than twenty years ago, when he had bought the picture and hung it with his own hands over his mantel. Even after the crucial scene of last night he had never forgotten [this *changed to* the curious] episode. It was the morning after he had seen Tilly Pratt in a graduating play; and though the girl had laid aside he[r] religious fervor [with *changed to* as easily as she had] the flowing robes and cowl of the Florentine Friar, she had still impersonated the militant idealism of Estbridge's youth. For he had loved Tilly, not for herself, but because she had shown him his own image. Like most men, [and all *changed to* according to the] analytical psychologists, he had identified his own dreams with the shape of a woman. "Yes, it was not you, Tilly. You were not Savonarola," he said.

For a grey quarter of a century hung now like a fog between the ample figure of the present Mrs. Estbridge and the girl who had bewitched him during his [first year *changed to* interne-ship] at Christ's Hospital. It was impossible for the most active imagination to create an illusion about the wife who invariably ruffled his contentment and devoured his time. Florid, robust, and bristling with activity, she had triumphantly checkmated him during the twenty years of their marriage. So relentless had been her rule, that he[r] victim, though still at bay, had been forced to accord a critical admiration to her performance. But for her amazing perseverance, he thought now, his whole life might have been different, and instead of missing the coveted chair of physiology at the University, he might have watched some of his early dreams acquire the outlines and [the semblance of *changed to* substance] of [realities *changed to* reality]. But for her he might have abandoned his profession as a means, no longer necessary, of breadwinning; and but for her, he added bitterly

after a minute, he might have used his great experience and his un-
doubted gift to raise the [standards of *deleted*] vision and accomplishment in the schools where doctors were formed. Yes, she had always
been at his elbow, holding him back. It was incredible; it was diabolical;
but she had done it for twenty years, and she was doing it still!

A convenient neurosis, cured now and then, but intermittently subject
to relapse in favor of some new doctor, kept Mrs. Estbridge in bed for
breakfast; and Estbridge had [come to *added*] [grasped *changed to*
grasp] eagerly this one rich hour of solitude. Between eight and nine
o'clock, no one invaded the dining-room where he sat at his simple breakfast which had been left by some servant who had vanished. If the telephone rang he did not answer it. If patients chose that hour to die, they
died without his attentions. There was no rustling of newspapers, no
slitting of fresh correspondence. The only sound in the room was the
bubbling of the coffee percolator; and while [this morning *added*] he
brooded over the meal, he was thankfully aware of the restful hush of
the place—of the mute service of inanimate things which surrounded
him.

"That's the last straw—to miss that appointment," he thought. "To
have worked for twenty years, and then to see the chair go to Adamson
—to Adamson who was my assistant [2] when he began." With the words
he rose hurriedly from the table, and crossing to the window, looked out
on the swaying ailantus tree. "There's but one way out, and no one could
blame me for taking it," he added under his breath.

The sound of the opening door made him wheel quickly about, and
he shivered with a nervous movement of protest as he found himself
facing the commanding form of his wife.

"Doctor Railston says I may begin to get up for breakfast," she remarked affably, as she passed to the head of the table, and took he[r]
place behind the archaic silver service she had inherited from some Pratt
who had figured in history. "So I planned a little surprise for you."

While she smiled benignly upon him, Estbridge realized that she had
become, by the authority of metaphor and fact, an immovable body.
Though he had longed for years to forbid her the room, he knew that he
was morally powerless to do so. Her presence [now *added*] was merely
part of [a definite *changed to* the whole] plan; and in the very instant
that he perceived her design, he understood that he was incapable of
making an effort to thwart it. Just as she had victoriously substituted herself for his profession and for the few hours at the end of his day, she

[2] "To Adamson who was my assistant" is underlined in the manuscript, suggesting a contemplated revision here.

meant now, he saw, to devour the one brief interval of time he could call his own. Not content with destroying his happiness, she was opening, with the best possible intentions, an attack upon the intellectual side of his work.

"You drink too much strong coffee," she said as her competent glance swept the table. "Bates tells me you sometimes fill the percolator twice."

He had fallen back into his chair, and while his lip tightened with exasperation, he watched her ring the bell and order bacon and eggs. From the moment when she had entered, she had become the dominant figure. She was a woman, and by virtue of her womanhood she had made the breakfast table her ally. By every law, by every custom she was fulfilling the domestic tradition; and without disturbing a convention, without disobeying a religious behest, she was ruining his life. Society was on her side—God, he felt for one bitter moment, was on her side. Had she been violent or vicious, he might have withstood her; but her authority was rooted in virtue, and before the tyranny of virtue he was helpless.

While she sat there, calmly waiting for her breakfast, he surveyed her large handsome face with a resentful gaze. From her stiff iron grey hair to her firm and massive figure, she presented a picture of matronly rectitude. The very perfection of her type was the thing he found it hardest to forgive in her. She was born to be "a good manager", and it was not to be expected that her inherited talent should stop short before the man whom fate, or his own folly, had delivered into her hands. With children to occupy her, she might have found, he realized, other outlets for her benevolent impulses; but there were no children, and as the years went by he had ceased his early rejoicing that his wife lacked the inclination for public reforms. From a firmly efficient management of her household, she had passed, without perceptible loss of either firmness or efficiency, to the management of his clothes, his diet, his exercise, and the number and the brands of his cigarettes. With an unholy dread he saw that it was only a question of time—perhaps of days—before she would begin to "manage" his hospital.

"I want you to eat more breakfast, John." She was pouring a plentiful supply of hot milk into her coffee. ["]And it is really absurd of you to fancy that you can think while you eat."

From the oblong mirror over the sideboard the reflection of his own features flashed back at him, and he stared at his distinguished face as if it had been the face of a stranger. Although they were exactly the same age, he became suddenly aware that he looked at least ten years younger than the capable lady whom he had married. Science had kept him young in return for the passion he had lavished upon her. In his bright blue eyes, which grew hard enough on occasions, still glistened the eternal enquiring spirit of youth. His dark hair had silvered, but it was still thick, and his compact and muscular figure had escaped the increasing weight which sent most of his contemporaries into belated training.

"Thank heaven for this holiday." She was beginning to ramble. "[tere *changed to* There] won't be any need for you to rush off this morning. If it's Christmas, it might as well be a merry one."

She was in an amiable mood, and it was plain to him, after the first moment or two, that the scene of last night had barely ruffled the surface of her composure. Well, of course, if a thing like that didn't ruffle one! A smile, half of humor, half of irony, twisted his lip, while there floated through his mind a sentence from one of his lectures on mental deficiency: "To be unable to recall experience and to profit by it is a common characteristic of the morons." [3]

When she had skewered the last bit of bacon on her fork, and not before, Mrs. Estbridge raised her eyes again to her husband.

"Have you heard that the chair of physiology has been given to Adamson?"

"Yes, I heard." A flush rose to Estbridge's face, staining his scholarly brow under the silver hair. The board of trustees had not only passed him over—they had passed him over for Adamson, a young fellow with merely a fair record and, as Estbridge told himself now, with a hopelessly limited horizon. If not Estbridge, it must, of course, have been Adamson—but by all that was fair and honest, it should have been Estbridge! What other man in New York combined his venturesome imagination with his sound knowledge and understanding of modern achievement? [4]

"How did you get the news?" he asked after a minute. Was it possible that here also she had helped to defeat him? In the old days when he had tried to make her share in his ambition to be a leader of young men, he remembered she had laughingly said to him more than once: "But that sounds very foolish to me. What's the use of standing up before a lot of Jews and telling them things that are all in the books anyhow?"

"Aunt Clara came in last evening," she replied, and added with a scarcely perceptible emphasis: "after you went out. Uncle Timothy rushed the appointment through, and would hear of no one but Adamson. He insisted on having a practical man——"

[3] This quotation is italicized in the revision.
[4] A shorthand scribble, perhaps "rewrite," is in the margin opposite this paragraph. The reference to Adamson seems to call for work.

So it was out at last! Old Timothy Pratt, his wife's uncle, had won over the board of trustees to Adamson—old Timothy Pratt, who had trebled an inherited fortune though he never got up before mid-day.

"Of course I knew that your uncle was opposed to me," said Estbridge, "But I had counted on Jim." Until that instant he had not realized how much he had counted on Jim Hoadly.

"Poor old Jim." Mrs. Estbridge's voice was faintly patronizing. "He did his best, but he is hardly a match for Uncle Timothy. I wonder why he doesn't come here any more?" As she paused she reached for the jar of marmalade and helped herself to an even spoonful. It was Mrs. Estbridge's proudest boast that she let nothing impair her appetite.

"I trust that Aunt Clara at least is pleased." Estbrook had recovered his humor, if not his temper.

"Not at all. On the contrary she asked me several weeks ago about the advisability of her speaking to Uncle Timothy. She seemed to feel, and quite naturally, I think, that Uncle Timothy ought not to—at least that he ought not to appear to be leading a fight against you——"

"Indeed!"

"But, of course, when she asked me frankly, I was obliged to tell her what I thought——"

His nerves jerked, and pushing back his chair, he walked quickly to the door.

"Yes, John, when she asked me for the truth, I was obliged to speak it. Even as things are now, I was forced to tell her that I rarely see you, that you show signs of irritability—you know you do, John—that you are overworked, and that any well-wisher—"

The volume of sound was interrupted by the sudden entrance of Bates, who felt, doubtless, that if the doctor had taken to entertaining at breakfast, the butler was entitled to be present. But even if the sombre Englishman, compressed to silence by generations of servitude, had miraculously acquired the gift of fluent speech, it would have availed him little against the torrential overflow of directions which followed Estbridge into the hall.

"John, it is snowing hard." The voice pursued him with the imperious accents of destiny. "If you *will* [ital. *added*] go out, don't forget to put on your overshoes."

One overshoe was already half on, but prying it off, Estbridge kicked it furiously under the hat-rack. "It would be an interesting experience," he muttered to himself as he slammed the door behind him, "if some rainy day she should remind me to put on my hat. I wonder what the devil I should do if she did?"

As he plunged through the snow in the direction of Fifth Avenue, he felt that his body vibrated in every cell and fibre with rebellion. It was a revolt not only against his wife, but against the whole world of women. At the instant he saw all women as victorious over the lives and destinies of men. As for his wife, he knew now, as he had known for years, that he had never loved her—that he had never perhaps loved any woman. He was passing the mansion of Mr. Pratt, just a few blocks south of the Park, and as he glanced up at the high windows, framed in snow, he felt that he wanted to curse the pompous old mandarin still asleep in his bed.

"Why shouldn't I cut it for good?" he asked again as he had asked an hour before. "By God, I will cut it for good! I'll take the post that is still open at Shanghai!" The wish which had created the thought evolved from a simple impulse into a practical idea. He saw before him a definite vision of freedom, and he saw the ten vigorous years ahead of him crowded, not with vain attempts, not with frustrated efforts, but with adventure, accomplishment, and reward.

The door of his office swung back into emptiness, and he rejoiced for the first time in the holiday which had relieved him of his usual staff of helpers. As he turned, still with the thought of Shanghai in his mind, to an atlas on the table of his waiting-room, he saw a woman's figure dimly outlined against the glass of the door. "Can it be Judith Campbell?" he thought while a tremor passed over him. Then, flinging the door open, he fell back a step, and stood waiting for her to cross the threshold. "What an angel you are to come to me through the storm!" [5]

She entered slowly, wrapped in dark furs to the chin, and he had an impression even before she spoke, of the softness and grace of her manner.

"I felt that you would be here, and I couldn't let Christmas go by without seeing you for a minute." Stopping beside the table, with its litter of last year's magazines, she gazed up at him with the strange gentleness which had first drawn him to her—that rare gentleness, he found himself thinking now, which alone can make a woman the equal of men.

"I wanted to bring my little gift," she said. "Last year I should hardly have dared." While he watched her take from her muff the white package, with its red ribbon and spray of holly, he became aware that her body like her mind was compacted of delicate graces, of exquisite surprises. Though she had been for years the professor of philosophy in a college for women, she was as feminine in appearance as any early Vic-

[5] An "X" in the margin opposite this paragraph indicates Miss Glasgow's dissatisfaction with it.

torian heroine of fiction. She was, he realized forcibly at the instant, everything that his wife was not and could never become. His wife was a dull woman with an instinct to dominate; but Judith Campbell—he felt this as he had never felt it before—was a clever woman with an instinct to yield.

"Your coming begins my Christmas," he said, and the words sounded so inadequate as he uttered them that he went on more rapidly: "I am so glad. It is your book. May I open it?"

She shook her head with a little laugh that had a yielding and tremulous grace. "After I go, I can stay only a minute."

The slender figure in the heavy furs had the look of a cypress-tree that sways and bends under the storm. Through the veil of dotted net her large grey eyes still gazed at him with an enigmatical softness. Even her intellect, in spite of its flashing brilliance, gave him this impression of softness and grace, as if its strength were tempered by sympathy. Though she had always appeared in her spiritual detachment to stand above the more commonplace aspects of passion, he had sometimes wondered if her perfect response to his moods meant a gradual change in her friendship. Could her delicate intuitions remain insensible to the inevitable course such things take?

And yet only at this moment did he realize that his will was drawing him to her. Against his [judgement *changed to* judgment], against his ideals, against his teaching and his habits, the will to live was driving him away from his work to the love of a woman. To his profession, and his conception of what it might some day become, he had dedicated both his intellect and his passion. For twenty years his marriage had been sufficient to keep him out of casual temptation; and his friendship for Jim Hoadly had supplied him, as he blindly supposed, with all that he required of sympathy and understanding. But at this instant, looking back on his association with Judith Campbell—on their first rare meetings at joint boards, on their occasional walks in the Park, on an evening now and then at some waterside restaurant during the summer, on the substantial help he had been able to give her in her work, and more than all on the ready comprehension with which she had met him from the start—looking back on all these things, he saw, with a luminous flash of understanding, that the miracle of renewed youth had occurred. While he stood there he felt like a man who had gone shivering to sleep in the winter, and had awakened to find the scented air of spring blowing in his window.

"There is something else I must tell you." Her soft voice quivered for an instant. "I had this morning the offer of the presidency of Hartwell College."

He breathed hard with suspense, yet he could think of nothing to say except the obvious: "But that's in St. Louis."

"Yes."

"And you will accept it?"

"Yes, I shall accept it."

"That means you will live in St. Louis?"

"That means I shall live in St. Louis."

The parrying had restored his composure. "You have always wanted something like that more than anything else in the world."

"I told myself this morning that I had always wanted such a place more than anything in the world."

The note of hesitation in her voice made him look at her quickly. He had always supposed that her face was too strong, too intelligent, to conform to any standard of beauty, but he recognized now, with a start, that she embodied the complete and absolute perfection of womanhood. And he felt that he wanted her as from his youth up he had wanted the unattainable—as an hour ago he had wanted the chair of physiology that went to Adamson.

"You deserve it," he said after a pause. "It is the outcome of your work, and the crowning of your ambition."

"Yes," the word faltered on her lips. "I suppose it is the crowning of my ambition." Though her age was thirty-eight there was the shyness of a girl in her eyes, and by her shyness and the quiver of her lashes as he looked at her, he knew that she loved him.

"I wish," she [added *changed* to pursued] slowly, "that I had no ambition."

"But would you give it up?" It was a simple enough question, and yet after he had put it, he stood watching her as if he were in a laboratory awaiting the result of some physiological experiment.

"Crowning a woman's ambition often makes her a beggar," she answered quietly, adding after a minute. "What a shame it is about Adamson!"

He laughed grimly. "Yes, I did want that; more, perhaps, than you wanted Hartwell. But that's over now. Who knows, after all, if it wasn't something else that I wanted?"

Her look touched him like a caress. "If I could only give you what I have."

"And yet it is the highest honor that could come to you."

She smiled, a little wearily he thought, as she answered:

"That is why I would give it to you."

"Judith!"

She had moved a step nearer the door, and stopping there at his call, she looked back with a startled glow in her face.

"Judith, would you give it up if I asked you?"

"If you asked me?"

"Would you stay—would you give it up if I asked you?" The glow in her face seemed to pervade her whole body while she stood before him transfigured.

"I would give up the whole world if you asked me."

"You would sacrifice your ambition—your future?"

A laugh broke from her lips. "I haven't any ambition—any future—except yours." It was as if the passive substance of her nature had flamed into energy.

He walked to the window, gazing down on the city, which loomed in bizarre outlines through the storm. "It's this way with me," he [said *changed to* began] impersonally, as if to the street. "An hour ago I made up my mind to quit New York for good. You know most of the reasons. All of them now since you know about Adamson. I have made up my mind to begin over again, and for once to get down to some real work—something genuine—in China. I told you about the post in Shanghai. Well, I am going to take it."

She drew her breath sharply, and though he still looked away from her, he felt her very will had passed into the flame and fervor of his.

"For twenty years I have thought that my hour would come," he [added *changed to* said] in a voice which he tried in vain to make as guarded as his manner. "It has come now."

"It has come now?" Her words were scarcely more than a sigh faintly drawn.

"It is here, and I want to grasp it while I have still the courage. I want to grasp it before it escapes me."

Though she looked as if she would yield—as if she would dissolve at a touch, he did not stretch out his hand to her. He had made his appeal and she had answered it.

"Yes, if I go, I must go while I have the courage. I must go now—to-day," he went on, gaining confidence while he watched her drooping under the weight of her furs. "I must go while you will go with me."

As he moved a step nearer, she swayed towards him, and for a moment he held her close with a gentleness that was strangely sacramental for a lover. Neither spoke until she released herself, and threw back her veil with the gesture of one who is casting aside the burden of years.

"Wherever you go, I will go with you," she said.

"You will go with me to-day?"

She glanced with brightly questioning eyes at the clock. "Is there a boat on Christmas day?"

He laughed, and with the sound he looked suddenly boyish. "Oh, enchanting professor of philosophy! No, there isn't a boat, but we'll catch the noon train to Chicago. To-morrow we'll go on to San Francisco, and after that the way will be easy. You have an hour. Will you be ready?"

"It will not take me an hour. I can get what I need in San Francisco."

He was allowing her only an hour, she knew, because to go at all they must go without thinking. They must act at once as each had dreamed so often of acting, in obedience to the divine, indomitable impulse. They must follow with bandaged eyes the spirit of adventure.

"And I'll go after burning my boats. I shan't even look over my papers. There must be no compromises." Then, as if craving movement, action, certainty, he glanced at the clock. "I'll telephone my man to send my things to the train. There will be a sudden call to Chicago. In exactly fifty-five minutes will you meet me in the Pennsylvania Station—by the gate?"

"I shall not fail you. I shall never fail you."

With the promise she had gone; and crossing to the window of the outer office, he looked down on her figure making its way through the storm. In the midst of thronging pedestrians, of noisy motors, of newsboys frantically crying the extras, he watched her press evenly forward until at last the whirling snowflakes gathered her in.

Well, that was over! He had made his decision; he had burned his boats; and no good could come from looking back over his shoulder. While he stood there gazing down into the street, he felt that the flame and glory of his hour was still with him. His nerves no longer reacted jarringly to his surroundings. He was aware of a complete, harmonious adjustment to the circumstances of his life. Destiny for once moved in obedience to his will. It was all so easy—this quick shedding of the husks of the past, this putting forth, with renewed growth and vigor, in a strange soil amid an alien people. What fools men were to talk of convention and experience! All one needed was the will to choose, the courage to act promptly.

Turning to his desk, he mechanically rang for his secretary, before he remembered that the day was Christmas. Then, reflecting with a smile that he couldn't very well use her for the business on hand, he began hurriedly filling his black portfolio with check-books, manuscripts, and letters which required personal answers. While he sorted his papers, littering the floor with what was not needed, and lighting a fire in the grate in order to burn certain documents which he wished to destroy, he found himself thinking, not of the post at Shanghai, not of the future with Judith Campbell, but of the chair of physiology which had been given to Adamson. The hurt had not healed. Though he told himself passionately that life without Judith would not be worth living, he was aware that beneath his happiness the wound to his ambition still throbbed.

He had been barely ten minutes at his task when an imperative knock on the door forced him to open it.

"I might have known who it was," he thought moodily as he turned the knob. "What an ass I was not to hide where he couldn't find me."

Jim Hoadly was a big man—so big that he seemed to fill the space in the doorway, and his mere physical bulk had always possessed a curious fascination for his classmate. To-day, however, Estbridge was conscious of a latent antagonism, of a secret revolt against all the qualities he had once admired in his friend. It was as if the demon of the inopportune had suddenly entered.

"I knew I'd find you here," began the caller, while he shook the snow from his shoulders with a vigorous movement. "No," he went on gaily in reply to the question in Estbridge's eyes, "I didn't even try at the house." A minute afterwards, as he passed through the doorway of the inner office, he broke into a low whistle of astonishment. "Whew! Quite a wind blowing, isn't there? and a conflagration on top of it!"

"I lit a fire, that's all." Estbridge was trying to smile unconcernedly.

"If I remember rightly it isn't your first fire either," retorted Hoadly, drying his sandy beard with his fingers. "You know, Jack, I always said you could act when your hour caught you."

"My hour?" Estbridge's glance flew to the clock. "Well you were right, Jim, my hour has caught me, and I am acting. I'm leaving at twelve o'clock—for the future."

A grey light, as if from the sombre sky outside, sobered Jim's merry features. "Do you mean to kill yourself, Jack?"

"Kill myself?" Estbridge laughed with joy. "No, I am going to live. For the first time in my life, I am going to live!"

Though Hoadly had led a life of singular detachment, twenty-five years of journalism had made him a shrewd interpreter of the emotions of others. "Shall I go through the form of enquiring," he asked airily, "if you intend to begin this new existence alone?"

"Alone? No."

"You won't mind my asking, I suppose, if Judith Campbell goes with you?"

For a moment Estbridge looked as if he were about to show resentment. Then his manner grew flippant, and he replied carelessly: "Well, why shouldn't you know? I want you to know before anyone else. You won't have a start of more than twenty-four hours over the papers at that."

"So it's the famous professor of philosophy!" Jim's tone was measured in its calmness. "I must say I find it hard to follow these feminists. But, Jack, you can't do it!"

"Who's to stop me?" Estbridge's voice was sharp with defiance.

"I am."

The thought of physical violence shot through Estbridge's mind, and he retorted angrily. "Don't try that game, it is dangerous."

"Oh, I don't know," responded Jim drily. "I've tried it before now, and I'm still living. But, come, Jack, you can't toss aside an old friend so easily. At least you can't do it until you have offered him a chair," he added, flinging himself into the worn leather chair facing the window. "I may sit down, I suppose, while I argue. Great Jove! How many poor devils, I wonder, have sat here before me?"

"You may sit down and you may argue," replied Estbridge, "but you won't mind my not listening to you, I hope. My train goes at twelve o'clock."

"Has it ever occurred to you to make an inventory, mainly in the interest of science, of what you are leaving behind?"

"It has. I am leaving behind a life that gets nowhere, and one that bores me to death."

"And to ask yourself what the lady is giving up in return for the doubtful constancy you offer her. By George, Jack, have you thought to tell her that the only thing you ever loved in any woman was your own reflection?"

"If that's all you know about it?"

"It isn't all, perhaps, but it's a good bit. You aren't the first analytical psychologist who has identified the world with himself, and, God permitting, you probably won't be the last."

"If that's your game, my boy, you are wasting time."

"Well, after all, you are dodging my question about the lady."

"Have you read her book on 'Marriage and Individuality'?" Estbridge glanced at the package on the table.

"No, I haven't, but I can make a good guess as to what it is all about.

There is not much to be said on that subject, I fancy. It is take it or leave it—that's all. But, granting that she doesn't lose much as she sees it, she doesn't stand to win very big stakes either, does she? Does she, now, really? Come, Jack, as a married man, nearing fifty, don't you agree with me?"

"If I do, how is the case altered? Of course I am not worthy of her, but what, in heaven's name, has that got to do with it?"

"You realize that your wife will never divorce you?"

With a shrug Estbridge went back to his papers. "Have I lived with her for twenty years without discovering that?"

"And the end will be, I suppose," Hoadly's voice had grown rasping, "that you will feel yourself bound to Judith Campbell until—until she comes between you and something that you want more than you want any woman. There is an instinct in you stronger than love, Jack, and God pity her when she crosses it. I have always said that your Grand Inquisitor was a humanitarian crossed in his purpose."

Estbridge's face darkened. "There are barely fifteen minutes left, and I've as much as I can attend to."

"Don't let me delay you." Rising from his chair, Hoadly held out his hand with the casual manner of an attorney who continues to smile pleasantly in the face of defeat. "You aren't allowing yourself a great deal of time, are you?" As he reached the door he glanced back, and [added *changed to* said] carelessly. "By the way, I forgot to tell you about Adamson. But I suppose you have heard?"

"I heard this morning," replied Estbridge sharply, "I wish the University well of him."

"Then you haven't seen the extras?" The door closed with a slam, and Hoadly turned back into the room. "He's dead, you know—run over this morning in West Fifty-ninth Street. I heard it two hours ago." For a moment he hesitated, and then added maliciously. "I suppose we'll have a hard time now to replace him."

"Adamson!" The portfolio he had picked up slipped from Estbridge's grasp, and he stood staring incredulously into the face of his friend. "Why hadn't you told me?"

"I came down for that, not just to wish you a Merry Christmas—but the news went quite out of my mind when I found myself in the midst of this romantic episode. After all, life is so much more engrossing than death, isn't it?"

"Adamson?" Estbridge was repeating the name blankly. As if awakening from the effects of a narcotic, he stretched out his hand with a groping uncertain gesture. Not only his tone, but his face, his look, even his figure, appeared to have altered. It was as if an entirely different set of nerve cells had begun acting at the instant—as if the molecular rhythm of his brain had run down, and then started feverishly with fresh waves of energy. He was like a man who had died and been born anew in an instant; and, watching him, Hoadly realized that his friend was now living with a different side of his nature—with other impulses, with other vibrations of memory, with other automatic reactions.

"So Adamson is dead, and the place at the University is vacant!"

Over Jim Hoadly's impassive features a smile that was slightly sardonic in its humor flickered for an instant. "You have just time to catch your train," he said, and added gravely, with a vague movement toward the portfolio, "the snow makes traffic difficult."

At the reminder the exultation faded from Estbridge's look, while his anxious gaze sought the face of the clock, and hung there as if drawn and held by an irresistible magnet.

"Yes, there is just time," he repeated; but he did not turn, and his shoulders did not stoop for the overcoat which Hoadly held waiting behind him.

"You had better start or you'll miss it," said Hoadly again, after three minutes in which he had watched the struggle with his smile of flickering irony—like the smile of some inscrutable image of wisdom. "It would be a pity to miss that train, wouldn't it?"

But the clock ticked slowly on, while Estbridge stood transfixed, bewildered, brooding, with his eyes on the hands which travelled inevitably toward the appointed hour.

Editor's Note

A twenty-three page typescript with manuscript corrections was among Ellen Glasgow's papers at her death and is now preserved in the University of Virginia Library. The story was written between 1918 and 1925, probably nearer the latter date. It has been folded in thirds to fit a business envelope, suggesting that it might have been sent out for an editorial opinion. However, the manuscript corrections are incomplete; they are precise and careful on the first few pages, but they soon thin out, exposing many typographical and stylistic flaws. I have silently corrected the typographical errors and included all her manuscript corrections in this edition of the story. At several points Miss Glasgow has expressed displeasure with a section, once by underlining it, once by an "X" in the margin, and once by a hasty scribble in the margin. I have indicated these places with footnotes.

Ellen Glasgow customarily made two drafts before having the final version typed for her publisher. This is plainly a second draft without the final polish. Before passing on this draft, Miss Glasgow would probably have smoothed out several awkward shifts in point of view and a few of the ponderous observations of Jim Hoadly. But the famous Glasgow irony is already there full strength. It dominates the story just as the fireplace portrait of the Italian monk Savonarola presides over the destiny of Dr. Estbridge. Like Savonarola, Dr. Estbridge tries to reform his world but stands convinced of vanity at the end.

An even more appropriate symbol of the "prosperous failure" of Estbridge is the solitary ailantus tree in his garden, the substitute for the Italian garden he planned in his youth. The ailantus (usually spelled ailanthus and sometimes advertised as the Tree of Heaven) is a fast-growing, pulpy, showy tree with clusters of disagreeable-smelling flowers. This tree, which says all that needs to be said about the outward attractiveness and inner softness of Dr. Estbridge, is one of Miss Glasgow's most appropriate nature symbols. In *Barren Ground* this kind of symbolism was to become a major informing device.

Miss Glasgow may be attempting to explain her ill-fated engagement to Colonel Henry W. Anderson just after World War I. Was she considering the necessity of throwing over her literary career and subordinating her desires to a man? Is she the professor of philosophy, ready to follow her lover anywhere? And did Anderson, like Estbridge, have an instinct stronger than love that might replace her with, say, Queen Marie of Roumania or the governorship of Virginia?

The egocentric male and the naïve, idealistic female have already become stereotypes in the Glasgow album, but while she tries her best to understand the male ego, Miss Glasgow finally riddles Dr. Estbridge with scornful epithets. Such a wife entitles him to pity, but such an escape—to Shanghai with a potential college president—is impossibly cruel. Only one thing could be more selfish than to run away under such conditions, and that would be for Estbridge next to drop Judith Campbell in order to advance himself professionally. Presumably he does just this.

William W. Kelly has just published for the first time "The Professional Instinct," with a three-page preface, in *Western Humanities Review*, XVI, No. 4 (Autumn, 1962), 301–17. His opinion of Mrs. Estbridge is higher than my own, and he believes the manuscript is closer to Ellen Glasgow's final copy than I do, but we agree on its date, style, and tone.